Jonathan turned around to see Anne staring at his half-naked torso. He remained silent.

"Do you miss the sea air?"

Wiping his damp forehead with his arm, Jonathan leaned on the axe, pausing to breathe in the invigorating scent of pine, birch, beech, elm, and poplar mingled with the mustiness of the earth and the fragrance of wildflowers.

"No. The sea has its beauty, but it is just as beautiful out here. It makes a person see things in a whole new light."

Anne said softly, "Living close to nature makes one appreciate the simple things."

"Like water!" Jonathan exclaimed.

Setting down the axe, he picked up a bucket and went in search of a stream. Filling the bucket to the brim, he quickly retraced his steps, but before drinking he offered the first dipper to Anne.

"You see, I do know how to be a gentleman." Their hands touched, and their eyes met. Then, before he had time to think, he had gathered her in his arms.

Jonathan groaned, closing his arms about her as he pulled her into the curve of his hard body. Bending his face to meet hers, he kissed her, the tip of his tongue stroking her lips as deftly as his hands caressed her body.

In response Anne moaned, turning her head so that his mouth slanted over hers and his tongue sought to part her lips. "Jonathan . . ." Anne was trembling. Never in her wildest dreams had she realized how primitive and powerful desire could be.

Though he wanted to give in to his desires, he pulled away and stood looking down at her for a long, aching moment. "Anne . . ."

His voice was cold. Like a splash of icy water. "What is it?" Anne asked.

"I . . . I shouldn't have . . ."

"Shouldn't have kissed me? It was I who kissed you." She reached up and touched his face, hoping to rekindle the desire that had sparked between them. "Besides, we have been far more intimate on several occasions, as I remember."

"I know but you aren't my captive now."

Her voice was soft and seductive. "Then perhaps I wish that I were . . ."

BOOK YOUR PLACE ON OUR WEBSITE AND MAKE THE READING CONNECTION!

We've created a customized website just for our very special readers, where you can get the inside scoop on everything that's going on with Zebra, Pinnacle and Kensington books.

When you come online, you'll have the exciting opportunity to:

- View covers of upcoming books
- Read sample chapters
- Learn about our future publishing schedule (listed by publication month *and author*)
- Find out when your favorite authors will be visiting a city near you
- Search for and order backlist books from our online catalog
- Check out author bios and background information
- Send e-mail to your favorite authors
- Meet the Kensington staff online
- Join us in weekly chats with authors, readers and other guests
- Get writing guidelines
- AND MUCH MORE!

Visit our website at http://www.zebrabooks.com

INDIGO SEA

Kathryn Hockett

ZEBRA BOOKS
KENSINGTON PUBLISHING CORP.
http://www.zebrabooks.com

ZEBRA BOOKS are published by

Kensington Publishing Corp.
850 Third Avenue
New York, NY 10022

All Kensington titles, imprints and distributed lines are available at special quantity discounts for bulk purchases for sales
promotion, premiums, fund raising, educational or institutional
use.

Special book excerpts or customized printings can also be created to fit specific needs. For details, write or phone the office of
the Kensington Special Sales Manager: Kensington Publishing
Corp., 850 Third Avenue, New York, NY, 10022. Attn. Special
Sales Department. Phone: 1-800-221-2647.

First Printing: January, 2001
10 9 8 7 6 5 4 3 2 1

Printed in the United States of America

Once again, to Rick and Aric . . .
And to Lou Rogers who has been a special friend in
a time of crisis.

*"My bounty is as boundless as the sea,
My love as deep; the more I give to thee
The more I love, for both are infinite."*

—William Shakespeare,
Romeo and Juliet, II, 2

Author's Note

In the dark of the morning of November 17, 1558, the clamor of bells announced the death of one queen and the accession of another. Mary Tudor, whose reign had been clouded by religious unrest and persecution, was gone forever. Elizabeth, daughter of Henry VIII and Anne Boleyn, now reigned. She inherited a dangerous legacy, the religious unrest that existed in England. Elizabeth, however, handled the "thorny" issue with skilled diplomacy. She united the country and won the love of her subjects. Unlike Mary, who was half Spanish, Elizabeth was totally English and more cherished because of it.

The chief danger to Elizabeth came not from within the country but from the intervention of France and Spain. Fortunately for England, the two countries were adversaries, which diverted their attention from English pursuits. Elizabeth played the two against each other with consummate skill and courage and in this way was able to avoid war. The queen was at her best in her negotiations and dealings with Spain. She dangled the promise of her marriage—first to Philip, then in turn to his son—like a carrot before a donkey's nose. Elizabeth was the most eligible woman in Europe and delighted in that fact. All the while England grew strong and prospered.

The Spanish king kept peace with England while English privateers made war upon Spanish colonies and ships. Small English ships took all the ocean for their province, using the British coast as lairs. They sailed forth to seize their plunder from wealth-fattened Spanish vessels without regard to the propriety of the taking. Though Elizabeth publicly disowned them, she privately encouraged them and did not disturb them. She even took her share in their spoils. She was in some ways a "pirate by proxy." She needed the wealth to build her own fleet of ships and also seemed to sense, in these privateers, the beginning of her navy. When the Spanish ambassador threatened war, she countered with the threat of marriage to a French Prince, thereby creating an English-French alliance.

An uneasy peace dragged on until continual English raids on Spanish ships and Spain's involvement with supporters of the rival Catholic claimant to the English throne, the imprisoned Mary Stuart, severed relations. It was a trying time for Elizabeth, whose popularity had begun to slip. In towns and villages there was unrest and talk of schemes, spies, plots and foreign agents, or traitors.

In the year 1586, nearly thirty years after her coronation, both Philip and Elizabeth prepared for a war that would decide the mastery of the seas and theological domination. Philip ordered his best admiral to prepare the largest armada history had ever known in order to invade England and dethrone the English queen.

It is amidst the beginnings of this turmoil that a handsome, daring privateer finds his destiny intertwined with that of a lovely young woman of Spanish-English heritage. Swept up in the furor of impending war, their love and desire will face the ultimate trial.

PART ONE

THE GOLDEN DEVIL

England, 1583

"The prince of darkness is a gentleman."
—Shakespeare, *King Lear, III, 4*

Chapter One

The air was cold and damp. Fog swirled above the ocean, engulfing the ship in its grip as the vessel maneuvered its way through the waters of the Bay of Biscay. Shadows moved through the murky mist as men aboard the ship went about their duties, bumping into one another from time to time, grumbling as they tried to see through the eerie vapor.

"Can't see our hands in front of our faces."

"How's a man supposed to go about his business when he can't even see past his nose?"

Staring out from the helm of his English ship, as if he could penetrate the thick mists with his piercing hazel eyes, Jonathan Leighton, captain of the *White Griffin,* also felt an uneasy sense of isolation and frustration. He could not even see the coast of Brittany, much less catch sight of the ship he had targeted as his prey. He uttered a curse beneath his breath.

"Bloody damn! Curse this fog."

His swearing was echoed by Edmund Falkhearst, his short, rotund, jovial first mate. "Aye. This ungodly mist is going to keep us from our quarry. Don't ye think so, Captain?"

Indeed, it was impossible to catch sight of the Spanish

merchant ship both men knew was on its way through the shimmering blue water. Even so, Jonathan was stubborn.

"I haven't given up yet." He clenched his jaw. "Nor *will* I!"

"Then neither *will* I!" Falkhearst stared up at his captain. Tall, blond, and arrogantly handsome, Jonathan Leighton was a man who inspired loyalty. There was hardly a man among the crew of a hundred and ten who did not admire the captain. Falkhearst even suspected that they would have followed their leader to hell and back if Jonathan asked them to.

Jonathan closed his eyes for just a moment, imagining a ship overflowing with gold coins, so many coins that its sides bulged as it bobbed on the water. "I have heard that the *San Pedro* is richly cargoed. It would be the greatest misfortune if they sailed right by us, fog or no fog."

For all his life Jonathan had been surrounded by merchants and sailors, hearing tales of untold wealth on the Spanish Main, that sprawling dominion surrounding the Caribbean Basin and the ring of islands bordering it. Even when he was just a boy, those stories had invaded his dreams. Someday he too would sail the ocean, he had vowed, ignoring his father's stern rebuke at such youthful imaginings. The fulfillment of his dreams, however, was long in coming.

As eldest son of an impoverished baronet and a wealthy wine merchant's daughter, he had been confined to the land. First there had been the years he had helped his father, then the many months he had been confined to Oxford pursuing his education. All the while a toughness, shrewdness, and ambition developed within him which could not be quenched. Someday he would have his own ship. It was a desire that had driven him.

"By my faith, I say that ship will not elude us, Cap'n!" Falkhearst hit his open palm with his fist. "No ship has ever escaped ye."

Jonathan's tone was determined. "Nor will, if I have my way!"

"Ye will find a way. Ye always do!" The corners of

Edmund's mouth tugged up in a grin, one that was promptly returned. "In truth, I think ye most surely are the devil ye are said to be." The Spaniards called Jonathan "Diablo Dorado," *golden devil*.

"Devil am I . . . ?" Jonathan crossed his arms, feigning anger.

"Let's just say that I thank the fates that we be allies, not adversaries, Cap'n. I wouldn't want to fight ye. I doubt God's angels themselves would—"

The ship slammed into a wave, bringing a shower of water washing over the deck, nearly unbalancing Jonathan's wide-legged stance. Though Falkhearst tumbled to the deck, Jonathan quickly regained his footing. Reaching down, he helped Falkhearst up, issuing his orders in a deep, booming voice as he did so.

"Roll up the sails. Reduce speed. Caution is the word until the fog lifts." Despite his lust for treasure, Jonathan would never put his crew at risk of a collision.

"Aye, Captain." A tall, lanky sailor and his short, skinny companion hurried to obey. For the moment danger was averted.

Even though peril had been avoided, Jonathan Leighton would not allow himself the leisure of relaxing his tense muscles until he knew that everything was completely under control. Walking to the railing, he gripped the wet wood and continued his watch, looking out over the ocean as if he could will the fog to lift.

Dressed in a plain leather jerkin, coarse sailcloth trousers which hugged his muscular legs like a second skin, and a white linen shirt, the sleeves of which were rolled high above his elbows, he looked more like a sailor than the English lord that he was. He looked, in fact, like a privateer, and that was the way he wanted it. It felt good to be unencompassed by the walls or the often-strict discipline of Elizabeth's court. Standing upon the deck of his ship, he felt the alluring excitement that always beckoned him to adventure.

Queen Elizabeth chose men of untitled birth to surround her at court, raising them up in favor. Jonathan caught her eye for he was the epitome of the Elizabethan man—a gentleman, poet, and philosopher, whose longing for adventure shone with fervor in his eyes. That he was also blessed with the striking attractiveness of face and body that the middle-aged queen found fascinating was to his advantage. Within months Elizabeth had elevated him to the ranks of the young, handsome men who frequented her court. Jonathan Leighton had become a lord.

He soon fled the rigors of court life, however, and joined a gallant group of newly created noblemen who crossed to France to fight for the Huguenots. Later he turned his restless energy against Spain, volunteering to aid the Dutch against that aggressive country. By the age of twenty-three he had more than proven his bravery and skill upon the seas; by twenty-four he had taken command of his own ship. At the age of twenty-five he received a privateer's commission from Elizabeth and in return captured a Spanish convoy of silver bullion off the coast of Panama. Returning the treasure to Elizabeth, he had been richly rewarded by the queen's own hand, dining freely with her aboard his ship. If there was now a price upon his head, he didn't care. Jonathan Leighton scoffed at danger.

At the age of thirty-two, Jonathan had everything he'd ever wanted, the freedom of the sea when he wanted it and days at court when that was his desire. He had all the wealth he could ever want. His life was filled with adventure. He was content, or so he told himself over and over again. And yet . . . there were times when he felt somehow unfulfilled.

"Cap'n . . . ?" Falkhearst's voice jerked Jonathan from his thoughts "What are we going to do? About the the fog, I mean."

"I don't know." Jonathan shook his head. "It's all that stands between me and Spanish gold!"

"Well, if you ask me, Cap'n, what we need is a wind to blow the fog away." Falkhearst was inexorably pleased with his idea. "Aye. Wind! If only . . ."

Jonathan put his hand on Falkhearst's shoulder as he looked deep into his eyes. His lips curved up in a grin.

"They say I'm the devil. Shall I conjure up a rousing gale that will lift the fog? Shall I, Falkhearst?"

Falkhearst's eyes widened as he bobbed his head up and down in a silent yes.

Jonathan mumbled a mock incantation half in jest, half in seriousness. He was amazed when, as if by a miracle, his spoken wish was granted. Only moments after he had uttered the words, a wind began to blow, lifting the veil of mist and rending the fog into shreds.

For just a moment Edmund's eyes held a touch of superstitious fear. "God's teeth, ye are the devil! Ye are for sure."

"I am no devil. Just a very lucky man." Jonathan hoped such good fortune would last, for even before the curtain of fog dispersed, he sensed the Spanish ship, felt it was out there, knew that with every nerve in his body. At last it came into view.

"No merchant ship but a galleon!"

The towering, four masted vessel with stacked decks looked awesome, dwarfing the *White Griffin*. Jonathan's ship was a race ship; built close to the water to give her more speed and maneuverability, but she was outgunned and out-manned.

" 'S death! Shall we make preparations to sail away from her, Captain?" The helmsman shouted.

"Nay, we'll go after her. Unfurl the sails. All hands to battle stations. Better to be the hunter than the hunted."

"But Captain—"

"Proceed as I have ordered, helmsman. I have not come this far to turn back empty-handed." In his heart Jonathan knew that intelligence won out over braun any day, and he had that in full measure. Give up? It was not in his blood to turn coward. He knew well that he could outsail any ship, be it merchant or galleon. "Prepare to ram them."

"Not only are ye a devil, but ye be bloody mad!" Edmund Falkhearst's jaw dropped open as he stared in awe at his captain.

"Of course I am mad, and proud of it. Daringly mad. And that is why I have been so successful." Before the other man could say a word, Jonathan strode away. They would fight and they would win, for the alternative was too dastardly to contemplate—death or a life of cruelty condemned to a Spanish galley as a slave.

From the deck of the *Serpiente de Plata,* Anne Blythe Morgan Navarro looked out to sea, thankful that the fog had lifted so that she could catch sight of the shoreline in the distance. Brittany. The sight of its shores meant she was closer to her homeland. Next would be Normandy. Then at last the ship would enter the English Channel, bringing her home.

"England . . ." she whispered. How precious that name sounded. She had never realized until now how eager she was to return. But she was! For a moment she almost forgot that she would be bringing a new husband with her.

Turning her head, Anne looked at her ring-bedecked and velvet-clothed spouse. There were many words that described Enrique. He was charming, intelligent, and attractive in an older man sort of way. His hair was dark brown, threaded with gray, his nose not bulbous or overlarge. His eyes were a pleasing shade of brown, his lips a bit thin but not unappealing. Tall and lithe, he had the physique of a much younger man, belying his forty-nine years. Most important of all, however, he was "manageable," for Anne had no intention of allowing any man to interfere in her life, husband or not!

Manageable! She smiled. Indeed, throughout the journey Enrique had constantly deferred to her whims and wishes, even in the matter of the marriage bed. Anne had insisted they wait before consummating their union, and Enrique had agreed, though the worshipful and heated looks he had cast her way informed her that he was as anxious to bed her as she was to reach England.

Anne shrugged at the thought of the upcoming wedding night. The idea caused neither passion nor breathlessness to consume her. Perhaps it was because she had given up all thoughts of love long ago. Reason ruled her life now and not foolish dreams of romance. She had married Enrique Navarro only because her father had insisted that it was a most prestigious match. As newly appointed ambassador's aide-designate to England, Enrique was one of Spain's most eligible men.

That was not to say that she did not believe in love. Quite the contrary, she did. Most emphatically so. Her parents had been proof of that. Anne had waited for just such an idyllic love story to enfold for her, but after many years of waiting she had given up. She hadn't met anyone who made her heart skip a beat. Worse yet, she was of the opinion that all of the foppish lords who surrounded the queen, jumping and groveling at that aging harridan's every command, were simpletons. How could she give her heart to any of them? Thus, at twenty-seven she had still been unwed.

"The finicky spinster," her disappointed suitors had labeled her.

Anne didn't care what insults they cast her way, especially when the most important man in her life was on her side. Her father! In her eyes there was no man on earth who could equal Richard Morgan, foremost councilor and advisor to the queen. Even now, with his black hair touched with gray, he was a magnificent man—strong, handsome, with a special gentleness reserved for her. She was the apple of his eye, a truth which made her very proud. If only she could meet such a man!

But after allowing dreams to cloud her thoughts for so long, she finally had to cast aside childish visions of love. Love just did not exist for her. Thus, after many years of waiting, she had given in to her father's wishes that she aid an alliance between Spain and England by agreeing to marry the newly appointed official.

A gust of wind took her unaware, and Anne laughed as she brushed several strands of black hair out of her eyes. Salt spray splashed her face as she gazed out at the ocean, but she barely noticed. She had inherited more than just her father's looks; she also had his temperament. She was stubborn, strong, with a love of excitement and adventure. If she was willful as well, then so be it. A woman should know her own mind!

"I like to hear you laugh." Coming up behind her, Enrique put his arms around her waist, bringing her close against his chest in the first gesture of affection he had shown her since the start of the voyage.

"I will give in to my mirth more often once we reach England." As she spoke she leaned back against him, closing her eyes. Though Anne was of Spanish blood on her maternal grandfather's side, she had hated Spain. The court had been lavish with velvets and silks, more than a match for England's splendor, but there had been little laughter among the coldly aristocratic courtiers.

"And did you not like my country?" She thought she heard a slight annoyance in his tone.

"Yes. It . . . was . . . was very colorful." In truth, the court of Philip of Spain had been gloomy, but Anne was gracious enough to keep this opinion from escaping her lips. "It's just that I was homesick."

"And is England colorful?"

"Most definitely."

"Then I too am anxious to reach this England of yours. I have no great liking for the sea. Too turbulent."

His words were a reminder of last night's storm, a gale that had brought forth Enrique's fear. That he had shown panic had somewhat lessened Anne's opinion of him. Perhaps bravery was not one of the words that described her new husband.

Anne's father had braved much fiercer storms and had faced execution in the days of Mary Tudor's reign. If not for the grace of God, he would have been burned at the stake, with her mother at his side. Opening her eyes with a start, Anne realized she would never have been born had that happened. How foolish then to fret over a few riotous waves.

"The ocean does not frighten me," she said, pulling away so that she could appraise Enrique again. He was not unattractive; indeed, she had heard it declared by many that he was handsome. Why then did his touch leave her so cold? It was a question she had no time to answer as the shrill sound of a trumpet rent the air. It was a chilling sound, one that caused Anne to stiffen until she saw the reason for the blare. It was the sight of a ship that had caused the alarm.

"Por alli, por alla. Un barco . . . otro barco. Siguiente detras." In his fright, her husband had lapsed into Spanish, babbling at the top of his voice, telling the others what was already known, that a ship was following them.

"It is just an English ship." Glancing out at the blue expanse of ocean, she saw clearly that the English flag flew from the mainmast. The words, however, died in her throat. It was indeed an English vessel, but as she looked on in dismay Anne could see that it was bearing down on the *Serpiente de Plata* at a murderous speed in an obvious intent to fight them. "God's nightgown!"

Puffs of smoke billowed from the English ship as it fired upon the galleon. The deck shuddered as wood splintered the railing. Anne sucked in her breath at the sudden impact. Men swarmed the deck, brandishing their weapons, preparing for battle. Cannons boomed as smoke billowed in the air. Grasping the railing, Anne uttered an oath of indignation at the approaching ship, damning them as fools. There was every possibility she might be killed by her own countrymen!

Chapter Two

Jonathan gripped the rail, shouting orders to unfurl the sails and proceed at top speed. "For England and the Queen!" he exclaimed.

His words were enthusiastically echoed by his men. "For England and Elizabeth!"

Patriotism guided them. Greed egged them on. Vengeance drove them. Anger boosted their bravery. They were furious at the Spanish for closing all trade and bagging all treasures for themselves.

For Jonathan there was a much more serious reason that goaded him on as well—the death of his cousin. Condemned to the galleys of a Spanish galleon, the youth had died a miserable death. The tortured account he had heard from one of his cousin's shipmates filled Jonathan's soul with a thirst for revenge against the hated Spanish.

"They'll pay in spades for what they did . . ."

Jonathan watched as his skilled sailors maneuvered the sails of the *White Griffin,* allowing the ship to take advantage of the wind. Speeding upon the sea like a sailfish, the vessel nearly took flight, overtaking the galleon with majestic determination. The sleek English ship veered sharply, angling in the direction of the galleon, then ramming it full speed at the bow. The impact caused debris and men to be hurled in the air. Like a huge whale, the Spanish vessel was wounded. The Spanish would be forced to fight a defensive battle.

Jonathan knew that Philip would put an even higher price upon his head for what he was about to do, but he didn't care. He could outwit, outsail, outfight, and yes, outrage, any Spaniard alive.

The roar of cannons shattered the silence of the sea. The air was filled with the suffocating stench of smoke and powder. The sound of cannon fire was defeaning, nearly drowning out Jonathan's commands as he strode back and forth across the deck. He was unrelentless and unmerciful in his quest for victory because that was the only way he knew how to be. To show one moment of weakness would not only bring about his own death but the deaths of his men as well. These Spanish were a bloodthirsty brood who, like sharks, would devour a man if given but half a chance. That was why he had decided to attack instead of sailing away. Ships that had tried to play fair with the Spaniards were now at the bottom of the sea, their captains little more than skeletons, keeping the fish company.

"Fire! Again, fire!" A volley of cannon balls cut to pieces everything in their path, damaging the hull and deck of the galleon before the Spaniards had time to counterattack. They had been taken totally unawares.

The riggings and mizzenmast of the galleon came thundering down, sending the bloodied bodies of Spanish soldiers flying across the deck. A fire erupted suddenly, bringing about total confusion and panic as many aboard the Spanish ship scrambled about, looking for ways out of the melee. Even so, the Spanish ship managed to get off a volley against the *White Griffin,* damaging the sails and foremast. The ship's figurehead of a white griffin was suddenly minus a wing.

"They intend to hit us broadside, Captain." Edmund Falkhearst stated the obvious.

"Reload!" Though he kept his silence, not even baring

his soul to the grizzled old man who had been his first mate since he could remember, Jonathan knew that if the Spaniards were given a chance to retaliate in full force, they could blast the English ship out of the water. He would not allow that to happen, at least not while he lived and breathed. The three-hundred-ton vessel was his home and the men who followed him as dear to him as brothers.

Aiding the men himself, Jonathan worked frantically, cramming the cannon with powder and ball, ramming it down the muzzle again and again. The huge guns were fired with deadly accuracy, shrouding the ship in cannon smoke just as surely as the fog had.

A shrill trumpet blast signaled another phase of the battle. Grappling hooks hauled the Spanish galleon alongside the *White Griffin*. At last to the shout of "for God and Saint George," the vessel was boarded.

As the ship rocked from the force of cannon fire, Anne wrapped her arms around the thick, round wood and hung on for dear life. Her heart thudded in her breast as she watched the battle from her position behind the mainmast of the *Serpiente de Plata*.

"They're going to kill us all!" Though she knew the attackers were her own countrymen, she was apprehensive about her fate just the same.

"Señora, go below!"

Anne ignored the shouted order. She would not go below. A fire had broken out on one of the lower decks, and she knew instinctively that though it was a tumultuous place to be, she should stay right where she was.

"Stay calm. Don't panic!" she whispered to herself, forcing herself to maintain her composure. She looked on in stunned shock and horror at the crimson, blood-stained deck. In her wildest dreams she had never imagined such a scene.

How long the battle raged, she couldn't say. All she knew was that it seemed the fighting had gone on for hours. Ropes hung like spider's webs connecting the invading ship to the Spanish vessel. Like spiders, the English sailors were dangling from the lines.

Vicious hand-to-hand fighting followed, smearing the deck with blood. It was a terrifying sight, enough to make any other woman swoon, but Anne held her ground, refusing to give in to any such weakness. She had to do something! She wanted to stop this carnage before it was too late. But what could she do? The answer came to her immediately. She was English. They were English. Perhaps she could reason with this English pirate-of-a-captain!

"*Date prisa!* We must hurry. There is a small boat lowering on the other side." Rushing toward her, his face as white as the galleon's sails, Enrique took hold of her hand, tugging frantically.

"I can't leave," she answered emphatically. "I must make these Englishmen listen to reason. I may be the only one here who can ensure any measure of sanity."

For just a moment she was ashamed that she *was* English, for surely the attack had been without warrant. Now the Spanish ship had been shattered by cannon fire and manacled to the side of the English ship by grappling hooks and overrun by English sailors, who were hacking at everything that moved.

"We must leave or we will be killed. *Por favor, querida.*"

Anne could feel her husband's hand trembling and frowned at him. Maybe he was a coward, but she was not. Reaching for a sword that had fallen to the deck during the fighting, she hid the weapon beneath the folds of her gown, just in case the ship's captain would not listen to reason. She moved forward, but Enrique tried to stop her.

"Stop quaking, Enrique, and let go of my hand. I will not desert this ship and leave the others to their fate. Not when I might be able to make the leader of this pack of jackals listen to reason."

"And what makes you think this bloodthirsty devil will listen?"

Anne squared her shoulders, suddenly sure of herself. "I

am Richard Morgan's daughter. The captain will hear me out when he finds out who I am.''

Frantically her eyes searched for the man in authority and settled on a tall, arrogantly handsome rogue who strutted about as if he were a king. This had to be the man she sought, and so she strode forwrard. Summoning all her courage, she met him eye to eye. She had expected sea-blue eyes to gaze back at her but was startled when she saw they were hazel, a mixture of green and brown. Hypnotizing eyes.

''Señorita?'' He looked at her warily, cocking one golden brow. To her mortification, Anne could not speak. *''Habla inglés?''* Because of her dark hair and the fact that she was aboard a Spanish vessel, he assumed she was Spanish.

His mocking smile incensed her beyond reason. Anger blazed in her eyes as she finally found her voice. ''You fool. You imbecile. You dolt. Of course I understand English. I *am* English.'' She squared her shoulders again and haughtily thrust out her chin. ''And you, sir, are a simpleton and a barbarian to do what you have just done. This ship carries the Spanish ambassador's aide to his post at Elizabeth's court.''

Though Jonathan was startled by the news, he did not show it. ''Indeed?'' Sensing a presence behind him, he whirled about and lashed out with his sword at the Spaniard who thought to take him from behind. In moments the unfortunate Spaniard joined his companions on the deck. Wiping his sword with his hand, the ship's captain acted as if there had not been any interruption. ''The ambassador's lackey you say? How unfortunate.''

''Unfortunate? It is much more than that!'' Anne could see that the English captain had divided the crewmen into two groups, who were surrounding the Spaniards in opposite directions, encompassing their enemies between them. ''You must stop this at once!''

''At once?'' Jonathan snorted in disgust. He wouldn't take orders from any woman except the queen.

''Yes, at once!''

The crewmen looked frightening, and for just an instant

her bravery failed her as she looked on in horror. Using bows and arrows, knives and pistols, slashing and thrusting with cutlass and pikes, the Englishmen were brutal. She had the helpless, sinking feeling that her intervention had come too late.

"Stop it?" Jonathan clenched his jaw as he looked down at her. "I think not. Not until I am sure that we have won. I will not doom my men to the dark dungeons or to a life as a galley slave. Unlike you, I have no liking for Spaniards. They are treacherous, greedy, and evil."

Anne was infuriated. "And just what are *you?*"

Jonathan was stung momentarily by the anger and loathing in her eyes. He was used to looks of a far different nature from women. "I am captain, and what I say is law."

"Captain? Is that what you call yourself?" His sun darkened face was an unusual contrast to the blond of his hair. He reminded her of a fierce Viking, those bold rovers who had raided England's shores so many centuries ago. "I think you are more of a pirate!" she mumbled beneath her breath.

"I'm a privateer!"

"A thief is what you are. When we arrive in England, I will see that you answer for what you have done." Anne winced with pain as she felt him grasp her wrist. "Take your hands off me. My father is Richard Morgan. He will see you hanged for this." She took his silence to be alarm and smiled. "You have heard of him, haven't you?"

He certainly had. Morgan was a man all Englishmen admired. Jonathan wasn't anxious to earn such an influential man's scorn and anger. "I've heard of him."

Anne was smug. "I thought so."

Her arrogance irritated him. "And I've heard he has a shrew for a daughter. One who is outrageously spoiled."

His hazel eyes raked over her, taking in every detail with a connoisseur's eye. He could not deny the fact that she was a beauty. Her face was her mother's, oval with a slight widow's peak at the forehead. Hair so dark brown that it was nearly black tumbled to her waist, unrestrained by the crimped curls or braids that were so in vogue. Her skin was smooth and fair, her features delicate, but it was the eyes that fascinated him most. Fringed by long, thick, dark lashes, they were sapphire. Those enormous eyes widened as she looked up at him, flashing fire in her silent rage.

"How dare you say such a thing!" Her indignation brought a flush to her cheeks, which emphasized her high cheekbones. "Insolent rogue." She glared her resentment as his eyes continued their roving. "Undoubtedly you are of common stock. You have the manners of a cowherd's son."

"And you have the temperament of a witch. With a viper's tongue."

Just as suddenly as he had grabbed her wrist, he now let her go. Had she been another woman, he would have enjoyed humbling her and turning her anger into desire, but with bodies lying dead upon the decks he had lost any craving for fierce lovemaking. Even so, the thought of scooping her up in his arms and carrying her to his cabin made him smile.

"What are you grinning at?"

"I was just thinking how delightful it would be to put you over my knee and give you the spanking your father undoubtedly never gave you." He moved forward as if to do just that, then just as quickly whirled around and strode away. He had better things to do than to quarrel with Richard Morgan's haughty daughter.

Anne watched in outrage as he turned his back, dismissing her. A yearning for vengeance flooded her, a desire to have him at her mercy. Would he be so cocksure if he was dangling from a rope? She doubted it. Clenching her fists, she watched him, then reached for the sword she had concealed in her skirt. That would make him listen. Oh, how she wanted to carve her inititals into his thick skin.

Unaware of her thoughts, Jonathan set his crew to the task of taking prisoner all the Spaniards who remained alive. The sight of the bodies lying sprawled upon the bloody deck sickened him. He was not as callous to death as most men thought. It was just that he adhered to the code of kill or be killed.

"Open the cargo hold. Howard! Edmund! Let us see what our labors have brought us."

The clatter of an overturned barrel caused him to turn around, but far from being unnerved, Jonathan laughed at the sight he saw. Dressed fashionably in her scarlet silk gown, the full skirts bobbing up and down as she moved, the dark-haired English beauty strode forward, a sword held high in her hand.

"Careful, my fair English rose. . . ." It seemed her purpose was to wound him. Far from feeling threatened, Jonathan was merely amused. "Your thorns may prick your own flesh."

In answer Anne brought up the weapon, using the stance her father had taught her when they sparred. She was very familiar with the use of sword and pistol. Her father had taught her how to handle both in case the need arose. Now, at this moment, she thanked him.

"I will not fight a woman."

"Then suffer the consequences!" Anne moved forward.

"Now look here, I've never had an opponent who wore a skirt and a farthingale and I don't intend to start now." Aiming the point of his sword at the deck, Jonathan thrust it into the wood.

"I repeat. If you will not fight, then you will suffer the consequences."

"You will have to strike down an unarmed man." His piercing eyes dared her to do just that.

"I should, just to see the look of surprise in your eyes." Anne took a step forward, but before she could make another move a commotion caught not only her attention but Jonathan's as well. "Enrique!" In her encounter with the English privateer, she had forgotten all about her husband. Now, to her consternation, she saw that he was poised haphazardly over the railing with the intention of jumping into the swirling water. "Enrique, no!"

"Do not be foolish, señor, or you will be food for the fish." Hoping to avert a tragedy, Jonathan stalked ever so slowly to where the obviously frightened man was perched.

"I give you my word that no one will harm you. The fighting is over." Had the situation not been so serious, it might have brought a chuckle to his throat. One moment he was facing a sword-armed woman; the next he was trying to coax some Spanish chicken down from his roost. "Come down, señor."

Anne was appalled at her husband's actions. "Enrique. Please." What kind of man would do such a foolish, cowardly thing? Obviously she had misjudged him.

"No. No. I do not trust you. Why would you spare my life when you have killed so many others?" Ignoring his wife's pleas, Enrique Navarro glanced warily about him, grasping the rail with both hands. Preparing himself for flight, he threw one leg over the ship's baluster, straddling it. The sight of his unfortunate countrymen seemed to wipe all else but self-preservation from his mind. To leave the ship, to get away, appeared to be all he could think about.

"Enrique. No!" How could she have married such a sniveling coward? She ran forward, hoping to catch him.

What happened next seemed more nightmare than real, more dream than actuality. One moment Enrique was clinging to the railing, the next he was gone. A violent wave jarred the ship, sending Anne's husband over the side. Anne heard a scream and realized it had come from her own throat.

In the next instant she was looking over the ship's rail, watching in horror as the ocean swallowed her struggling husband.

Chapter Three

Anne stared in confusion at the swirling waters, watching as a dark head bobbed up and down, then disappeared. "Enrique!" she screamed, leaning over the rail. "No!"

Strong hands grasped her firmly around the waist, pulling her back to safety. The captain's voice growled in her ear, "Careful, or you will join that fool in the ocean!"

Anne struggled furiously. She had to save her husband. "Let me go! I have to help him!"

"How? By jumping in the water?"

Whirling around, Anne pushed frantically at the captain's chest, trying to get away. She couldn't stand idly by while her husband drowned! "I must try to save him!"

"Save him? Join him in his stupidity, you mean!" Jonathan had nothing but contempt for cowards. Even so, he shouted to Falkhearst and the others to cast ropes into the ocean for the Spaniard to grab on to. "Haul him in! I have some questions I'd like answered."

"Aye, aye, Cap'n."

Anne watched the captain out of the corner of her eye as he stepped away from her, then waved his arms about issuing orders for an attempted rescue of Enrique. He was doing everything in his power to save her husband, including sending out three small boats to search for him. In her state of mind, however, Anne cast the ship's captain in the role of black-guard, blaming him for Enrique's fate. If he hadn't attacked the ship, Enrique would be by her side, not struggling in the sea.

"Captain. Captain. We've searched every inch of the ocean and can find no trace of the Spanish gentleman." Edmund Falkhearst came bounding up, bowing politely as he passed in front of Anne. "I think for a fact that he must be dead."

"I'm not surprised." Dutifully, Jonathan said a silent prayer for the Spaniard's soul and an audible prayer for the souls of all who had died.

Dead. The word stung Anne. Her husband was gone.

Fearing that she might swoon, the dark-haired first mate held out his arm, but Anne fiercely motioned him away.

"He's drownded, he is. Poor bloke." Obviously smitten by Anne's beauty, he stood staring, wringing his hands. "Nothing to be done about it. Nothing at all. Though I did try to find him, honest I did."

Anne stared at the man wordlessly, feeling more guilt than grief. Guilt that she felt no overwhelming sorrow at Enrique's demise. She willed herself to cry, but tears would not come. What kind of woman was she that she could remain so unmoved?

Jonathan was always uneasy with women's emotions. They confounded him. He sought refuge from having to deal with a teary-eyed woman by tending to his captainly duties. "Call back the boats, Edmund. I need every man. We need to transfer the cargo to the *White Griffin*." He was unprepared for the fury that was unleashed on him.

"Cargo! Cargo? Is that all you can think of? You heathen! You cutthroat! You've killed him, you and your greed." Numb to sorrow, she gave vent to another emotion that had welled up inside her. Anger.

Turning to Jonathan, she scalded him with her words. In reality, however, it was herself that she was storming at all the while. She should have done something to stop Enrique. Now he was dead and no amount of wishing or self-incrimination could bring him back.

"Enrique . . ." It seemed like some ghastly dream. He couldn't really be gone. It seemed so useless, so senseless. Why, oh why, had he done such a stupid thing? "I should have been by his side, not sparring with some egotistical pirate," she said in self-reproach.

"Do not blame yourself for what happened, madam. I assure you that I do not!"

"I do not blame myself, I blame *you*. It is but another of the wrongs you have done for which I shall make you pay." Putting her hands upon her hips, she stared at him only to find him mimicking her stance. Oh, how infuriating he was!

"I had no part in this. The gentleman jumped to his own doom." He clenched his jaw in stubborn ire. "May I ask just who that whey-faced poltroon was?"

Anne winced. She herself had been disappointed in the way her husband had reacted. Lowering her eyes, she said softly, "That man was the ambassador's aide I told you about. And . . . and my husband."

He took a step towards her, his chiseled features expressionless. "For that you have my apologies, madam." Though his tone was cold, in truth he thought it a deplorable fact. A woman with as much spirit as this one needed a man, not a milksop. Were he this beauty's husband, he would have fought for her, given his very life's blood to save her from her captors, not taken the coward's way out. The thought of her being married to the Spaniard bothered him, though he could not truly say why. It was none of his business.

Despite the tragedy of the situation, Anne was fascinated by the captain's obvious masculinity. He had a broad chest, muscular arms, a flat, taut stomach that spoke of strength every time he moved. Though she refused to admit it, the very sight of him made her heart quicken. Perhaps that was why she cast him such a surly frown, fearful he might guess how his manly presence affected her.

''What is to be done with me?'' Anne had heard rumors of what happened to female prisoners. Like the treasure aboard ship, they were treated as part of the spoils. Was rape to be part of her ordeal?

She looked warily at the tall English sea captain who had braved her anger as calmly as he braved the combat. He was looking at her with the indulgence one might give an ill-tempered child, seemingly reading her mind as he said ''I will do my best to see that you are quite safe and comfortable for the remainder of the voyage. My cabin lacks luxuries, but I'm certain it will do. As to your husband, what has been done has been done, and nothing in this world can change it.''

''Your cabin?'' Anne seldom felt fear, but the thought of being near this virile man caused that emotion now. Somehow she sensed that she had met her match. She could not cajole her way with this one. ''As your prisoner?''

''As my guest.'' He bowed, taking his leave of her. Ignoring her protestations, he set his crew to the task of emptying the hold and was pleased at the stock of wealth that met his eyes. Gold, silver, and jewels were piled high; this treasure would most definitely placate Elizabeth's censure. That bold lady had the true heart of a pirate when it came to silver and gold.

''We are rich, Captain. 'Twas our luck to come across such riches in the fog.'' Standing with parchment and quill in his hand, Edmund Falkhearst carefully made log of each thing of value. ''Riches from the New World I would suppose, though I can't imagine why they were not unloaded in Spain. Did I not know better, I'd say our poor deceased dignitary had it in mind to bribe someone, else why was a ship headed for England filled with such a hoard? And yon lass calls *you* greedy.'' He motioned with his head towards Anne, who was watching as her own possessions were being transferred to the English vessel.

''I've been wondering the same thing. Perhaps our interception of the Spanish ship was more timely than we suppose.''

Busying himself with pulling at the rope of a hemp loading net, easing a cargo of gold down into the opening of his own ship's hold, Jonathan pondered the matter. He couldn't help but wonder if there was more to the dignitary's jumping overboard than he had first imagined. Perhaps it had been something more than a mere act of cowardice. Suppose the ambassador's aide had fled from the ship in order to escape questioning? If that was the case, then how much did his widow know? She was English, that much was undoubtedly true, but that did not mean she could not be involved in a plot. Indeed, since the Papal Bull of 1570 had made the assassination of Elizabeth lawful in the eyes of the Catholic Church, attempts on her life were being actively encouraged by the Pope. Hadn't Francis Throckmorton recently been caught sending information abroad?

England and Spain were at odds, and yet this English-woman had married a Spaniard. It aroused his suspicion. Although it was true that her father was an advisor to the queen, it would not be the first time that a man in such a position turned traitor. Like Throckmorton, Richard Morgan was a staunch Catholic, had in fact been one of Mary Tudor's councilors until he was arrested for treason. He had been saved from an untimely death by the intervention of a *Spanish* dignitary; a man who, it was found out later, was his wife's father.

"And Anne Morgan's grandfather!" At that thought, he stiffened. Anne Morgan was herself of Spanish blood; why had he not remembered that fact? He pondered what he knew about the young woman. She had been pampered, spoiled by an over-indulgent father, and allowed to come to court only infrequently. Though she had many offers for her hand from titled Englishmen, she had scorned them all, with her father's approval. "Until she married a Spaniard." Jonathan gritted his teeth as he remembered her weak, cowardly husband. Perhaps not so cowardly after all, but instead wary of betraying his guilt.

"The English lass is a beauty, isn't she, Captain?" Jonathan felt the stab of a quill in his ribs. "Isn't she, Cap'n?"

"What?" He realized he hadn't heard a word Edmund had been saying.

"I said the Englishwoman is a bloomin' treasure. Worth her weight in Spanish gold. Were I a wee bit younger, I'd have it in mind to soothe that poor forlorn widow. A woman like that should not sleep alone."

"Most definitely." Jonathan smiled dangerously as an idea came to mind. He knew he had a golden tongue and that women flitted around him like butterflies. Jonathan had enjoyed many flirtations; all types of women had succumbed to his charms, from innocent young maids to sexually unfulfilled matrons. Now he intended to add the widow to his list of conquests. It would be for the good of England, he told himself. He would charm Anne Morgan and find out if he was right about her husband having been involved in a plot.

"The widow . . ." He smiled as he thought how their clash of wills had only just begun.

Chapter Four

Fiery sparks exploded in the night air. Red and orange flames licked at the galleon. Wisps of smoke curled up towards the sky as the *Serpiente de Plata* burned like a funeral pyre. Anne watched the final destruction of the Spanish vessel through the mullioned window of the captain's cabin, feeling helpless for the first time in her life.

It was too late for Enrique. Too late for the men aboard the ship. Too late to undo the barbarous acts of that ... that pirate! She had been powerless to keep Enrique from jumping to his doom, too late to aid the conquered men and perhaps just as unable to control her own destiny. It was an unsettling thought.

What about me? What happens now? Just what was the captain going to do? Would he be honorable? "Ha!" She had no illusions about him being an honorable man. He was a murderer, a plunderer, and a thief. The openly lustful way he had been looking at her made her assume that he was a philanderer as well. No doubt he stole women's hearts and virtue with just as much abandonment as he had stolen the Spanish gold.

She had no reason to believe he would be a gentleman.

Even after having learned that the man who had fallen overboard was her husband, the captain had shown no respect but instead had condemned her husband, all the while looking at her with a heated gaze that had nearly scorched her. He had given her no reason to believe that he would show her the respect due a widow.

Widow! She was a widow! How strange that thought was now. Only a few hours ago, she had been a newly wedded bride, sailing back to England with her husband. Now when she returned, it would be alone.

Perhaps there were no certainties in life after all. It was an unnerving thought for someone whose life up until now had been so secure and predictable. Now Anne realized that one brief moment could completely alter the course of one's life and possibly even destroy it. It was an unsettling thought that deeply troubled her as she stared out into the night.

For the moment her fate was in the hands of a dangerous man! Whether she liked it or not, the English captain had her destiny right in the palm of his hand and she deeply resented him for it.

"What is he going to do?"

She had begun to doubt that she would come to any serious harm. So far she had been treated with deference by most of the crew. *He wouldn't dare allow his men to violate me.* She was, after all, the daughter of Richard Morgan. Even that overbold pirate would have to be cautious.

For just a moment, she smiled. There was nothing quite as fierce as an enraged father. Even this Captain whats-his-name would have to account for her safety or explain the reason why she had come to serious harm. As to the poor unfortunates who had been captured, she could not say the same. For them, there was only the dank darkness of the ship's lowest deck. Had she been Spanish or of lowly English birth, she might have suffered a similar fate or worse.

But what about her virtue? Rape. It was an ugly word, and yet she had heard stories of what happened to women who were so unfortunate as to be captured by men with no code of law. Seafarers. Privateers. Violent men. Wrapping her arms around herself, she closed her mind to such thoughts, confident that despite his faults, the privateer captain would not dare even contemplate such a thing.

Or would he? She shivered as she remembered the way the captain had caressed her body with his eyes, taking in every curve. His gaze had been bold. Brazen. Lustful. There was no doubt of what he had been thinking. Or planning?

Anne's attentions were drawn to the low, wide bed, and she stiffened. If he makes but one attempt at touching me, I'll make him wish he had never been born. Her eyes sought out a weapon and found it in the large brass lamp that balanced on a table near the bed. If it became necessary, she would wield it without remorse. Maybe that would knock some sense into the shameless captain's head.

"But it will not be needed," she whispered to herself. Once more she assured herself that being Richard Morgan's daughter would cause the captain to use caution in his treatment of her.

The captain had been gruff, bold, and rude, it was true, yet he had come to her aid once or twice. She remembered her humiliation when one of her leather-bound trunks had broken open during the loading, revealing her more intimate feminine apparel. Three of the rougher seamen had thought to have some fun at her expense, parading about holding her petticoats, corsets, farthingale, and chemise to their bodies, swaying about like women. The captain's intervention had saved her further embarrassment as he had given stern orders that she was not to be molested. For that at least she thanked him, if she did not totally trust him.

A small china basin and pitcher balanced precariously on a table near the window, and Anne busied herself with washing off the grit and the grime of the battle. The stench of smoke offended her nostrils, and she hurried to change her clothes, searching to find where her trunks of clothing had been placed. Finding one trunk, she looked through it for something appropriate. A woman in mourning was expected to wear dark-colored gowns with high, choking collars, and so she chose her dullest dress, one of dark brown velvet with large full sleeves banded in three places by gilt ribbon. Carefully braiding and coiling her hair, she put on a cap of brown velvet trimmed in lace with points coming down in the center of her forehead and on both cheeks. A ''Mary Stuart'' cap, she'd heard it called and shuddered at the fate of that poor woman who even now languished in some lonely tower as prisoner of the queen.

She too was made a widow by men as ruthless as those who strode the deck outside the door. One of those seamen obviously thought to be a visitor, for she heard a loud knock at the door.

''Whoever it is, go away!'' Anne ordered shrilly, fearing that it might be the captain. She didn't want to confront him again so soon

''It's me, Edmund Falkhearst. I've brought light for the tapers, and yer dinner.''

Anne remembered him, a paunchy, always laughing man in his older years who had shown her kindness when her husband had jumped over the rail. ''Are you alone?''

''Aye!''

Opening the door, she was greeted with his grinning, cherub-like face.

''I'm not very hungry.'' The thought of the galleon's defeat deeply troubled her. It had been senseless, unnecessary for that English pirate to attack. ''How could I be after what has happened?'' Her heart was filled with pity for those who had died and those who were now held prisoner. ''How can I think of only myself when others are suffering?''

''What's happened has happened. 'Tis the way of things.'' He pushed through the door, setting a tray on a round table near the bed. The cabin was tiny, much smaller quarters than she had enjoyed on the Spanish vessel, and the little man nearly collided with her as he turned around. ''Don't need to think those Spaniards would not have done the same. Why, our lives would not have been worth a farthing if Jonathan hadn't struck first.''

''Jonathan?''

''The captain.'' He seemed to sense that she was inter-

ested. "Jonathan Nathaniel Leighton is his name." He thrust
out his chest proudly, as if talking about himself. "He's the
queen's own privateer."

Anne mumbled beneath her breath. *The queen's privateer.*
He seemed to deem it a lofty title for himself. "I doubt that
Elizabeth would sanctify what has been done. She is most
assuredly a peaceful lady."

"Peaceful, yes. But she is also a woman who knows the
value of gold."

"Indeed. When I tell her what happened, she will be as
horrifed as I am. She'll clap your Captain Leighton in irons
and throw away the key!" Anne punctuated the sentence
with a shake of her head.

"Imprison Jonathan?" He laughed. "Not hardly. She'll
pat him on the back and take her own share of what we
bring back. Why, Jonathan was granted a commission by
her very own hand."

Anne drew herself up to her full height. "Would you
imply, my dear sir, that the Queen of England knows of this
piracy at sea and would condone such actions by one of her
captains?" Anne was aghast.

"She bloody well does and will. She encourages piracy."
His voice lowered conspiratorily. "How else do ye think
she hopes to finance a fleet of her own ships?" His voice
lowered to a whisper. "But don't tell anybody." With a
chuckle, he fidgeted in a small leather pouch he carried at
his waist and pullled forth a wick that was used in firing
powder. Standing up on tiptoes, he used it to light four tapers
that rose from brass wall sconces. The flickering candles
gave light to the room, casting wavering shadows. "There,
that will make the cabin more pleasant for ye."

"Thank you." Anne gave him a half smile. "But I will
not be comforted until I see the white cliffs of home." She
thought it was a burst of sudden shyness that made him
avert his eyes. "It shouldn't be long now. Two days. Perhaps
three." *And then we'll see just how arrogant your captain
will be,* she thought. She sincerely doubted the little man's

story about the queen's attitude towards piracy. "We'll be home soon."

"Depends on the wind." He stared hard at his feet, not even lifting his eyes to look at her as he made for the door, but he did flash her another smile as he passed through that portal. "Think again about yer dinner. I gave ye a share of my own rations, I did. The cook's a magician with such paltry fare. Beef cooked in beer, cheese, a biscuit and some wine. Being that it's Friday, there's even chick peas."

Closing the door behind him, he left Anne and she was surprised by how much she wanted to call him back. He had been pleasant company. Without his presence, it was quiet in the room except for the faint roar of the sea outside. She was suddenly very lonely.

This is all just a dream, she thought, sitting down upon the bed. I'll wake up and find Enrique bending over me, and we'll share a laugh or two about how fanciful I can be. As if to prove that it was indeed a nightmare, she pinched herself, finding to her woe that it hurt. Not a dream then, but reality. Enrique was dead, she was the guest of an English privateer, and the galleon she had sailed on had been consigned to the sea.

Guest. Prisoner. She thought it to be a fine line indeed between the two in her situation. What was this man like, this man she had just learned was named Jonathan Leighton?

Anne looked around as if hoping to find the answer within the confines of the room. There was nothing soft or gentle in what she saw. No velvets, satins, or silks. A few Turkish rugs on the floor were his only concession to luxury. It was a very masculine room, and she decided immediately that it must reflect the captain's personality.

Maps were nailed to the wall haphazardly, dotted with colors, telling the story of places that had been visited or soon would be. So he was an adventurous man. Charts and nautical instruments covered the large wooden desk that was securely fastened by nuts and bolts to the wooden floor; books tumbled from makeshift bookcases. Surprisingly, it appeared that he was a studious man. One corner of the cabin was piled with canvas, sailcloth, and rope, representative of a man who made his living by skimming the sea. An open chest at the foot of the bed revealed one dagger, two pistols, and three swords. Proof that he was a violent man.

Anne put all the pieces together to form the completed mosaic of Jonathan Leighton, but found several pieces missing. Did he have a softer side? Had he ever been in love? Did he laugh? Did he cry? Was he as vulnerable as other men? If someone pricked him, would he bleed?

Anne remembered the sight of him, his shirt torn and dirtied from the battle, his leather doublet stained by blood, his hair a flash of gold in the sun. He kindled an emotion within her that was frightening in its intensity. Hatred? She told herself it was, yet a voice seemed to whisper that she lied. There was a magnetism about him that drew her to him, and this deeply troubled her. The thoughts that tugged at her mind were unseemly for any woman, much less a widow. Enrique was dead and this English captain was partly responsible! She must remember that.

"Enrique! Enrique! Enrique!" As if to exorcise herself of any thoughts regarding Jonathan Leighton, Anne forced herself to think her husband's name. Leaning back on the bed, she closed her eyes, wrapping her arms around a big stuffed pillow, lost to a haze of dreams as the soft sway of the ship and the soft thumping of the waves soon lulled her to sleep.

Chapter Five

The soft glow of moonlight illuminated the red cross of Saint George on a field of white which was the insignia of the *White Griffin*. Standing on the quarterdeck, Jonathan Leighton felt an overwhelming sense of pride in his ship as he watched the flag flutter in the breeze. It was as fine a vessel as had ever sailed the seas.

"And thankfully a sturdy boat. . . ."

To Jonathan's relief, the three-masted vessel had escaped any severe damage from the day's fighting. The ship had sustained a broken mast, crushed bowsprit and beakhead, broken beams in the ship's hull, minor damage to the sails, and a shattering of the figurehead's left wing. Considering the magnitude of the battle, however, the *White Griffin* had been very lucky. Despite its injuries, the ship could still sail without any major hindrance. Therefore, Jonathan had made the decision to change course and sail away from England and not towards it. Due to his suspicions concerning the Spanish diplomat and his determination to investigate his suspicions, he didn't want to arrive in England too soon. He needed a few more days so that he would have time to question the widow and find out why so much gold was aboard the Spanish ship.

"Who in England was that cowardly husband of hers going to bribe?" he whispered to himself. It was a question that troubled him deeply in these turbulent times of plot and counterplot.

"Cap'n . . ." Standing with his cap in his hand, Edmund looked forlorn as he approached.

"What is it?" Jonathan's first thought at seeing the little man's frown was of the *White Griffin*. "Was there more damage done to the ship than I first concluded?"

Falkhearst shook his head. He sighed. "It's . . . it's about the widow. I . . . I looked in on the lady, just like yer told me, Captain."

Jonathan curled his lips in a mocking smile. "And was she hospitable?" He could well imagine that Edmund's hangdog look was the result of her scolding.

"Aye." Edmund sighed again. "And as gentle as a lamb."

"Gentle?" Jonathan cocked one brow in surprise. That was hardly a word he would use to describe her.

"And . . . and just about the prettiest sight I ever did see. . . ."

Jonathan could remember the widow's loveliness in his mind's eye, but he refused to admit aloud that he thought her to be beautiful. "Pretty is as pretty does, or so they say," he grumbled.

Falkhearst ignored Jonathan's barb, saying softly, "She's taking what happened today much harder than yer think."

Jonathan stiffened. "Then perhaps I will pay her a visit tonight, to make amends and give my condolences to the bereaved lady." Though usually a patient man, he was consumed with a sudden impatience to pay the widow a visit. To interrogate her, of course.

"I don't think ye should, Jonathan." The first mate's voice was so low that Jonathan barely heard him.

"What?" Jonathan cast a critical eye overhead as two of

his crew scrambled up the rigging, walked along the yard-arms, and secured the sails.

Falkhearst repeated, "I don't think yer should." The look on his face was the epitome of compassion. "The poor lady is broken-hearted. Why . . . why, she wouldn't even take a bite of what I brought her."

"Then she will just have to go hungry." Jonathan was annoyed. So the haughty chit had charmed Edmund. "That woman is trouble! Put away your sympathies and look at her realistically, Edmund! She's cunning and dangerous."

Falkhearst clucked his tongue. "Oh, no . . . .no. She's a bit spirited perhaps but . . . but I like her."

"You *like* her!" Jonathan was incensed by Falkhearst's seeming betrayal.

Falkhearst hurried to explain. "I . . . I think we might have misjudged her, Captain. She doesn't look like a spy or a traitor to me."

Jonathan's voice was a deep rumble. "And just what does a traitor look like?" Perhaps she was more dangerous than he had feared. Certainly she had quickly wound Edmund around her little finger. "Are they perchance taller? Fairer of hair?" Jonathan touched the tip of Falkhearst's nose with his finger. "Do they all have crooked noses?"

Edmund was taken aback. "Why, I . . . I don't know, but I . . . I don't think *she* is one." He twisted his hat so fiercely that he nearly tied it into knots.

"Well, I do!" Jonathan roared. "They come in all shapes and sizes, including pretty packages." He paused for a moment, then asked, "You can't trust your eyes when it comes to spies. You can't even trust reputations. For example, would you have suspected Throckmorton, Edmund?"

Falkhearst shrugged. "I . . . I don't know."

"No doubt the others didn't know either, because they misjudged him and thus trusted in his loyalty. We both know the consequences of that error in judgment. Luckily he did not succeed, or there would be another woman wearing the crown of England on her head right now!"

Jonathan paced up and down the deck, deep in thought.

He was loyal to Elizabeth and considered her a skilled diplomat who had brought about not only his prosperity but the prosperity of others. More importantly, she had maintained the peace.

"I can't take any chance of harm coming to the Queen. You know that there are still those who would see Mary Stuart sit upon the English throne." That his own cousin was suspect he determinedly pushed out of his mind. "It's a troubled time in England. Spain is instigating—"

Falkhearst put his hand on Jonathan's arm. "I just don't want to see the pretty young widow hurt, that's all, her having just lost her husband and all. She isn't some light o' love, she's a lady. A fair English rose, just like you said, and—"

"A rose with thorns!" Falkhearst's infatuation with the woman made Jonathan all the more determined to expose her perfidy. "And until I can reassure myself that she really is innocent, I intend to go ahead with what I have planned."

He would try to get the information without using force, but if that became necessary, he was prepared to bully and threaten. Hopefully it would not come to that. He hated to make of Richard Morgan an enemy, at least not just yet.

"But . . . but Cap'n . . . couldn't you just let the lady be for a while until . . ."

Jonathan turned his back in disgust, not wanting to hear any more of Edmund's foolishness. It was obvious that his first mate's opinions had been tempered by his infatuation. Why, the next thing he knew, the entire crew would be smitten. He had to find out the truth and quickly so that he could get the ship back to port and then get on with the normalcy of his life. Grumbling beneath his breath, he climbed the ladder to the first mate's tiny cubicle and pushed open the door. A clutter of disarray met his eyes. Edmund was most definitely not a well-organized man.

"Edmund acts as if I intend to beat her," he mumbled beneath his breath. "What kind of man does he think I am? Didn't I give the lady my own cabin?" It was a grand act of generosity, he thought, sharing this room with Edmund when he could have kept his own quarters. Despite the rough life at sea, he was still a gentleman.

Muttering all the while, he sought to make himself present-able, washing himself, exchanging his seaman's garb for those of a gentleman. Unlike some of the other sailors, Jonathan kept his face smooth-shaven, a streak of his own vanity, and so he found a razor and scraped his face. Shaving, however, was no easy task for there were no mirrors in the cabin, and he could not see what he was doing. Nevertheless, he somehow managed. When he was fully satisfied with his appearance, he climbed down the ladder to his captain's cabin, which was right below.

Opening the door, he found the room bathed in gentle light, illuminating the lovely vision that was curled up in the middle of the bed. Jonathan drew in his breath as his eyes traveled over her appreciatively. Against the light green of the quilt, her form was clearly outlined, as was the dark mantle of her hair. She looked alluring lying there, her ankles and calves peeking beneath the hem of her dress, her full breasts rising and falling as she breathed deeply of sleep. Long, dark lashes shadowed her cheekbones, and he could not help but think how softly feminine she looked when she was not quarreling with him. Despite himself, he had to admit that she was beautiful. Was it any wonder that Jonathan felt something stir within him? Desire? Lust? Or another emotion he could not quite define? Whatever it was he was mesmer-ized by her as he made his way across the deck.

She was certainly the prettiest hellion he'd ever con-fronted. A hellion who looked more like an angel as he looked down at her. Conflicting emotions warred within him. He found himself suddenly wanting to comfort her, to assure her that all would be well, an insane desire to take her into his arms and never let her go. Was it any wonder that Edmund had been so bemused? Could he really blame him?

She looks so sad. He wanted to see that generously curved mouth turn up in a smile, see her deep blue eyes look upon him with favor. He wanted to . . .

No, by God! Fiercely he tore his gaze away. It had been his intention to wield his charms on her, not the other way around. What was the matter with him? He reminded himself coldly of the situation. He had found her aboard a ship loaded with Spanish gold headed for England. This seemingly innocent lovely had drawn him into a quarrel while her husband was initiating a cowardly suicide leap from Jonathan's ship so he wouldn't be interrogated.

She was in on it. Bereaved widow be damned. The Spaniard leaped to his death rather than take the chance of being executed. His suicide was an act of guilt.

Aide to the Spanish ambassador indeed. That man was up to more than a diplomatic mission. Jonathan had seen the man's face and knew a devious look when he saw one. What's more, he would be a blithering fool if he let the widow's womanly appeal sway him from his purpose. Folding his arms across his chest, he braced himself for combat as her eyelids fluttered open.

"You!" The ship's captain was staring down at her, his hazel eyes nearly burning her with his gaze. "What are you doing here?" Instinctively Anne drew away, distrustful of his intent. How could she have believed even for a moment that such a man could be a gentleman?

"What am I doing here indeed! It is my cabin." He wanted to rage at her but remembered himself. Honey was much surer bait than vinegar. "I left a few of my personal items behind and came to claim them." To uphold the lie, he gathered up a few items lying on his desk. "I hope I did not disturb your sleep."

"Obviously you did," she exclaimed, eyeing him up and down with contempt.

He ignored her barb, forcing a smile. "For that I apologize. It is my hope that you will be comfortable here."

"Comfortable?"

She gave him a measured look, trying to decide if he was being truthful or just snide. He seemed to be in earnest, much to her surprise, and thus she relaxed. He did not look as threatening now. Away from the deck, he didn't look any more menacing than any other man at court did. He had changed into a doublet of brilliant green decorated with buttons and piping of dull gold. He wore short trunk hose of a darker hue decorated with brown appliques and close-fitting cantons of gold. The captain looked dashing, she couldn't deny that. From the toes of his brown leather shoes to the top of his head, he looked dashing and handsome.

Jonathan called upon all the charm he possessed as he said, "We started off on the wrong foot, so to speak. I regret that. I would like to make amends and show you I am truly sorry for what happened."

"You are sorry?" It was the last thing she expected to hear him say.

She watched silently as he reached into an old wooden chest and pulled out a bottle of wine. Filling two tankards he retrieved from a nearby table, he held one forth for her to take. "Let us call a truce between us."

"A truce?" Anne scrambled from the bed and stood looking up at him warily. What was his motive? She had hardly expected his solicitations, considering the rude and arrogant way he had acted up on deck.

Jonathan sought to pacify her obvious distrust. "Your husband's death was most unfortunate, but you must agree that it was no fault of mine."

She shook her head defiantly, not willing to so easily forgive what had been done. Whether or not he was responsible for her husband's death was a matter of opinion.

"Oh, wasn't it! Have you so easily forgotten what happened?"

What a stubborn woman. Was she going to hold a grudge forever? "I have not forgotten. However, if you remember correctly, it was your husband's decision to, shall we say, take his leave of the ship. I did not push him." He struggled to maintain his composure, but he was perilously close to losing his temper. "There is no reason for us to be hostile towards each other, don't you agree?"

He could not expect her to so easily brush the matter aside, Anne thought. Enrique was dead. She had to at least show proper respect for his memory. "Had you not attacked the ship, he would not be dead. Because of that you are responsible, sir."

Jonathan bristled at her words yet maintained his smile. This matter of pleasantry was going to be difficult to feign if she continued to bait him. Stubborn woman. She was exasperating. Any other woman would have cheerily complied and absolved him of any guilt. "I only did what had to be done to save my own life and the lives of my men."

Your Spanish friends were not as innocent as they seemed, and neither are you, he thought sourly. That she continued harping on the subject seemed to speak of her own guilt. One would have thought that the Spaniards were her kinsmen, but she was English *and* a subject of the queen. How could she let herself forget that?

"Save the lives of your men, indeed!" Anne wasn't falling for his excuse. "It did not seem to me that you were threatened by the Spanish vessel. What's more, I know that the intent of the ship's captain was to sail peacefully to England."

"Landing at which harbor?" He blurted the question without a second thought, then amended his tone of interrogation. "Where was your destination?" He stared into the depths of his tankard as if he could find the answer there. "Near the coast of Lancashire? Northumberland? Yorkshire?"

The northern counties were notoriously sympathetic to those who aligned themselves with Mary Stuart. They wanted to turn the country back to Catholicism. It chilled him to the bone to think that perhaps the gold and silver had been meant to pay an army to march against the queen.

"We were headed for London. Isn't that where most ships put into port?" She was incensed and confused by his questioning. His curiosity about their destination didn't make any sense at all. "My husband had an appointment there. One he will not be able to keep now. I will have to inform—"

"With whom?" Seeing that she had not even touched

her wine, he bade her drink. He would get her woozy with wine to loosen her tongue. "Who was he going to see? Who was his appointment with?"

"With Howard Morley," she answered matter-of-factly, seeing no reason to be evasive. Realizing that she was thirsty, she took a drink.

"Howard Morley and the queen. And of course my father."

"Of course." So, Richard Morgan was in on it too.

Seeing that at last she had partaken of her wine, he refilled her cup. He doubted the queen was to be among those assembled for the supposed meeting.

"And what of the gold? Who was that intended for?"

"The gold?" Why on earth did he keep interrogating her? Suspicion concerning his motives pricked her. Was he perchance hoping to use her answers in some other foul scheme? Was he planning another act of piracy? Well, she would not be a part of his crime. "I don't know about any gold."

She was lying. He knew it. She must have stood there watching while it was being loaded. That much gold didn't just suddenly appear out of nowhere. "The gold that was in the cargo hold. And the silver. Certainly it was not your dowry." He laughed as if to make light of the matter.

"It was not." Whatever foolish game he was playing, she was tiring of the play. Questions, questions, questions.

"Then what was it?"

Her entire body was aware of him as he took a step towards her. "What do you mean?" she asked warily.

He was determined to find out the answer. "Was it a present? A bribe?"

She looked at him incredulously as he grasped her by the shoulders. "I'm sure I do not know." She should have pulled away, but she did not. Instead she glanced at him questioningly, trying to perceive his motives, trying to read the inner workings of his mind.

"I think you do." Though his voice was low and husky, the insistent pressure of his fingers gave her a warning of his anxiety. "I think you know a great deal. I also know that I intend to find out just what was, or perhaps still is, ticking away in your mind."

She didn't know the answer to the questions he was asking but realized what he was insinuating. "You will find out nothing!" Her eyes were dark and fiery sapphires, caressing him with anger as she said, "Unhand me, you—you pirate!"

"Pirate am I?" He laughed, deciding to end the questioning for the moment.

"Yes. Pirate!"

Seeing that a lock of her hair had come undone from its pins, he reached out to capture it, brushing her hand with his fingers as she reached up to secure the stray curl. The mutual touch of their fingers was surprisingly sensual for such a simple gesture, and for a moment Jonathan was silent. Then he said, "I would rather say that I merely want to aid the Spanish in redistributing their gold."

"Distribute it." She noticed rough calluses on the palms of his hands, a small scar by his forehead, the only visible signs of a seafaring life now that he'd clothed himself like a proper English gentleman. There was a cleft in his chin that she had not noticed before. Anne almost reached out to touch it, but quickly controlled the impulse, whispering, "Steal it you mean."

There is something about this man. Something that confounds my common sense. He's unprincipled, dangerous, arrogant, and much too bold, and yet I can't help but wonder what it would be like to have his strong fingers touch and caress me. I can't help but wonder what it would be like to lie in his arms and . . .

She flushed at the thought, angry at herself. Enrique was dead. She must remember that! She must also remember that it should have been his hand that straightened her hair, his fingers that stroked her, not this English pirate's. She drew away, casting the captain an angry glare. He wasn't anything like her husband.

Oh, no. Enrique and Jonathan Leighton were as different as night from day. Enrique was controllable. Manageable.

He had given in to her every whim. She might be able to say many things about this Jonathan Leighton, pirate extraordinaire, but she could never say that he was "manageable."

Jonathan was fascinated by the intensity of those thickly lashed blue eyes as she studied him. He intrigued her. The thought made him smile. She was not as angry as she pretended. Just as he was drawn to her, she was likewise drawn to him, though he doubted she would ever admit it.

"Steal? You accuse me unjustly."

There was a spark of passion between them that he no longer wanted to deny. Why should he? When a man lived a dangerous life, he knew well that he had to live for the moment, without second thoughts. Therefore, it seemed natural to encircle his arms about her in an embrace.

"Ah, madam, you wound me with your words. How I would like to hear compliments instead from those sweet lips."

With an oath that was halfway between a curse and an imprecation, he bent down and captured her mouth in a searing kiss that left Anne breathless. His lips flamed on hers, moving, searching, plundering, igniting a fire in her blood that she struggled to control. There was danger in such feelings and in the insane urge she felt to press herself closer, to cling to him. Pulling violently away from his embrace, she slapped him across the face, not so much in anger as in sudden fear, an emotion she rarely felt.

"You devil! You whoreson. How dare you." Stunned and shaken by the depth of her reaction to a mere kiss, she lashed out in the only way she knew, with words. "I am not some foolish, shy young maid that you can seduce. I am a woman . . . . a . . . a married woman."

"Very much a woman." The passion of their kiss, the fierce hunger he had felt at her nearness, the nearly uncontrollable desire that had surged through his body shook Jonathan to the core. Never had just one kiss affected him this way. He wanted to possess her so completely, so powerfully, that she would forget that any other man existed, especially that cowardly, devious husband of hers.

"A . . . a woman who is in mourning, sir."

"As you keep reminding me. Or are you reminding yourself?"

His question hit home. She felt the need to remind herself again and again. "I must think of my husband and show proper respect."

"Why? He didn't think about you when he jumped." Jonathan had nothing but loathing for the foolish Spaniard. "He thought only of himself and how fearful he was. He didn't seem to care that he was leaving you behind to answer for his misdeeds."

He would sincerely enjoy seducing and taming this lively young widow. Traitor, spy, or not, she intrigued the hell out of him, more so than any other woman he had ever known.

"He made the choice to die. But you are very much alive. I could tell just how alive by how you responded to my kiss." Reaching out, he touched her lips with his fingers to remind her.

Anne pulled away. She felt threatened by him. He was not the kind of man who understood the word no. Anxiously she eyed the open trunk that displayed Jonathan's weapons, just in case she had need of them. He, however, sensing her intent, positioned himself between the trunk and the glowering woman.

For the first time since childhood, Anne started to cry. Not because of sadness, but from a sense of frustration. For the first time in her life, she had met her match, and she didn't like it at all.

Jonathan misunderstood her emotions. "He was not worth your tears. In truth you should not mourn him. He was a coward. He left you behind to take his share of punishment."

"Punishment?" Intent on easing her way towards the safety of the door, Anne paused. "What do you mean, punishment? Fie, sir, it is you who are the pirate, not my husband and not I."

Jonathan was tired of having her call him a pirate, especially when it was her husband who had seemingly instigated treachery. ''I am an English patriot. My duty is to keep the enemy off balance, to prevent them from bringing money or supplies to those whose thought it is to overthrow the queen—*anyone,* be he Spanish or English, whose purpose it is to raise an army to dethrone Elizabeth. Any enemy of Elizabeth Tudor is my enemy.''

Anne crossed her arms across her breasts and stepped back. He was talking about rebellion. What did that have to do with Enrique? With her?

Jonathan continued, ''I will not let any gold reach England that might be used for such a deed. Particularly Spanish gold. Do you get my meaning?''

There was a long, uncomfortable silence between them, broken only by the creaking timbers of the hull as it suffered the slap of the sea. Anne stared, her heart hammering in her breast, her lips frozen in a gasp as she at last realized what he had been thinking all along. The expression on his face told her all too clearly what he believed and clarified the reason for his questioning. It seemed so impossible, so ludicrous, but he seemed to think that the gold found aboard the *Serpiente de Plata* was to be used against Elizabeth. Why, he actually seemed to think that she was involved!

''God's nightgown!'' Her eyes widened as she put her hand up to her mouth. She was angry. She felt humiliated. She was appalled. Jonathan Leighton was accusing her of being a traitor!

Chapter Six

The wind ruffled the sails and whipped at Jonathan's hair as he stood on the deck. "That woman is trouble!" he grumbled, running his fingers through his hair in a frustrated attempt to brush it out of his eyes. "Trouble!"

Though Jonathan could at times be a stubborn man, there was no way he could argue with the truth. He had made a mistake in thinking that he could tame the haughty widow, much less trick her into revealing the details of her husband's plot against England. She was either innocent of any kind of treasonous act or too intelligent to be unmasked. In the meantime, her very presence was already creating havoc among the crew.

"Trouble," he said again.

Slowly but surely she was seducing his usually loyal sailors with a smile here and there and a look of promise in those wide blue eyes. Now there was an ever-present tension between his men as they vied with each other just to find ways to please her. Why, even the ship's cook had fallen under her spell, using his newfound culinary skills to whip up a special recipe for tomorrow night's dinner just to gain her favor.

Bloody damn! One would think she was the queen of England, the way they tripped over themselves just to please her!

Worse yet, Jonathan had to be on guard, for there was more than just a hint of a conspiracy in the making. He had heard disgruntled whispers concerning his decision to delay their arrival back in England. It was no secret that some of the men were anxious to return home with their spoils and to be reunited with their loved ones. These sailors, who had not been ensnared by the widow's charms and viewed a woman's presence on ship as a bad omen, openly blamed her for their woes. Suspicion and peril hovered in the air.

A flock of seagulls screeched as they circled the crow's nest, as if adding their voices to the argument. "Go home. Go home," they seemed to say.

"Not until I know why there was so much gold aboard the Spanish ship or why the Spaniard jumped overboard," Jonathan mumbled to himself. He had to find out the truth. Was the lovely, dark-haired widow a spy and a traitor to England or as innocent as Edmund Falkhearst professed her to be? And what about her husband, Enrique Navarro? Had he been in league with all those who plotted Elizabeth's downfall or just a man who had been in the wrong place at the wrong time and then had acted out of cowardice?

Jonathan was well aware that the security of the realm was constantly threatened by plots and counterplots that centered on putting Elizabeth's cousin Mary Stuart on the throne. The Papal Bull of ten years before had made the assassination of Elizabeth lawful to any would-be revolutionists and traitors. It was no wonder then how much the queen depended on her brilliant "spymaster," Sir Francis Walsingham. Thanks to him and his network of secret agents in Spain, France, and Flanders, several plots had been uncovered before they could be carried out. Plots that were often financed by Spanish gold. Gold just like the treasure that had been discovered on the *Serpiente de Plata*.

"I must find out . . ."

Jonathan touched his tongue to his lips, tasting the salt

from the sea. If the lovely widow wouldn't tell him, then he would have no choice but to turn her over to Walsingham for questioning.

Aye. Walsingham would know how to loosen her tongue.

Jonathan remembered what had happened to Francis Throckmorton, a man devoted to the overthrow of Elizabeth. The traitor had been sending abroad information on the lay of the land and making up a list of sympathizers to Mary Stuart's cause when he had been caught by Walsingham's men. Tortured in the Tower, he had told all he knew of the plotting between Mary Stuart, her Guise relations in France, and the Spanish ambassador in London.

Tortured! Jonathan cringed as he suddenly envisioned the lovely widow stretched out on the rack. No! He didn't want that. He would have to find out the necessary information himself before they returned to England.

Thoughtfully his eyes narrowed as he stared out to sea for a long, long moment. Oh, how he loved the gentle slap of the wind on his face, the ever-changing hues of the water, the creak of the ship, the smell of tar and brine.

And the woman? How did he really feel about her? Had she already gotten under his skin more than he realized? Was he just as vulnerable to her beauty and charms as poor Falkhearst? If he wasn't, then why was he so anxious to protect Anne Morgan Navarro from Walsingham?

What was the truth? Had he been so anxious to justify his confiscation of the gold aboard the Spanish ship that he had convinced himself of a plot that did not exist?

Suddenly Jonathan looked over his shoulder towards the hold. If the widow wouldn't confide in him, then perhaps he could get the information from someone else. The prisoners.

The hold was a dark, musty, odorous, gruesome place. A place for rats and spiders. Hardly the place he wanted to visit unless there was no other choice . . .

''Falkhearst . . .'' His voice was carried by the wind. ''Falkhearst!''

His first mate answered the call in an instant, clicking his heels together as he offered a salutation. ''Aye, aye, Cap'n.''

"The prisoners. How are they faring?" He looked Edmund directly in the eye, trying hard not to reveal his innermost feelings.

He shrugged. "As well as can be expected under the circumstances, Captain. You know Spaniards. They are an ever-rebellious lot. And dangerous to boot, I'd say."

"I see." Straightening his shoulders, Jonathan stood with his chin held high, his mouth set with determination. "Have any of them been questioned?"

"No, sir," Edmund answered matter-of-factly. "Should they have been? Because if so, I don't remember you issuing any orders and . . ."

"That's because I didn't." Jonathan put a gentle hand on Edmund's shoulder. If he had been particularly hard on the little man today, he was sorry. "I don't expect you to be a mind reader, my friend."

Edmund swallowed. "Then . . . then you aren't angry because . . . because we had a little disagreement about . . ."

"No."

Falkhearst grinned, obviously relieved to be back in the captain's good graces. "You told me to see that the widow was comfortable."

"And is she?"

Edmund shook his head. "Quite so."

Jonathan laughed softly. "At least she hasn't convinced any of you to paint the ship pink. That in itself seems to me to be at least a minor victory."

"A small victory. Aye, aye, Captain." Edmund roared with laughter, then just as quickly sobered. "All joking aside, I think Annie is as fine a lady as I have ever met. You'll soon see."

"Annie?" For just a moment Jonathan resented the camaraderie that had sprung up between the young widow and his first mate. A camaraderie from which he was excluded. Indeed, it seemed that as much as Anne Morgan Navarro liked Edmund she loathed Jonathan. What was more, she made no secret of her dislike.

Edmund blushed. "It's wot I calls her."

"Well . . ."

He suspected that it would have pleased Anne Morgan Navarro to know that she occupied a great deal of his thoughts. In fact, he could not get the young woman out of his mind. Her image hovered just in front of his eyes at all times, even when he was on deck staring out to sea. Now why was that?

Jonathan cleared his throat. "Now about the prisoners. Are there any who have accepted my offer of amnesty?"

"One," Edmund answered. "Seton by name. An Englishman." He looked nervously down at his boots. "The others said . . . said you could go to hell," he repeated. "They said that is where a devil always resides."

"Oh, is that so!" His tone was merciless. "Cut their rations of food and water, Edmund."

"Cut their . . . rations," he repeated, then shuddered. "But Cap'n. They're human beings."

"Who would have had no qualms about putting their swords through our gullets." Jonathan quickly made his decision. Slowly he made his way to the steps that led to the lower decks and beckoned Edmund to follow.

It was dark in the hold. Dark, damp, and silent. Wooden ships were cheerless places, reeking with the stench of bilge water and rotten meat. The odor of mold and rot assailed Jonathan's nostrils as he opened the trapdoor to the hold.

"Light a torch, Edmund. I want to get a look at our prisoners," he exclaimed, squinting against the sudden burst of light that Edmund sparked.

There were twenty prisoners in all, chained together at the wrists and ankles. Jonathan hardened his heart as he looked at them. They were dirty, ragged, and shackled, but at least they were alive. That was more than the Spanish would have granted him and his crew, had they been defeated and a far better fate than they granted the slaves they had begun to traffic in.

"I am by nature a very reasonable man," Jonathan began. "I might even be persuaded to send you back to Spain if I get the right answers to my inquiries."

In a jumble of Spanish, he asked the questions that were preying on his mind, the same questions he had posed to Enrique Navarro's widow. He was rewarded by a purposeful silence. Either the men didn't know the answers, or they were determined to die martyrs' deaths.

"So. You are a stubborn lot," Jonathan exclaimed. "But I can be patient if necessary. I assure you, however, that Francis Walsingham will not be as patient."

"Walsingham!" The voice was a croak. "You would turn us over to him?"

Taking the torch from Edmund, he held it just inches from the man's face. "I would! Without a qualm."

Stark terror contorted the man's features. Obviously he had heard of the queen's spymaster and his manner of extracting information. "No, Señor, please . . ."

Jonathan knew at once that he had found a man who would save his own life at any price. He would soon be babbling. "Unchain him, Edmund."

What followed was a purposeful, if stressful, hour of questioning in which at least a few of Jonathan's inquiries were answered. He learned that Enrique Navarro was all that he had suspected and more.

Clad in her chemise, petticoats, and other undergarments, her long, dark hair falling loose about her shoulders, Anne lay tangled in sheets and blankets. For a long time she lay quietly, staring towards the door, listening to the creak of the wood and the sloshing sound of the ocean against the ship. She couldn't sleep. The dark was just too depressing, the room too gloomy a place to find peace. She felt trapped and desperately alone. Strangely enough, she missed Enrique's snoring.

Enrique.

Visions of his death haunted her, tormented her. Would she ever forget the expression on his face as he went over the railing? Or the way he seemed to float towards the foaming sea in slow motion? Or the way he seemed to reach out for her at the last moment, as if changing his mind about his fate?

Enrique, why did you jump ? Why did you stoop to such a drastic and spineless action? Why? His death had executed all of their plans together with one fatal, swift, and foolish action. His death had made her a widow before she had really become a wife.

Widow. The reality pricked her. *It's too late for any kind of happiness.* His cowardice had ended any hope of a future together. Once again she was on her own. Alone.

Closing her eyes, she tried to conjure up her dead husband's face, only to open them again quickly as another visage hovered in front of her eyelids. The captain! His face haunted her, his words taunted her, and the memory of his accusation pushed sleep even farther from her mind.

"I am an English patriot. My duty is to keep the enemy off balance, to prevent them from bringing money or supplies to those whose thought it is to overthrow the queen," he had said. "*Anyone,* be he Spanish or English, whose purpose it is to raise an army to dethrone Elizabeth," he had scolded, staring at her so intently that she had felt the heat of his eyes. "Any enemy of Elizabeth Tudor is my enemy. I will not let any gold reach England that might be used for such a deed. Particularly Spanish gold. Do you get my meaning?"

She had, for he had made his accusation as plain as the nose on his face. He suspected Enrique of involvement in a plot to overthrow the queen, and he assumed that she was her husband's accomplice.

Enrique the leader of a rebellion? It was ridiculous. Or was it?

The truth of the matter was that Enrique *had* acted suspiciously, skulking around while she was sparring with the captain. What's more, his face had been as pale as a ghost's when he realized the ship had been boarded by the English.

Was there a sinister reason for his leap from the rail? Or had he merely been too terrified to think rationally? And the gold. Why had there been so much treasure on board? And why hadn't she been told about its presence?

Was there any truth to the captain's accusations?

Anne mulled it over in her mind, trying to decide on the guilt or innocence of her husband. There was no denying that Enrique had panicked when he realized that the English captain had won the battle. Nor was there any denying his act of cowardice in leaping into the ocean. The question was, why had he been goaded into taking his own life rather than resigning himself to becoming the English captain's prisoner? Had he been terrified of the questioning he knew was to follow? Was her husband guilty as charged? Or was there another explanation for his actions?

Tossing and turning on the bed, she was besieged by doubts and suspicions. At last her questions drew her towards the table like a sleepwalker. There, fumbling with the tinder-box, she retrieved a flint and steel for striking a spark. Relighting the candle, she picked it up, using it to light her way as she opened the door. Cautiously she paused, waiting to be intercepted. When no one halted her progress, she draped a blanket around her shoulders to cover her near nakedness and continued.

It was quiet. At night, shipboard life slowed its pace. Half the crew was sleeping while the other half stood watch. Anne gracefully glided past row upon row of hammocks. *Seeking what? Going where?*

The ship bobbed up and down on the ocean, surrounded by water. Unless she wanted to jump to her doom as Enrique had done, she was trapped. Although there were no bars on the captain's cabin door, she was his prisoner.

Prisoner!

Touching her fingers to her mouth, she remembered the captain's kiss and felt a strange ache coil in her stomach. Fear? Or did the captain's nearness inspire some other reaction?

I hate him! Trembling, she gathered the corners of the blanket around her body, trying desperately to forget the flame in her blood that the memory of his kiss evoked deep within her. The truth was, his hot, soft, exploring mouth, strong arms, and husky voice tormented her with yearning.

His warm caress of mouth and tongue had ignited a host of sensations that Enrique had never been able to spark.

No! She wouldn't feel this way towards that arrogant brute. She wouldn't! The feelings that stirred inside her were wanton and disloyal to her dead husband. *I'll die before I'll let him touch me!*

Die? Would she? Making her way towards the ship's railing, she leaned over the edge, staring at the swirling, salty water below. No one was watching her. She could slip over the railing and plunge into the icy, dark waters.

Sometimes it takes far more courage to live than to die, she thought. It took strength to face consequences head on. Was she up to the task? Could she be a worthy adversary for the captain of this vessel?

Yes! Let the captain do everything within his power. She would fight against him with every ounce of strength and fortitude she possessed.

Once again Anne looked down at the waters. Would she jump? Never! She would stand up against the captain and do everything in her power to make him pay for what he had done. Enrique was innocent. The captain was the guilty one. His accusations were false, little more than subterfuge to hide his own blame.

I will make him wish that he had never fired that first shot from his cannon. I will make him repent all the lives that were lost during the battle. I will make him regret the moment he first set eyes on me. I will get back to England, expose his piracy to the queen, and smile as he is marched away in chains.

The silent vow she made gave her newfound strength as she made her way back to the cabin. There, seeking the safe haven of the bed, she pulled the covers over her shoulders, closed her eyes, and tried once again to get some sleep.

Alas, sleep was elusive despite her tossing, turning, and counting black-faced sheep. Ordinarily the swaying motion of the ship and the sound of water lapping against the side would have lulled her into slumber, but not tonight. Her mind was much too active with thoughts of revenge to fall into oblivion.

Suddenly she had the feeling that someone was in the room.

Slowly, carefully she opened one eye just a slit. The captain was standing near the bed, his hands upon his hips, a strange gleam in his eyes. What was going to happen now? Would he fall upon her like a savage? Would he show some finesse? Or was the captain here merely to start another quarrel?

Anne couldn't think; she could breathe. Her ears filled with a soundless rushing as she waited. *If he dares to put one hand on me, I'll . . . I'll club him over the head with the lamp.*

Surprisingly, he did nothing. Uttering a soft curse, he merely blew out the candle she had left burning on the desk, turned on his heels, stalked out of the room, and closed the door behind him. How curious, how strange, how confounding. What had been the purpose of his visit? Anne had no idea. Would she ever understand the man? Or herself?

It was dark in the first mate's cabin except for the flickering fire of one lone taper. Staring at the candle's flame, Jonathan sat rigidly on the edge of the bed watching the glow as he sorted things out in his mind.

If the prisoner he had questioned was telling the truth, and he believed that he was, for there had been no reason to lie, the gold that had been confiscated *had* been destined for enemies of Elizabeth. Under a barrage of questions, the young Spanish sailor admitted that the treasure was to have been used as payment for the abduction and possibly the assassination of the queen.

Another plot to free Mary Stuart and put her on Elizabeth's throne!

To date there had been many attempts to free the imprisoned Scottish queen. Even so, Jonathan sensed that there was something more sinister about this aborted plot. He suspected that Philip, the king of Spain, was somehow involved. If not, then how could Philip explain Spain's newly appointed ambassador's aide, Enrique Navarro, having been neck deep in the conspiracy?

At least the widow had not lied about her husband's newly acquired position. But undoubtedly she had lied about everything else, including her knowledge of what was going on. Unless she was deaf, dumb, and blind, she must have had at least some suspicion about her husband's intentions.

Deep inside him he had hoped that he was wrong and that Anne Morgan—Anne Morgan Navarro—was as naïve about the situation as she pretended to be. But she wasn't!

" 'Tis a pity that females are not allowed on stage," he muttered to himself, "for surely that woman would have made a consummate actor."

Indeed, she had put on a worthy performance tonight, complete with the tears that had fallen from those beautiful blue eyes. For a fleeting moment, he had actually wanted to believe her plea of innocence. He had almost felt sorry for her.

Sorry? Bloody Hell! Her husband had been on his way to a meeting in London with someone whose job it was to "remove" the queen. Moreover, there had been something else afoot, something grandiose and far-reaching. But what?

Jonathan clenched his fist. It was too bad that the Spaniard had jumped; otherwise Jonathan would have taken great delight in forcing him to confess everything. No matter what he had to do, he would have made the sniveling coward reveal the details of the conspiracy, including the names of the conspirators. A list that included Anne Morgan Navarro. Jonathan could only wonder.

He scowled as he realized how close he had come to being taken in by her declaration of innocence. If he hadn't stormed out the door, if he had spent another minute with her, she might have been able to change his mind about her guilt and his own actions.

Thankfully he had listened to his brain and not his heart and sought the answers among the crew of the ship.

What he had learned held some surprises. First and foremost, it was not a merchant ship he had attacked, but the *Serpiente de Plata,* a ship owned by Enrique Navarro. The *Serpiente de Plata* had set out at the same time, taking the exact route the merchant ship, the *San Pedro* would have taken. Undoubtedly Navarro had hoped to land in London, unload his treasure, and deliver it before the substitution was discovered. Unfortunately for him, Jonathan's quest for riches had ruined his plans.

Whom was he going to meet? Exactly what were the plans? Did Enrique's widow know?

After interrogating the Spanish sailor, Jonathan had gone back to his cabin to have it out with the widow. She had been asleep, spoiling his need for further argument. Worse yet, she had looked as innocent and beautiful as an angel. Why, even now her face haunted him and he could not get her out of his mind. It was a very dangerous sign, a reminder that he was just as vulnerable to her charms as poor old Falkhearst who snored so loudly from the cot across the tiny room.

Oh, no. Not him. He wouldn't allow himself to be seduced by her bereaved widow ploy or her protestations of guiltlessness. He'd find a way to force a confession out of her if it took forever.

How? How am I going to get her to confess and confide the details of the plot? Chicanery? No. She was much too intelligent a woman to be tricked into incriminating herself or her dead husband. Bribery? He doubted that would work. The woman came from a family that had no monetary needs. Force? No, he didn't have enough evidence at this point to justify strong-arming the woman.

In frustration, Jonathan sprang from the bed to pace the confines of the small room. Back and forth, back and forth. Monotonous. Tiring. All the while the candle burned down to a nub, at last leaving Jonathan in total darkness. Hoping exhaustion would aid him in securing his slumber, he returned to bed but couldn't sleep no matter how hard he tried. His mind was just too active. Too troubled by all that had happened. Worse yet, he was bothered by the lovely young woman's scorn of him. It pricked his pride.

Pirate, am I?

She had called him by that name in a scathing tone. As if he was the only one who plundered. The truth was, there were more pirates than a rational man could count, for on the seas there were no laws, rules, or regulations. On the ocean, trade existed by permission of piracy. Ships both large and small used the inlets off the British coast as lairs to sail forth and seize what they could with no fear of Elizabeth's condemnation. Perhaps because she saw in these brazen and bold buccaneers her future admirals. Men like John Hawkins and Francis Drake had already made names for themselves. Jonathan was determined to follow their example.

It was not an impossible dream. Hadn't Sir Walter Raleigh done the same? A New World existed beyond the western seas, a place of dazzling wealth. He had been there and seen for himself. Great treasure fleets sailed home from the Spanish Main, Spanish galleons filled with incredible plundered riches. English captains such as he wanted only their fair share. It was time Spain's once-unchallenged dominance was contested, and he was just the man to do it. With Elizabeth backing him monetarily, he would be unconquerable! In the meantime, however, it was to Jonathan's advantage to protect the Queen of England.

"They will never depose her. Not while I am alive!"

"Jonathan?" Edmund's mumbled exclamation of his name reminded him that he was not alone.

"My muttering awakened you. I'm sorry."

"Don't be, Cap'n. I've been drifting in and out of sleep, troubled by what we learned tonight. Poor Elizabeth. She's a good queen, a fine woman. Why can't she just rule in peace?" Hearing a soft "meow" outside the door, Edmund quickly rose from the bed, lit a taper, and opened the door to allow a big gray tabby cat entrance. "There you are, Walsingham."

Falkhearst had named the cat after Elizabeth's great

spymaster, and indeed the name seemed fitting, for the cat was as successful at hunting out rodents aboard the ship as his human counterpart was at tracking down the "rats" who plotted against the queen.

"I was worried when ye didn't show up for yer dinner."

"He was undoubtedly busy chasing those pesky rats below deck." Despite all his precautions, Jonathan's ship had its share of the annoying, thieving creatures. The hungry rodents gnawed through casks and sacks to get to the ship's store of food and even gnawed on the wood of the ship's hull.

"Aye. Walsingham is as fine a mouser and ratter as ever there was. An important part of our crew, I'd say." Picking the cat up in his arms, Edmund lovingly scratched him under the chin. "Why, without him there to guard our foodstuffs, we might all go hungry."

Jonathan smiled as he looked at the plump cat and his equally rotund master. They were like two peas in a pod. Both loved eating and napping. Both were congenial by nature. Both had a knack for getting into trouble. They belonged together.

"If he can root out and destroy as many rodents as Walsingham has traitors, then I'll be deeply in his debt." Remembering his interrogation of the Spanish sailor, Jonathan frowned. "I hate to say I told you so, but . . ."

Falkhearst blinked, then looked Jonathan directly in the eye. "I don't care what the sailor said about her husband. I still think Annie is blameless, just like she said she was."

"Oh, you do, do you? And just why is that?"

"Because I have good insight into people's natures, that's why. I can see into their hearts." Sitting back down on the cot, Edmund cradled the tabby on his lap as he spoke. "That's why the moment I laid eyes on ye, Cap'n, I knew I wanted to sail on yer ship. And I wanted to be the best first mate ye ever had."

"And you have been, Edmund." For just a moment, Jonathan's anger at the situation softened. "And the best friend I've ever had. I would trust you with my life. As a matter of fact, I have."

"Then listen to me and believe what I tell ye. I don't think Annie knew anything about the conspiracy. She was merely being used by that scoundrel of a husband of hers. He must have played on a woman's need to be loved and somehow deceived her.''

"Deceived her?" Jonathan shook his head. "No, I think Anne Morgan knew exactly what she was doing when she married that popinjay Spaniard. She wanted power, Edmund, not love."

"All women want love. It's part of their nature. Annie is no different. But she made a mistake in picking that man for a husband."

"As I recall, Anne Morgan was courted by several English courtiers. She rejected every one of them.''

"Perhaps because she needs a man of stronger mettle than the likes of the queen's hangers-on. Perhaps she needs a man like you, eh, Cap'n? A gentleman."

Jonathan bristled. "Just what are you saying, Edmund. Spit it out!"

"I'm saying that ye got off on the wrong foot with Annie. Ye treated her a mite badly, but it is not too late to make amends.''

"Make amends! How? By betraying my own country and queen so that I can stand in line to be the next man in that lady's bed?"

"Ye are attracted to her. Admit it."

"Nay!" His protestation came much too quickly. Jonathan balled his hands into fists. He didn't want to feel the way he did, but somehow he couldn't help it. Damn it all, he *was* entranced by her, but he'd jump overboard before he would admit it to Falkhearst.

"Then why else are ye being so stubborn about going home? Why do ye insist on floating about in the ocean like some leaf upon the wind?"

"The widow knows more than she is saying. I intend to find out how much more."

"Ye are making a prisoner of her, that's wot. But not for the reason ye are stating. Ye want her here because she fascinates you. But keeping her here like a trapped bird will do no ye no good. No good at all. It will merely create trouble, for you and for her.'' Edmund sighed. ''Take what I say as more than just a warning, Cap'n. Take it as a premonition.''

Chapter Seven

The early-morning sun lit up the eastern horizon with flames of orange, purple, and pink light, but Jonathan had much more on his mind than sunrises. Standing solemnly on the quarterdeck, he cast a critical eye at his men as they scrambled up the rigging and along the yardarms. Each and every one of them seemed to have his head on a swivel, and Jonathan knew why in an instant. *She* was on deck!

"Leave it to a woman to cause havoc among a usually loyal and orderly crew," he grumbled beneath his breath.

Jonathan remembered Edmund Falkhearst's warning. Oh, yes, there was potential trouble brewing, but it wasn't of his making. Instead he put the blame squarely on her shoulders. Dressed as she was in a carnation-pink gown that amply displayed her bosom, a high lace collar and seven strings of beads around her neck, and a farthingale beneath her skirts, she was highly visible, just as she intended. Well, this wasn't Elizabeth's court, and the men assembled were not courtiers with nothing but money and time on their hands.

"Attention to your duties!" Jonathan shouted, angry that he should have to remind his crew to keep their minds on what they were doing. ''I'll have any man flogged if his lapse in attention causes this ship any trouble.''

Jonathan was angered and rightly so. The crewmen's lack of full concentration to their jobs created potential problems. Manning a ship meant constant watchfulness. Every job was essential. The helmsman at the wheel had to make certain that he steered the ship on the correct course. Just the right combination of sails had to be rigged, for if there was too little sail the ship did not move speedily enough through the water. Contrarily, if there was too much sail and a strong gust swept over the ship, the wind might snap an already damaged mast.

Sailors worked aloft with no safety nets to guard against a fall. A mistake usually brought fatal results, for either the falling sailor would plunge into the icy sea and face the danger of drowning or break his body on the hard wooden deck below the mast. Jonathan knew he could not take the risk of his men being distracted, woman or no woman.

''Good morning, Captain.'' Anne had tossed and turned last night, but although she had gotten only a few hours of troubled sleep, she had so carefully dressed and coifed her hair that it hardly showed. In fact, she looked radiant as she crossed the deck to speak with the captain. More importantly, she knew that she looked her best. And why not. She had spent a long time on her morning dressing ritual.

''You should stay down below,'' Jonathan complained, refusing to give her the satisfaction of knowing that he noticed how attractive she looked.

As for Jonathan, his disheveled appearance matched his mood. He was tired and he was cranky and it showed on his face. Last night he hadn't gotten even a wink of sleep. Falkhearst had snored loudly enough to wake the dead, the cot he had slept on was as hard as a rock, and even if he hadn't been bothered by the discomfort of his sleeping arrangements, he had been so angered by the plot against Elizabeth and thereby perturbed by this woman and her pretense of innocence that his mind had been a jumble of angry thoughts.

"Stay down below, indeed," she answered brusquely. Anne clenched her teeth. Oh, why must he always be so unpleasant? "I refuse to be cooped up."

"You refuse . . ." He swore beneath his breath. She was spoiled, headstrong, and haughty, a combination that always riled him. "Do I need to remind you that I am the captain?"

"No, I think your swagger and arrogance is enough reminder of that," Anne replied.

Jonathan ignored her sarcasm. "Why, madam, I thought you would want solitude, considering your state of mourning. But then, perhaps amongst the noble widows of Spain mourning is done much differently." He pointed towards the skirt of her brightly hued pink gown.

For just a moment Anne was taken off guard. "I am certain that all widows grieve deeply, whether they are English, Spanish, French, or countryless." She touched her skirt. "When I set off on this voyage, it was as a bride. I don't have any black dresses in my trunks for I was not planning on being a widow so soon. As for solitude, I don't need your recommendation as to how to mourn my late husband. I mourn him in my own way."

Her verbose, emotional response rendered him speechless and made him feel a twinge of guilt for just a moment, but he quickly recovered, using anger as a shield for his moment of weakness. "Be that as it may, must I remind you that we have work to do up here on deck?"

Anne forced a smile, though she wanted to spit in his eye. "Far be it from me to interfere in your work, Captain. Go right ahead with what you are doing. Believe me, I can be very good at finding my own amusement and staying out of trouble. I don't need any help from you."

His eyes raked over her. She was a stunning, animated, intelligent woman who knew how to make the most of her allure. In truth, he couldn't really fault his men. They would have to be blind not to have noticed her. "You are a distraction."

That was probably as close as he would ever get to giving

her a compliment, Anne thought. "A distraction?" She smiled.

Jonathan was loath to give her even a hint of a compliment. "Your dress, madam. It's bright." He laughed. "Why, you remind me of a bird I saw in the New World. A flamingo, they call it. An awkward, long-necked, lazy bird that spends its time standing on one leg."

The mocking tone in his voice sparked the anger she had sworn to keep under control. So that was what he thought of her. "How dare you! I am not lazy or awkward and I never have been." Before she went to Spain, she had worked side by side with her father on his estates. When there had been the threat of crop failure, she had even toiled with him in the fields.

"So say you. But I'll give you the benefit of the doubt on that point," Jonathan shot back. "As a matter of fact, I'll put you to work. Let's see. There is caulking the decks, splicing the ropes—or perhaps you would like to go aloft." He pointed to the sailors balanced precariously on the yards high above.

If he meant to frighten her, Anne was determined to hold her own. "Lend me a pair of breeches and I'll do any kind of work you need." She looked towards the sailors who dangled in the air on ropes and rope ladders like monkeys. "There. I'll go up there."

Bloody damn! Jonathan could see that she meant it. Foolish woman. She probably would climb up the rigging just to prove a point and fall and kill herself in the bargain. How would he answer to her father for that? "I ought to call your bluff, but as it is I don't have any more time for tomfoolery, madam."

"I wasn't bluffing," Anne shot back. When she was a girl, she had climbed trees with her brother, taking great delight in her ability to climb higher and faster than he could.

"Well, I was, but I don't want to have to fish you out of the ocean or patch up your broken bones." He waved his hand in the air as if dismissing not only the subject but her as well. "If you want to play at being a crewman, then do as you are ordered and go below."

"No." Anne stood her ground. "I will take no orders from you." It was always what the mighty and powerful captain wanted. Well, she wasn't one of his crew. "Unless you insist on locking me in the hold with your other unfortunate prisoners, I'm afraid you are just going to have to suffer my presence up on deck."

Jonathan was perilously close to losing his temper. "Perhaps I should do just that. Lock you up!" Oh, but the very thought was tempting. An hour or so in the ship's prison and she would not be so high and mighty. "After all, in my mind you are just as much suspect as the others keeping the rats company down there."

How dare he talk to her that way! Oh, what an exasperating human being. "Whatever suspicion might be whirling around in your brain, you are wrong."

Biting back a sharp retort, Jonanthan merely shrugged. "Wrong, am I?"

"Yes, wrong." Though the others were intimidated by him, she refused to grovel.

His eyes were hard, his voice stern. "If so, then I need to be convinced, for even you must admit that the evidence suggests otherwise."

"Evidence?" There was no proof against her husband or against her.

His words were loud and staccato. "Your marriage, madam. To an enemy of England."

The way he spoke the word "marriage" made it sound as if she had committed some sort of a crime. Still, although she knew it was none of his business, Anne told him the political reason she had married the Spanish ambassador, explaining that the match was to aid in an alliance between Spain and England. A match instigated by Elizabeth herself.

He scowled. "With you as the prize." Jonathan raised one brow suggestively. Why that seemed to bother him so much he really didn't know, and yet it did. Perhaps because it showed how shallow and vain she really was. Just like all the other women at court whose only interest was money and title.

For just a moment Jonathan was reminded of Catherine Neville, the lovely, auburn-haired young woman who had broken his heart so many years before. Though she had spoken of undying love, she had quickly forgotten that avowal and married a French nobleman nearly twice her age. He put all thought of her from his mind as he stared at Anne.

Anne swallowed the anger that his arrogant attitude inspired. "If you must put it that way, then yes." She paused, then continued, her eyes condemning him despite her efforts to hold her temper in check. "You attacked a peaceful vessel on a home-coming voyage. Nothing more. Enrique and I were coming home."

"Bringing with you quite a surprise, or so I would wager." There was utter contempt in his tone.

She struggled to keep a level head. Last night she had lost her temper, but today she was determined to remain calm no matter what the provocation. "If you mean something sinister in that remark, the answer is that there was no surprise."

"Oh, come now. Surely your husband had something up his sleeve." His attitude annoyed her, as if he expected a confession

"There was no ominous surprise, as you will learn for yourself once we get back to England and you speak face to face with the queen." Looking out towards the ocean as if by so doing she could see a familiar landmark, she asked, "Which will be when?"

There was a long silence before he answered. "When I decide."

His voice had a cold edge that made her shiver. Were they going back? The answer was obvious in his eyes. She realized then the true danger she was in. She had somehow come into the path of a man intent on carrying out some sort of vendetta against an imagined crime.

"No . . ." She swallowed a sob. She wouldn't give him

the satisfaction of knowing he had finally made her feel real fear.

"I do not intend to go back to England until I know who was to be the recipient of the gold. And don't play innocent with me. One of the Spanish sailors talked. I know all about your husband's intentions." Folding his hands across his chest, he waited expectantly, as if anticipating a confession.

"You know nothing at all. If one of the sailors spoke otherwise, he was lying." Or trying to save himself from being tortured.

"I think that you are the one who is lying." Jonathan's unrelenting gaze met hers in a duel of wills. "If you want to go back to England, then you had better tell me what you know. I want the names of the English traitors who were in league with your husband."

"I don't know what you are talking about. My husband was not involved in any plots."

"He was! What's more, I will not sail to London until you have given those names to me."

"Then we will be sailing on this ocean forever, for I don't know anything about plots or names or even why that gold was aboard, unless it was intended as a gift for the queen."

"Gift." He laughed derisively. "I'm afraid you will have to come up with a much better story than that."

Thrusting back her shoulders and staring at him defiantly, she blurted, "I don't have to come up with any story at all. 'Tis you who need to come up with an alibi for why you killed innocent men and committed piracy."

Though Anne sounded as if her emotions were under control, she was unnerved by the turn of events. The ship was surrounded by water. There was no way that she could escape. So she really was at the captain's mercy. Or was she?

Shielding her eyes against the glare from the water, Anne gazed upward at the sailors perched so precariously high above. There were so many men and all of them gawking at her. Captain Jonathan Leighton was not the only male aboard. Though he was in control of the ship now, that did not always have to be. Perhaps she could use her womanly wiles and therein find a man, or men, who would go against the captain and help her . . .

Jonathan had never felt so isolated as he did now. Whether in reality or in his imagination, it seemed that his crewmen were all against the decision he had made concerning the widow. Even Falkhearst who had always been steadfast in his loyalty, frowned at Jonathan whenever he looked his way.

Just what does he want me to do? Sail on back to England as if nothing happened? Well, he couldn't do that. Particularly now that he knew that what he had suspected about that Spaniard was true. He was Elizabeth's enemy. Knowing that, Jonathan could do nothing other than what he was doing. He owed a lot to Elizabeth, especially loyalty. His crewmen would have to abide by his decision.

Jonathan reflected on his crew. Each and every one of them meant a lot to him. They were more than just sailors, they were a substitute family. He felt a camaraderie for them, a genuine affection. He was protective of them.

Jonathan had thought carefully about each crewman before taking him on. He had chosen Falkhearst as his first mate. Though Edmund was overly fond of his ale, he was plucky, always made him laugh, and defended him on all matters. As his most steadfast friend, he trusted him. Howard Seton was another sailor he had targeted for that reason. George Andrews was one of the few crewman who could read and therefore made a fine purser in addition to his other duties. Tall, with bright red hair, he reminded Jonathan of a fierce Scotsman.

Then there was Jason Wentworth, the rawboned, pale, skinny young crewman who always looked at Jonathan as if he worshipped him; Thomas Weatherly, who had dreams of captaining his own ship; Henry Bowsprint, whom Jonathan had rescued from a grim nobleman's dungeon. The list went on and on.

Jonathan's thought turned once again to Anne Morgan. What about the widow? Was she the most beautiful traitor that England had ever known or was she really as inculpable as she insisted?

He was going to find out the truth about Anne Morgan Navarro if it was the last thing he did. He had to know if she was a traitor. And if she was? Was he prepared to see her head decorating London Bridge?

Jonathan shuddered. If she was guilty, if she had been involved, there had to be another way. Perhaps he could take her to the New World, where she would be far away from courtly intrigue. And what then?

All sorts of thoughts danced around in Jonathan's head. All of them ungentlemanly, all with the same outcome— he and Anne Morgan together in bed. Oh, yes, he lusted for her, and yet strangely there was something more. Something he couldn't quite put into words.

Fool . . . she hates you! He had seen to that. But how did he really feel about her? Was Falkhearst right? Was his decision to stay out at sea a matter of lust and not loyalty? Was he besotted with the woman? Was he?

"Cap'n." Whirling around, Jonathan saw Falkhearst standing behind him, his bald head shining in the sunlight. His tone held a gentle scolding as he said, "Cook said ye didn't eat a bite of breakfast."

"I wasn't hungry. There were just too many things on my mind."

"I would imagine." Falkhearst cocked his head to the side, looking up at him. "And just about all of them had to do with Annie, I'd say."

"She's exasperating."

Edmund laughed. "She's a woman. They are all that way."

"She is more exasperating than most."

"Because she knows her own mind. She's proud, strong, and as smart as a whip." Edmund spoke as fondly of her as he would have spoken of a daughter. "She's the first woman ye have met who is a match for ye."

It was true, but Jonathan was loath to admit it. "Oh, she's smart all right. Too smart for her own good. Look at the trouble she has gotten herself into."

"Bah!" Edmund shook his head back and forth as he clucked his tongue. "I don't want to hear any more accusations concerning her. Annie's no traitor. I know it, and you know it too, deep down."

"Do I?"

"Yes, and if ye want a bit of my advice, I'd say ye need to change yer strategy a mite."

"My strategy."

Edmund was blunt. "Stop barking at her like a mad dog every time she comes near."

"I don't bark."

"Excuse me, Cap'n, but ye do." Suddenly losing his newfound bravado, Edmund Falkhearst looked down at his shoes.

Jonathan's attitude softened. Edmund meant well. He put a hand on the little man's shoulder. "But as you know, my bark is much worse than my bite. So you see, your Annie is safe from any retribution, at least for the time being." He added a warning, however. "But if she gives me any real trouble, or does anything to disrupt my ship, I will act accordingly."

Chapter Eight

It was amazing what could be accomplished when one persevered, Anne thought as she critically assessed the changes she had made to the captain's cabin. What once had been a bleak, drab, uninteresting room had now been transformed into comfortable, colorful, habitable quarters, albeit with a definitely feminine touch.

"A bit gaudy but definitely interesting," she whispered to herself with a self-satisfied smile. The captain had stubbornly insisted that she stay below decks, so she had made good use of her time by redecorating. If her efforts were perplexing to his manly ego—well, so be it!

If the captain insists on holding me a prisoner and sailing endlessly about in the ocean, then I will make certain that at least I feel at home. With that thought in mind, she had enlisted the aid of several of the crewmen to carry trunks and large wooden boxes filled with her belongings to the cabin and to remove the captain's belongings and place them in the ship's storage area.

The maps that had been nailed to the wall had been replaced with two scenic paintings that had been gifts from King Philip of Spain to the "newlyweds." Now they had a temporary place of honor on the captain's wall. The charts and nautical instruments that had been piled chaotically on the captain's desk had been replaced with a tablecloth, a marble statuette of an angel, a vase, and an array of various gold and silver bric-a-brac which had likewise been wedding gifts. The canvas, sailcloth, rope, and wooden chest had been removed. In its place were Anne's trunks and a small, carved wooden chair. The most striking change, however, was the wine-colored coverlet and lace pillows that now covered the bed.

"It will do, at least for now!" Anne said softly, mentally taking note of the other changes that needed to be done to improve the room's decor.

She watched two well-muscled sailors fill a brass tub, also requisitioned from among her belongings. After having spent the morning unpacking and decorating, she was looking forward to a warm bath, for she knew she'd feel much better once she felt the warm cocoon of water surrounding her. It would relax her and give her time to think and to plan.

"The water should be nice and warm for ye, lass," the freckle-faced sailor said with a Scottish brogue as he made a little bow in front of her. It was obvious that he was very eager to please.

"Aye, we warmed it specially for you on the cook's stove," the other sailor announced proudly. Bending down, he dipped his elbow in the water. "Perfect. Not too hot and not too cold."

"Even so, be careful that ye don't catch a wee chill . . ." The younger of the two sailors gazed down at the water with a look of aversion that spoke of the fact that he had probably had few baths in his lifetime, if any. Illogically, there were still those who thought that bathing brought on illness. Even the queen had a suspicion and an aversion to bathing and used perfume to freshen her person instead. Anne had no fear or prejudice against submerging herself; as a matter of fact, she rejoiced in such luxury.

"I'll be careful," Anne replied, picking up a towel and silver bottle that contained bath perfume and liquefied soap.

"We only filled the tub halfway, just in case the ocean gets turbulent." The other sailor grinned. "Wouldn't want the water to spill all over the floor and make puddles. Of course, if it did spill I'd be more than happy to come mop it up." He looked her up and down with an expression that spoke of his longing to be in her good graces. "All you'd have to do is whistle."

"I'll remember that." Thanking the young sailors for their help, Anne closed the door on them. Padding across the hard wooden floor on bare feet, she pinned up her hair, sprinkled perfume in the water, then began to strip off her garments one by one, folding them neatly and placing them on the bed.

Stepping into the tub, she lowered herself to a sitting position, then leaned back. The water was just the right temperature. The sailors had gone to a lot of trouble just to please her. Which was more than she could say for the captain.

"Well, I have no care of what he thinks or does." She took smug satisfaction in knowing that she was slowly winning the captain's crew to her side just as she had planned. "I can add two more sailors . . ." Holding up her hand, she smiled as she counted on her four fingers. "The freckle-faced sailor, the tall lad, the balding crewman, the one with the dark hair . . ." *And don't forget dear Edmund.* The first mate was her staunchest advocate. He had made her comfort his primary duty. More importantly, he had been very kind to her in a grandfatherly sort of way, whereas the other men's interests obviously were more of a carnal nature.

Anne had learned at court how to manage men, including how to flirt and make unspoken promises that one had no intention of keeping, promises made with a batting of long-lashed eyelids or a slight smile. She was in fact quite skillful at keeping her virtue while men seduced her, but only in their *minds.* She had even kept Enrique at arm's length during the voyage. Now she knew her experience in such matters and her womanly charms would help her win the captain's crew to her side.

Picking up the bottle of liquified soap from the rim of the tub, Anne worked some into a lather as she mentally formulated a plan of action. She had to find out where the ship's weapons were stored and then think of a way to free the Spanish sailors who were being held prisoner.

If the only way to get back to England was to commandeer the ship, then she would have to do just that. After all, the captain was the one who had declared war. Besides, she felt in her heart that somehow her husband's death had to be avenged.

Anne had heard through the grapevine that the captain had cut the prisoners' food and water rations. That made the matter of the "mutiny" and takeover of the ship even more important.

If there was no one else who could come to their rescue, then she would have to take on that duty herself.

Raising her leg, Anne luxuriated in her plan and in her bathing. Somehow she had to get her hands on the key that the captain wore around his neck. The key Edmund had let slip was the key to the leg irons the prisoners wore. She had to have that key to free the prisoners. More importantly, she had to get into the ship's hold. That was the first step. Then she would have to subdue the captain to keep him out of the way while she unshackled the sailors. Then there was the matter of swords, knives, and guns. If she was going to gain control of the ship, she needed weapons, though she hoped in her heart that her inspired mutiny would be bloodless. There had been too much violence already.

"There must be a way to take over the ship in a civilized manner," she thought aloud. She didn't wish the captain any harm and intended only to lock him in the hold until they reached England. In the meantime, she would call upon Edmund Falkhearst to take over as captain. In her opinion, the always-pleasant little man would make a fine ship's commander.

Leaning back and closing her eyes, Anne gave in to several

fantasies of *her* mutiny. In one version Falkhearst was dressed in the captain's garments as he strode up and down the deck issuing orders. All the while Jonathan Leighton, barefoot and dressed only in a wooden barrel, cowered by the railing, pleading for forgiveness.

"Forgive you?" Anne shook her head. "Never!" Pointing towards the railing, she was merciless as she ordered him to jump over the railing.

"Jump?" His eyes were dilated with fear. "I'll drown."

"You won't drown. You can float all the way back to England in that barrel." She laughed aloud at the thought of the arrogant captain bobbing up and down in the barrel as he floated down the Thames River. It was a punishment that suited a pirate!

In another fantasy it was Anne herself who sported the captain's boots, hat, white linen shirt, sailcloth trousers, and leather jerkin.

"What shall we do with the prisoner, Captain Morgan?" the freckle-faced sailor was asking. "Shall we hang him from the yardarms or tie him to the mast?"

"Neither," she murmured. "Captain Jonathan Leighton deserves a sentence that is much more creative than—"

She was in the process of running her soapy hands up and down her leg, immersed in her thoughts, when she heard the door creak. The sudden unwelcome feeling that someone was staring at her swept over her. Turning her head, she was startled to see the captain. As usual, he was scowling. Didn't the captain know how to smile?

"Just what do you think you are doing?" he shouted, making no secret of his anger. Bartholomew and Andrew had abandoned their posts. When he had inquired as to their whereabouts, he had been informed that they were attending to their duties below. Their duties, he fumed. Acting as ladies' maids. Bloody hell. For the moment Edmund Falkhearst's advice about how to react to "Annie" was forgotten.

Anne was aghast that her quarters should be invaded without so much as a tap at the door. Even so, she couldn't keep sarcasm from her tone. "Doing? Why, I believe it's called taking a bath.'' She laughed, and although her first instinct was to shield her bare breasts from his view, she didn't make any such attempt to cover herself. If he was hoping to embarrass her by bursting through the door, she wouldn't let him know he had succeeded. ''Perhaps you ought to try it sometime, Captain. It does wonders for a foul mood.''

''Bath be damned.'' He ignored her derision, getting right to the point. ''You are using precious water that should be used for better purpose than your vanity.''

So that was all that irked him. For a moment, Anne had feared that he had overheard her mumbling and sensed her intentions. ''Such as?'' Provocatively she ran her soapy fingers between her breasts.

''Dr ... drinking.'' Jonathan's eyes strayed to the full mounds that were only partially hidden by the soapy water. Oh, she had a lovely body, all right. As well she knew. He, however, wasn't going to ogle her like a lovesick seal, he thought, forcing himself to look away. ''Andrew and Bartholomew should have known better than to waste the ship's supply—''

She wondered if he was just trying to start another quarrel or if he really was such a miser. ''Waste, indeed!'' Anne leaned back, watching him all the while. ''Surely there must be plenty of water aboard. And even if there isn't, it hardly seems to be a critical matter, considering that we're completely surrounded by the ocean.''

Her devil-may-care attitude annoyed him. Still, remembering Edmund's admonition not to ''bark'' at her, he tried to maintain at least some semblance of civility as he answered, ''Ocean water is full of salt and therefore undrinkable.'' Picking up one of the buckets, he grumbled as he set it aside. ''And even if it wasn't unfit, my men should know better than to go against my rules.''

''Oh, of course, Captain.'' Putting her hand to her forehead, Anne mimicked the salute she had seen the crewmen give him. As she raised her hand to her forehead, one bare breast was fully exposed just for an instant, but long enough for Jonathan to be granted a tantalizing view.

For just a moment he forgot his avowal to ignore her allure as his eyes focused on her soft, womanly flesh, but as she leaned back down in the water, he remembered himself. With a grumble he strode about the room concentrating on the alterations that had been made to his quarters. As if inciting insubordination wasn't bad enough, she had totally "womanized" his cabin from top to bottom. He strongly suspected that she had gone out of her way to irritate him.

"Bloody damn. What have you done?" It looked like a woman's boudoir and not at all like the quarters of a seaman. The colorful bedspread was the primary target of his ire. It took all his self-control not to strip it from the bed and throw it out the porthole.

"Very tasteful, isn't it?" She goaded with a sweep of her hand.

He looked towards the bed and seemed to imagine a couple in the throes of lovemaking. Suddenly he realized he was imaging himself and her. Hastily he looked away.

"I've refined your cabin, Captain, and made it more comfortable."

"Comfortable for whom?" That popinjay husband of hers, he thought, but did not say. He swallowed the string of swear words that were brewing in his throat.

"Why, for anyone who occupies it." Pointing to a bucket of water, she requested with mock sweetness, "Would you please bring that closer? I need to rinse off some of this soap."

Grumbling beneath his breath that *he* was not a lady's maid, Jonathan nevertheless complied. "You have monopolized the time of my crewmen for mere foolishness," he swore, secretly savoring the sight of the lovely bare flesh so prettily presented to him out of the corner of his eye. "Now those two crewman will be put to the task of swabbing the deck because they left their posts. All because of you."

He was trying to make her feel guilty. Anne clenched her jaw to keep from losing her temper. All the while she was wishing that they could change places so that she was the captor and he the prisoner. *I'd put him in chains and give him only bread and water,* she thought, *just as he has done to the men down below.* She could guarantee that the captain would not be so righteously proud and arrogant then.

"I suppose you would not listen to any request I might make for clemency for them."

"I would not!" Jonathan had to demand respect from his men. If he faltered, it could mean total anarchy. "Orders are orders."

"Tyrant," she mumbled.

Jonathan could read the resentment in her eyes and sensed that she was thinking of ways to get revenge on him. He would have to keep an eye on her. She could be dangerous, particularly where the Spanish prisoners were concerned. He'd have to keep the key to the hold on a chain around his neck at all times or she might find a way to sweet-talk one of the crewmen into setting the prisoners free.

Out of habit, Jonathan walked over to the desk, swearing loudly when he realized his compass wasn't there. "How is it possible for one woman to change strong, able-bodied men into weak, gullible, lovesick nincompoops so quickly," he mumbled.

"What did you say?" Only the word "nincompoop" had been audible, a word she wanted to call him at the moment.

"I said that you should finish up with your bath and quickly." Turning his back, Jonathan strode towards the door. He needed his damnable compass.

Anne stretched her fingers toward the handle of the bucket he had set down, but it was still just out of reach. Beneath her breath, she uttered a swear word she had learned from her father.

Jonathan grinned. "If you were a lady, you wouldn't make such a reference to a man's lack of legitimate birth," he goaded her.

"And if you were a gentleman, you would help me," she countered.

With a shrug, Jonathan picked up the bucket and handed

it to her, his fingers brushing hers as he did so. It was a brief caress, but at the same moment their eyes met just long enough for Jonathan to come to a disturbing conclusion. Whether he liked it or not, Anne Morgan Navarro fascinated him.

"Thank you . . ." Anne felt the overwhelming attraction too. Taking the bucket handle from his outstretched hand, she stiffened, troubled by the strange shiver that rippled through her. It was a strange sense of excitement that had set her heart pounding. A giddy feeling.

What kind of a woman am I? she reprimanded herself silently, sternly. Enrique, poor dear Enrique. He was not even cold in his watery grave, and yet here she was tingling at another man's touch. A man she barely knew. A man who, in a manner of speaking, was responsible for her husband's death. An arrogant, ruthless man!

Anne was determined to remember the captain's transgressions, and yet, even though every time they were together they ended up arguing, somehow being with him made her feel vibrantly alive. Alive while Enrique was dead.

Once again Anne's body tensed at the thought of what had happened to her husband. Death had struck him so swiftly, so unexpectedly, that she hadn't completely come to terms with the reality of it all. Now guilt was added to her emotions. Guilt that despite all that the captain had done, she was attracted to his strength, good looks, and maleness. Perhaps that was why she felt the need to suddenly mention her late husband.

"Enrique always washed my back for me when I was in the tub," she informed him.

"Oh, he did, did he?" Jonathan's face flushed with annoyance—yes, and jealousy. Damn. It was as if an apparition had suddenly entered upon the scene. Enrique Navarro's unwanted ghost. "Well, unlike your departed husband, I don't have time for foolishness."

"Foolishness!"

"Yes, foolishness." Putting one foot up on a wooden chair by the tub, he freely gazed at her, comparing her in his mind to other women he had known. Try as he might to find her lacking in desirability, her appearance had the opposite effect. Was it his imagination or was she really the most enticing, seductive, if strong-willed female he had ever laid eyes on?

Her eyes alone threatened to enchant any man who gazed too long into their depths. "Bloody damn!" *And I am weakening,* he cautioned himself. It wouldn't be long now until he was just as infatuated as the others. "Hurry up with your bath and get dressed. I have need of a woman's nimble fingers." One of the sails needed mending. Jonathan was willing to allow her up on deck if she would mend it.

"My fingers are very nimble. Just what is it you need, Captain?" Anne purposefully made her voice seductive. Perhaps if he came closer, there was a way she could get her fingers on the key that dangled so temptingly from around his strongly muscled neck.

The way she said "captain" sounded stirringly intimate on her lips, and he felt a surge of blood course through him. Fleetingly the thought flickered through his brain that it was the first time he'd been with an attractive woman for a long time without it ending up in bed. Taking a deep breath, he tried his damndest to keep his expression from registering the sensations she unleashed.

"Oh, woman!" His breath was shaky. Keeping his hands to himself at this moment was just about the hardest thing he had ever had to do. And then again, perhaps he didn't need to restrain his passions. This was a grown woman, a widow, not some untried girl. She was well past the blushing stage.

All the passion Jonathan had kept so carefully controlled burst forth. Compulsively he moved close to her. His fingers roughly traced the contours of her face, then moved down to caress her neck and her shoulders.

"Your skin is soft," he rasped. Her head whirled in a dizzying awareness of him as he captured her slender shoulders in his hands, pulled her out of the water, and then drew her wet, bare flesh close against his chest. "I want you," he breathed.

The length of his hard, muscular body felt hot against her own as he lowered his head to press his lips to hers. His kiss took her breath away. It was infinitely more pleasing than she had remembered. Returning his kiss with an unrestrained abandon, she felt desire spread languidly through her body. It worked its way up from her knees to the top of her head. A warm, tingting feeling . . .

Jonathan's kiss went far beyond a mere touching of lips. His tongue searched the contours of her mouth in a gentle, exploring caress that intensified her newly found passion. With an increasing measure of boldness she mimicked the gentle exploration of his lips and tongue, helpless against the powerful tide of desire that consumed her, a quivering sensation that shot through her body as she felt his hand slide down to cup the soft fullness of her bare breast.

How long he kissed her, she did not know, having lost all awareness of time. Her world was in his arms, his nearness her only reality. Wrapping her arms around him, she ardently embraced him, pushing all inhibition from her mind.

Lifting his mouth from hers, Jonathan stared down into her flushed face, his breath coming quickly between his parted lips. "Anne . . ."

He was totally ruled by his emotions. For once, her anger was gone and she was warm and responsive in his arms. Was it any wonder that the heat of his body was steadily climbing? He swallowed, trying to calm himself, but it was impossible now. He wanted to take off his clothes and join her in the tub. He wanted to touch her, learn every secret of her body. He wanted her to touch him too.

Taking her hand, he placed it on his hardening manhood and felt her shiver. "I want to make you forget anything and anyone."

Anne groaned as she wound her arms around his neck to pull his mouth to hers in another kiss. Desire was like a fever, and she reveled in the sensations flooding her body.

Compulsively Jonathan's hand closed over her breast to

begin a slow, leisurely exploration. Then, dropping his head, he kissed the valley between her breasts. Despite the fact that he was well experienced with women, this was strangely different. His feelings were more heated, his passion more out of control. Because of his anger? Or was there another reason?

He was awed by the loveliness of her soft, velvet skin, the firm young breasts that rose to meet his caress. He savored the expression that chased across her face, the wanting and the passion that were so clearly revealed. Tugging at his shirt, he was anxious to remove his constricting garments. He wanted to feel the softness of her breasts against his naked chest, wanted to . . .

"Ahem."

Turning his head, Jonathan looked towards the door. They were not alone. Edmund Falkhearst was standing there. The little man's mouth was open as if in shock and he was staring intently at Jonathan.

With a gasp, Anne sat back down in the water, modestly shielding her breasts from the little man's view.

"Don't you ever knock?" Jonathan asked, without even trying to hide his irritation.

"I . . . I was . . . just going to . . . to look in on . . . her to see if she needed anything," Edmund answered, blushing as he hurriedly glanced towards the tub.

"The widow is doing fine . . . just fine."

"Of course she . . . is, Cap'n . . ." Falkhearst looked at Jonathan, then at Anne, then back at Jonathan. "I'm sorry, Cap'n. I . . . I didn't realize. I didn't . . ."

"Nor did I." Jonathan sought a way to salvage the moment. Taking Edmund firmly by the arm, Jonathan led him towards the door. If he was lucky, this intrusion wouldn't ruin his amorous intentions entirely. "Come, we have to talk."

"Aye, we must. They're causing more trouble than anticipated." Falkhearst looked back at Anne, blushing furiously. "I'm sorry to have interrupted—yer bath, Annie."

Jonathan opened the door. "Say farewell."

Edmund waved. "Farewell."

Anne heard the door close but waited for just a few more moments before she reached for the nearby towel, stepped from the tub, and wrapped the towel around her body. Edmund Falkhearst had said something about trouble. That word piqued her curiosity. Tiptoeing to the door, she was determined to learn more information.

"Bloody hell! They have to be stopped at all costs," she heard the captain saying as she put her ear to the door.

"Aye, they are proving to be more of a problem than I ever supposed," Falkhearst answered. "They're smarter and more resourceful than I might have ever guessed they could be."

"What about Walsingham?"

Anne gasped at the very mention of the name. Anne always thought of Elizabeth's secretary of state as a spider who had spun a web of espionage that stretched from Edinburgh to Constantinople. Oh, how she loathed Walsingham! He was brilliant, it was true, but with a streak of cruelty that had touched all those unfortunate enough to come under his scrutiny. He was called a "searcher of hidden secrets, a man who knew how to win men's minds and to apply them in his own uses."

"Walsingham?" she heard Falkhearst reply. She leaned closer. "There are too many and alas, there is not enough time for Walsingham to deal with them *all* before we are ruined, Cap'n."

"Then we'll just have to find another way to get rid of them," the Captain answered in a menacing tone.

"How, Cap'n? Poison them? Bludgeon them? Smother them? Or just grab them and throw them overboard?"

Jonathan's voice was determined. "It doesn't matter. Just get rid of them."

"But—but Cap'n, I—well, I—"

"You're too kind-hearted, Edmund." There was a pause. "Come. Let's go below and take a look at the dangerous bastards. Then we'll decide how to destroy them once and for all!"

Anne shuddered as she put her hand to her mouth. The captain's cruel words rang in her ears. "Get rid of them. Destroy them," he had said.

So, the captain was even more ruthless than she had ever supposed. Without a moment of hesitation or even a thought of mercy, he had coldly declared his intention to murder the prisoners in the hold.

"No!"

Opening the door, she started to go after Falkhearst and the Captain to stop them, but her common sense overruled her emotions. What could she do alone? She was naked, unarmed, and outnumbered. At least for the moment. But if she remained calm, she might think of a way to free the prisoners.

She had to get the key to the hold and find a way to procure weapons. At least that way she could give the prisoners a chance to defend themselves against a cold-hearted pirate with no mercy!

"Tonight." There was no time to wait now. After hearing the Captain's conversation with Edmund Falkhearst, Anne knew she had to act and do it quickly.

Rats. If there was one thing that Jonathan couldn't abide, it was those thieving, destructive, pesky rodents! They always meant trouble on board a ship. If they were not eating up the ship's food supply, then they were gnawing at the wood of the ship as they carved out hiding places and nests. Now, according to Falkhearst, they were overrunning the *White Griffin!*

"Rats!" Jonathan had a more personal reason for disliking them as well.

As he followed Edmund Falkhearst to investigate for himself the severity of the rodent situation, he shuddered, remembering a time when as a boy he had been punished by his overly strict father in a manner that still troubled him. He had been locked in the cellar of the family's London townhouse along with the rats and the spiders.

For three days he had languished down there without any light, food, or water, listening to the chatter of the rats, wincing as they crawled over his hands, feet, or stomach or brushed against his face.

When at last his grandfather had freed him from his dark, damp, frightening prison, he had learned that his father had forgotten to release him before going away on a long journey. Though his father pleaded for his son's forgiveness when he returned, though Jonathan had granted him exoneration, he had never really forgiven his father, nor forgotten. It had been but one of many things that had tarnished their relationship over the years.

"How many do you think there are?" he asked Falkhearst now as they climbed down the ladder that led to the hold.

"I counted at least thirty, but probably more." Edmund jumped down from the ladder.

"And you say they are eating anything and everything?"

"They've invaded an alarming number of our sacks of grain, they have chewed into the wheat barrels, gobbled up big chunks of cheese—why, they've even eaten the maggots in the biscuits." Falkhearst wrinkled his nose in disgust. "They don't seem to be as finicky as the men. They'll eat whatever is in their path."

"Have you set traps?" Jonathan's boot soles made a loud thump as he dropped down beside his first mate. Walking up and down, he examined the holes and tears in the boxes, barrels, and sacks with a frustrated grumble.

"Aye. Only to find them empty. Rats are sly little blokes!"

"Certainly more than a match for old Walsingham, or so it would seem," Jonathan said wryly.

"Aw, Cap'n, the poor puss is doing his best. He's a good ratter, just like I bragged he was. It's not his fault that they breed faster than he can catch them."

Jonathan smirked as he envisioned the overweight Tomcat. "If Walsingham had to rely on the rats for his food, he would catch them. But I fear you have spoiled and pampered the cat so much he's nearly as bad as some of the queen's courtiers."

Falkhearst laughed. "Forsooth, Cap'n, ye insult the poor creature with that remark. With all his faults, my dear Walsingham is worth thrice any of those wastrels." Falkhearst quickly came up with an idea. "Perhaps we need more cats."

"More cats!"

"I heard that Raleigh's ship has four ratters aboard."

"Four? Then we will go him one better. We'll have five." Falkhearst chuckled. "With Walsingham as their captain."

Jonathan started to tell Falkhearst that cats were solitary creatures that were very bad at taking orders, but seeing how that idea pleased Edmund, he kept quiet on the matter. Meanwhile he expressed his intention to search the alleyways of London for stray cats once they came ashore.

"Aye." Falkhearst was cheered by the idea. "We can head right towards London to get them. Shall I issue the order to change course and—"

Jonathan's booming "No!" caused Falkhearst to jump.

"But Cap'n . . ."

"There are still some questions in my mind that I need answers to before we go back." Spying a rat, balancing precariously on one of the wheels of cheese on the cheese rack, he gave chase, only to come up empty-handed. "Damnable nuisances . . ."

"Unanswered questions," Edmund repeated, blushing as he asked, "is that what you were doing with Annie then? Interrogating her?"

Jonathan glowered. "What I was doing with 'Annie' is none of your business."

Edmund shook his head sadly. "Ah, Cap'n, Cap'n. Why won't ye listen?"

Jonathan was stubborn. He didn't need Edmund's advice. "I know how to handle women."

Edmund mumbled beneath his breath, "Ye think that ye do."

Jonathan's ego was on the line. "Not only will I soon have Anne Morgan Navarro eating out of my hand . . ."

Remembering the way she had clung to him, he added, "And sleeping in my bed, I will soon know the names of every man, be he from England or Spain, who was involved in that Spaniard's plot. Then and only then will we return to London."

Chapter Nine

The plan began as a fantasy, a scenario Anne played out in her head as she paced up and down in the captain's cabin. The desperation of the situation, however, forced the seed of the plot to take serious root in her mind. It was dangerous and yet, what else could she do? She was the only one who could save the prisoners. How then could she think only of herself?

She had no other choice. There was no time for anxiety. No time now for caution. No time to fear the man with golden hair who for all intents and purposes held her captive.

Hurriedly Anne dressed in the mannish riding clothes she had worn in Spain, round hose, and doublet, and pulled on her boots. If she was going to act like a man, she had to dress like one. Besides, skirts got in the way.

Wrapping her arms around her body, she paused, remembering for just a moment what it had been like like to be touched by . . .

"No!" She wouldn't allow herself to think for even a moment of what might have been if the captain were not a ruthless monster intent on seeking bloody revenge for an imagined deed. Anne forced herself to harden her heart against him. Whatever she had to do she would do without any qualms. Even so, she gasped at the sound of tapping on the door.

"Anne. Anne . . ."

It was the captain's voice. Quickly she readjusted her scheme. She had planned to catch him unawares in the hold below, render him senseless, and then take the key. Now, however, she had to deal with him here in her cabin!

"I'm coming." Anne tried to still her trembling hands; then she opened the door.

Jonathan was all smiles. "I remembered your admonition to knock." He looked her up and down, raising one eyebrow as he noted the way she was dressed.

"I was going to take a stroll on the deck, and I didn't want to be conspicuous, but come in," she said with a wide sweep of her hand.

"It wouldn't matter how you were dressed, men would notice you," Jonathan said softly. "I did, however, prefer you naked. You have a beautiful body."

Anne hid her darker emotions with a feigned smile. "Why, thank you, Captain Leighton."

As Jonathan appraised her, Anne let her eyes appraise him. The torchlight haloed his golden hair and emphasized his chiseled features, the strong line of his jaw, and the mystifying depths of his hazel eyes. Oh, but he was a handsome man, and he made a dashing figure. Too bad his looks didn't match his character.

Remembering his boast to Falkhearst, Jonathan was bold. "I'm sorry that we were . . . uh, interrupted before. I came back with the intention of continuing what we had begun."

For just a moment Anne feared she might be too late to save the men below. Just how long did it take to commit murder? "The . . . the matter that Edmund needed to discuss. Did you take care of it?" she asked softly, trying to keep the tremor from her voice.

Remembering the rats, Jonathan grimaced, then shook his head. "No. 'Tis a matter I will deal with on the morrow."

He held out a bottle of wine he had taken from the hold. "I thought we could make good use of this."

Anne eyed the bottle and smiled sincerely. "Oh, I'm certain that we could," she said as seductively as she could, thinking all the while that, unwittingly, the captain had furnished the weapon that she needed.

Feeling confident in the outcome of his visit, Jonathan found two mugs and poured the wine. He set the bottle down. "I must admit that this is from your ship. I must further admit that England has no equal to the wine from King Philip's stores."

Again Anne smiled, hoping that the same could be said for the strength of the king's bottles. "I see that somehow you knew that I prefer the red," she said, picking up her mug of wine. She took a long gulp, letting it warm her and hoping it would give her courage.

Jonathan finished his portion, then poured himself another drink. When he was through, he took off his jerkin, pulled off his boots, and tugged at his shirt impatiently. "Now, where were we?"

Anne moved closer to the bottle, hoping to pick it up and hit him with it while he was preoccupied. Alas, she was not quick enough.

"Do you want me to . . . uh, help you undress?" Jonathan asked, feeling more than a bit smug that the seduction was progressing so well, at least up to this point.

Anne laughed. For the first time since she had first met him, the high and mighty Captain was ill at ease. "Perhaps it would be more pleasurable if we undressed each other, Captain." Anne had no intention of taking off her clothes. "I'll undress you first."

Jonathan had never really heard her laugh before, and he couldn't help thinking how melodic and pleasant her laughter was. As if she moved in slow motion, he noted infinite details about her as she undressed him. Gestures, expressions, the way she moved, and of course those incredible sapphire eyes. He couldn't help remembering how it had felt when he kissed her. Her mouth had been so soft, and she had been so . . .

"You are so strong," Anne whispered. Reaching out, she stroked his arm, tightening her fingers on his flesh as her hand moved downward.

Just the touch of her hand ignited Jonathan's passion. His heart thumped wildly as blood surged through his body. For just a moment the world centered on her and the promises she made with her eyes, lips, and fingers.

"Jonathan . . ."

He felt her breath ruffle his hair, felt the sensation continue down the whole length of his spine. He couldn't think past the point of wanting to be inside her, longing to be sheathed in her warmth. His breath caught in his throat as her fingers moved inside his waistband, over his stomach, and then stroked his maleness.

"Close your eyes and I'll take you to heaven, Jonathan," he heard her say.

"Mmmmm. I'll bet that you will," he answered, closing his eyes to await the feel of her lips on him. "And then I'll take you to the stars . . ."

He didn't see the upraised bottle, didn't even know that it was hovering in the air until he felt it crash against his skull. Then, as everything went black, it was too late for caution.

Anne held her breath as she stared down at the crumpled form lying on the floor. "There . . . I've kept my promise. Sweet dreams, Captain." Purposefully she slipped the key-chain from around his neck and put it in her pocket. She moved towards the door.

"Wait . . ." He might have a thicker skull than she imagined.

She had to tie him up and gag him so he couldn't call for help. "If I have to, I'll sail the ship myself, but I am going home and I am going to keep you from murdering those men!"

Searching for something to tie around his ankles and wrists, Anne had to settle for the laces of her corset, which she tied as tightly as she could. She gagged him with one of her silk stockings, then stepped back to admire her handiwork.

"That's the closest you will ever come to my underthings in this life, Captain," she taunted softly.

Stepping back she tried to ignore the odd tingle in the pit of her stomach, a feeling she tried to ignore but which was still with her as she made her way to the lower levels of the ship. Keeping to the shadows, clutching the key, she hurried to the hold.

It was dark in the hold. Dark, damp, and eerily silent except for the grunts and groans of the men on the other side of the hold. Worse yet, it smelled of sweat, bilge water, and mold. All in all it was a thoroughly disgusting place, Anne thought as she made her way to the prisoners.

Footsteps echoing above her, accompanied by the unnerving chattering of rats, sounded in the stillness as she listened. Deciding nonetheless that it was safe to light a lantern, she pulled one off the wall. Striking a flint against the iron, she sparked a fire, then sighed with relief at its soft glow. Slowly, stepping carefully, she made her way towards the sound of snoring.

Reaching the prisoners, Anne saw that only one man stood in the way of freeing the men. Slinking back in the shadows, she set down the lantern and moved forward again. Hefting a large piece of wood she found on the floor nearby, she soon rendered that guard senseless.

Picking up the lantern again, Anne moved closer to the prisoners. "Wake up," she exclaimed in Spanish, kicking at the grate with her foot. "I've come to help you."

"Help us do what?" one of the prisoners asked.

"Escape," she answered, taking the chain with the key from around her neck.

"Who are you? Is this some kind of trick?"

"No," she answered, bringing the light closer to illuminate her face.

"Señora Navarro . . ." There was deference in the man's tone.

"Did you bring weapons?"

"No, but I think I know where some are stored." Hastily she fumbled with the key and unlocked the iron grate. Lifting it up, she moved through the opening.

It was cramped inside, with just enough room for the men to stand. Even so, the tallest Spaniard bumped his head as he bolted to his feet. *"Dios!"* he swore angrily. "How anxious I am to get out of here."

"Patience. I'll have you free soon enough," Anne replied, putting the key in the lock of his shackles. She shuddered at the thought that men should so confine their fellow men.

Suddenly the Spaniard grabbed her from behind, pressing himself tightly against her body. It was one of the dangers of being a woman.

"Mmmm, you smell so good."

For just a moment Anne regretted her bravado. She was frightened. Still she clung to her calm. She had to show strength, or she was doomed. There were those who preyed on fear and weakness.

"Well, you do not. You smell like a goat!"

Ignoring her insult, he buried his face in her hair. "Do you know how long it has been since I have had a woman?"

Turning her body sideways, Anne aimed her knee at the man's crotch. With a groan he clutched at himself. "No, but I know you will never have another woman as long as you live if you try that again." Shaken but determined not to show it, she pulled a pistol out of her belt, aiming it at the prisoner's private parts. There was only one bullet, but that was enough. "Now, do you want to be free?" she asked the others.

The answer was unanimous. *"Sí!"*

Anne freed another man and then another. When she was finished, she slipped the chain with the key around her neck for safekeeping. "Follow me. And hurry!" Somehow maintaining her calm, she made her way back to the upper deck with the prisoners following close behind.

* * *

Like an angry wind, the rumble of voices filled the air. It was so loud that Jonathan could hear the noise through the haze of his awakening mind. His head throbbed, but he forced himself to open his eyes. For a moment confusion dazed him, but as he tried to reach up to touch the knot at the back of his head, as he realized that he was tied up, he remembered being hit. He also knew who the culprit had been.

"God's whiskers!" he mumbled against the silk stuffed in his mouth. Anne Morgan Navarro had hit him, then trussed him up like a goose on a spit. Angrily his gaze sought her out. She was gone!

What was going on? Why did she do this? Not because he had made advances surely, for she had been only too willing. A woman's revenge? Had she nearly cracked his skull because of her husband? Or had there been another reason?

Angrily Jonathan mumbled against the cloth covering his mouth. He had to get free. He had to find her. Jonathan winced as a dull pain slashed through his head. He was going to have quite a bump. A reminder not to trust a woman, or at least *that* woman, ever again.

Outside the door he heard the sound of shouting, the clash of swords, and the all-out noise of fighting. Something was going on. Something far more serious than a woman's betrayal.

Jonathan cried out as loudly as he could, trying to bring someone to his aid. He had to get free, had to get a sword in his hand, had to take command of whatever was going on.

Hating his desperation and the feeling of helplessness that overwhelmed him, Jonathan crawled awkwardly toward the door. Lifting up his feet he struck at the door again and again. All the while his anger was steadily growing.

I have to get free and when I do—he kicked at the door— *I'll*—

"Cap'n?"

There had never been a more welcome sound than Falkhurst's voice. Jonathan banged the door with his bare feet as hard as he could, willing the little man to open it. After repeated banging, the door was opened at last.

"Cap'n!"

For just a moment all Falkhearst could seem to do was to stare down at Jonathan, his mouth agape. Jonathan's angry, muffled words, however, soon moved the first mate to action. First he took the gag from Jonathan's mouth.

"Who did this to you, Cap'n?"

"Who do you think?" Jonathan croaked. He moistened his dry mouth with his tongue, cringing as Falkhearst laughed, no doubt at his unclothed status.

"Annie did this?" Falkhearst shook his head. "God's body. Ye surely did have her eating out of yer hand, just like ye said."

Jonathan stiffened at the reminder of his boasting. "If you say I told you so, I'll have you keelhauled," he threatened as Edmund fumbled at the laces that tied him.

"Oh, now, I wouldn't be so foolhardy as to say *that,* but I might say—"

"Don't say anything. At least not at the moment," Jonathan answered, holding on to Edmund as he stood up. He was dizzy. The crack to his head no doubt. Even so, he was first and foremost a captain, despite his injury.

"What's going on? Mutiny?"

Edmund shook his head. "Somehow the prisoners got out of the hold, got their hands on weapons, and are trying to take over the ship."

"The prisoners!" Jonathan reached up for the key around his neck. It was gone. He knew who had taken it. "Somehow, indeed! Someone seems to have aided them. And that someone was your precious Annie." What was more, her actions were confirmation of her guilt. Despite her protestations of innocence, she had been part of the Spaniards' plot all along. And now she had instigated a fight.

"Cap'n, don't—don't jump to conclusions. Please—"

Falkhearst's eyes were pleading.

Jonathan was too angry to say a word. Hurrying to don his garments, then retrieve his sword and pistol, he made his way to the main deck, with Falkhearst right on his heels. He was greeted by total chaos.

His sailors were nose to nose with the prisoners as they fought. Some had been wounded and were stained with blood. Jonathan was saddened to see that three of his own men fought on the wrong side. Mutineers.

All of the men were growling, snarling, scowling, and blustering in their act of confrontation. Some held clubs in their hands, poised in the air and ready for blows; others brandished knives whose sharp points gleamed in the moonlight; a few held swords. All looked wrathful and menacing. And right beside them stood Anne Morgan Navarro, holding a sword in her hand.

It had begun, but Anne's heart was not in the action. Though she was surrounded by men, though she felt in her heart that what she had done was right, she felt alone. More alone than she had ever felt in her life.

She sought the captain's eyes as they stood across the deck from each other. He was expecting her to show weakness, expecting her to back down. Well, she wouldn't.

"Put down your weapons," Jonathan ordered.

Ignoring his command, the combatants started their fighting anew.

Jonathan did not even pause. Aiming his pistol high above their heads he squeezed the trigger and fired. The explosion shattered the air.

"By God!" Startled, all of the men froze, looking as immobile as statues. Slowly, one by one, they turned their heads in Jonathan's direction, focusing their attention on him.

"So far I've let you live so that you can face trial, but if any of my men are maimed or killed, I'll give the order to cut you down without any mercy shown."

"Mercy?" Anne took a step forward. "I heard with my own ears how much mercy you intended to show." She quoted what she had heard the captain say. "You said you were going to destroy them all."

"What?" Jonathan shook his head in confusion. Had he been hit on the head that hard? No. She was merely trying to justify her actions. "You are talking nonsense. I said no such thing."

"You *did!* Upon my oath as an Englishwoman and a loyal subject of the queen, you said just that to Edmund Falkhearst."

"Then upon your oath as an Englishwoman, you lie!"

With her legs spread apart, her long hair tumbling around her shoulders, she stared him down. "I am not lying. Perhaps you didn't realize that I heard the two of you talking, but I did. Remember?"

Jonathan didn't remember, but Edmund Falkhearst did. "Lord love a duck!" He looked at the captain, then at Annie, then at the captain again. He had to clear the matter up. "Cap'n, we were talking about the—"

"Throw down your swords. Upon my oath, I will not allow harm to come to any of you," Jonathan said, nodding towards the prisoners.

"Don't listen!" Anne was determined to see this thing through to its fateful conclusion. She had no reason to trust the captain. "Fight while you have the chance."

The prisoners lacked her spirit. They were weak after so much time spent below decks. They were outnumbered. Each of them knew that any kind of serious battle would end in their defeat.

"You give us your word that we will arrive in your country alive, señor?" At Jonathan's nod, the sailor threw down his sword.

For a long, drawn-out moment there was silence; then slowly each Spaniard relinquished his weapon. Anne, however, held tightly to the sword in her hand, unwilling to face the punishment she knew she would face.

"You. Landers!" Jonathan pointed the pistol at a short, dark-haired sailor. "What is the meaning of this? Are you so enamored of the Spaniards that you would turn against your own?''

Landers took a halting step forward, nearly tripping over another's sailor's outstretched leg. ''I was acting in defense of a lady.''

Jonathan swore beneath his breath. ''How chivalrous of you, but must I remind you about the penalty for mutiny?''

The sailor paled. Anne looked on, horrified. She had never meant to cause harm to any of these men, only to thwart the captain.

''Throw down your sword and I will spare your life. I'll hang you by your toes and not your neck.''

Looking first at the captain, then at the ship's railing, then at the captain again, Landers was obviously scared. For a moment Anne thought the sailor would foolishly make a run for it and jump over the rail. Instead he threw down his sword.

''I'm sorry, Captain, but—well, I'm not the only one who abhors what's happened since we came across that damned ship.'' He looked towards the others for support. ''I want to go back to London. We all do.''

Though the others didn't say a word, Jonathan could read the same message in their eyes. In that moment, he realized that Edmund Falkhearst had been right all along and he had been wrong. Stubbornly so. Even so, his pride held fast. He couldn't admit the error of his judgment in front of his men. He could, however, give the order to go back to England, which was what he did now, amidst loud cheers.

Anne watched the captain warily. Could he be trusted? Could she believe him? If so, then at least some good had come from her bold actions.

In a booming voice, Jonathan gave orders for the prisoners to be ''relocated'' in their quarters below. He also gave orders for the mutineers to be locked in the hold beside them.

''And so it is over, just like that?'' Anne asked.

''Just like that,'' Jonathan answered.

''And are you going to lock me in the hold as well?''

Rubbing the bump on his head Jonathan answered, "I should lock you there but I'll content myself with locking you in my quarters instead." His head hurt like hell, but it was his pride that was wounded even more severely. For a moment he had actually thought that she desired him and that she wanted to become his lover. All the while it had been nothing but a ploy to get her hands on that key.

"That bloody key!" he mumbled. Seeing it around her neck he reached for it, his fingers brushing her throat as he undid the clasp. She could feel the current of anger in his heart as he touched her. His eyes were cold, the pupils narrowed as he looked at her.

To her horrified amazement, Anne felt treacherous tears fill her eyes. She blinked them away furiously. She had done the right thing! She knew it in her heart. Though he would not admit it, the captain had been in the wrong.

"Now we are truly enemies. Is that what I am to suppose?" she asked.

Jonathan stiffened. "I don't know how I feel. All I know is, since the day we first met, you have caused nothing but trouble." Reaching up, he touched the bump on his head.

"Only because you made a prisoner of me and accused me of things I had not done." Anne looked him right in the eye. "Whether you believe it or not, I am and always have been loyal to the queen. I would never cause her harm."

"And you think that I would believe you now?"

Anne held her head up. "To be honest, Captain, I don't really give a bloody damn if you do or don't. I know the depth of my character and the strength of my loyalty. That's all that really counts." Turning her back on him, she made her way back to her quarters.

Chapter Ten

The wind sang in the taut sails of the *White Griffin* as the ship pushed her prow into the frothy sea heading towards England. True to his word, Jonathan had set a course for London.

Looking out the open porthole, Anne watched as the vessel moved rapidly through the shimmering blue water, stirring up waves. *So at last I am coming home,* she thought.

A flock of seagulls screeched as they flew by, as if protesting the invasion of their tranquility, and Anne thought how she wanted to add her voice to their cry. True to his word, Captain Jonathan Leighton had kept another vow as well. He had locked her in his cabin and had issued stern orders that she should be carefully guarded at all times. Even so, the thought of at last seeing England's shores calmed her disquiet.

Anne touched her tongue to her lips, tasting the salt from the sea as a spray of foam caressed her face. That and the smell of the ocean were her most poignant memories of the voyage she had taken with Enrique. They had planned to return to London together. Now Anne was coming home alone.

"Widow . . ." The word had an ugly ring to it. Moreover, having lost a husband meant that by custom she would be expected to "suffer." For at least a year she would be condemned to wear black, to hide away on a country estate, isolated from all companionship. Even so, she was thankful to be alive and eager to see the queen. Oh, what a story she had to tell!

Thoughtfully her eyes narrowed as she stared out to sea for a long, long moment. Strange. She was eager to be home and yet she realized that there was something special about sailing. She loved the gentle slap of the wind on her face, the ever-changing hues of the water, the creak of the ship, the smell of the morning air. She could understand a man's devotion to the sea. But she would never understand a man's thirst for piracy, she amended, thinking about the man who had so drastically changed her life.

"Jonathan Leighton, you . . . you . . ." In her anger she couldn't even think of a bad enough epithet for him.

"He's not as bad a bloke as all that," a voice said behind her.

Anne whirled around to see Falkhearst standing there, his sailor's cap in his hand.

"Considering that he has taken away my freedom and is treating me as a prisoner, it will take a lot of talking to convince me of that," she countered.

"He's doing what he thinks has to be done to avoid any more trouble. If that means that his harshness has caused ye harm, then I'm truly sorry. Were it up to me . . ."

"I know." Anne smiled at him fondly. "You have shown me every kindness. No matter what happens, I want you to know that I consider you a friend."

Edmund Falkhearst blushed. "I . . . well, I . . ."

"If, when we reach London, you would like to leave this ship and the harsh command of its captain, I'm certain that I could use my influence to find you lucrative employment."

Falkhearst gasped. "Oh, no! I could never leave Jonathan. He needs me."

Anne scoffed. "He doesn't need anyone but himself!"

Falkhearst was anxious not only to defend his captain but to soften her opinion of him. "He's been good to me and good to the others."

"So good that he has made pirates out of them," she scoffed.

"Privateers."

"One and the same." To Anne the words were synonymous. "Oh, for the life of me I can't see why this entire crew didn't mutiny when they had the chance."

"Mutiny?" He was horrified. "Why, each and every man respects Jonathan and would never betray him." Falkhearst hurried to explain. "A seaman's life is hard. Ordinary men are attracted to shipboard life because life on the land is even harder. Some on board joined Jonathan's crew because they could not find work elsewhere or because they had been severely abused by those who stick their noses in the air and turn their heads to poverty. Jonathan has given them—given us—a chance."

"To plunder?"

Edmund Falkhearst shrugged. "Jonathan merely takes from the Spaniards what they have stolen from the dark-skinned people. I would say it is tit for tat!"

Anne had heard fearful rumors about how the people of the New World were treated. Stories she did not quite believe. Still, true or not, she could not condone what Jonathan was doing. "Two wrongs do not make piracy right."

"Perhaps not. But if you could see the good Jonathan brings about by giving a goodly bit of his treasure to the poor in London, ye might soften yer heart a bit towards him."

Anne was stunned. "He gives his money to the poor?"

"Aye, to the children, the old, and the widows who have naught been remembered by anyone else. After Elizabeth's father, Henry, God rest his tortured soul, threw the priests out and sacked their monasteries, there was nowhere for the poor to go. Few people cared. But Jonathan did."

Great waves swelled, rising and falling to batter at the ship with heavy slowness, shattering into a froth of spray as it hit, and Anne thought how like that fearsome wave the captain was. Uncontrollable, unconquerable, unpredictable. And charitable? It was a new dimension of the captain's character.

"It doesn't matter what your captain is like. Once this ship touches the shore, we will never see each other again." For that she should be grateful. But was she?

Anne had brooded over Jonathan Leighton's stubbornness during the day, and at night he had intruded himself into her dreams. Over and over again she relived that moment when he had kissed her, touched her. Only in her dreams she hadn't pulled away from him but had been warm and willing, moaning with delight as their bodies had caressed. He had whispered that she was beautiful, caressed her tenderly, had smiled as he kissed her, had ...

"No matter what you say, I know what I heard and thus do I judge him!" she cried out, quickly pushing such thoughts away.

Anne closed her eyes, disturbed by the pictures that flitted before her eyelids. Scenes of fighting. Images of cannon fire, of pillage, and of blood-washed decks. She could hear the wounded crying for help, see the dead lying lifeless all around.

Faces floated through her brain, their expressions pained and condemning. Faces of those who had suffered the captain's brutality. Faces whose voiceless accusations tortured her emotions. Worst of all, she remembered the way he had spoken of ridding himself of the prisoners. She put those thoughts into words, condemning him anew.

Gently Edmund touched her arm. "Let me see if I can remember the gist of what was said." He thought a moment. "They are proving to be more of a problem than I ever supposed. We'll have to find a way to get rid of them. Let's go below and take a look at the dangerous bastards."

Anne remembered very vividly all that was said. Now it was her turn. "He said he would have to find a way to get rid of them ... destroy them, is what I remember he said.

'Twas a murderous and cold-hearted thing to say about any man.''

"Aye, that it would be, if Jonathan had been talking about the prisoners. But ye see, he wasn't.'' His hold on her arm tightened. "We were talking about the rats.''

Anne was disbelieving. "Rats?''

Edmund Falkhearst nodded. "Aye, the rats. I came to tell the cap'n that Walsingham couldn't quite manage them all.''

"Ah-ha! Walsingham!'' Anne flung the name in the little man's face as she pulled away from him. "I doubt that the queen's secretary of state would condescend to a problem with rodents on your captain's vessel.''

"This Walsingham would.'' Promising to be right back, Edmund left, but only for a moment. When he returned, he held a big gray tabby cat in his arms. "Señora Navarro . . . Annie . . . I give ye *Walsingham!*''

"No!'' Anne didn't want to believe, for it would mean that she had made a ghastly mistake.

Edmund set the cat down. "Here, Walsingham. Come here Walsy, Walsy, Walsy.'' Purring loudly, the cat returned to his arms, all the while staring at Anne with his yellowish-green eyes. Edmund scratched him under the chin. "Walsingham here is the ship's official ratter, though his days as supreme feline are numbered. There are just too many rats, and the devils are clever. Jonathan is going to get more cats when we reach London.'' He squared his shoulders. "Thanks to my advice, that is.''

Hesitantly Anne reached out and stroked the cat, remembering how it had been a cat that brought her parents together. Her mother, a merchant's daughter, had been alerted to an intruder in the storeroom by her orange tabby cat, Saffron. That intruder had been her father. That first meeting had been the beginning of a love story that had always warmed her heart.

"Perhaps in this instance I was wrong about your captain. . . .'' She conceded.

"And in other ways too,'' Falkhearst hurried to say. "Maybe if ye give yerself a chance, ye could come to—''

"No!" Anne answered quickly.

The very thought of anything happening between the captain and herself filled her with a strange sense of panic. Loving a man like that would destroy her. No matter what Edmund Falkhearst said, Captain Jonathan Leighton was cold, calculating, and heartless. He would take her, mold her to his whims, use her, then, when the wind was right, leave her to go sailing. Just like the man who had broken her grandmother's heart. A sailor's first love was always his ship.

The ship bobbed up and down on the waves in time to the melody Falkhearst played on his squeeze box. The creaking of the rigging and the slap of waves against the hull added percussion as voices blended to sing the first mate's ditty. If the crew of the *White Griffin* warbled slightly off key, the look on their faces and the joy of their impending homecoming made the song worthwhile.

Standing at his favorite place at the rail, Jonathan listened, tapping his toe to the rhythm of the song, then joining in the chorus.

"Oh I left my wife, for a sailor's life
to go bounding over the sea,
I gave up my pride to sail o'er the tide,
It's a life on the ocean for me.
Then anchors up, and fill your cup, we'll drink until
    we drown.
And when we come home we will not be alone 'til
    the next time our ship
leaves town. . . ."

"We will not be alone . . ." Jonathan sighed. He would be. Unlike the others, he had no one waiting for him. Which was just as he had always wanted it, he told himself. No strings. No ties to bind him. That was how he wanted it, and yet . . .

Oh, but the moon was so glorious, he thought. Huge and silver, it was like a gigantic ball balancing in the sky. And the night air was cool and refreshing. The only thing missing was someone to share it with.

Jonathan shook his head. No, he wouldn't allow that train of thought to cloud his brain. Besides, the moon, the sky, the stars, and the fragrant breeze had nothing to do with his contentment. It was the gold down below. Gold for the men and the queen. And the children. Enough to give them not only food, but clothing and toys. Jonathan smiled at the thought.

"Cap'n . . ." Falkhearst was flustered as he hurried to Jonathan's side. "For the umpteenth time, won't you reconsider . . . ?"

"And let the widow hatch up some other dangerous scheme against me?" Jonathan was adamant. "No!"

"But—but she did what she did and all because of the rats—"

"The rats?" Folding his arms across his chest, Jonathan said beneath his breath, "Aye, the ones who plotted Elizabeth's downfall, with whom I am certain *your* Annie was consorting."

Edmund sighed. "Ye must listen, Cap'n." He sputtered it out without even taking a breath. "It seems that Annie overheard us talking about the rats and how we needed to get rid of them. She misunderstood and thought we were going to . . ." He made a slicing gestures with his index finger at his throat.

"To kill . . . ?"

"The prisoners."

Instead of soothing Jonathan's temper, the very thought riled him anew. "She thought I was such a bastard that I could cold-bloodedly get rid of men in such a way?" He cringed at the thought.

"Annie knows the truth now." Giving Jonathan a not-so-gentle nudge, he advised, "Go talk with her. Ye haven't spoken a word to her since the hubbub day before yesterday.

If ye but listen to her and allow her to listen to you, then all the misunderstandings between ye will be cleared up."

"Talk with her and open myself up to her scheming again." He shook his head obstinately. "No, thank you. I'd as soon be flogged."

"The way ye are acting, ye should be," Falkhearst said beneath his breath. Throwing his hands up in the air, he added, "I won't say anything more about it, but just remember that I tried."

Looking out the porthole, Anne watched as England's shore came into view. She was nearly home! That thought made her feel vibrantly alive and strangely invincible.

So the captain thinks that he can keep me locked up like a naughty child who is being punished for a misdeed? Well, perhaps it is time that he meets his match!

Having eavesdropped on conversations between the sailors, Anne knew that the captain was anxious for a meeting with the queen, undoubtedly so that he could cajole her into believing his lies about Enrique. She suspected that to be the true reason for his having imprisoned her. Well, Anne had a little surprise in store for the arrogant captain. When he swept into the anteroom for his audience with the queen, she would already be there ahead of him.

But how? The door was locked tightly, and there was no way to pick the lock. Nor was she able to convince any of the sailors to let her out of the cabin, even for a moment. But what about the porthole? Was it large enough to squeeze through?

Putting her hands around her hips, Anne measured her body, then calculated the measurements of the porthole, coming to the conclusion that there was about an inch to spare. Certainly a tight squeeze, but manageable. And dangerous!

Sticking her head out the open porthole, she watched the waves warily. The ocean was calm at the moment, but it could be temperamental. She was an expert swimmer and had "taken to water like a fish," her father had said. Even so, was she skilled enough to brave the ocean? Did she even dare contemplate anything so risky?

Tugging at her skirts, Anne cursed her woman's garments. There was no way she could fit through the round opening with a skirt and farthingale. She would have to strip. Was she brazen enough to do so?

Yes! At the moment freedom was the most important thing in her life. Stripping off her skirt, farthingale, under-linens and wire undergarments, Anne stood by the porthole garbed only in a chemise and white hose. Taking a deep breath, she stood on the chair she had dragged near the porthole and squeezed through, feet first. Swinging her feet toward the ship's curving side, she clutched precariously at the porthole's rim as she grasped for a rope that dangled from the upper deck. Ignoring the pain in her hands as she moved, she shinnied downwards, dangling only a few feet from the waves.

"It's not too late to turn back," she breathed.

Her stomach threatened her with nausea as she swayed to and fro. Only by the greatest effort did she suppress a scream. Ignoring her lurching stomach, she forced herself to remain calm. This was not really so very different from that tree limb that she had clutched so many times before at the lake when she had challenged her brother to a swim. What was more, the waves would sweep her to shore.

Looking up, Anne could see the sailors swarming across the deck and climbing the rigging as they made ready to sail up the Thames. She could see Captain Jonathan Leighton as well, looking very formidable, as usual. Balancing himself against the rocking and swaying of the deck, he shouted at his men.

Heart pounding, every nerve in her body vibrantly alive, Anne made her decision. She could do it! She would do it! For Enrique's sake and for her own.

Chapter Eleven

Jonathan squinted against the sunlight as the *White Griffin* entered the estuary and sailed up the River Thames, the waterway that divided London into northern and southern halves. No matter how many times he sailed up the river, he always felt the same flutter in his breast to know that he was coming home. It was a feeling that intensified as the ship drew closer.

"London . . ." It was the jewel of England, a bustling, prosperous city with buildings on both banks of the river and on London Bridge. Like a giant man-at-arms, the great Tower of London rose to the sky, as if guarding the city.

The docks of London were filled to capacity with ships of every size and variety, from fishing boats to large merchant vessels resting at anchor. It was a veritable forest of masts, flags, and banners. Three four-masted galleons were riding at anchor, their cargoes of tobacco, olives, sugar, cacao, and other New World luxuries having been unloaded. It was a reminder to Jonathan of his fondest dream of an expedition to the New World. One day soon it would be his ship just returning, he vowed. In the meantime he would be more than satisfied with his own cargo of Spanish gold!

The docks were bustling with early-morning activity and people. There were sailors dressed in white, their sunburned faces matching the red of their jaunty caps; young women saying tearful good-byes to the men they feared they might not see again; warbling merchants hawking their wares, and people from foreign lands whose colorful garments could be seen even from a distance.

London was a seething mass of noise and motion. It was a city of loud noises—the yells of traders, the brawling of apprentices, the sound of horses' hooves on the cobbles. It was a cacophony of confusion. Because those talking were competing with the other noises, even normal conversation seemed to be loud.

London was a vast commercial huddle that hugged the river, a wide swath of buildings and people. Entertainment, from theaters to bear-baiting arenas and taverns flourished on the south bank. Citizens crossed the river by boat or over London Bridge. The Thames was everyone's thoroughfare. There was not only commerce on the river, but also gilded barges that carried those of wealth and power to their destinations. In truth, Jonathan thought, the river is becoming nearly as crowded as the streets.

A long time ago, London had been contained within the confines of old Roman walls with gates to let people in and out. Now it was outgrowing its enclosure. Inside the walls were the steeply pitched roofs of three-storied, gabled houses, church spires, turreted towers, and chimneys that belched smoke over the hazy skies of the city.

With a regretful sigh Jonathan could see from afar how quickly his beloved city was bursting at the seams. Even London Bridge was crowded with shops, stalls, and three-storied wooden houses, like a city within a city.

Striding to the quarterdeck, he cast a sharp eye upon his crew as they took in the ship's sails and secured them. Anchors and cables were proved, the ship laid to rest.

''I know you are anxious to visit the taverns, Landers, Wentworth, Seton, and Andrews. So am I. Let's get this ship unloaded and then we'll draw straws to see who goes ashore.''

A rousing cheer met Jonathan's words. Then each and every sailor bent his back to the task at hand. Soon the ship was swarming with sailors, from the foremast to the rigging and yardarms to the deck.

Suddenly a startled oath rent the air. ''She's gone. Captain! Captain! The woman. She's not in your cabin.''

''What?'' Jonathan crossed the deck in three long strides.

''I—I looked everywhere,'' Thomas Weatherly insisted. ''She's nowhere to be found.''

''Look under the bed.'' She was small, and there was just enough room for her to hide.

''I did. She wasn't there.''

The cabin was small. Jonathan knew there weren't many places she could duck into or under. Still, if he knew Anne Morgan Navarro, she would find some nook or cranny in which to hide just to annoy him.

''Go back and look again,'' Jonathan demanded. ''And don't come back until she's found.''

It was an order young Weatherly obeyed until Jonathan, tiring of waiting, sent Andrews to aid him in his search. They both returned, their downcast eyes telling him that she could not be found.

''God's blood!'' Jonathan swore. He immediately ordered a search of the whole ship. ''She's a woman, not a ghost— she has to be here somewhere.''

The search lasted two hours. In the end, Jonathan had to admit the truth. Anne Morgan Navarro could not be found.

''Captain . . . Captain, I . . . I know it sounds strange, but . . . but I think that she slipped out the portal and jumped into the ocean.''

''Jumped?'' The memory of Enrique Navarro's leap from the railing came back to Jonathan's mind. ''No!'' She wouldn't have been as foolish as that popinjay. Would she?

''Of course, that's it, Captain,'' Landers exclaimed. ''The portal was open and there was a chair pushed up against the side of the ship right beneath it. And her garments were strewn in a path to the chair. I remember that she . . . she was most tidy. She would have folded up her clothing unless . . . unless she was in a great hurry.''

Jonathan didn't know quite what to think. He was both appalled and fearful to even think of anyone, much less a woman, jumping into the sea. Even so, he didn't want any of his crew to sense his true feelings for the woman. Thus he reacted like a bear, an exasperated expression on his handsome face. ''She's my prisoner, an enemy of the queen. We must find her!'' He barked out orders to set sail back to open water. Meanwhile, Jonathan tried to control his growing panic as he contemplated her fate.

The turbulent sea tugged Anne under. Her ears were filled with a roar as the darkness enveloped her. Dear God, what had she been thinking of? She was going to drown! Her lungs were burning for want of air, and yet she held her breath. Kicking her legs furiously to propel her body upward, she was rewarded when she reached the surface. Gulping in the sweet nectar of air, she prepared herself for another assault.

The waves were furious, throwing her back and forth like two gigantic hands. ''Help me! Oh, God, help me!'' she sputtered when her head came up again. The water was so cold that it drained what meager strength she had. She had never guessed that it would be so cold or so violent.

''I never should have jumped,'' she said, realizing she had overestimated her prowess. ''Never . . .''

She fully realized now what it must have been like for Enrique in his final minutes. Instead of consigning her to her fate, however, it increased her determination. She wanted to survive so desperately. It wasn't her time to die. But how long could she survive in the water? The shore seemed so much farther away once she was in the water than it had from the ship. She was exhausted. Even so, she wouldn't give in to death.

Strange, she thought, but the less she fought the water,

the fewer times it took hold of her. With this thought in mind, she ceased kicking and thrashing her arms about and tried to work with the rhythm of the rolling water, telling herself over and over again that she was at the lake and that her brother was swimming right behind her.

Up and down, rising and falling, she let herself drift with the waves, saving what strength she was able to. Could she somehow maneuver herself towards the land? Eventually. It seemed to be wiser, however, to attract the attention of one of the fishing boats that skimmed the harbor.

"Help me! Help! Help!" She cried out over and over, her anger and determination giving her renewed strength. Jonathan Leighton had to get his comeuppance. She wouldn't let him get away with piracy!

The shadowy form of a boat loomed more than a hundred feet ahead. She could see its stern hugging the ocean. Taking a deep breath, she opened her mouth to scream, but a wave sent a froth of water and in the end she came up choking. For one agonizing moment, she thought the waters would claim her. But no! She wouldn't give in. Gathering all her strength, Anne tried to scream again, and this time a loud shriek rent the ocean's noise.

"What's that, Edgar? Did ye hear a scream?"

"A scream? If I did, it would have had to come from a mermaid! How much of that whiskey have ye been drinking?"

"Shhhhh! Listen, I heard it again."

"A mermaid, singing to lull us beneath the waves? I didna hear anything."

Somewhere in the vast expanse of water, a woman was crying aloud, her voice frantic but clear. "Help! Help me."

"There. Ye see! Let's follow that sound. Pull with' the oars, Edgar."

Anne's watery prison seemed endless. Having swallowed some of the ocean's water, she felt nauseated and she choked back the bile that rose in her throat. The boat was moving closer! If she could just hold on to her strength a little longer . . .

"Ye're safe!" A deep voice was speaking as strong hands pulled Anne from the water. She exhilarated in the feel of solid wood beneath her as she was yanked into the boat. Lying in an exhausted sprawl of arms and legs, she closed her eyes.

"What on earth is a girl doing out here?" A round cherubic face peered down at Anne. "Are ye a mermaid?"

"Yes!" she gasped, hoping that might put an end to his questioning.

"Well, I'll be a tinker's ass."

"She isn't a mermaid. Must have been on a ship out there," he grumbled, nodding his head in the direction of the *White Griffin*, which now bobbed up and down as it rested at anchor. "Shall we take her back?"

"No!" Opening her eyes, she darted them back and forth warily. "The captain . . . the captain will lock me up again."

"Lock ye up?" The man exchanged looks with the other fisherman. "Wot kind of a man would lock up a woman, captain or otherwise?"

"A bastard, that's who," answered the other.

"Take me in to shore. I must see the queen." She was adamant on the subject.

"The queen?"

"I was on a ship. The captain attacked and stole the gold aboard for his own. He . . . he was the cause of my husband's death. I think he locked me up to keep me from telling the Queen but I jumped in the sea through . . . through the portal."

"Well I'll be. Ye jumped."

"Yes. I wasn't going to let him win. He's a pirate!"

"Pirate is he?"

"Well he'll give ye no more trouble. We'll take ye to the queen."

Anne sighed. She had no other choice but to trust them. She closed her eyes once again. She was shivering from the chill, but she was covered with a soft piece of canvas. The waves were rocking the fishing boat back and forth up and down back and forth. Anne lost all track of time as she lay huddled and quaking with cold on the hard, wooden boat bottom. She barely noticed how uncomfortable it was she was so tired. So weary.

"Lie back and save yer strength," a deep voice said.

Anne was too exhausted to do otherwise. Closing her eyes, she succumbed to the wisps of darkness that reached out to touch her.

The water glinted green and foamy as it caressed the shoreline. Hugging the waves the ship gently dipped and pitched as it strained at the anchor that held it in the bay. For the first time since he had taken to the seas, Jonathan didn't even notice. Instead he was haunted by his actions and reactions.

"Dear merciful God!" The image of Anne's lovely face hovered before his eyes. Bitter despair enveloped him. Though they had looked high and low, Anne Morgan Navarro was nowhere to be found. She was gone! And it was his fault! Edmund Falkhearst's premonition came back to haunt him.

"Cap'n. What in the bloody hell is going on?" Edmund Falkhearst cast Jonathan a bone-chilling stare.

"She's gone . . ."

"Gone?" if Falkhearst was uninformed concerning Anne Morgan Navarro, he was the only one. Jonathan decided that during the search of the ship, Falkhearst had been down in the hold with the gray tabby.

"She slipped out the porthole and . . . and jumped."

Despite his usual good nature, Edmund swore violently. "What have ye done, Cap'n?"

Jonathan clung to one last hope. Edmund had treasured Anne right from the first. Perhaps he was hiding her. "The question is, what have *you* done, Falkhearst." He grabbed the little man by the front of his shirt. "Where is she? Where are you hiding her?"

"I'm not hiding her, but I wish that I had. I wish that I had stolen a rowboat and rowed all the way back to London.

Anything to keep this from happening." Tears filled the
little man's eyes. "Oh, poor, poor Annie . . ."

Falkhearst's show of grief was sincere. Even so, Jonathan
ordered another search of the ship, this time including the
hold where the prisoners were kept. Like the other searches
before, however, this one ended up with no sign of Anne
being found.

"I knew it. I knew it. I told ye, but ye wouldn't listen.
Damn yer pride!" Falkhearst's anger shone through his
tears. Then all at once, it was as if he couldn't stem the
rage that consumed him. Though he had always served
Jonathan faithfully with unfaltering devotion, he suddenly
hurled himself at his friend.

Though Jonathan was taller and stronger than Falkhearst
and could have ended the mayhem with one blow, he held
back, suffering the little man's assault. It *was* his fault. He
had been stubborn. In retrospect he realized that he had been
wrong to try and subdue a woman as spirited as Anne Morgan
Navarro.

A well-aimed punch connected with Jonathan's jaw, but
he didn't even wince. It was as if he wanted to feel some
physical pain. Perhaps then he could concentrate on something besides the ache in his heart.

The other sailors subdued Falkhearst quickly as Jonathan
rubbed at his injury. Though he could have given orders to
have Falkhearst flogged or worse, he limited his punishment
to be a cooling-off period in the hold.

"My fault . . ." Jonathan mumbled as he watched Falkhurst being carried away. He should have listened to Edmund
when he had explained Anne's rash actions. Instead he had
been hell-bent on punishing her. It was a thought that tore
at his very soul. Now Anne was gone, and nothing he could
do could bring her back.

Chapter Twelve

London swarmed with people. Open carts, coaches, drays, horses, and wagons clogged the streets, their occupants openly staring at the wet, bedraggled, half-naked woman draped in a blanket who walked along the street. Even so, Anne would not be daunted in her efforts to talk to the queen before Captain Leighton did.

The voices of the vendors hawking their wares, the church bells, the grumbling of shoppers haggling over the price of their purchases was as welcome to her as a familiar melody. Elbowing her way through a crowd, she added her presence to the confusion. She'd missed London. Only now did she realize how much.

I'm English through and through, she determined, still fuming as she remembered how Captain Leighton had dared to question her loyalty and make accusations. Well, soon the matter would be settled once and for all and the captain clapped in chains for his act against the Spanish ship. If the queen also instructed him to get down on his knees and beg Anne for her forgiveness—well, it would be an added boon.

Trying to get used to walking on land again, she crossed the street carefully so as not to be run over by the carts and wagons in the street. Church spires, steeply pitched roofs of gabled houses, and turreted towers all formed a jagged landscape against the sky. Chimneys and smokestacks billowed dark gray smoke from the forges and furnaces in the workshops below. Like a well-kept garden, the majority of the people had flourished under Good Queen Bess's reign.

"I'm home! Where I belong," Anne whispered as she half ran, half walked towards Whitehall Palace.

She made her way by foot and by barge beyond Fleet Street, through Temple Bar to the Strand, the thoroughfare that led to where the queen was now in residence. It was only when she saw the walls of Whitehall that she began to lose her newfound confidence. Putting her hand up to her still damp, straight hair she regretted the lack of time she had taken with her appearance.

Anxious to tell her story to the Queen, she had borrowed an overlarge pair of boots, tan canvas trousers, and a blanket from the fishermen, thanked them for their timely rescue, then hurried down the docks towards Whitehall with little care of how she looked. Arriving at Whitehall had been the most important thing on her mind. Now as she combed her fingers through her hair, she longed for a fashionable coiffure and to be donned in her finery.

You have to continue; you cannot go back now because of vanity, she scolded herself as she approached the palace. Surely the queen and everyone around her would be sympathetic. Besides, her bedraggled state only emphasized the torment she had suffered at the captain's hands. With that thought in mind, Anne squared her shoulders, held her head up high, and announced herself to the guard at the front gate with as much pride as she had ever exhibited. Despite the fact that he gawked, then guffawed, she was admitted. Hearing the gate click shut, she swallowed, counted to ten, then moved forward.

The walls were of dark wood paneling. At either end of the room were tall windows draped with lustrous brocade curtains. Raising her eyes to the ceiling, she could see swirls of ornately carved wood. Row upon row of royal portraits adorned the walls, including those of Henry VIII, Mary Tudor, the boy king, Edward VI, and of course Elizabeth in all her finery. Oh, what a contrast Anne made to those portraits, dressed as she was.

"The moment has come," Anne said, taking a last look at Elizabeth's portrait as if to reacquaint herself with the monarch who held such massive power in her ring-bedecked, slim-fingered hands.

Stepping inside the crowded anteroom, she looked about her. Inside strolling musicians idled about with lute and harp, singing vibrant melodies. There were dozens of servants in attendance, as if pampering the queen was the most important business of the realm. Elizabeth was seated in her carved chair in the chamber, clothed in white, as if she really took seriously her claim to be a virgin queen.

It was a bright world Anne entered, just as she remembered it to be. She was aware of the ladies in their silk, brocade, and velvet gowns, looking like bright peacocks, their hair piled high, their faces painted. Gems sparkled like stars as they moved, making them look somehow unearthly, as though they came from another sphere. All around her their eyes were staring, hostile, amused, mocking, and curious.

"Such attractive people," Anne whispered, "but it is only a surface beauty." She knew that beneath the finery lurked hatred, envy, jealousy, and greed. Was it any wonder that Anne's father, mother, and brother spent as much time away from court as they could?

Anne walked slowly through the room, hardly even noticing the splendor of the furnishings. Her attention was fixed on the woman in the ornate chair at the end of the chamber, under a canopy of the royal colors of green and white. The crest of the Tudors was above her head. Around the queen, like planets revolving around a sun, stood a circle of men, their faces turned towards the queen with expressions of mock adoration. Their jabbered flattery held a jarring tone of insincerity.

The muted sun's rays cast flickering light against the rich-hued tapestries and draperies of the chamber, dancing upon the gold threads that swirled their way across the fabric of her white velvet gown. A stiff, lacy ruff rose behind her head and framed her bright red hair and painted, pale-complexioned face. A long rope of gold and pearls glistened against her bodice, emphasizing the long lines of the slim figure she was so famous for. Her face was thin, her bright red hair most obviously a wig. As usual she had gone to great lengths to provide the appearance of a younger woman.

Suddenly two of the queen's guards crossed their pikes in front of Anne's face, halting her before she had a chance to get within forty feet of the queen. "What is your business?" one of them snarled, scrutinizing her clothes, or rather lack of them, and thereby deciding she did not belong within. Anne stated her purpose in coming, then watched as the reason for her visit was announced to the queen by one of the young pages.

Elizabeth was shocked at first, then amused, then curious. "Well . . . ?" Her eyes traveled assessingly from the top of Anne's wet head to the toes of her booted feet.

For just a moment Anne wondered if the queen even recognized her in her sorry state. "I'm Anne Morgan Navarro, your majesty."

"I know who you are," the queen exclaimed in a tone of annoyance. "Though you look at the moment much like a wet puppy, I would recognize that profile anywhere. Richard Morgan's profile."

"And my own!" Anne declared. She realized that it would have been far better to have talked with the queen alone. Sensing that to be an impossible request, however, she spoke right up. "I have returned from Spain, though not in the manner that my husband and I had planned."

"So I would hope," Elizabeth answered caustically. Several of the courtiers giggled.

Anne ignored them. "I seek an immediate audience with you."

"You have it." When Anne faltered, she said sternly, "Speak up, girl."

"If you remember, your majesty, I was recently married

to Enrique Navarro, the newly appointed ambassador's aide designate to England.''

''Of course I remember.'' Seeming to tire of the fawning attention of her male courtiers, she motioned them away. ''It was a great mistake.''

''What!'' Anne halted. It was not the reply she had expected. Her heart hammered in her chest until she was certain it would burst. Remembering her manners, she dipped into a curtsy, spreading the blanket like a skirt. ''My . . . my marriage was partly to aid an alliance between Spain and England.''

''Spain be damned!'' Elizabeth exclaimed. ''A pox on Philip and on all of them.''

Anne was aghast. Obviously something unforetold had happened. ''Your majesty . . . ?''

Elizabeth motioned with her hand. ''Get up, get up, get up.''

Anne straightened, looking right at the queen as she squared her shoulders and adjusted the blanket more strategically. ''What has happened? I don't know what has piqued your ire.''

Not one to mince words, Elizabeth spelled it out. ''Walsingham has learned of yet another plot to put Mary Stuart on *my* throne. That man who was once married to my sister, God rest her soul, is under suspicion.''

''Philip?'' Remembering Captain Leighton's accusation, Anne paled. This turn of events certainly complicated matters. ''But certainly Philip has proven to be a friend to your majesty. And as to the Scottish queen, her past ties with France, his sworn enemy, surely makes him loath to help the captive queen take your place.''

Elizabeth snorted. ''As long as he held hope that I would marry either him or his sniveling son, he played a game of patience. It appears now that he may have had a change of heart and allegiance.''

''But surely you have been misinformed—''

''I have not!'' The queen sat forward in her chair. ''Walsingham's network of secret agents in Spain, France, and

Flanders have sent regular reports. Based on these missives, I've decided to expel the Spanish ambassador, Mendoza, from England and to give open aid to the Netherlands in their fight against Phillip.'' She smiled. ''Tit for tat.''

''And Enrique . . . ?''

''Will be expelled as well. So you see, your return to England will be brief, my dear.''

Anne moved closer. Far away Elizabeth had appeared to be beautiful; up close it was obvious that she had lost whatever beauty she might have once possessed. ''It hurts my heart to have to tell your majesty that she will not have to expel my husband.'' She took a deep breath in an effort to maintain her composure. ''My . . . my husband is . . . dead.''

''Dead?'' Now it was Elizabeth's turn to be surprised. ''How?''

''We were set upon by pirates. They stole the gold aboard the ship and imprisoned everyone on board. Enrique . . . suffered a . . . a mishap and fell overboard.''

There was a long pause as Elizabeth digested this information. Anne wasn't sure whether to breach the silence or wait for the queen to speak again. She waited.

''I am sorry for your loss,'' Elizabeth said at last.

''Thank you, your majesty.''

''What of the gold?'' Elizabeth's thin lips tightened, the wrinkles at her eyes and mouth seeming more pronounced beneath her heavy makeup. Her expression was grim. She rested her lovely, long-fingered hands on the arms of the chair, gripping tightly as she tried to manage her poise.

''As I said, it was confiscated.'' Anne smugly supposed that no matter what the queen's feelings were for Phillip and Spain, she would not condone piracy.

Elizabeth motioned with her ring-bedecked hand. ''By whom? Who stole the gold?'' She looked Anne up and down, raising one brow as she once again assessed her half-naked state. ''And other things.''

''Captain Leighton, who sails the *White Griffin,*'' Anne answered. Now at last the captain's misdeeds had come to light. She wondered what the punishment would be and guessed that it would be imprisonment in the Tower. Well, perhaps it was a needed lesson.

"Jonathan?"

Anne nodded. "Captain Jonathan Leighton."

The Queen scowled. "I know his full name. Jonathan Nathaniel Leighton." Elizabeth looked long and hard into Anne's eyes. "Jonathan has served me well. There has never been a blemish on his name or reputation."

For just an instant Anne forgot herself and, remembering all that had occurred on the *White Griffin*, she lost her temper. "Well, I fear there is now. Jonathan Leighton is a pirate!"

Elizabeth was visibly upset. Her hand kept going to her throat. At last she rasped, "Pirate, did you say?"

For a moment Anne feared that her boldness might have angered the queen, but then, as she stared at her, she realized that beneath all the paint and finery she was much the same as any other aging woman. Deciding that the truth had to be told, she began.

The story tumbled from Anne's lips, as many details as she could elaborate upon. She told of the peaceful voyage, the sudden attack, the dismay she had felt upon finding herself at the mercy of one of her own countrymen. In a whisper she spoke of Enrique's untimely death.

"The gold. What of the gold?" Anne was unnerved by Elizabeth's hawklike countenance. Her eyes seemed to skewer her as she looked directly into her face.

"Jonathan Leighton has it." Anne felt her confidence return. "I said he was a pirate, and I mean that with all my heart. Perhaps you thought you knew him, but I can assure you that you do not know the real Captain Leighton at all."

A nerve twitched in Elizabeth's face. "There is something foul here. But I will get to the bottom of it. Of that I can assure you."

"Thank you, your majesty." Never had Anne felt so relieved. Soon this would all be over.

Suddenly the queen's mood brightened. She smiled, then reached out and patted Anne on the head like a puppy. "Perhaps that moment has come."

"What moment?" Anne turned her head and followed the direction of the queen's gaze. A man stood in the doorway, waiting to be announced. His golden hair looked like the sun; his muscled physique captured every feminine eye. It was Jonathan Leighton. Anne knew his good looks did not match his heart. She shot a quick, furtive glance at him from under her lowered lashes, hoping against hope that he wouldn't recognize her, and shrank into the shadows behind Elizabeth's throne. She was relieved that he was not looking at her at all. Standing tall and erect, his attention was focused on Elizabeth.

Though he was still shaken by Anne Morgan Navarro's apparent death, Jonathan's voice was steady as he said, "I would like a word with Elizabeth if you please."

The guards at the gate recognized Jonathan, allowing him to enter without a pause.

The maze of corridors at Whitehall were crowded with courtiers and servants alike, passing each other as if in mock procession. All eyes turned towards Jonathan as he walked by, curious as to the long procession of sailors who followed him.

"I have something for the queen," Jonathan announced. Looking at Elizabeth, he boldly winked. "Something that I will give to her once we are less encumbered by eyes."

"Such an impetuous man!" Elizabeth's tone had lightened. "But then, I have always liked men of daring." Elizabeth put her hand to her temple and pondered the matter for a long, long time. "You know how much I favor you. Of all the lords, you are among those I hold most dear."

"You majesty does me too much honor. I am overcome," Jonathan whispered.

Anne stiffened as she watched the enfolding scene. Why, instead of immediately being hailed by Elizabeth as a villain, the Captain was being treated like some reigning favorite! It was enough to make her gag.

Beckoning him forward, Elizabeth placed her hand on

Jonathan's shoulder. "I take great delight in welcoming you back to court. Lord Vickery is amusing, but frankly, his vanity can sometimes be a bore." She spoke the next words loudly enough for that lord to hear. "I believe he needs to have you here just so his head does not get too puffed up! With a bit of competition, he may learn to be more humble and to remember that I have raised him up and I can bring him down."

"Your power is absolute, your majesty," Jonathan said, barely suppressing a sad smile. He had come to offer Elizabeth her share of gold, and his conscience screamed out at the price that had been paid. Anne Morgan Navarro's life.

"Yes. And I can grant any wish." Elizabeth's mood was gradually improving, and her fond smiles clearly affirmed that despite all that Anne had told her, Jonathan was in her good graces. "Knowing that, what is it you would wish for, Jonathan?"

Jonathan closed his eyes and hung his head. Were it within her power to grant him a chance to relive the day, he would have gladly taken it in lieu of any other prize. Perhaps then he could make amends and listen to Falkhearst's advice. Surely then he would never have treated Anne so wretchedly.

"I fear that what I wish for cannot be granted." He wanted Anne to come back to life.

Elizabeth stiffened. "My power is absolute."

"Of course it is," Jonathan hurried to explain. "I only meant that were I able to do so, I would undo a certain deed."

"Undo?" Elizabeth studied him intently. "I think I know of what you speak." Hurriedly she shooed the courtiers away until only she, Jonathan, and Anne were left in the room. "There is someone here who claims that you have willfully wronged her."

Jonathan looked at Anne, recognizing her in an instant. He could never forget that face or those huge blue eyes. For a moment he was certain that he was looking at a ghost. "No. It can't be!"

Anne's eyes met Jonathan's across the distance of the

room, and she knew at once that the moment of truth had come. Despite the fact that Jonathan had the queen's favor, she held her ground. Right would win out in the end.

Jonathan stared long and hard at the dark-haired young woman who at the moment was the most beautiful sight he had ever beheld. At last deciding that Anne was flesh and blood and not a spirit, he asked, "How did you get here?"

She felt her cheeks burn under his scrutiny. "I swam!"

"Swam?" It was a feat that was astounding.

"I had a little help from two fishermen," she conceded.

"God bless them," he whispered. He started to say that he was truly sorry for much of what had occurred, but the queen silenced him. She was not used to being ignored.

"This young woman has made serious accusations against you. How do you plead?"

"Guilty," Jonathan answered. "Guilty of zealously ridding my queen of her enemies and bringing back to England the gold that was targeted to be used against her." Gold from which he hoped he would be given his share.

"There is no proof of that!" Anne was incensed. Oh, his answer had been clever, but even so she hoped the queen would be fair in her judgment. "Captain Leighton is merely toying with words to make his piracy justified, but my husband was not involved in any plot. The gold was to be a gift for you."

Elizabeth tightened her lips. "Then if the gold was for me, you should not care who the giver is."

Anne gasped. So, her trip to Whitehall had been a waste of time. The queen was a horrible woman! She didn't care a wit about the discomfort Anne had suffered aboard the *White Griffin* or about Enrique's death. All she cared about was her gold. "God's blood, she is as big a pirate as he," she said beneath her breath.

Elizabeth tapped her on the shoulder with her fan. "Speak up, girl. What did you say?"

"I said I hope that you and Captain Leighton enjoy your gold." It was obvious that they were in league with each other. The rumors were true. Though the queen disowned the privateers who prowled the seas, she not only wouldn't disturb them but took her cut of the proceeds. Anne hadn't wanted to believe it, but the truth was like a slap in the face.

Elizabeth pursed her lips. "There are times when you can be a most insolent pup. But perhaps a period of repose in the country will calm you, as befits a newly made widow."

This woman, queen or otherwise, thought of life as a game! Oh, how Anne wanted to scold, but she dared not say a thing. Even so, it was only by biting her tongue that she maintained her silence. Jonathan Leighton was being forgiven for any wrongdoing. As a matter of fact, he was being rewarded while she was being banished to the countryside. Glowering at Jonathan, Anne begged to take her leave.

There were no good-byes, no formal dismisal. Elizabeth's attention had shifted to the man garbed in canvas trousers and leather jerkin, the dashing Captain Leighton. She motioned him over to take a place at her side.

Damn them both, Anne thought. Without looking back, she hurried across the shiny marble floor and swept through the doorway.

With a lump in his throat, Jonathan watched her go. Somehow, some way, he had to make amends or suffer Anne's hatred forever.

Chapter Thirteen

The great hall of Whitehall Palace echoed with the voices of the brightly colored, heavily bejeweled, gaudily dressed lords and ladies assembled in the gigantic room to celebrate Captain Jonathan Leighton's successful voyage. Sounds of laughter, the buzzing of voices talking about the latest gossip, politics, or matters of a more serious nature blended with the music being played.

Elizabeth certainly knew how to celebrate, Jonathan thought. And why not? With the gold he had given her, she could well afford tonight's gathering.

In the far corner of the hall, on a raised dais, musicians strummed, plucked, and tooted their instruments in accompaniment to the clamor and talk of courtiers and guests. A boisterous crowd amused themselves by dancing, flirting, and playing at dice, yet all within hushed to a silence as a fanfare trumpets and drums announced the entrance of the queen.

Elizabeth Tudor, sole ruler of England for twenty-five years, stood with head held high and shoulders back as she assessed the crowd. Ever so faintly she smiled, then made her way regally into the room as all heads turned her way.

In a room full of gilt and glitter, she shone like a star despite her age. Dressed in a gown of white and gold, the sleeves and bodice of which were sprinkled with sequins and jewels, she looked every inch a queen from the tip of her red-bewigged head to the hem of her voluminous skirt.

"You see, Jonathan," she whispered as he walked beside her, "no matter how many plots are hatched against me, I will win out in the end. Do you know why?"

"Your beauty and intelligence make you an unbeatable rival," he answered. She was unequaled in diplomatic skill. Some called her the wisest woman that ever was. She had the advantage of conferring directly with ambassadors in French, Italian, or Latin and thus didn't need interpreters and intermediaries. Her enemies condemned her publicly but privately admired her.

She smiled. "It's been said that I have the mind of a man in a woman's body, but in truth I think that if given a chance, any woman can be an intellectual match for any man."

Remembering Anne Morgan Navarro, Jonathan quickly agreed.

"My father so wanted a son that he divorced Catherine of Aragon, challenged the pope, beheaded my mother, and married several times. If only he could see that it was his daughter who has become England's greatest ruler."

The queen enjoyed the adulation; in truth she savored it, surrounding herself with handsome men who vied with each other to be her favorite. Courtiers impoverished themselves just to entertain her, poets smothered her with sonnets expounding on her beauty, musicians strummed songs to her praise. Even so, the position of queen's favorite was often a tenuous one, for Elizabeth Tudor was quick to anger and unforgiving when crossed. Was it any wonder then that Jonathan felt the prick of apprehension as he followed the tall, thin, red-haired monarch into the hall?

One false move, one wrong word, and despite the gold I could find myself sitting in the Tower, he thought. Had it not been for that, he would have run after Anne when she left Elizabeth's presence instead of just watching her go.

After the evening's celebration was over, however, he planned on finding her so he could tell her how he really felt.

The queen's procession passed through the line of groveling courtiers, reminding Jonathan anew of the perilous position he found himself in, all because Elizabeth had looked upon him with a favorable eye. The court was filled with ambition, jealousy, and intrigue, and even now he could feel the eyes appraising him, wondering what must be done to send this latest favorite toppling from his lofty perch. Well, he would fool them, he thought. The first chance he had, he would set sail and absent himself from these vultures.

But first I will search every London inn to find Anne. She thought the very worst of him, and that deeply troubled him. He could only keep his fingers crossed that his instincts were right. It was dangerous to travel at night. Jonathan supposed that she would find someplace to rest for the night and then set out for the country at dawn's first light.

It seemed to be a never-ending march past doublets and gowns, but at last Elizabeth reached the far side of the room and seated herself gracefully upon her high-backed chair despite the hindrance of the wheeled farthingale beneath her gown. Motioning to the place beside her, she said but one word, "Jonathan!" The honor did not go unnoticed by those assembled, yet the taste of victory was as dead as ashes in Jonathan's mouth. He would have preferred to be sitting beside Anne. "I am honored, your majesty," he murmured nonetheless.

Quickly his eyes appraised her, and he thought she looked undeniably awesome dressed in all her finery. She seemed at that moment to personify the glory of England.

"Ah, Jonathan," she sighed, "I know that you have expressed a desire to put out to sea again, but we need men like you at court."

Jonathan pointed toward the men who smiled at the queen with adoration. "You don't need me. Here I would be but one among many. At sea I can be unique in the manner in which I serve you."

Reaching up her long-fingered hand to brush wistfully at her ruff, she sighed. "You are the kind of man I am always drawn to—tall, strong, and courageous. I need your kind of man here. But I am wise enough to know that a man like you must have freedom."

"Thank you, your majesty." Jonathan was relieved. He felt so out of place here dressed in wine-colored doublet and trunkhose, oyster-hued nether hosen that clung tightly to his legs, and a stark white ruff around his neck. The garments were as constricting as the life here at court. He was far more comfortable in his canvas trousers and leather jerkin.

Jonathan knew he was the antithesis of the queen's other current favorite, Roger Pembroke, a tall, dark-haired man with mustache and well-trimmed beard who stood watching him as a hawk watches a dove.

"He thinks I'm competition," Jonathan said to himself. And why wouldn't he? Elizabeth made a game of pitting men against each other for her favor. But Pembroke was wrong. Jonathan didn't want to take his place. He was a bold man, an adventurer who relished action and travel; Roger Pembroke was a courtier who was more prone to wield a pen than a sword.

Jonathan loathed the man. His dislike of the vain, arrogant popinjay was intense and for good reason. From the moment Jonathan had set foot in Elizabeth's court, Roger Pembroke had made it obvious that he was to be an enemy. He had babbled vicious rumors, made Jonathan the butt of a hundred jests, and in all ways tried his very best to get Jonathan banished from court. Only by his intellect and a reasonable measure of good luck had Jonathan survived.

"Since I have favored you with the privilege of sitting by my side, I feel it is only fair that Lord Pembroke be given the honor of partnering me in the first dance," Elizabeth exclaimed, playing at her games again. In a flash of green and gold, Roger Pembroke offered her his arm. "Musicians, you may begin!"

Hurrying to obey, the court musicians lifted up lute, viol,

brass, woodwind, and sackbutt to begin a lively tune. Elizabeth loved to dance and pirouetted with the energy of a woman half her age. Jonathan watched from afar, grateful for a chance to think about Anne again.

She was fond of Falkhearst. Perhaps it would be wise to have him be Jonathan's go-between. At the very least Jonathan wanted a chance to tell her that he no longer suspected her of conspiracy against the queen. He might even go so far as to humble himself before her and apologize, something he had never done before for any human being. In this case it was necessary, however, for he had done the widow a grievous wrong.

Elizabeth herself had opened his eyes by revealing to him in their meeting that she and Walsingham had known all along that Enrique Navarro was suspect and therefore dangerous. Because of that, Elizabeth had fostered a marriage between the Spanish diplomat and someone known to be loyal. Anne. It had been the queen's hope that Anne would be useful in keeping her informed of the devious Spaniard's doings. Thus Anne had been an unsuspecting pawn all along.

Falkhearst had been right.

"So you are making a name for yourself on the sea, just as you said you would," a soft voice said behind him.

Jonathan recognized that voice as belonging to a woman he had once given his heart to. Gweneth Carleton was her name, and she was a tall, achingly lovely young woman with eyes as dark as the night and tawny hair. It was a striking combination.

"I should have listened to my heart, Jonathan."

"But you didn't." She had listened to her longing for affluence and power.

"And now I find myself trapped in a marriage with a man old enough to be my grandfather."

"But a man nevertheless your husband." Jonathan's eyes strayed across the room to the man she had married, a nobleman who had long been an advisor to the queen. A very powerful man.

"We were good together, you and I." Her voice was wistful.

"That was a long time ago."

"Not so long that I have forgotten."

Jonathan's answer was cold. "Well, I have." What had happened between them was over. It had ended in his head, if not his heart, long ago. From that time forward Jonathan had sought out the company of women he could bed, then leave upon the morrow.

"Please Jonathan . . ."

Jonathan spoke slowly, trying to maintain his calm. "You belong to another man." Jonathan was wise enough to know that a liaison with Gweneth could well be the one weapon his enemies could make use of. No woman, no matter how lovely, was worth such a price.

"Another man? Fie, you use the term lightly, sir. Were my husband a man, I would have no need to cast my eyes elsewhere. Henry Carleton has long been impotent." Gweneth's face was flushed, and she sought to cool herself by fluttering her feathered fan before her face.

"That is your misfortune."

How strange, Jonathan thought, that prior to meeting Anne Morgan Navarro, he had thought often about this woman with the tawny hair. To put it simply, he had lusted after her. Now he found it easy to decline what she wanted to offer.

"You are cruel, Jonathan. Even so, I know a part of you still cares for me." Her voice, at first but a whisper, had grown louder. "Tell me . . ."

"Your husband has had another attack of gout, madam," Elizabeth declared, coming up behind them. The queen's tone was scathing as she looked Gweneth in the face. The green haze of jealousy colored Elizabeth's eyes. "A good wife would go to him."

Gweneth quickly recovered her poise. "Of course. I was but complimenting Captain Leighton on his capture of the Spanish ship." She looked at Jonathan with longing. "He and I are old friends."

"So it appears." Elizabeth's eyes moved from shoulder to hem and back again, surveying this radiant vision. Gweneth's gown surpassed even Elizabeth's own, as had been the intent. Even more eye-catching was her youth and the curves of her voluptuous body. Elizabeth was not a woman who would suffer competition in silence. She was queen. She ruled here. "But duty calls you elsewhere. Go to your husband, woman."

Gweneth quickly obeyed, leaving the hall. Elizabeth watched her go, then turned again to Jonathan. "You made a wise choice in leaving that one behind."

Jonathan shook his head. "The truth is, she left me."

"Then instead of wise I'll call you lucky, for by my word, she will come to no good end." The queen shrugged. "But come, let's have no more talk of her. We have other matters to discuss."

Those "matters" included her proposal that Jonathan join with Sir Francis Drake in a voyage to the New World. Though Jonathan was intrigued by the idea, though it had always been his dream, he put the queen off, asking for three days to think about it. First and foremost he had to settle the matter between himself and Anne. What he wanted was a chance for a new beginning, as if they were becoming acquainted for the first time—under much different circumstances, of course.

Strange, he thought with a smile, he had never before put any woman ahead of his ship and his quest for adventure. But then again, never before had he met any woman like Anne.

Shaking his head in amazement, he thought of how she had reached London by swimming, a bold action that not even he would have attempted. Perhaps, when all was said and done, he had truly met his match.

Anne lay awake in the small room at the Swan's Neck Inn for a long, long time, tossing and turning in an effort to fall asleep. Mulling a dozen things over in her mind, she found that sleep evaded her.

Have I been wrong? Was Enrique involved in a plot against the Queen? Is that why he married me? To get closer to Elizabeth? Propping herself up on one elbow, she felt angry with herself. She may have been played for a fool! Somehow she had to find out, for it changed everything! But how was she going to learn the truth?

In a chilling moment of reality, she realized how. Walsingham. The Queen had spoken of missives that had been intercepted and plots that had been revealed. Spying was Walsingham's speciality. Even so, the thought of dealing with the man who had brought down Mary Stuart, was unnerving. Walsingham had done little to hide his hatred for Mary, Queen of Scots, and any woman or man who thought to free that noble queen.

"I'm a loyal Englishwoman," Anne breathed. "I have no need to fear him." Unless in his zeal to protect the queen he ensnared someone innocent in his web.

Anne shuddered as she remembered seeing heads atop London Bridge. That could be the fate of someone who made the wrong move or said the wrong thing, perhaps even herself if she was not careful. And what of Captain Jonathan Leighton? Though she had lied to herself, despite everything she was drawn to him. He was not the kind of man one could easily forget. Could she put him totally out of her thoughts as she languished in the countryside?

"I must!" She and the captain came from two different worlds. Or did they? Had her anger blinded her to what the future might have had in store if she had not judged him so quickly?

She lay back down on her side, her head resting on one outflung arm, her dark hair tumbling across her face and spilling like a dark tide onto the pillow. She closed her eyes, but though she counted sheep, separating them by color, she couldn't relax enough to sleep. She was therefore vibrantly aware when someone entered her room. Feigning slumber she nonetheless opened her eyes just enough to catch sight of the intruder. It was one of the sailors she had freed from the hold the night she had tried to instigate mutiny. Entering quietly, he lit a candle on a table by the door and stood watching her.

"I'm not asleep," she informed him. "And I see that you are not locked up!"

"I escaped!" His voice quivered with fear.

"Escaped?" She watched the door. "Are there others?"

He shook his head. "No, Señora Navarro. The guard was distracted and forgot to lock my leg irons. I got away."

Anne sat up in bed. "Why did you come here?"

"I followed you and waited until the path was clear because you tried to save us all once before." He threw himself at her feet. "Please . . . I do not want to hang!"

"And should you?" There were so many unanswered questions in her mind. "Was my husband involved in anything to do with harm to Elizabeth?" When the sailor remained silent, she asked, "Was he?"

Though he didn't say a word, the look in his eyes answered the question.

Dear God! She started to tremble, then calmed herself by saying aloud, "Well, at least it's better to know. Now I will not have to brave an audience with Francis Walsingham." But what about the sailor? Could she turn him in?

Despite her resolve that she should, his pale face and the pleading in his eyes deeply stirred her. She wished so many things. Most of all she wished for the tranquility and peace of mind she had when life was so much simpler.

"Please, Señora, help me."

Walsingham was like a huge spider. He knew everything. If he got wind of her compliance in his prisoner's escape, she would be lost. And yet . . .

"Come." Anne stood up. Taking refuge behind a small partition, she dressed haphazardly, then called out, "We'll leave at once."

For a moment his expression held hope, yet he asked, "Where are we going?"

"They will be searching all of London for you. We need

to leave at once. You can go with me as far as Canterbury
and take a ship from nearby Dover. Hopefully Elizabeth's
anger will not have touched there as yet and a ship can be
found."

"*Gracias,* I will do as you say."

"You must never tell anyone that I aided you. It could
mean my life."

He nodded. "If I even thought I might talk in my sleep,
I would cut out my tongue."

Anne had purchased some clothing on her father's credit
at one of the shops on the street near the inn. Now she
gathered it together. Having kept the fisherman's blanket
and trousers, she handed them to the fugitive. "Put these
on."

He hurried to comply. Then, when they were ready to
travel, they opened the door. Keeping to the shadows, they
vanished into the night.

Jonathan took leave of the bargeman and stepped ashore.
Looking over his shoulder, he ascertained that no one had
followed him, then made his way on foot towards the Swan's
Neck Inn, a half-timbered, whitewashed building with a
thatched roof and boxed windows that looked over the
Thames.

"She has to be here." Jonathan had visited several other
inns in hopes of finding Anne, only to come up empty-
handed. Not a man to give up; he had given Anne's description to several people as he walked along. An old woman
remembered having seen a female of Anne's description
making several purchases at some of the shops, then heading
in the direction of the inn.

Drunken laughter, singing, and boisterous carryings-on
emanated from within the dwelling as he walked to the door.
It was the kind of place that a woman like Anne would never
have frequented had she not been in dire circumstances.

Opening the creaking door, he found himself face-to-face
with a tall man with a crooked nose who beckoned him

inside. Accustoming his eyes to the dim light, Jonathan let his gaze roam over the contours of the room, searching for a glimpse of Anne's slim form. Seeing no sign of her, he turned to the innkeeper.

"I'm looking for a woman."

The man laughed. "Aren't we all!"

"I mean a certain woman." There was a faraway look in his eye as he described her. He was remembering how she had looked in the bathtub. "Her name is Anne Morgan Navarro, though I am not certain that she would give out her real name."

"There is an Anne Morgan."

Jonathan's heart raced. "Where?"

"Upstairs in the room at the end of the hall. The one with the broken door hinge."

Jonathan took the stairs two at a time. He was in a hurry—until he reached the door. Suddenly he felt tongue-tied. Just what was he going to say to her? He leaned against the door, surprised to find that it was open.

"Strange . . ." Hesitantly at first, then more boldly, he stepped inside. "Anne?"

The bed was rumpled and showed evidence that someone had been sleeping there. The window was open just a crack to let in the night air. A chair in the corner had been tipped over, as if the occupant had been in a hurry. Hurry to do what? Leave? It seemed to be the reason.

Why? Why would she leave in the middle of the night? It was a dangerous and foolhardy thing for a woman to do, but then Anne was no mere woman, that he knew firsthand. "Something doesn't feel right . . ."

Running back downstairs, Jonathan questioned the innkeeper. Anne had paid for her room in advance; thus there was no reason for him to be anxious to track her down.

"Was she alone?" Jealousy that she might have had a visitor stabbed at Jonathan.

"Aye, at least I suppose, but then it's never been my habit to stick my nose into other people's business," the innkeeper replied.

"Were there any messages, anything at all that might have caused her to leave suddenly?"

The innkeeper shook his head. "I thought she was still abed."

"Do you know where she went?"

The innkeeper looked down his long nose. "If I didn't even know she was gone, then how would I know where she was going?"

Jonathan started to ask another question, but suddenly it seemed that a hundred voices shouted it out at once, "Fire!"

"Fire?" It wasn't an unusual occurrence, so Jonathan didn't run to look out the window with the others.

"At the dock—a ship. It's burning like a cinder."

"The dock?" Jonathan joined the other patrons at the window, looking in that direction. He saw a huge torch flaming on the water, an inferno devouring the skeleton and sails of what had once been a ship. The smell of smoke filled the air as the riggings and mizzenmast came down in a fiery crash.

Silently Jonathan said a prayer, then ran towards the dock as fast as his legs would carry him. Climbing into a longboat, he rowed so hard and so fast that his hands were blistered as his eyes were given confirmation of his greatest fear. The ship going up in ugly flames was the *White Griffin!*

Chapter Fourteen

Flames sprayed in all directions, licking hungrily at what remained of Jonathan's ship. The fire was devouring everything in its path. All that he owned.

"Falkhearst!" With horror, Jonathan realized that he had ordered the little man to be locked in the hold. "No!" Like someone possessed, he tore off his doublet and boots. He couldn't let Edmund die.

Flames leapt upward, threatening to demolish everything in their way. Timbers crashed down as flames ate away at what remained of the ship. A rational man would have admitted that there was no chance that Edmund Falkhearst could still be alive, but at the moment Jonathan wasn't rational.

He faltered for just a moment; then, despite the hopelessness of saving his first mate, he dove into the ocean and swam towards the ship. All the while the flames from the burning ship danced higher and brighter.

The smell of smoke permeated the air, burning his eyes and obscuring his vision as Jonathan moved towards the burning ship. He closed his eyes for just a moment. When he opened them, he gasped. Clutching a broken piece of the mizzenmast with one hand and a totally drenched Walsingham with the other, Edmund Falkhearst bobbed up and down in the water.

With a shout, Jonathan lunged forward. Reaching Falkhearst, he grabbed him by the shirt and swam with all his might back to the longboat. Thick smoke billowed through the air, stealing away their breaths. The brightness of the fire nearly blinded them. All around them, the fire raged out of control, licking at them with scorching heat. Only when they had reached the boat and Jonathan had rowed for several minutes could they stop coughing.

"The ship, Cap'n . . . the ship . . ." Falkhearst gasped, choking violently as he tried to take a breath.

"Everything I own is nothing but cinders, and yet seeing that you are alive, old friend, makes me realize what's really important."

"Cap'n . . . I'm sorry that I hit ye . . ."

Jonathan silenced him. "I don't want to talk about it, Mundie," he whispered, using a nickname he hadn't used for a long, long time. "What was done was done. All I know is that you are a sight for sore eyes. I thought . . . I feared . . ."

"Landers used the honor system. He didn't lock me in."

"Thank God for Landers."

"I would have stayed for the duration of my punishment, but I smelled the smoke."

Cool air rushed to meet them, the faint wisps of a sea breeze. It was a balm to their lungs and their souls. "And went in search of Walsingham . . ." Jonathan's eyes touched upon the cat who was now sitting at Falkhearst's feet, licking himself and acting as if nothing much had happened.

Edmund cherished the cat with his eyes. "I couldn't let anything happen to Walsy. He's my best friend—that is, next to ye, Cap'n."

Dark gray smoke swirled in the air behind them like an ominous thundercloud. They watched from a safe distance as the flames consumed the ship. "Damn them!"

"Damn who, Cap'n?"

"Damn whoever set fire to my ship." Jonathan didn't know who the culprit was, but in his mind was a long list of suspects, including Anne Morgan Navarro. She had been angry when he triumphed over her concerning the queen. But angry enough to instigate the burning of his ship? Shaking his head, he tried to get that thought out of his brain. He had suspected her once before and it had gotten him into trouble.

"Do ye think the Spaniards did this?" Edmund asked, staring out to sea.

"More likely someone English with loyalties where they shouldn't be," Jonathan answered.

Another thought crossed his mind, but he quickly pushed it away. Elizabeth wanted him to do her bidding, it was true, but surely she wouldn't burn him out just so that she could have him in her power? But what about one of her councillors? Roger Pembroke was a fierce rival, yet it would benefit him far more if Jonathan was out to sea. Henry Carleton? He had been angry when he saw Jonathan talking with his wife. Walsingham? Surely the queen's spymaster would have no reason, and yet it was just the kind of thing a man like him might do if the ends justified the means.

Silently Jonathan rowed, staring at a sleek ship he passed with a figurehead of a dragon. It reminded him of a Viking ship.

"*The Pendragon* is its name, after King Arthur's father. It's a fine ship, Captain," Falkhearst declared, taking note of the direction of his captain's gaze.

"Captain?" Jonathan expelled his breath in a long, sigh. "Am I? If so, I'm a captain without a ship."

"But not for long. You'll get another."

"Will I?" Because Falkhearst was a good friend as well as a first mate, Jonathan confided, "The *White Griffin* was all that I had. I lost everything with that fire." A lifetime of working and saving. Financially he was bankrupt. And emotionally as well.

"Everything?"

"Except for my townhouse. And a farthing or two."

"I'm sorry, Captain. What are you going to do?"

There was nothing else he could do. Remembering the queen's proposal that Jonathan set sail with Francis Drake, he knew it was his only answer. He had to have another ship. The only problem was, it would put him in the queen's debt again and mean that in many ways he was no longer his own man.

The moon glowed like a golden coin in the night sky, shining its mist of light upon the two horsemen traveling up the rocky, pitted road. Having purchased two horses on her father's credit, Anne and the escaped sailor rode at a furious pace. Both were near exhaustion. All that both had suffered seemed to be catching up with them. As for Anne, all she knew was that her body pricked and pained in a dozen different places. Even so, she was determined not to pause or rest even for a moment.

Had she been wrong in helping Juan? Anne wasn't certain. She had put her own security at risk to help a fellow human being, yet there was something about the fugitive that troubled her. For one thing, the details of how he escaped seemed to change each time he spoke of it. There was a burn on his hand that Anne had noted when they were saddling up the horses, yet Juan refused to take time to have it tended to. Moreover, he would not meet her eye when she had asked him how he had been burned.

C'est la vie! Anne told herself. She had made her choice; now she must live with it.

It was deathly silent when at last Anne and Juan decided to rest. Hot mulled wine would be a welcome boon when she reached Canterbury. Her father's brother, Roderick, or rather Father Stephen, was at the cathedral there and she knew that she could count on him to help not only her but Juan as well. Second only to her father, Anne trusted her uncle more than anyone else in the world.

Heading for a clump of trees, Anne dismounted, thinking about the time her father had been a fugitive. He had once ridden nonstop to give Queen Mary Tudor warning, only to be imprisoned in the Tower because of a lie. Monarchs were easily led by their councillors, her father had always warned. ''Trust only yourself.''

Juan dismounted and came to stand beside her. ''I fear that I am used to riding ships but not horses, Señora. I do not think I can travel any farther.''

''We must.'' It would be risky to travel in the light of the day. They had to go as far as they could while it was still dark. ''Once we reach Canterbury, my uncle will see that we find passage out of England.'' She felt the need to caution Juan one more time. ''But by your honor, do not speak a word of what either I or my uncle have done to help you. There are going to be troubled times between Spain and England.''

''Trouble that your queen and that whoreson of a captain began,'' Juan hissed. His frown changed to a smile. ''But perhaps they will be repaid for what they have done.''

''It takes two to make a quarrel, Juan. The captain wronged me as well as you, but I am going to forget about it and put it in the past. Seeking retribution is often futile and more often dangerous. If you have nothing in your heart but anger, it can turn to poison.''

All Anne wanted now was peace and the love of her family. Closing her eyes, she could visualize the stonework and tall towers of her father and mother's home in Norfolk. Oh, how she wanted to feel the security of their comforting arms.

Hoofbeats! Anne was certain she heard the sound of horses. Had they been followed, or was it a coincidence that horses were coming this way? She knew the dangers that often lurked behind the bushes in the night from thieves, robbers, and the like, but worse yet was the fear that Juan was being followed, that somehow he had been recognized at the inn.

''Someone is coming. Shall I kill him, Señora?''

''No!'' No matter what happened, Anne didn't want the blood of any Englishman on her hands, nor did she want to see Juan killed. ''Hide! In the bushes.''

"But the horses—"

"Are black." She could only hope that they would blend with the night. "The shrubbery will hide us all, I hope." Superstitiously, she crossed her fingers as she ducked behind a bush just as a several horsemen raced over the grass-carpeted ground.

Scarcely daring to breathe, Anne watched the shadows that rode past them, heard their shouts, the soft plop of their horses' hooves as they slowed down. For a moment Anne feared the horses had been spotted, then shared a smile of relief with Juan as the riders moved on. Time passed slowly, measured by the rhythm of their hearts, and at last Anne felt of a certainty that they were safe.

"The horsemen are headed for Maidstone on the River Medway." It was a marketing center where many Spanish shops that sold goods from the New World were located. No doubt they assumed that the fugitive was headed in that direction. Even so, Anne knew they had to be careful. "I know a shortcut."

Though she knew the pathways she had chosen were not as comfortable, that there were no inns at which they could stay, they had to make do with the inconvenience, for every inn within riding distance would be suspect by Walsingham and his men.

Until Anne reached Norfolk, she was in danger, yet thinking about the love of her family brought her a strange feeling of calm. She had made it this far, and that said something for her courage. Though one phase of her life had ended before it really began, it seemed suddenly as if a new one was opening.

PART TWO

STORM OVER ENGLAND

London and the North Counties, 1586

"There's a mist on the glass congealing,
'Tis the hurrican's sultry breath;
And thus does the warmth of feeling,
Turn ice in the grasp of Death."

—Bartholomew Dowling, *The Revel, Stanza 6*

Chapter Fifteen

There was nothing better in this life than returning home a hero. Jonathan squared his shoulders, feeling proud of himself and not at all humble as he stood looking at the door of the Devil's Thumb, a half-timbered tavern in the City. The tavern was popular with sailors and sea captains, and he always felt at home here and welcomed the company and conversation.

Indeed, he had much to talk about. Though he had left London as an impoverished man because of the fire, he was returning home a wealthy and renowned man who had made a name for himself sailing to the New World. Only his new friend, Sir Francis Drake, exceeded him in notoriety.

In fact both their names were synonymous with England's prosperity and fledgling exploration of the New World. Spain had risen to wealth by the grace of Columbus and Pope Alexander VI, whose arbitration decrees had awarded nearly all of the Americas to Spain. Jonathan, Raleigh, Drake, and other daring seamen, however, had not been afraid to go up against Spain's power. Like annoying mosquitoes, they had raided ships and colonies, pricking the Spaniards until they weakened them.

At first it had seemed impossible to dislodge Spain from her dominance in the New World, for she had hundreds of colonies and England none. Each year immense riches passed from the mines and found their way into Philip of Spain's coffers—that was, until he and Drake, financed by friends and the queen, entered and plundered the port of Vigo in northwest Spain, sailed on to the Canary and Cape Verde Islands, crossed the Atlantic, raided Santo Domingo, and carried on their own private war with Spain. Now Jonathan had returned with his spoils.

Jonathan paused only another moment, then pushed open the creaking door. Four tavernmaids, all pretty, all buxom, turned their heads to stare at him as he stood in the doorway, but he ignored them. Since first catching sight of England's shores, he was obsessed with one woman only. Anne. Strange, but during all the excitement of his adventures there hadn't been a moment when he hadn't thought about her, wondering where she was, what she was doing. Her period of mourning was long since finished. Had she remarried?

Of course she has. She's a beautiful woman, he chided himself. *Did you think she would wait for you?* If she had thought about him at all during the last three years, it would have been in anger, for their parting had been anything but amicable. It was a reality that Jonathan deeply regretted.

Noise emanated from within the back parlor, distracting him from any further thoughts. Drunken laughter, chatter, singing, and boisterous carryings-on came from the patrons. It was, in fact, crowded to the beams with men in their cups. Even so, several eyes turned towards him as Jonathan entered the large room.

"Isn't that Jonathan Leighton?" asked a sailor Jonathan recognized as once having been in his crew.

"God's whiskers, it is," said another.

Jonathan was recognized despite the fact that he had changed. His body was leaner and harder, his skin a swarthy olive from the sun, a striking contrast to his pale gold hair and short-clipped beard. Dressed in an emerald-green doublet, a sleeveless leather jerkin with standing collar, thigh-high boots fastened by straps to the waist of his buff-colored trunk hose and under-doublet, he cut a dashing figure as he strode across the room. Suddenly he was barraged by a dozen questions.

"Did ye give those Spaniards their due?"

"Did yer show them not to toy with Englishmen?"

"Did some of your men really get eaten by monsters?"

"Are there really men with red skin in the new lands?"

"Do headless men there have mouths in their chests and eyes in their shoulders?"

"Are there birds of every color?"

"Is it true that the women kill their men like black widow spiders after they have gotten them with child?"

Jonathan put up his hand. There were still individuals whose only knowledge of the New World was through the old myths. "I'll answer one question at a time. But first, let me quench my thirst."

It was musty and smoky inside. Firelight danced and sparked; glowing candles illuminated the scarred wooden tables, the uneven plaster on the walls, the bowed beams of the ceiling. The plank floor was sprinkled liberally with a mixture of rushes and sawdust that was in desperate need of a good sweeping out. Still, this had always been Jonathan's favorite London tavern.

"Jonathan?" A familiar face smiled up at him.

"Falkhearst!" The little man was a welcome sight. Jonathan gave him a fierce hug. "I missed you!"

Edmund hugged him back. "And I, ye."

"You should have gone with me. The sun burned us to a crisp, the ocean dashed our longboats to shreds, our supplies ran short, but we had a grand time."

Falkhearst threw back his head and laughed. "It sounds as if I would have had an uproarious time too." His eyes misted with tears. "I missed ye, Cap'n, I did. But it's good to have ye back."

"It's good to be back!" He looked Falkhearst in the eye. "And I understand why you wanted to stay here." Falkhearst had had enough of the seafaring life and wanted to—as he called it—get his land legs again. Besides, he was getting older and wanted a more settled kind of life and something to eat besides oatmeal, fish, dried peas, salt pork, and sea biscuits. "What are you doing now?"

"As a matter of fact, Cap'n, I work here for another sea captain."

"Sailing? But I thought—"

Falkhearst grinned. "Captain Ryan Paxton owns this tavern now. It belonged to his mother, God rest her soul."

"Paxton?" Jonathan had a limited acquaintance with that captain, but from all he had heard he was a good man.

"Once a sailor, always a sailor, it seems," Falkhearst continued. "Thus the good captain can't give up his ship. While he's away sailing, I overlook the doings at the Devil's Thumb and keep everything shipshape."

"It's a good living?"

"Captain Paxton has been good to me . . ." Falkhearst looked up at Jonathan. "But not nearly as good to me as ye." His voice quavered. "I'll never forget that when yer ship was burning, ye came back to save me."

"I didn't save you, you saved yourself and Walsingham." Looking around the room, Jonathan spied the fat gray tabby cat guarding a mousehole in the wall. "I see he's still a mouser."

"And always will be. Just like a sailor, he's always on duty." Falkhearst laughed. Wiping his hands on his coarse white, bibless apron, Falkhearst gave Jonathan's back a hearty slap. "But come. I will not have you stand." He led Jonathan to a table in the corner. They were followed there by several of the patrons who were anxious to have their curiosity assuaged.

Jonathan was again barraged by questions. Remembering his promise, he answered them.

"Was it all that you had heard? Paradise?"

"It is a lush, rich land in some areas. There are trees that are three times taller than any in England, with no leaves except at the top. And grass that rises all the way up to a man's waist. And flowers, and birds, and strange animals . . ."

His eyes took on a faraway look as he talked. There were times I thought it to be paradise." His eyes darkened. "But there were other times, when disease and the ever-biting bugs tormented us, when I thought it to be hell."

"What about the people there? Are they anything like us?"

Jonathan shook his head. "No. The brown-skinned men there are most uncivilized. They go naked and have strange ways."

"And the women? Do they kill their mates?" asked an old man.

"A tankard of my very best ale for my friend!" Falkhearst thundered.

The tavern maid looked at Jonathan's handsome face, broad shoulders, slim hips and waist with admiration, openly ogling him.

"Step lively now," Edmund scolded the maid when she seemed more intent on staring than in going about her work.

"No. The women are beautiful and very skilled at weaving and other wifely duties," Jonathan was saying. "Some of the Spaniards have taken them as concubines."

"Yer ale, sir." The tavern maid came back quickly, serving up the ale with a wide smile. Hopeful of Jonathan's attentions, she lingered just a moment after setting down the tankard. Licking her lips, she offered up a silent invitation. Jonathan shook his head, though he did give her an extra farthing.

"And no there are no men with mouths and eyes in the wrong places," he continued. "Except for their coloring, the men and women in the New World have two arms and legs just like us. If they are as wild as the land on which they live, they are nevertheless human. A fact the Spaniards too often forget." He shuddered as he remembered some of the brutal treatment. "As a matter of fact, we freed five native chiefs who were being tortured. They are our allies now."

"What about monsters?"

Jonathan's face clouded as he remembered that one of the

men had been eaten alive. "There are creatures—serpents—called alligators. Unfortunately, they like the taste of men."

"Like dragons?"

"Smaller, but just as ferocious. And there are bright red, purple, yellow, and green birds. More beautiful than peacocks. They are called parrots."

Falkhearst pointed to a boy wearing the queen's livery who was coming towards them. "Do you know him, Cap'n?"

"No." Jonathan sincerely hoped that the lad was there in search of someone else, but his hopes faded as the boy approached him.

"Are you Captain Jonathan Leighton?"

"I would like to say no, but I am honor bound to tell you that I am." Jonathan suspected that Elizabeth was overly anxious to get the crown's fair share of the cargo aboard his ship.

"I have come to bring you back with me. It is a matter of utmost urgency, Captain Leighton."

"Surely not so urgent that I have not time to finish my ale."

"*He* wants to see you right away."

"He?"

"Sir Francis Walsingham. He wants you to follow me to his chambers at Whitehall."

"What on earth can he want with *me?*" Jonathan leaned back in his chair, not in the least eager to be confronted with the man. To put it bluntly, he didn't trust him. Walsingham was always up to some plot or other.

"You must come immediately, that's what I was told."

There was no use tempting Walsingham's anger. Swearing aloud, Jonathan rose to his feet, determined to get the meeting over quickly so that he could return to the tavern.

Trying to make himself comfortable in the hardbacked chair, Jonathan leaned back and stretched his legs as he waited for his meeting with Sir Francis Walsingham. What was it about Walsingham that always bothered him despite the fact that he had few dealings with the man? The ghoulish manner in which he went after his enemies, Jonathan thought. The man was cold. Calculating. Deadly, if a man were on the wrong side . . .

"For a man so anxious to speak with me, he isn't hurrying," Jonathan declared, standing up to pace up and down the long corridor.

At last the sound of shuffling footsteps alerted him that someone was coming. He was surprised, however, to be greated by William Cecil, Lord Burghley, and not Walsingham. The white-haired Lord Burghley moved slowly, a result of his gout.

"So, you have come, Captain Leighton."

As if he had a choice, Jonathan thought. "I thought surely 'twas a matter of some urgency, else I would not have been tracked down."

"Anything concerning Elizabeth is always a matter of urgency."

"Of course."

"How was the New World? Filled with Spaniards, I would suppose."

"Aye, Philip has sent a great many to colonize the land."

"It was most astute of him, for I now believe that the Mediterranean will cease to be the center of the white man's civilization and power and that the age of the New World is upon us." He pulled at his long white beard. "We need to establish colonies there in the name of the Queen."

"And quickly." Jonathan assumed that was why he had been summoned. "I plan on doing exactly that, but first I want to sit back and enjoy my life for a while. A man can have his fill of wandering."

"I hope that is true," Burghley answered, totally confusing Jonathan.

"Why would you hope that? I thought—"

"The task at hand for you will take place on land," Lord Burghley explained. He beckoned for Jonathan to follow him.

* * *

Moonlight streamed through the mullioned windows as Jonathan walked into the large room. He was surprised to see that not only Walsingham but Elizabeth waited for him within.

"Your majesty," he said with a bow.

She gave Jonathan time to admire her and to conjure up the necessary compliments; then she motioned for him to come forward.

"I see that the air and the sun of the New World agree with you. Perhaps the next time you visit you should take me with you."

"Perhaps I should."

She frowned. "I fancy that had I been a man, I might have made quite a privateer."

"I think you most surely would have," Jonathan replied with a wry smile, thinking that in some ways she already was a royal privateer. Although she stayed on land, she gave orders to her men, then hugged her spoils when they returned. "Then again, you could always put on male attire and travel incognito."

"Hm. Perhaps you are right about that." The queen laughed. "I'll let Burghley and Sir Francis rule while I test the waters and see this New World for myself."

It was a joke, of course. Burghley and Walsingham were the two men she trusted with her life, yet even so her demeanor always reminded them that she was in control and that there could only be one ruler of England.

"What think you, Jonathan? Do I dare turn England over to these two and go cavorting around the world with you?" The queen's eyes traveled assessingly from one to the other of her ministers. Jonathan did likewise.

Walsingham, a dark-haired, swarthy-skinned man of lithe physique and stern countenance reminded Jonathan of a crafty weasel. He lived for his work, enjoyed it with ferocity, and served his queen well. Integrity. Obsession. Dedication. Those were the three words that defined him. His intent was to protect the realm, to ensure peace and prosperity. His dark eyes scrutinized Jonathan now, and he thought how anxious he was to get out of the spymaster's sight.

If Walsingham reminded Jonathan of a weasel, Elizabeth's elderly adviser brought to mind a wise old owl, one who had counseled the queen very well all these years. Burghley had a prudent yet relentless policy that had been a factor in Elizabeth's success.

Burghley had grown old in the queen's service. His once-red hair and beard were now so gray as to be almost white. Bundled in his robes of office, a dark, fur-lined gown pulled close about the ruff at his throat, the flaps of his black wool coif-cap pulled down over his ears, he looked as stately as the queen and nearly as formidable.

As Jonathan assessed the queen's councilors, they were in turn assessing him. For a long time it was uncomfortably silent, but at last Elizabeth said, "As much as I enjoy conversing with you, Captain Leighton, there was a purpose in summoning you this eve." Her eyes squinted as she looked at Jonathan. "Gentlemen, which one of you wants to tell our captain here what is afoot?"

It was Burghley who spoke first. "Do you remember three years ago when you attacked the ship of the Spanish ambassador's aide, imprisoned the crew, and took the gold aboard your ship, the *White Griffin?*"

Jonathan did, very vividly. "How could I forget?" He only hoped that matters between England and Spain hadn't changed suddenly so that he would have to be made a scapegoat not only for that action but the raids upon Spanish ships and colonies in the New World. That was often the queen's way. He held his breath.

Burghley continued. "Do you remember Enrique Navarro?"

Walsingham spoke for the first time. "What was *his* fate?"

"I had nothing to do with that," Jonathan said decisively but defensively. "That sniveling coward was afraid to be questioned. He jumped overboard and drowned.'' He looked Walsingham right in the eye. "Why?"

It was Burghley who answered as he thrust his gout-gnarled hands into the furred sleeves of his gown, a habit he was known for. "Do you remember his widow?"

"Anne," Jonathan exclaimed. "Yes." How could he ever forget her?

"Do you remember that the Spanish ambassador, Mendoza, was told to leave England?"

"Yes. . . ." He also remembered the look on Anne's face when she had been told. It had been a minor victory for Jonathan at the time, but in the weeks to come he had regretted not only that but many other things.

"It was her fault!" Elizabeth's thin lips tightened, and the wrinkles at her eyes and mouth seemed more pronounced beneath her heavy makeup. Her expression was grim. "I had to get rid of Mendoza because of her," she hissed, gripping her chair tightly as she tried to manage her poise.

"Anne?" Jonathan shook his head, coming quickly to her defense for fear of a serious reprisal. "I'm certain she had nothing to do with it."

"Not Richard Morgan's sniveling daughter. I mean Mary Stuart, the captive Queen of Scots. It was because of her that I threw Mendoza out of the country."

Jonathan sighed with relief. Elizabeth was not angry with Anne.

"We have had this discussion a dozen times or more. As long as Mary lives, she will be a constant threat to the queen." Though it was Walsingham who spoke, Burghley's expression clearly said he felt the same way. It seemed that for the moment they had forgotten all about Jonathan as they vented their anger and frustration towards a problem they were unable to eliminate.

"How well I know." Elizabeth's voice was carefully controlled. "I have no love for her, but she is still a kinswoman and an anointed queen. I do not seek her death. To do so could well lead to my own undoing. When blood is let, the hounds often seek more."

Seek her death? Jonathan didn't want anything to do with that sort of assignment. Though he had never met her, Jonathan had heard glowing accounts of Mary's beauty and generous nature. He supposed that was at least one reason Elizabeth grew angry whenever she thought of her rival. Mary had always had an undeniable sexual allure, which drew men to her. They wanted to protect her. Even some of Elizabeth's own courtiers.

Elizabeth might have been attractive once, but the passing years had touched her cruelly. It had been many years since her own hair had sufficed to frame her rouged and powdered face. The once luxurious tresses were now rumored to be thin and threaded with silver. It was said that wigs had long been her refuge from the ravages of time.

"Paulet is said to keep an unending watch over her," Burghley was saying, "but if you have heard that she no longer has ideas of obtaining her freedom, then you have heard amiss." His frown was fiercesome, his brows furled together as he stroked his white-frosted beard. "She will never change."

Elizabeth shook her head. "I have heard that she has offered, if released, to withdraw all claim to the English crown, never more to communicate with conspirators, to live anywhere in England according to my choice, never to go more than ten miles from that residence, and to submit to surveillance by neighboring gentlemen."

"Do not trust her." Walsingham and Burghley spoke the same words simultaneously.

"She speaks openly against you." Walsingham's words had the desired effect, for Elizabeth's mood quickly turned back to anger.

Though he had been ignored for a moment, Jonathan now realized he was the pivot of Walsingham's and Burghley's attention.

"I have learned that Phillip has covertly taken Mary's side and plans to take action against Elizabeth. He now fears England more than France. France is too involved in its own civil war to be a threat in the New World. But England . . ."

Walsingham's piercing eyes skewered Jonathan, as if to remind him that he and Drake were to blame.

"Mary and Philip . . ." Elizabeth did not like that prospect at all.

Walsingham strode to the table and pulled a stack of papers from a satchel. "By a variety of desperate devices she has managed to correspond secretly with the French and Spanish ambassadors, with her adherents in Scotland, and with representatives of the pope. Letters have been smuggled in and out, in the washing, in wigs, in the lining of shoes." Walking back to Elizabeth, he held the missives towards her. "This is a collection I have gathered during her long captivity."

Elizabeth waved the papers away. "I don't need to look." She mumbled more to herself than those in the room, "Throughout the years, so many have come under Mary's spell, even some of her jailers. What is this web of fascination that she weaves?"

"I have uncovered every plot in time." Walsingham's mouth grimaced in a rare smile. "I even have agents among the students and priests of the Jesuit College in Reims. They keep me informed. Every man has his price."

"And every woman?" She beckoned Jonathan to come closer. "Plots, plots, plots—how I am tired of them."

Jonathan remembered that Ridolfi, a Florentine banker active in London had been first, then Norfolk, a member of her own family. Then there had been Francis Throckmorton, Catholic nephew of the queen's late ambassador to France, who had joined Mary's cause and thus been executed.

Walsingham cleared his throat as he continued. "Were it the Scottish harridan who had you within her grasp, dare you imagine she would hesitate to sign your death warrant?"

Elizabeth shook her head. "Nay, I will not hear of it!"

Walsingham lifted his head sharply. "Tell her, Captain Leighton. Tell her that she must give her consent."

Jonathan kept silent. He wasn't going to feel responsible for such a terrible thing as the Scottish queen's execution.

His silence came at a deadly price, for Walsingham looked daggers at him.

'You must consent! It is the only way your safety and that of the realm can be guaranteed. Do not tie my hands behind my back, majesty!''

There was a long silence. Elizabeth sat unmoving, staring at the three men. Lowering her head and folding her hands in her lap, she exhibited a demeanor that had an air of resignation, as if she knew it to be the only way. Even so she did not say the words that gave them permisson.

"Jonathan knows if you don't," she whispered. "If I have any hand in an anointed monarch's death, then I pave the way for my own. And that is the end of it!'' There was another long pause before she said, "Captain Leighton . . . Jonathan . . . tell me about your adventures. What do you think of the lands to the west?''

"I think we need to lay a claim to them, your majesty. There is much more than gold to be had there, as you already know. Much more.''

"I heard you and Drake proved to be a worthy match for Phillip's captains.'' Elizabeth grinned, exposing her darkened teeth.

Jonathan gave Elizabeth an abridged story of what had happened after she financed thirty vessels to sail forth against the Spanish Empire. "We kept them off balance at least and let them know that we are a force to be reckoned with. I think Drake wanted to single-handedly defeat Philip,'' he said with a sigh. "We didn't, but at least we made a mark.''

Suddenly Walsingham interrupted. "Forget all this talk about the New World. We have trouble right here in England!'' His voice softened. "You are to go at once to the North Counties.''

"The North Counties?'' Jonathan's cheek twitched with irritation. He didn't like being relegated to the position of Walsingham's errand boy, nor did he want to act as one of his spies. "I have a ship to run. My time is valuable.''

"Your time belongs to the queen,'' Walsingham snapped.

"Your first mate, Steffington, will captain your ship in your absence."

"Steffington will captain *my* ship?" Jonathan looked towards Elizabeth, hoping she would contradict the order. She did not.

"Jonathan, Jonathan. You have been shipbound for the last three years. You need a rest. I am giving you one."

"By taking away my ship?" He was incensed.

"It is still your ship. I am merely borrowing it and you, but not together. I have need of you in Stafford. You have an acquaintance there, and that acquaintance will prove to be useful."

"Your majesty. I do not know anyone there."

Elizabeth adjusted an earring. "You do. Anne Morgan Navarro by name."

At the mention of her name, Jonathan felt heat surge through him. "Anne?" The conversation was coming back to her again after a multitude of interruptions.

"She is living with her brother there. Edward Bowen Morgan by name."

For just a moment Jonathan feared that somehow Anne was involved in a plot to free Mary Stuart. If so, he would not take any part in her downfall. He had too many regrets as it was.

"If you think that I can get in Anne Morgan Navarro's good graces, you are wrong. The last I remember, the lady hated me because I caused the death of her husband."

"He isn't dead." Walsingham's voice was as staccato as a pistol shot.

"What?" Jonathan was shocked by the allegation. Thinking Walsingham to be in ignorance of the truth, he said, "You must be wrong. I saw him jump from the railing of my ship. All of my sailors searched the ocean for him. He vanished."

"He isn't dead," Walsingham said again.

"That's impossible!"

"Not for a man like him." Walsingham explained that he had learned that Enrique Navarro's "suicide" had been faked so that it would be thought that he had died. "He crawled back aboard your ship and lived there all the time you were out to sea."

"No . . . it can't be. . . ." He had vanished into the ocean's depths. And yet his body had never been recovered, so it was possible. . . .

"He lived off the stored food in the hold, like a rat!" Walsingham explained.

"Rat," Jonathan repeated. Suddenly it all made sense. "Falkhearst's rat problem." It hadn't been the rats who had torn into the food stores. It had been Enrique Navarro, a rat of another kind. Worse yet, he must have had help from at least a few of Jonathan's crew. Or his conniving widow. "Does his . . . does Anne know he is alive?" Had she been the one who helped him survive aboard the ship? If so, then she was a most worthy foe and a very convincing liar.

"No. She believes that he was drowned," Walsingham said, clearing her of any perfidy in Jonathan's mind. "I think Navarro wanted it that way. However, we have reason to believe that he will try to contact her sometime in the future."

"He is alive," Jonathan repeated, still astounded by that information.

"Navarro is living in France under an assumed name with the Spanish ambassador, Mendoza. The diplomat that was expelled—"

"Yes, I know." Jonathan hoped his tone did not reveal his annoyance. So Enrique Navarro had been more danger-ous and cunning than he had ever realized. "So, what is it you want with me?"

"I need someone to watch over the widow. Someone who is loyal and loves his queen." Walsingham knew just what to say so that it was impossible to say no. "I want you to renew your acquaintance so that if Navarro does try to contact her, I will be immediately informed."

"You want me to become a spy!" Jonathan said the word with loathing.

"Elizabeth and I have not forgotten your desire for a ship. . . ."

It amounted to blackmail. Even so Jonathan was trapped, and he knew it. Besides, he had to admit to himself that his interest in Anne Morgan Navarro, widow or no, was the driving force that goaded him into saying, "I will leave with the first light of dawn."

Chapter Sixteen

Though winter was only just coming to an end, the weather was mild in Stafford. Anne looked out the bedroom window of her brother's manor house, appreciating her view of the rolling hills and pasture, blue ribbons of water winding a path through the valleys, and leafless trees raising their branches as if to pray. There was a serene beauty to the countryside that always touched her.

I'm at peace here. And sometimes lonely, though she would never have admitted it to anyone for all the world.

Standing in her undergarments, Anne poured water from a pitcher into a small china basin, hurriedly washed her face, then plaited her long, dark hair and fashioned it into coils on either side of her head. Dressing in a dark-green gown decorated with gold, she thought about how the routine was always the same. Out of bed by the cock's fourth crow, then pull the nightgown over her head, put on her underthings, lace her corset, put on her farthingale, fasten up her petticoat and gown, and slip on her neck and wrist ruffs. Then Anne brushed her hair, wondering all the while what sense it made to spend such time on her toilette when she never saw anyone other than her family and their few servants.

"I could go about half naked and there would be few people to notice," she lamented. In truth it was isolated in the country, with none of the social events she had grown used to at court. It seemed at times as if being a widow was nearly as bad as being dead.

During her mourning period, Anne had tried to pass the long hours with embroidery, reading, gardening, or at play with her brother's pet spaniels, but she had sorely missed dancing, riding, and swimming. Now she was out of her mourning, but still strangely melancholy.

She missed Jonathan Leighton. How was it possible for a man one barely knew, a man one always argued with, to become so very integral to happiness? Without him, loneliness had taken on a new meaning.

Anne tried to think of other things lest she give way to melancholy. At least she was away from the queen. Remembering her last audience with the aging monarch, she frowned. Elizabeth might know a great many things, but she didn't know the first thing about how to treat people, unless they were handsome men.

Anne looked out the window again, trying to convince herself that she was glad she wasn't in London. The city was too crowded. This area consisted mainly of a broad belt of rich pastureland, crossed by canals and gently flowing rivers. To the south were several square miles of moorland and forest that was once a hunting ground of Plantagenet kings, or so Edward had told her. To the northeast were the oaks and hollies of the vast Needwood Forest. To the southwest was the River Trent, which meandered through the countryside touching on several towns.

Stafford itself was a charming country town located on the River Sow. Grouped around the village green was a church with fine chancel arch and nave arcades dating back to before the Norman Conquest, a market square flanked by half-timbered cottages and shops, and one or two seemingly busy inns.

Most of the men in Stafford were farmers. Most of those were sharecroppers; some were tenants paying a fixed rent;

a rising proportion were freeholding yeomen. Enclosures of common lands continued just as they had in the past, for pasturage proved more profitable than tillage. Though serfdom itself was gone, evictions of tenants by enclosures had generated an unhappy class of laborers who sold their brawn from farm to farm or from shop to shop. Always kind of heart, her brother paid his workers more than the usual wage.

Sitting on the velvet-cushioned, high-backed chair in her bedroom, Anne watched as rain drops, not snow, gently spattered the window. She had thought to spend only a few days with Edward and his family, but the few days had turned to nearly three years, a time in which she had hidden away from the rest of the world and been the perfect widow.

Anne remembered that things hadn't always been so routine. She reflected on the frantic ride to Canterbury with Juan. Keeping her promise, she had enlisted the help of her uncle. Dressing Juan like a priest, he had easily slipped the fugitive on a ship bound for Spain. Though she had not heard a word, Anne assumed that he had arrived safely.

As for her, after a long visit with her father and mother, she had set out for her brother's estate in Stafford. He and his wife had welcomed Anne into the household with a warmth and protectiveness that had made leaving an impossibility. There were times it just felt good to be with family.

Anne thought about her brother with a loving smile. Edward was rugged in build, which belied his gentle nature. He was versatile and resourceful, much like their grandmother, Blythe Bowen. His wife Margaret, a decisive, strong-willed woman with auburn hair, seemed a perfect match for him.

The romance between the two had happened suddenly and quickly. Though Margaret was just seventeen, she had known upon first meeting the eighteen-year-old, red-haired Edward that he was the only man she wanted to marry. With that thought in mind, she had pursued him with a vengeance, asked him to marry her, and prodded him to elope with her when their parents insisted they wait. Like Anne, patience was never one of Margaret's virtues.

The marriage, if not a perfect one, was as close to idyllic as most people could ever hope for and had produced a daughter and a son. Margaret and Edward were truly happy together and cherished their family. This contentment made Anne long for what they had.

Even her brother's two-storied family house was perfect, or nearly so. The house was built of plaster and brick under a roof thatched with straw. There was a pond in the front yard upon which ducks and geese swam about, an old mill building complete with a waterwheel, a pumphouse, and a barn. There were apple and cherry trees near the mill. Terraced land flanked the pond and fed it with water from a gently moving stream.

Inside, the walls were adorned by tapestries. The cabinets, tables, chairs, chests, and bedposts were cut and mortised in walnut and oak. All of the bedrooms had embroidered coverings, feather mattresses, and silk canopies. What Anne loved most of all, however, were the gardens that in spring had primrose, hyacinth, honeysuckle, larkspur, sweet William, marigold, Cupid's flower, love-lies-bleeding, love-in-the-mist, lily-of -the-valley and roses, white and red for the Houses of Lancaster and York.

"Someday I want a home like this . . . and the love my brother and sister-in-law have," she said wistfully, wishing she could be just as happy.

"What, up already, Annie?"

Recognizing Mary, her young niece's voice, she turned around. "I couldn't sleep."

"What a little early birdie you can be." Mary yawned. "I, on the other hand, wish that I could sleep, but I have a hundred chores to do. I guess they just don't care that I'm still a child."

Seven-year-old Mary had been named after her mother's grandmother and not after the Scottish Queen. Even so, in these tenuous times, her name had often made her the target of teasing, playful and otherwise.

"Why am I always the one to have to churn the butter,

sweep the floors, and do the scrubbing? Why doesn't Taddie have to do anything?''

"Because he's a boy. He helps your father," Anne explained, remembering when she had said the very same thing to her mother.

It troubled Anne that although the queen was a woman and therefore should have understood the plight of her sex, there were few opportunities for young females. All organized education of girls had been ended by Henry VIII's dissolution of the nunneries, yet primary education was offered to any boy in reach of a town. In hopes of aiding her niece's future, therefore, Anne had taken it upon herself to tutor the child in both English and Latin.

"My hands will look like an old woman's before I'm seventeen. I'll end up an old maid.''

"Not here you won't," Anne said gently, tugging on her niece's long dark hair. "There are lots of boys who will grow up to be handsome men. You'll find the right man someday.''

"How can you be so sure? *You* haven't!''

"Merry-go-up, what a thing to say." At first Anne was perturbed, but then she realized that the girl had only spoken the truth. Though there had been a few countrymen who had played court to her, Anne was still unmarried.

"Are you still pining for your dead husband, Aunt Annie?''

"Yes," Anne answered, because it was easier to say that than to explain that she remembered a brief moment of passion and kisses from a sea captain.

The years that had passed had mellowed her resentment of Jonathan Leighton. She realized now that her anger had been as much out of fear of his virility as anything else.

"Do you think you will ever get married again?''

"I don't know. . . .''

There was silence, then out of the blue Mary asked, ''Did you like kissing?''

"I did . . . very much.''

Mary wrinkled up her face. "Well, I didn't like it when Harry kissed me."

"That's because you haven't grown up yet. There will come a time when you will like it. . . ." Once again Jonathan's face and the memories of that fateful voyage caressed her thoughts.

"You're daydreaming. Of your husband?"

Anne hadn't thought much of Enrique at all the past year and a half. In truth, knowing what she did now, she never would have married him just for the sake of prestige. Marriage was meant to be for love. It was something that was meant to be forever . . .

"Aunt Annie, what are you thinking?"

"How hungry I am." Taking her niece's arms, she led her towards the stairs.

Margaret was already working in the kitchen by the time Anne and Mary arrived downstairs. A pot of porridge bubbled on the stove. The enticing aroma of bread baking in the oven made Anne realize just how hungry she really was. Forcing herself to ignore her gently growling stomach, however, she joined Margaret in the task of peeling the potatoes that were to be fried for the morning meal.

"How strange it is to think that these come from the New World," Margaret announced, hefting the potato in her hand. "I think my darling Edward was wise to get hold of them and plant them here. You can cook them so many ways."

Anne's brother was not only a prosperous merchant who shipped his goods all the way to London, he grew many of his own products. He had tried planting the strange leafy plant, tobacco, also from the New World as well, but the cold of the north was unsuitable. Besides, having caught his young son smoking a pipe had changed his mind about the wisdom of having such a sinful weed around.

"It is a wicked thing," he had said.

"You are old-fashioned, brother dear," Anne had teased, informing him that the smoking of tobacco was fashionable at court. "I'm told there are seven thousand tobacco shops in London and separate rooms just for smoking."

Edward had responded that he should blame London's newest indulgence on Drake, Raleigh, or Leighton, who had sailed to the New World and brought back the tobacco that now was the trend in the city.

The New World, Anne thought, immediately thinking about Jonathan again. She had heard that he had gone there with Drake and that he had made quite a name for himself. Closing her eyes for just a moment, she could almost imagine him standing on deck with the wind blowing in his tawny hair. What might have happened if she had met him before she married Enrique?

"Edward says that the guilds have been hamstrung," Margaret was saying. "There are too many regulations. How glad I am that my dear husband is so inventive. Unlike some of the others, he has not lost any markets."

It was true. Edward was a clever promoter who gathered capital, bought up raw materials, distributed these to shops and families, bought the product, and sold it for a large profit. His barn was a miniature factory, his workers employed in a variety of ways. The women wove and spun flax and wool, sewed and embroidered, prepared herbal medicines, and experimented in the art of cookery. The men not only farmed but distilled liquor and delivered her brother's goods to market in dozens of towns.

Under Elizabeth's reign, there had been a laborious code enacted that was supposed to banish idleness and unemployment. It required every able-bodied youngster to serve as apprentice for seven years until he was twenty-three. Every willfully unemployed man under thirty not having an income of forty shillings a year could be forced to take employment as directed by the local authorities. In the countryside all healthy men under sixty could be compelled to join in harvesting. Even so, Anne's brother never took advantage of anyone but paid them such a fair wage that he had many men clamoring to work for him.

It was silent in the room. After breakfast the women, including young Mary, were engrossed in their stitchery. Though the two female servants took care of the heavy cleaning, there was always mending to be done as well as embroidery. Sewing was something that Anne did but never enjoyed. She wanted to do something adventurous, not prick her finger on a needle twenty times a day!

"Woman's work," she scoffed. Far better to be a farmer . . . or a sailor. Or a ship's captain.

Life in her brother's house left little room for adventure. Anne and Margaret often did the cooking and the dishes on top of other light duties. Breakfast was at seven, dinner at eleven or twelve, supper at five or six. The main meal at noon was plentiful. Anne smiled as she remembered Enrique saying that the English stuffed themselves more than any other people on earth. Perhaps that was why so many persons suffered from gout.

"Listen . . ." Sewing in slow motion, then pausing, Mary attuned her ears to a sound.

Anne cocked her head too. She could hear the faint sound of wheels hitting against the stones outside, the clop of hooves. "Edward is home." There were times when Anne really missed London and enjoyed her brother's bits of gossip.

"Come on!" Mary was the first one down the stairs, then Margaret. Anne followed, sweeping from the room with a rustle of skirts. Their footsteps blended together on the stairs—Margaret's heavy tread and Anne's lighter step; Mary's footfall was nearly soundless.

They caught up with Edward Morgan just as he was unloading one of his wagons. Tall, with red hair and beard, he was a handsome man and the spitting image of his mother, Heather Morgan. "Ah, my three ladies . . . see what I brought you."

Mary's gift was a doll, dressed like the ladies at court, including silk stockings, a ruff, and a farthingale. Margaret's present was a silver necklace and Anne's a book, *The Faerie Queene* by Spenser.

"It's about chivalry and knights and has political allusions I know you will enjoy."

"Knights . . ." Mary was eager for Anne to read it to her.

"Edward, do tell. What is happening in London and at court?" It was Margaret who spoke. "What of the queen? Is she ever going to marry?"

"I think not, for if she does England will have a king and not a queen. If she takes a husband, he will be the one to rule England. She knows that and thus remains a maid."

"A virgin?" Margaret raised one eyebrow. "I know she makes such a claim, but I doubt that she speaks true. There was talk of Leicester several years ago. She loved him, methinks." She wound her arms around Edward. "Just as I love you."

For a long time the two satisfied themselves with hugging, forgetful that there was anyone else around. Then Mary cleared her throat. "Sometimes I think you two are like lovebirds."

"That's exactly what we are," Edward replied. Gently he kissed his wife on the lips. She in response whispered something in his ear to which he replied, "What? When?"

"It's due in four months."

Edward gave out a loud whoop of joy. "I'm going to be a father again!" He turned to Anne. "Did you hear that, sister dear? You are going to be an aunt thrice over."

Edward spent several minutes trying to think up names, both boys' and girls'. One of the names mentioned was "Jonathan".

"I like the name, though I have a feeling I am carrying another girl," Margaret said wistfully. "If it is a boy, though, I would like to call it Jonathan after a certain captain with whom your sister is well acquainted." When Anne looked puzzled, she said, "You sometimes talk in your sleep."

"Ah-ha, the captain who kidnapped you, eh, sister dear?" He grinned. "I'm in a mood to tease. Guess what sea captain is soon to be our new neighbor?" It was a marvel, he related, that while his business was selling and shipping goods, their new neighbor owned not one but three ships, all gifts from the queen.

"A sea captain is going to live in Stafford?" Anne deduced that he must be very old.

"No. In fact, he is young." Edward put his hands on his hips. "Give up?"

Anne shook her head. "There is no use my guessing. I don't know the names of any captains except for Hawkins, Raleigh, Drake, and—"

"Jonathan Leighton!"

Anne's face flushed, then turned pale. "Jonathan Leighton is coming here?" She felt dizzy and clung to her brother's arm for support. "Oh, my God . . . Jonathan. . . ."

The wheels of the wagon seemed to be constantly moving, with stops made only at night or in case of personal need. It was an exhausting and uncomfortable journey to Stafford over rough and rocky roads. Anxious to arrive as quickly as possible, Jonathan kept a rigid and often harrowing schedule that left little time for comfort or relaxation. He did in fact keep the same strict discipline for himself that he did for the men on his ships.

Jonathan traveled from London to Oxford to Coventry and beyond, staying at whatever inns were available, passing through village after village until Falkhearst, who had accompanied him on an ale-buying journey for the tavern, insisted that he felt much like the gypsies they had heard about.

"This wagon is as rough as a deck in the worst storm. Even so, I'd settle for a bruised prat any day," Edmund Falkhearst said, rubbing his sore buttocks, "just for a chance to sail with yer again, Cap'n."

"I hope you still feel that way when this journey is over," Jonathan answered, thankful that Falkhearst had come with him. Not only did it make the journey more companionable, but the two men could take turns at the reins. Jonathan had put a great many of his personal belongings in the wagon so that his stay in Stafford would be more comfortable. Falkhearst was going to use the same wagon for the barrels of ale he was to take back to London.

"I will, Cap'n. I will." Falkhearst suddenly remembered.

Take 4 FREE Books!

We created our convenient Home Subscription Service so you'll be sure to have the hottest new romances delivered each month right to your doorstep — usually before they are available in book stores. Just to show you how convenient Zebra Home Subscription Service is, we would like to send you 4 Kensington Choice Historical Romances as a FREE gift. You receive a gift worth up to $24.96 — absolutely FREE. There's no extra charge for shipping and handling. There's no obligation to buy anything - ever!

Save Up To 32% On Home Delivery!

Accept your FREE gift and each month we'll deliver 4 brand new titles as soon as they are published. They'll be yours to examine FREE for 10 days. Then if you decide to keep the books, you'll pay the preferred subscriber's price of just $4.20 per title. That's $16.80 for all 4 books for a savings of up to 32% off the publisher's price! Just add $1.50 to offset the cost of shipping and handling. Remember, you are under no obligation to buy any of these books at any time! If you are not delighted with them, simply return them and owe nothing. But if you enjoy Kensington Choice Historical Romances as much as we think you will, pay the special preferred subscriber rate of only $16.80 each month and save over $8.00 off the bookstore price!

We have 4 FREE BOOKS for you as your introduction to
KENSINGTON CHOICE!

**To get your FREE BOOKS,
worth up to $24.96, mail the card below
or call TOLL-FREE 1-888-345-BOOK
Visit our website at www.kensingtonbooks.com.**

Take 4 Kensington Choice Historical Romances FREE!

❥ *YES!* Please send me my 4 FREE KENSINGTON CHOICE HISTORICAL ROMANCES (without obligation to purchase other books). Unless you hear from me after I receive my 4 FREE BOOKS, you may send me 4 new novels – as soon as they are published – to preview each month FREE for 10 days. If I am not satisfied, I may return them and owe nothing. Otherwise, I will pay the money-saving preferred subscriber's price of just $4.20 each... a total of $16.80 plus $1.50 for shipping and handling. That's a savings of over $8.00 each month. I may return any shipment within 10 days and owe nothing, and I may cancel any time I wish. In any case the 4 FREE books will be mine to keep.

Name _____

Address _____ Apt No _____

City _____ State _____ Zip _____

Telephone ( ) _____ Signature _____

(If under 18, parent or guardian must sign)

KN070A

"I don't want to forget. The man who usually makes this journey always stops by Chartley to get empty barrels from the house of Amyas Paulet."

"Paulet?" Jonathan remembered that in the shuffle of jailers, Mary Stuart had been given over to Paulet's care. For a moment he was alarmed, then shrugged it off. There couldn't be much harm in retrieving empty barrels. Still, he cautioned, "Have no contact with the captive Queen of Scots, Edmund. They say she can charm the wings off a dove, and I know how sympathetic and kind a man you can be."

"It hurts my heart that she has been treated in such a surly manner...."

"Surly or not, consorting with her in any way would be considered treason. Just remember...."

"Aye, aye, Cap'n, I will...." Falkhearst let go of the reins with one hand so he could put his hand to his forehead.

"It's still early. We'll bypass the inns and head directly for Stafford," Jonathan announced, flicking the reins of the wagon. It was a decision he was to regret, for as they traveled along, the day proved to be most miserable.

A chill wind gusted. The skies overhead were dark with clouds that threatened a storm as the wagon creaked over the hill six miles from the town of Stafford. "There it is. Chartley Hall," Jonathan announced. "I've decided to go with you to get the barrels. That way I can protect you from yourself."

Chartley was situated on a hill rising from a fertile plain, an estate with a multi-windowed, gable-roofed manor house with a circular keep and towers. Around that manor house was a large moat.

"I would suppose this place has been chosen to house the captive queen because of that ditch," Jonathan said, noticing the direction of Edmund's eyes. "It is most suitable for security reasons, for I doubt it would be easy either for Mary to escape or for those who are unwanted to get beyond the walls."

Falkhearst scanned the manor house and grounds with a sad gleam in his eye. "I wonder how she is being treated."

"So far Mary Stuart has kept her head when there are many who would see it struck from her shoulders. In that she is lucky. Keep that in mind, Edmund."

When they arrived, Falkhearst went to get the empty barrels. Jonathan made a tentative exploration of the outer rooms of the manor house. The house was roomy and well built. It was an imposing structure, nearly as grand as Whitehall, but with a rustic splendor. Built of stone, it looked to be a sturdy fortress, too, but one that was comfortable inside. Jonathan had heard that the captive Scottish queen was in a less stringently guarded cage than she had been before. He knew why. Walsingham was setting a trap.

He remembered his own advice. "Be careful!" Still, as he caught sight of a chesnut-haired woman who sat by the window reading, he felt his heart lurch.

"Mary . . . ?" It couldn't be. It had to be someone else.

The woman responded to the name immediately, turning her head. In that moment Jonathan was stunned. This round-faced, plain woman couldn't possibly be Mary of Scots. No, she couldn't be. This woman was not at all queenly. Though he had heard that Mary had changed, Jonathan found himself staring. This woman looked so old. Not at all like the beauty that his cousin, Roarke MacKinnon, had described.

This woman with the unhappy face and matronly form could not be the legendary, beautiful Mary Stuart. She was dressed all in black, like one in mourning. It was a dress that was sadly out of fashion, its faded skirts puffed out by a Spanish farthingale, not the French version that Jonathan had seen at court. The woman's face was overly pale with lines at the mouth and eyes.

"Who are you? Why do you seek me out?" The voice was soft and soothing with just a hint of a rasp. Stoically she eyed Jonathan up and down, noting the dust of the road, the snags and tears of his garments. Jonathan thought he probably looked like a begger. Even so, he was treated with the utmost courtesy.

"My name is Jonathan Leighton. My cousin, Roarke MacKinnon, once served you."

Her sudden smile lit the room. "Ah, yes. I have fond memories of him and of Kylynn. Tell me, are they well?"

"Very. And happy."

Mary's eyes sparkled with unshed tears. "Good. Good!"

As Mary stood up, there was a regal bearing to her form, a pride that no amount of suffering could smother. All that remained of what she once had been was the elegant height to her rapidly thickening form and her long-fingered hands, yet she conducted herself like a queen.

"Jonathan Leighton. I have heard of you. You sailed to the New World and, I see, returned to tell about it."

"I did." Jonathan felt strangely tongue-tied. Despite his advice to Falkhearst, he realized that his own heart ached for Mary. He remembered that her captivity had lasted nineteen years. Nineteen! Still, there was a kindness in Mary that could be sensed when in her presence. Nineteen years, Jonathan thought again. And all that time Walsingham had done everything within his power to see her killed. What might have happened to Mary if she had never fallen in love with Bothwell? What if Darnley had escaped the plot against his life? What if Mary had never ventured onto English soil, had never asked her cousin Elizabeth for sanctuary? But all those ifs had come to pass. Now she was England's and Elizabeth's prisoner, and her confinement reminded Jonathan once again to be careful.

Chapter Seventeen

Never had a journey seemed so endless, or a road so long. More than once Jonathan had glanced impatiently at wheels that seemed to be purposefully churning slowly. *If I were on my ship, we would already be there,* he thought. His ship! Oh, how he missed the sensation and power of the waves as the prow skimmed along. Traveling on land was cumbersome, but then, perhaps he would always be a seaman at heart, even when he was on land.

Jonathan's feet ached from the uncomfortable shoes he wore, stout foot coverings of thick leather made for wear and not style. He had to admit, however, that his expensive leather boots would not have survived the journey. There had been times when the condition of the road meant stopping to help Falkhearst push and pull the wagon out of the mud, times when he walked instead of riding on a long stretch of road, just as he was doing now.

Although Jonathan was anxious and irritable, Falkhearst was whistling contentedly, flicking the reins now and again to keep the wagon trundling along at a steady if tedious pace. "Are ye anxious to see Annie again?"

"Yes . . . but I'm just not certain how she will react to seeing me."

Jonathan looked down at his garments. He hardly resembled a dashing sea captain now in his traveling clothes. He was dressed in a tunic of russet wool, buttoned down the front from the close, uncollared neckline to the low waist. The garment came to mid-thigh, brushing against his long breeches of light brown canvas. The coarse pants were tied at the ankles and bound with straps at a point just below the knees.

"She'll be glad!" Falkhearst winked. "Anne always cared for ye, even when you ruffled up her feathers."

"We'll soon see."

Jonathan and Falkhearst journied the rest of the way in comparative silence, Edmund taking in the scenery, Jonathan trying to sort things out in his mind. Anne had a right to know that her husband was still alive, and it troubled him that Walsingham had so adamently insisted that he not disclose the secret to her. *She'll find out the truth when Enrique Navarro comes back and accuses me of being a liar. . . .*

Would Enrique Navarro return to England no matter how much danger the journey would pose? Jonathan knew that if Anne were *his* wife, he would brave any danger to reclaim her, but the popinjay was a devious, strange kind of fellow. *Perhaps he'll stay in hiding and Anne will never even know . . .*

"Look, up ahead. There's a pond," Falkhearst said, interrupting Jonathan's thoughts.

"On someone else's land." Jonathan tried to get his bearings. The property that Elizabeth had "gifted" him with for his services should be near here. He took out his compass.

"They shouldn't care if we pause only to freshen up!" Falkhearst laughed. "Ye should see yerself, Cap'n. Ye are all gritty and grimy!"

"So I might imagine." Jonathan dusted himself off, then gave in to Falkhearst's suggestion. "All right, we'll stop, but only long enough to wash our hands and faces."

Jonathan got down from the wagon, moving towards the

pond as he looked at his compass. Though he hated to admit that he was lost, he knew he needed to glance at the map at least one more time. It was just one more example of how much better he navigated on water than on land. Suddenly an insistent, high-pitched barking startled him as two spaniels ran out of a nearby enclosure.

"Cider! Wart! What is it?"

There was something familiar about the voice. Jonathan drew back, then stiffened as a woman followed the dogs.

Though the face she saw was unshaven, the hair tousled, the clothing dusty from the road, Anne recognized the man in that instant. "Jonathan!"

Jonathan stood for a long moment, unsure of what he should do or say next. This wasn't the reunion he had desired. Always having prided himself on his dashing appearance, he loathed being caught looking like a begger. Where the devil was Falkhearst? Jonathan could see that the little man was hiding behind a tree like a would-be cupid. Jonathan was on his own. He forced a grin, bowing slightly as he said, "It's a pleasure to see you again, Anne."

Anne's blue eyes shone with an undisguised happiness. "And to see you, Jonathan." Subduing the spaniels, she looked at him for a long, long time. "How are you?"

In agitation he ran his fingers over his chin, disgruntled at the stubble there, then brushed at the dirt on his trousers. "Better than I look."

He shifted uneasily, more upset over this unexpected meeting than he would admit. He'd hoped to get a good night's sleep, then dress in his best garments before seeking her out. Instead, here he was standing before her covered with grime, smelling like horses.

"You look like . . . the Jonathan Leighton I remember." Even disheveled he was a strikingly handsome man. She hadn't forgotten just how pleasing to the eye he was.

"And you are looking lovely as usual," he said simultaneously, eyeing her up and down appreciatively from the top of her head to the hem of her mauve dress.

She hadn't gained an ounce. She still had an hourglass

figure, slim in the waist with full breasts and gently curving hips.

"The country agrees with you."

He'd almost forgotten just how beautiful she really was. Her cheeks were flushed, emphasizing high cheekbones. Her skin was smooth. Her sapphire eyes were wide and flashing a different kind of gleam. Not anger.

She tried to keep her voice calm and even, but she was overjoyed to see him again. There was laughter in her voice as she said, "I look *better* than I did the last time we were together, or so I would hope."

For just a moment Jonathan was at a loss; then he grinned as he remembered that her hair had been damp and straight and she had been dressed in the clothes of a fisherman. "Though I risk sounding like a flatterer, I can only say that you are always lovely."

Anne felt a shiver go up her spine as he took her hand in his long, hard-fingered grasp. His slightly roughened thumb rubbed over the back of her hand. "In case you hadn't heard, I spent some time in the New World. But I wanted to take a break from sailing so I purchased some land near here." He looked deep into her eyes. "We are going to be neighbors."

"So my brother told me . . ." In sudden embarrassment, Anne pulled away. She'd thought about him often, had wanted to see him again one day. Now that he was here, however, she felt uncomfortable, ill at ease. Something had changed between them. Somehow her feelings were different.

Jonathan noticed her reserve and solicitously drew back. He was careful in his choice of words. "There hasn't been a single day that has passed, even when I was on the ocean, when I didn't regret the way things were between us." He tensed, hoping that he could make her understand the depth of his feelings. "Is it possible, do you think, that we could . . . pretend that we are meeting for the very first time?"

Something in his intense gaze forced her to meet his eyes, but she quickly looked away. Oh, what was it about Jonathan that made her feel so flustered and yet at the same time so alive? "We were both stubborn," Anne conceded, "but time has a way of putting things into perspective. And yes, we can pretend."

This time when their eyes met, she didn't look away. She was motionless, frozen, suspended between past and future, sunset and dawn. If she had believed in magic, she would have insisted she was under a spell. Whatever was happening, it seemed as if at that moment her life was about to change.

"Anne . . ." The way he spoke her name, with so much tenderness, made her feel dizzy. This was a Jonathan Leighton she didn't know.

Jonathan felt a tug, more powerful than the tide, draw him forward. Bending his head, he started to kiss her, but Edmund Falkhearst's intrusion put an end to any amorous intention.

"I knew yer couldn't stay mad at each other, at least not for long." Squinting his eyes, he looked at her, saying, "If all the women in Stafford are as pretty as ye are, Annie, I just might take the cap'n up on his offer and stay here to settle down."

"I wish that you would. Your friendship was a very precious thing. I'd be happy if we could be friends again."

Falkhearst blushed. "What say ye, Jonathan? Do yer need me?"

Without even a blink of his eye, Jonathan responded, "I do."

"Well then, ye have it. What else can I do but stay and keep the cap'n out of trouble." Falkhearst's grin spread from ear to ear. "I'll take the barrels of ale back to the Devil's Thumb, tell Cap'n Paxton of my plans, gather Walsingham up in my arms, and be back before you can say 'Peter Piper picked a peck of pickled peppers' thrice."

"So I will have two seamen as neighbors." Though Anne's voice sounded cheerful, she was a bit perplexed by the suddenness of it all. She and Jonathan Leighton had met under harrowing circumstances. They had parted in anger.

He had been gone for three years without a word or a whisper in her direction. Now all at once he had come back.

"Seamen without a ship," Falkhearst reminded her. "Which I suppose will make landlubbers out of us."

"Landlubbers," Anne repeated, feeling a sense of uneasiness bubbling inside her. Perhaps she had spoken too soon. Perhaps old resentments and memories couldn't be swept aside so easily. "So you intend to stay."

"As a matter of fact, my ships have sailed without me," Jonathan replied, trying to keep the resentment out of his tone. Walsingham had seen to that. He insisted to the queen that after such a prestigious, sucessful time at sea, Jonathan Leighton deserved a time of rest and relaxation as a reward. The truth was, it was blackmail.

"They have sailed. . . . ?"

"I now have three." If he did everything that Walsingham instructed, he did. If he did not, then his loyalty would be in question and he might lose everything.

"Three." So she was right. The sea was in Jonathan's blood. How then could he so suddenly have a change of heart? "Your ship—or ships—are very important to you, aren't they?" she queried.

"Let's just say the freedom I feel on the ocean is important to me, yes. Seafaring keeps me out of the kind of political intrigue that can cost a man his head in these times."

"And yet you have come here to the country . . ." Doubt clouded her mind. Something more than the wish to make an apology had goaded him into coming here. But what? The Captain Leighton she remembered wasn't the kind of man who would be content without the feel of a deck beneath his feet.

Jonathan hurriedly sought a way to sooth her misgivings. "If I said that my coming here was by accident, I would be lying. The truth of the matter, Anne, is that I inquired about your whereabouts and in fact acquired the land nearby in hopes that we could become reacquainted."

"I see." She wondered if a man like Jonathan Leighton would ever really settle down. Country life was a radical change from what he was used to. It was quieter, less adventurous, and the sunrises and sunsets occurred on the same horizon every day.

Jonathan could sense that she was troubled and damned Walsingham's assumption that everyone but the spymaster was a simpleton. For just a moment he was tempted to tell her the truth, but what could he say. *Oh by the way, Anne, I was sent to the country to spy on you by the queen's diligent searcher of hidden secrets, the one who has cost so many people their heads. Though I came here because I couldn't forget you and hoped with all my heart that I might get you into bed, I also came to spy on you. I hope that doesn't make you perturbed in any way.*

"Jonathan won't say it, but I will. He has deep feelings for ye, Annie," Falkhearst blurted, hoping to ease the tension. "He came here to court ye as well as to make amends." He sighed. "Take it from an old sailor. Life on the sea can be adventurous but also lonely. There comes a time when a man wants a home, someone soft lying beside him, and mayhap the patter of little feet."

"And a woman with a dowry?" Anne asked caustically. Did the captain really want a home, a wife, and little ones running all about, or was his coming to Stafford merely to quench his temporary boredom? Did he think because she was a widow, she would jump into his bed? And what did *she* want?

Anne knew that her carefully planned future had been handed a crucial blow when the man she had thought to share her life with was killed. That didn't mean, however, that she was anxious to find herself wedded again. She was doing very well. *But does that mean you want to live the rest of your life alone?*

The answer was no. There were so many times lately when she lay awake feeling a fevered longing to be held, to be touched, to be loved. Even so, she didn't want to act in a way that made Jonathan Leighton think that she was the kind of woman who gave her favors too easily.

"I have no need of a woman's money," Jonathan said

dryly, wondering if they were going to start their old quarrels again. "I have ample wealth of my own."

Sensing another awkward moment, Falkhearst suddenly took Jonathan's left hand and Anne's right. "Everything is going to be roses and rainbows from now on. I feel it deep within my bones. Roses and rainbows. Ye can trust me on that."

"Roses and rainbows. . . ." Jonathan could only hope so. It was just as he had told her—he wanted to put the past behind them and begin again.

Somehow he would placate Walsingham and put all this spy business behind them. With that hope, he stared down at Anne, his eyes moving tenderly over her thick, dark lashes, the finely wrought shape of her nose, the curve of her mouth. He wanted to kiss her and would have if Falkhearst hadn't been present. Instead he found himself saying, "Would you like to come with us and take a look at my new quarters?" When she hesitated, he said, "Please. I may need a woman's advice on what needs to be done."

Anne brushed at the skirt of her dress. She felt a surge of excitement. Why not? "I'll need to change into riding clothes and saddle up a horse."

Even from a distance, Jonathan could see that the manor on his new estate was an imposing structure, though not without a rustic beauty. Walsingham had not been miserly when he had set up the props for his subterfuge. That the manor had once belonged to Thomas Gordon, a sympathizer of Mary Stuart's who had recently lost his head, made it even more devious. As they rode closer, Jonathan felt a chill sweep through him, though not from the wind.

"It's a beautiful manor!" Anne was not seeing it through the same eerie perspective as Jonathan.

Constructed of red stone, the manor was three stories tall with rising gables and several chimneys. Innumerable windows from story to story looked out on a landscape surrounded by trees. Jonathan wondered if the shrubbery had been planted to enable those who were involved in treason to be able to come and go without being easily detected.

"It's been dormant for a few years. It may need repairs."

"It might, Cap'n, but we'll soon put it in tiptop shape from bow to stern." Realizing that he had been using terms for a ship, Falkhearst laughed. "Aye, it will be shipshape in no time."

As they reached the manor, Anne was quick to dismount. Brushing off the tan skirt of her riding habit, she secured her horse, then moved towards the door. Entrusting Falkhearst with the horses and wagon, Jonathan quickly followed.

Staring at the double oak doors, he waited several minutes before he knocked. "From what I'm told, this comes with a staff of three servants, a housekeeper, a stable hand, and a gardener." All loyal to Walsingham if Jonathan was not mistaken. He would have to guard his every move.

"Servants who need to be taught discipline," Anne exclaimed after waiting a long while for the door to be opened.

At last it was answered by a tall, gray-haired woman with piercing brown eyes. "What do ye want?" She looked Jonathan up and down, then snorted. The dust of the road, the snags and tears in his garments, hardly defined him as the new lord of the manor.

"Something to drink would suffice for the moment," Jonathan answered. Only by putting his booted foot in the door did he keep it from being slammed in his face. "Open up. I'm Jonathan Leighton, and I've traveled too long and too far to be met with such impudence!"

There was a long pause before the door was thrown open. "Ye are Jonathan Leighton?"

"In the flesh!" Taking hold of Anne's hand, he led her through the doorway before the woman had a chance to close it again.

"Yer don't look much like yer description." She eyed Anne suspiciously. "And who is this?"

"Anne Morgan Navarro. Her brother owns the manor a few miles from here to the south."

"Navarro?" The woman frowned. "I didn't know that there were any foreigners nearby."

"I'm not a foreigner!" Anne hurried to say. "But you are extremely rude. Let's hope that you are better at your job than you are at remembering your manners." Her eyes were unwavering as she looked at the woman.

"Come this way." The woman turned and led them into the house.

It was dark inside despite the many windows. Anne could see why. All of the draperies and curtains were closed, making the interior appear shaded and shadowy. Swearing beneath her breath, she walked from window to window opening the coverings.

The sunlight spotlighted cobwebs on the lofty ceiling, dirt on windowsills, dust on the floors, and a general look of disarray.

"Why—this manor hasn't been dusted or cleaned in months, if then. And the rushes on the floor are moldy. They should have been thrown out and replaced with fresh rushes mixed with herbs." She looked at the woman accusingly. "How long have you been here?"

"A week." She answered Anne's look of dislike with one of her own.

"So you are new. Even so, you have had time enough to at least do the preliminary cleaning." Anne looked at Jonathan, saying beneath her breath, "If it were me I would dismiss her this minute."

Though he wanted to do just that, Jonathan knew that his hands were tied. Walsingham had insisted on staffing the manor with his people. "I'll give her another chance."

Surprised by his reaction, Anne picked up a nearby broom and immediately shouldered the responsibility for the house herself. Perhaps Jonathan Leighton had more need of her than he knew.

Over the next several days, that thought goaded her into tackling the cleaning with a vengeance while Jonathan made household repairs and assessed what work needed to be done on the land.

There were trees to cut down and stumps to be removed. Tough roots that were impossible to burn had had to be pulled or dug out. To be sure, it was arduous work, but there was work just as arduous to be done on a ship. So thinking, Jonathan reacquinted himself with the proper use of an axe and how it should be sunk into a soft log when the cutting was done. That kept the axe blade safe and in good chopping shape, he remembered. Through trial and error, he learned to cross-stake cordwood so it wouldn't tumble down, to split a log by placing it in the crotch of a fallen tree, to use a maul to split a stubborn log.

Taking time out to lean on the axe handle for a moment or two, he looked around and had to admit that it was unbelievable what he had done in such a short time. He felt infinitely proud of himself and proud of Anne. It seemed that when they worked together and were not at odds, they made a good team.

"So ... are you planning to leave all this work and go back to the docks?"

Jonathan turned around to see Anne staring at his half-naked torso. He remained silent.

"Do you miss the sea air?"

Wiping his damp forehead with his arm, Jonathan leaned on the axe, pausing to breathe in the fresh air, and nearly became intoxicated by the invigorating scent of pine, birch, beech, elm, and poplar mingled with the mustiness of the earth and the fragrance of wildflowers.

"No. The sea has its beauty, but it is just as beautiful out here. It makes a person see things in a whole new light."

Anne said softly, "Living close to nature makes one appreciate the simple things."

"Like water!" Jonathan exclaimed.

Setting down the axe, he picked up a bucket and went in search of water, finding the perfect place in an area where several large rocks purified a stream. Filling the bucket to the brim, he quickly retraced his steps, but before drinking he offered the first dipper to Anne.

"You see, I do know how to be a gentleman." Their hands touched, and their eyes met. Then, before he had time to think, he had gathered her in his arms, his mouth only inches from her own.

Anne's heart hammered in her breast, beating in rhythm with his. She was giddily conscious of the warmth emanating from his body, aware of an intense tingle in the pit of her stomach.

Jonathan closed his eyes tightly and clenched his fists, taking a deep breath as he fought for control. He started to pull away and was surprised when she slipped her arms around his neck. Then her arms tightened.

At that moment Anne didn't want him to be a gentleman, and her feelings showed in her expression. "Edmund is occupied. He won't interrupt us this time."

Something in her voice took him by surprise. He touched her, moving his hand slowly up her arm from elbow to shoulder as he explored, caressed, but it was Anne who initiated a kiss as she slowly raised her chin.

Jonathan groaned, closing his arms about her as he pulled her into the curve of his hard body. Bending his face to meet hers, he kissed her, the tip of his tongue stroking her lips as deftly as his hands caressed her body.

In response Anne moaned, turning her head so that his mouth slanted over hers and his tongue sought to part her lips. She mimicked the movement of his mouth, reveling in the sensations that flooded through her. She couldn't help thinking that it had never been like this with Enrique. She had wanted him to keep his distance. She craved Jonathan's closeness. When he kissed her, he made her feel as if the whole world shuddered.

Jonathan's desire was no less fierce than hers. He had known desire before, but never like this. His reaction to Anne's soft mouth opening to him, to her softness, to her warmth, to her flowery woman's smell, was explosive. For one moment he nearly lost his head completely. His hands pushed her back slightly as his fingers fumbled at her bodice, searching for her soft flesh.

"Jonathan . . ." Anne was trembling. Never in her wildest dreams had she realized how primitive and powerful desire could be, nor how fiercely and quickly her emotions could get out of control.

"I can't be satisfied with just kissing. I want you, Anne, in the full sense of the word," he breathed in her ear. "Come with me . . . inside. . . ."

An image of sweeping her up in his arms, carrying her to the bedroom, and making frantic, passionate love to her flashed in his mind. She had been without a man for three years, and he had been nearly as celibate. Why wait any longer? She was a widow, not some untried girl, and. . . .

No. She was *not* a widow! Anne's husband was still alive. If he made love to her knowing that Enrique Navarro lived, he would make an adulteress out of her, something for which she would never forgive him. In that moment Jonathan knew that an insurmountable obstacle stood between them.

"Jonathan . . . ?" Anne nuzzled his neck, remembering what Edmund had said about Jonathan coming to court her and about a man wanting a home and someone soft lying beside him. "Roses and rainbows. . . ." she murmured, closing her eyes.

Jonathan groaned, succumbing to the heated encroachment of her body and the shiver that flashed through him as she kissed the back of his neck. Though he wanted to give in to his sexual desires, he pulled away and stood looking down at her for a long, aching moment.

"Anne . . ." He wanted to tell her that her husband was alive, wanted to explain everything, but the fear that he might endanger her by doing so held the truth at bay.

His voice was cold. Like a splash of icy water, it doused Anne's sensual feelings. "What is it?"

"I . . . I shouldn't have . . ."

"Shouldn't have kissed me? It was I who kissed you." She reached up and touched his face, hoping to rekindle the desire that had sparked between them. "Besides, we have been far more intimate on several occasions, as I remember."

"I know but you aren't my captive now."

Her voice was soft and seductive. "Then perhaps I wish that I were ..."

Had he wanted to, Jonathan knew that he could seduce her with promises, make love to her, and satisfy his own desires. Once he would have done so and said to hell with the consequences. Now, however, Jonathan found himself putting Anne's well-being ahead of his own. Looking at her, he knew he wanted forever and all that went with it, not a quick roll in the hay and a fond farewell.

Anne was unlike anyone he had ever known. She was soft and feminine, yet at the same time strong and determined. She was the kind of woman who would jump off a ship and swim to shore despite the danger. She was the kind of woman who would brave Walsingham's anger if she thought him to be in the wrong. She was the kind of woman he had been looking for all his life, a woman he felt he could love deeply. There was only one problem, or rather two—Anne's husband and Walsingham.

Though he didn't say a word, Anne could sense the way he had pulled away from her not only physically but in his emotions. "I thought you said that you came here to begin anew."

"I did, but ... there are things in the past that have come to light and ... I ..."

"We had a stormy meeting, is that what you mean?"

"To put it simply, you hated me." And he didn't want to experience that angry resentment again.

"I was stubborn and angry and I felt guilty for having ... feelings for you that I ... never had for my husband." There, she had been truthful.

"You never loved him ?"

"No."

Her admission made his heart soar! But what did it matter? In all legalities she was still Enrique Navarro's wife. How was he going to explain that to her without telling her the whole story about Walsingham?

"But . . . but you married him and . . ."

Anne stiffened. "Is that what troubles you? Enrique?" Her eyes narrowed, her face flushed. "Do you still think I was his accomplice? Do you still think I was guilty of treason against the queen?"

"No, of course not! That demon has been put to rest once and for all." Only to be replaced by other problems that plagued his mind, such as a husband who had returned to haunt him and a man who was relentless in pursuit of that errant, dangerous spouse.

"Has it?" Anne could read something in his expression, a look in his eyes that told her that he was hiding something from her.

"Anne . . . please. You don't understand. . . ." He reached out to touch her, but Anne pulled away.

"I understand perfectly. When you can be forthright with me, when you can tell me what is in your head as well as your heart, then and only then will I talk with you again. Good day, sir." Turning her back on him, Anne walked away.

Falkhearst's eyes were downcast. "I'm sorry, Cap'n. I rode over to talk with Annie and give her your message, but she says to tell you that she meant what she said."

"She won't see me."

"Not unless you tell her what you are hiding." Falkhearst raised his brows in question. "What *are* ye hiding, Cap'n?"

"I can't tell anyone. Not even you!" Jonathan held his anger at Walsingham in check. He had wanted to give Falkhurst a message for the queen's spymaster telling him to go to the devil, but he felt it wasn't fair to get Falkhearst involved in his problems.

"Not even me?" Edmund was crushed.

"I don't want to put you in any danger," Jonathan explained.

"I'm not afraid. I'd go to hell and back for ye, Cap'n. I would." His unwavering stare gave proof of that.

"I know, and for that I am grateful. It's just that sometimes a man has to do certain things on his own." Determined to change the subject, Jonathan hefted a barrel and laid it in the wagon, then adjusted the ropes that would hold all the barrels securely. "Take care, Edmund. Even though it's the country, there are still dangers. London isn't the only place for ruffians, rogues, and murderers. Be on the alert!"

Falkhearst smiled. "Aye, aye, Cap'n. I'll try to have eyes in the back of my head as I ride along." Grabbing hold of the seat, Falkhearst pulled himself up. "And you . . . take care of yerself while I'm away." He paused. "Don't listen to what Annie says. Ride over there and bang on the door until she answers."

Jonathan shook his head. "It wouldn't do me any good. There are . . . things standing in the way of our happiness."

"But nothing ye can't fix." Falkhearst picked up the reins. "I'll be back as soon as I can, Cap'n, and then mayhap we can put our heads together like we always do. You were meant to be with Annie."

Chapter Eighteen

Sitting before the fire, clad only in her chemise, a blanket pulled around her body to ward off the night's chill, Anne watched the fire tickle the stones in the hearth. How long she sat staring at the flames she didn't know. Minutes? Hours?

The way Jonathan Leighton had kissed and caressed her was still seared into her mind. She couldn't get the taste of his mouth from her lips or rub from her skin the lingering sensation of how his hands had felt. Even now, several hours later, just the thought of the way he had touched her caused her body to ache with longing.

"He made me feel so alive!" she whispered.

She had spent three quiet, uneventful years in the country with her brother's family. Three routine, though peaceful, years. During that time she had thought often about Jonathan Leighton, reliving those days aboard his ship and wishing that she could undo some of the things she had said and done. Suddenly, out of the blue, he had appeared and it was as if the last three years had not happened.

He told me he regretted the way things were between us. He asked if we could pretend we were meeting for the very first time. In truth it had seemed like a new beginning. Being with him had seemed so perfect, so right.

He kissed me and I wanted to be in his arms forever. . . . The truth of the matter was that she cared about him more than she had realized. Perhaps she had right from the first time they met.

How had it happened? When had she fallen in love with Jonathan Leighton? Precisely when it all happened she didn't really know. All she knew was that she had fallen hard, irreversibly so. In addition to her desire for him, there was a deep caring, a wanting to be with him forever and ever. Now that she had seen him again, she hated to even think of returning to her old routine or her previous loneliness.

Closing her eyes, it was as if she could feel the warmth of his fingers as he stroked her hair. It was a glorious feeling. Her senses had been full of him—the way he smelled, like the fresh wind; the way he felt, so hard and strong; the sound of his heartbeat. She had heard a roaring in her ears, like the sound inside a seashell, as one of his hands threaded through her hair. It felt so good to be touched the way he had touched her. Despite the size and strength of his hands, Jonathan was surprisingly gentle.

But something went wrong. Jonathan's eyes had revealed that he was deeply troubled. His gaze hadn't been direct but had wavered back and forth as if he were hiding something from her.

Had the years changed him that much? He was a proud man, a stubborn man, a strong man, but always a man who spoke what was on his mind. The Jonathan she had known three years ago had been forthright, even when they were arguing. Today she had sensed that he wanted to tell her something, but for some reason felt that he could not. The question was why?

"I shouldn't have lost my temper," she whispered, "I shouldn't have walked off." Once again her spirited nature had gotten the better of her. She had reacted too quickly. Perhaps if she had been patient, Jonathan would have confided in her eventually.

Puzzling over the matter, she tried to sort things out in her mind, deciding that Jonathan's sudden appearance in Stafford was the key.

"He didn't come all the way to Stafford just to settle an old quarrel or to take me in his arms, yet his kiss . . ."

Leaning her head back, she tried to quench the flame in her blood that the memory of him evoked, but his hot, soft, exploring mouth and husky voice tormented her with yearning. She imagined his strong arms holding her, caressing her, thoughts that sent tickling shivers up her spine. He'd held her so tenderly, as if she were precious to him.

It couldn't all have been a lie.

Anne remembered the story of how her father had stolen her mother's heart. Even though she had heard the story over and over again, she had not really been prepared for the potency she had felt in Jonathan's arms today. But then the moment had been spoiled.

"What if . . ." Wrapping her arms around her knees, Anne curled up in a ball and closed her eyes. What if Jonathan was in some kind of trouble? What if the queen had sent him to Stafford in disgrace—what then? He wouldn't be the first man to suffer from the change in Elizabeth's moods.

Anne stood up. Padding on bare feet to the window to look out upon the night, she thought the matter over. She had been wrong to issue ultimatums. She should have been patient and left it up to Jonathan to tell her what was on his mind.

"Tomorrow . . . I'll visit the manor and tell him what is in my heart and tell him that no matter what is troubling him, it doesn't matter."

Snuffing the candle on the table by the bed, she slowly removed her chemise and undergarments, hanging up the clothes on the horizontal pole above the head of her bed. She slipped her nightgown over her head. Standing beside the soft feather mattress, she let her hair swirl about her shoulders, letting the long tresses tickle her back as she swayed from side to side. It was a sensuous, enticing feeling that sparked a yearning within her to have the captain beside her, loving her.

Anne suddenly felt the chill of the room. Getting under the covers, she pulled them all the way up to her chin. The quilt was thick, but even so, it was the thought of Jonathan Leighton that warmed her. Oh, to have him beside her, holding her tightly against him! Closing her eyes, she smiled at the thought, drifting off in a deep, contented sleep.

Something woke Anne in the middle of the night. Men's voices. Her eyes fluttered open. It must be well after midnight. Who would be at the manor at this late hour? Getting out of bed, she went to the window and looked out. There were shadows moving from the stables to the back of the house. Shadows of men.

Anne felt a sense of alarm. Who could it be? And why were they here so late at night? She sensed an emergency. Edward!

Putting on a robe, Anne hurried from her room in search of her brother, but though she searched from room to room, she couldn't find him anywhere. But she did hear voices. Instinctively she followed the sound.

The passageway.... There was an empty room below the first floor, a huge cellar that had been used to hide Protestants during Mary Tudor's reign to keep them from being burned at the stake. Anne realized this was where the men were going she clutched her robe tightly around her, then followed.

The air was chilly and damp inside the passageway. Anne shivered as she fumbled around in the dark, thankful that there was light up ahead.

"We have to do something, Edward. She's so close. Chartley is but a few miles from here."

"If we lift a finger to help her, we will all lose our heads."

"We're not asking you to commit treason. Only to help us get her out."

"How?"

"You're a merchant with wagons and access to Amyas Paulet and thereby to Mary."

"Where will you take her?"

"To France. To Spain. Or take her to the pope himself. It doesn't matter, as long as she is safe from Elizabeth and from Walsingham."

Anne crept closer. Standing as if in a ceremonial circle were twelve men. One of them, Sir Anthony Babington, whom she had met once before, was dressed elegantly in gold velvet and satin, a diamond studding his ear. Babington was a dreamer, an empty-headed popinjay with his head in the clouds. To Anne's way of thinking, that made him a dangerous man. Why was Edward having any dealings with such a man?

"I want you to meet John Savage," he was saying as he walked to the edge of the circle. There stood a bearded but balding, tawny-haired man. His garments bordered on ragged, the dark-green doublet worn in several places, the high white neck frill graying from lack of a proper cleaning, the breeches snagged here and there. The thigh-high boots and gloves the man wore were of buff-colored leather, but they too looked as if they had seen better days. He was a soldier of fortune if ever there was one.

"Edward, may I introduce John Savage."

Anne could see by Edward's expression that he was nervous. Her brother was not the kind of man to become involved in plots. He was gentle, kind, if perhaps weak at times, but not an intriguer. Babington, however, seemed to have him under his influence.

John Savage had the tone of a zealot. "There are others who would help us. Hundreds and hundreds of Englishmen in these northern counties who favor Mary Stuart over that bastard-born Elizabeth."

" 'Tis treason of which you speak."

"I prefer to call it a rescue mission."

Even from a distance, Anne could see her brother pale. "We'll end up on a gibbet!"

"We've taken a vow. We must do it." Babington appealed to her brother's sense of fairness. "It is not seemly that Mary remain Elizabeth's prisoner. Mary came to Elizabeth for aid, but her own cousin betrayed her. It is time the queen of Scots was freed! The northern Catholics feel the same. They'll help us.''

"Elizabeth will rue the day she put a woman of the true faith in a cage.''

"Aye!''

"Aye!''

"Now, introduce our guest to the rest of our assembled guests, Edward,'' Babington was saying.

Edward went around the circle, moving clockwise. "Edward Abington, Edward Windsor, Thomas Salisbury, Robert Barnwell.'' He paused to take a breath. "John Traves, Henry Donn, Chidiock Tichbourne, Charles Tilney.'' The men inclined their heads as their names were said. "Edward Jones, and last but not least, Gilbert Gifford.''

It was a strange circle of conspirators, men her brother would never have had any dealings with had it not been for their common goal of freeing the imprisoned Scottish queen. "The Enterprise,'' as Gifford called it.

"There are sixty-thousand foreign troops ready to aid the captive Scottish queen,'' he boasted. "I have but to give the word. Not only that, I have it on good authority that the King of Spain is building up an armada to use against Elizabeth.'' He expressed his determination that he was not afraid to die, if need be, for the cause.

"Die?'' Edward clutched at Babington's arm.

"I would gladly give my life if I knew that by my death Mary would be given her chance to rule here.''

John Ballard's enthusiasm soon calmed Anne's brother. He could not envision failure, he said. Not when there were so many ready to support the cause of Mary of Scots. "There are allies inside and outside England. Noblemen as well as peasants. The entire Catholic nobility of England will not hesitate to support us. The King of Spain is at our beck and call. The pope himself is with us. I know. He told me so with his own voice.'' An audible gasp said clearly that the assembly was impressed.

"We will bring England back to the Catholic faith. It will

be a notable moment in this country's history," Babington added.

Anne had heard enough to know that her brother was risking his life. The wheels of a conspiracy had begun to turn. If her brother didn't realize the dangers involved, she did.

She had to make him realize what was at risk. Aligning himself with these men could mean his life and the ruin of his family. Particularly if Walsingham got word of the plot.

"Now, let's ride. There are other men I want you to meet, a few miles from here."

Anne shrank back into the shadows as the men filed past her. They were going to ride off somewhere, and Edward was going with them! Since the time they were children, Anne had always protected her "little" brother. She felt the same need to protect him now.

She had to follow them and somehow head Edward off and convince him that what he was doing was wrong. And if that wasn't possible, then she had to make certain that he was not caught up in some kind of a trap. Though Mary of Scots had many followers here, so did Elizabeth.

It was cold outside. Heading towards the stables in her nightclothes, Anne questioned the wisdom of her actions not once but several times, and yet, what choice did she have? Edward was riding headlong into trouble, and there was no one else to save him.

Reaching the stables, she pushed through the opening, trying hard to catch her breath as she waited for her eyes to adjust to the darkness. It was quiet; only the nickering and pawing hooves of the horses disturbed the stillness. The others were already on the road. She had to hurry and somehow cut Edward off from the rest of the men.

"He has never been as good at horsemanship as I," Anne said. In truth, despite being female, Anne had always been better at everything than her brother. It was a fact that had goaded Edward in childhood.

Anne did not dare to light even a candle for fear that she might attract unwelcome attention, so she chose the first horse she came to, a dark animal that would blend with the night. Working in total darkness, she lifted a bridle from its peg on the wall, quickly untangling the reins. Calming the horse with soft words, she pressed the bit against the animal's mouth, then slipped the headstall over the ears. Fumbling about for a saddle, she located its bulk, then swung it upon the horse's back. Bending down, she fastened and tightened the saddle girth with a horseman's competent skill, her fingers trembling all the while. She had to hurry.

The moon glowed like a golden coin in the sky, shining its mist of light upon the rocky, pitted road. Anne rode at a furious pace, her eyes scanning the pathway ahead. If she knew Edward, he would be lagging behind the others. She would easily catch up with him.

It was dark and quiet in the bedroom, yet Jonathan couldn't get to sleep no matter how hard he tried. For once in his life he had acted honorably and unselfishly towards a woman, and where had it gotten him? She had turned her back on him and stormed away.

Where women, or at least that woman, were concerned, a man was damned if he did and damned if he didn't!

Putting his hands beneath his head, Jonathan closed his eyes. He wanted Anne. Wanted her so badly that it was nearly an obsession. Wanted her with a sexual hunger that not even a dunk in the stream outside could cool. Wanted her and needed her with a different kind of longing than he'd ever felt for a woman before.

He wanted more than her body, he wanted her heart. And he wanted it forever.

Jonathan thought of himself as a man who did not believe in dreams and who held few illusions. He knew mankind's faults and so guarded himself accordingly. Oh, how he had laughed at those romantic fools who wrote sonnets, love poems, and stage plays with ever-afters! Now, for the first time in his life, he knew what they were talking about when they wrote about love.

He could have made love to her but he didn't. . . .

He knew why. Anne was a decent woman. A woman of good character. A woman not at all like the kind of easy-loving females Jonathan was used to. That kind he could have at the wink of an eye, a dimpled smile, and the snap of his fingers. He didn't want that kind of relationship with Anne.

It was Falkhearst's fault. All that talk of settling down and listening for the patter of tiny feet made him think of things he shouldn't.

Jonathan's eyelids flickered as he thought long and hard about his past. First there were the unfortunate years of constant bickering with his father, then his rebellious years when he had packed his bags and taken off for London and the court. That had been followed by seafaring days accompanied by rum, women, and song. And now his days as Walsingham's pawn.

If Anne were in his place and he in hers would she warn him? Although once he had made accusations against her, he knew now that she was truthful, honorable, and loyal. She would tell him the truth. How could he do otherwise?

I'll send a message to Walsingham and tell him that no matter what he does with my ships, I will not be his lapdog! Then he would go to Anne and tell her the truth. And hope beyond hope that what she said was true, that she was not in love with her husband. With England and Spain at odds, it would be easy for her to get a divorce.

No! It wasn't possible! How could he have so easily forgotten that Anne and her family were Catholic? Her father, Richard Morgan, had helped Mary Tudor win her crown.

Even if she did not love her husband, even if he had transgressed against the crown, she would stand by him. And go to her own doom. Annulment then? No, it was out of the question. The pope was no friend to England or Elizabeth.

So what of the future? What could he really offer her? What did he have to give? Love? Never having experienced it in any form, Jonathan wasn't really certain just what that was, and even if he did, would it be enough?

"Mistress . . ." That was all Anne could ever be to him. She could never be his wife, not while her husband lived. But if Jonathan aided Walsingham in his quest to find Enrique Navarro, the headsman might do the rest.

No! Although Jonathan had killed men in the line of duty, that had been different. That had been combat. "Walsingham . . . !" He whispered the name with loathing. Anne wanted the truth. In his heart, Jonathan knew that he owed her that. Anything less would make a mockery of his declaration of love.

Rising from his bed, Jonathan paced up and down, then hurried to dress. When he was troubled, he often strolled the deck of his ship, but there was no ship for him now. But he could ride! When he was a boy, that had always calmed him.

It was deathly silent as he stepped outside. Jonathan gathered his cloak about him as he hurried towards the stables and saddled his horse. If this was London, he could have gone to the tavern and had some hot mulled wine, he thought as he rode off.

London . . . It made him think of Falkhearst. He had headed towards London a long time ago, but Jonathan knew that the wagon would slow him down. Should he try to catch up with him and ride back to London as well? It wasn't too late to go back and say the devil with Walsingham and Elizabeth. No, he had to talk with Anne first. He had to make her understand.

Jonathan rode fast and furiously, glad that concentration on where he was going obliterated his jumbled feelings about Anne. At last the late-night ride exhausted Jonathan and strangely liberated him too. If he couldn't sleep before, he knew that he could now. He would undoubtedly fall asleep the moment his head touched the pillow.

Jonathan reined in his horse for a brief rest before heading back, and in that moment he thought he heard the sound of horses. He attuned his ears. Yes, he heard the sound distinctly now. There were several horsemen. From the crest of a hill he watched as they thundered past, grinning as he saw that there was one horseman lagging behind. No—two!

"The last horseman is trying to catch up with the others." For the moment, Jonathan did nothing but watch. Then, as the riders passed by him, he realized the last rider was a woman. The long, flowing hair gave her away.

Anne was quickly closing the distance between herself and her brother. "Edward! Edward!" He couldn't hear her. She shouted again, only louder this time. "Edward, slow down!" A low-hanging branch nearly unseated her, but she was oblivious to all else but the sound of the hooves ahead of her, clattering loudly over the rocky terrain. She had to catch up. What if Edward was riding headlong into some kind of trap?

The wind slapped her face as she guided her horse furiously up the hillside. Suddenly a deer ran across the roadway, startling both horse and rider. Her horse whinnied, rearing and snorting. Anne strained desperately for the reins as her horse shied, then bucked and reared. Anne gasped, then screamed as she was thrown violently from the saddle. Her voice echoed in her ear before she hit the ground and was engulfed in total darkness.

Chapter Nineteen

Jonathan watched in horror as the female rider fell. He looked up ahead at the riders and realized that none of them knew there had been an accident. It was up to him to help.

Riding frantically towards the crumpled figure lying on the ground, he hurried to dismount, then ran towards the woman. Only when he reached her did he realize who it was.

"Anne!" Her eyes were closed. She looked frighteningly still. Bending over her unconscious form, he whispered a fervent prayer. Please let her be alive! Seemingly his plea was answered, for as he put his head to her breast he could hear her heartbeat. "Anne!"

Her breathing was even, though her face looked ashen. Apparently she'd struck her head when she was thrown from the horse. The cut on her forehead attested to that. Jonathan gently wiped the blood away with his fingertips. Cautiously he examined her, probing her arms and legs to determine if there were any broken bones. There did not seem to be, but still he was careful. He knew it could be dangerous to move her if she were hurt internally or had injured her spine.

"It's cold. I can't leave you here." She was not dressed for the night air. She was wearing her nightclothes!

A myriad of questions flooded his mind. Whom had she been riding after? Why was she dressed as she was? What had happened tonight?

"Anne . . ."

She mumbled something unintelligible, and moved her arms and legs, putting his mind to rest about a back injury. Still, a head injury could be serious.

He wanted her to awaken, he thought as he stripped off his cloak and used it to shield her from the chilled night air.

Carefully he picked Anne up in his arms, cradling her head against his chest. For a long moment he stared down, mesmerized by how vulnerable she appeared. He'd never seen her that way before. Even when she was his prisoner, she had never been defenseless. An all-consuming sense of protectiveness surged through him. The urge to safeguard her, to shield her, consumed him.

He looked in the direction of the manor house. It was too far to walk. There was no other choice but to ride with her in his arms. Holding her close, he somehow managed to pull himself up on the saddle; then he rode cautiously, carefully, towards the manor house.

If mounting the horse had been difficult, dismounting was an even greater test of Jonathan's skills, yet somehow he managed to get her safely to the door of his bedroom. Gently, he placed Anne upon the bed.

"Anne! Anne!" Oh, how he longed for her to open her eyes, to speak to him, even if her tone was angry.

Standing over her, he studied her quietly in the glow of the hearth fire. His breath was trapped somewhere in the area of his heart as he stared at the loveliness presented to him. She looked so fragile, yet so desireable. He tried to ignore the desire that stirred within him at the sight of her tiny waist, firm breasts, and long, perfectly shaped legs. Doing his best to make her comfortable and hide her allure, he covered her with a blanket.

Jonathan sat on the bed and brushed her dark hair aside to examine her head. There was a lump, "a knot the size of an egg." No wonder she was still deeply asleep, he thought. He'd had experience tending the wounded, knew a cold, damp cloth would bring some relief. Tearing a towel in two, he dipped it in the water pitcher on a nearby table, laid it on Anne's forehead, and sat back to wait.

"Anne!" Bending down beside her, he called her name over and over, his pulse quickening as he saw her eyelids flutter. "Anne."

She was so lovely, he mused, from the tip of her toes to the top of her dark-haired head. He let his eyes move tenderly over her in a caress, lingering on the rise and fall of her breasts beneath the blanket. For just a moment he gave in to temptation and kissed her soft, warm mouth. A parting kiss, he thought. A sad tribute to what might have been.

With a regretful sigh, he moved away from her yet kept a vigil. She was the kind of woman he had been searching for but a woman he could never hope to obtain. Enrique Navarro, that popinjay Spaniard, had married her, and as long as he lived she would be legally tied. And yet, if she would only awaken, perhaps he could accept that. He would try.

Jonathan sat unflinchingly by Anne's bedside all through the night, leaving only to light the fire in the bedroom fireplace or change the cold cloth on her head. He stared at her, entranced by the way the firelight played across the curves of her body beneath the coverlet, creating tantalizing shadows and reminding him of her beautiful body. "We might have been lovers that day when you were in the tub in my cabin if Falkhearst hadn't . . ."

"Ohhhhh!" The moan was soft, but audible.

"Anne?"

She was moaning, moving her head from side to side. It was the first hopeful sign she'd given of returning to consciousness. Reaching out, he touched her face.

"Oh, Anne." Seeing her eyelashes flutter again, he took

her hand, willing her to open her eyes. "Anne. Wake up . . . please. . . ."

She stirred, putting her hand to her temple. "Mmmmm. My head," she moaned. Instinctively she reached out, feeling disoriented, clinging to him, needing stability in a turbulent, whirling world.

The closeness of her softly curving flesh was nearly his undoing. The brush of their bodies wove a cocoon of warm intimacy that he relished. He was flesh and blood and not a saint, yet his passion was tempered with a more tender feeling. He swallowed with difficulty, longing to clasp her in his arms in a closer embrace. The feel of her body pressed against his was pure torture that was only relieved when she pulled away.

Light flickered before Anne's eyelids as she struggled to open her eyes. Where was she? She was confused. "What happened?" she asked softly.

"Your horse threw you." Pushing her hair aside, he examined her injury again.

His fingers were strokes of softness as he touched her, making her feel warm and tingly inside. She nestled closer, her face buried against his chest. "My horse . . . ?"

"Why were you riding in your nightgown?" It was still a bafflement. Certainly she was prone to doing unusual things. "Who were you following?"

Suddenly recognizing his voice, Anne's eyes flew open to find Jonathan sitting on the edge of the mattress, his fingers entwined in her hair. His unsmiling visage illuminated by firelight was the first thing her eyes focused on. She'd know that profile anywhere.

"Jonathan!" She remembered now that she had dreamed that he had kissed her. Had he? Her thoughts were hazy, and her head throbbed painfully as she sat up.

"Aye, I brought you here," he murmured huskily, remembering their brief embrace.

"Where is here?" She looked around her in confusion.

"My manor. My bedroom."

Her eyes widened as she turned her head. They stared at

each other, two silent, shadowy figures in the dimly lit room, each very aware of the other. The air pulsated with expectancy. Anne could not help but wonder what he was going to say, what he was going to do. Her eyes never once left him as he moved forward to gently brush her hair out of her eyes.

"When I saw you fall, my heart stopped beating. You mean a great deal to me, Anne!" The tone of sincerity in his voice deeply touched her. He knelt on the edge of the bed, causing the mattress to sag under his muscular weight. "You are so very special." *And I love you.*

Slowly Jonathan bent his head, cherishing her lips in a kiss. Gentle. A much different kind of kiss than he had ever given her before. Her lips parted in an invitation for him to drink more deeply of her mouth. He did, igniting a warmth that engulfed her from head to toe. Breathlessly she returned his kisses, tingling with pleasure when he began to hungrily probe the inner warmth. Following his lead, she returned his kiss, tentatively at first, then passionately, tangling her fingers in his thick, tawny hair.

"Anne!" Their kiss was his undoing. All he could think about was the pounding of his heart as he relished the warmth of her body. She'd haunted his dreams no matter how fiercely he'd tried to put her from his mind. And now she was here. How could he let her go? Even though a voice inside his head shouted out that he was playing with fire, that it was sheer insanity to tease himself so, he couldn't pull away. He wanted her too badly, was tempted at last beyond his endurance.

Capturing her slender shoulders, he pulled her up against him as his mouth moved hungrily against hers. Her head was thrown back, the masses of her dark hair tumbling in a thick cascade over his arm, tickling his neck. "Ah, Annie. Annie!" With hands and mouth, he sought to bring her pleasure.

A hot ache of desire coiled within Anne, surpassing the ache in her head. She couldn't ignore the heated insistence in her blood. There was a weakening readiness at his kiss, a longing she couldn't explain but which prompted her to push closer to him, relishing the warmth of his hands as he outlined the swell of her breasts beneath the blanket. When he drew his mouth away, she tugged his head down, seeking his lips eagerly.

Anne didn't understand this all-consuming need to be near him; she only knew that Jonathan alone aroused an urgent need within her, a longing to embrace him. She craved his kisses, his touch, and wanted to be in his arms forever. Dear God, she was helpless against this powerful tide that raised gooseflesh down her arms, up her legs.

"Jonathan." She moaned his name into his hair as his lips left her mouth. Soft sobs of pleasure echoed through the room's silence, and she was surprised to find that they came from her own throat. Her senses were filled with a languid heat that made her head spin. She closed her eyes, giving herself up to the dream of his nearness.

Agonizingly, gently, he traced a path from her jaw to her ear to the slim line of her throat until his lips found her breasts, tracing the rosy peak. Dear God, she tasted so sweet. He was mesmerized by her, by how right it felt to hold her in his arms, his hip touching her stomach, his chest cradling the softness of her breasts. The longing to make furious love to her overpowered him.

Anne stared up at him, watching as he studied her, and the look of desire she saw branded on his face reassured her that he cared deeply. She arched up against him, but through the haze of her pleasure she remembered.

"Edward!" He shifted his position, reaching out to smooth the tangled strands of hair away from her face, but she jerked violently away. "My brother—I have to warn him! I was riding to—to catch up with him—"

"Warn him of what?" He frowned, looking down at her.

She couldn't confide in him. She didn't dare confide in anyone. "Of . . . nothing."

"Nothing!" He rolled away from her, coming to his feet, standing with his legs apart, his arms crossed over his chest. His breathing was deep as he struggled to get control of himself, his emotions. He swore a violent oath. "A woman doesn't ride out in her nightclothes for no reason. Tell me."

Clenching and unclenching her hands, she sought to put her thoughts in order. She had been following her brother and those men—those conspirators—but she had fallen. . . . The deer. Her horse . . . and Jonathan. . . .

"I'm too late." It was an agonizing thought. Whatever had happened had already taken place. Edward's fate for good or for ill was in his own hands. Even so, she tried to get up so that she could find out what happened, but she was still too dizzy.

"For once in your life you are going to have to rely on someone else," Jonathan said softly. "Trust me, Anne."

Wordlessly they regarded each for a long long time, until Anne looked away. The pulse at the base of her throat fluttered wildly, her heart beating so frantically that she thought it would burst.

"Trust me." He leaned so close that she could feel his breath stirring her hair. It thrilled her, yet frightened her too. The effect this man had over her was unnerving. She wanted to melt into his arms, give herself up to the strange feelings he always inspired. But could she trust him with her brother's life?

Eyes wide in her pale face, she stared at him, following his movements as he strode away from her and paced the length of room. At last she said, "I need to know that Edward is safe. Can you ride to our manor and find out?"

"I can and will." It was such a simple request, and yet he knew that the fate of their relationship depended on learning to trust each other. Going to the door, he paused. "Try to sleep while I'm gone. And use the wet towel to ease the swelling. I'll be back as soon as I can."

Anne was asleep when Jonathan returned. Bending down, he nuzzled her throat. "Your brother is all right, Anne."

She sat up in bed. "Was he . . . was he there?" The worry

that he might have walked into one of Walsingham's traps had consumed her. The queen and her councilors had no pity for anyone consorting with the captive Mary Stuart.

"He left last night to go to Chartley. Apparently he had a business transaction of some kind with a man named Paulet." Jonathan was well aware that he was the man who was Mary Stuart's new jailer. "Your servants told me that he is expected to return this evening."

"He *will* return?"

"If he does not, then upon my oath I will go in search of him."

Anne sighed with relief. She knew in her heart that Jonathan would be true to his word. "Thank you!"

"You love your brother very much, don't you?"

"When we were little, I tagged along after him, even though I was older. And then there were times when I mothered him. Edward was always getting into trouble because he didn't see danger coming. I'd always be there to pick him up and see to his scraped knees and elbows." The corners of her mouth tugged down into a frown. "Once Edward told me that he felt as if he had lived in my shadow. He said that I was the gifted child who did everything right. He said that I was the sun in Mother and Father's eyes . . ." She paused. "Maybe I knew it to be the truth. Maybe I've always wanted to make it up to him."

"And I think that you have. Last night you nearly broke your neck to warn him." Of what?

Anne stiffened. "Not to warn him, just to give him a message."

Jonathan didn't argue. They were together, that was all that mattered. Whatever had driven her last night was no longer important. "How's your head?" he asked.

"Harder than I might have imagined," she answered with a sigh. "I'm going to survive."

Jonathan reached out and gently massaged her shoulders. "You're tense. Close your eyes and relax. Put everything out of your thoughts. . . ."

"I love the touch of your hands." Anne didn't sense the

kiss coming until his lips brushed hers. Her mouth opened to him like the soft petals of a flower. She loved the taste of him, the tender urgency of his mouth. Her lips opened to him for a seemingly endless passionate onslaught of kisses. It was as if they were breathing one breath, living at that moment just for each other.

Desire that had been coiling within Anne for so long only to be unfulfilled, sparked to renewed fire and she could feel his passion likewise building, searing her with its heat. They shared a joy of touching and caressing, arms against arms, legs touching legs, fingers entwining and wandering, exploring. Mutual hunger brought their lips back together time after time. She craved his kisses and returned them with trembling pleasure, exploring the inner softness of his mouth.

"Anne!" Desire writhed almost painfully within his loins. He had never wanted anything or anyone as much as he did her at this moment. It was like an unfulfilled dream just waiting to come true.

Pushing the blanket aside, Jonathan's palm, firm and warm, slipped down the front of her nightgown, cupping the full curve of her breast. Lightly he stroked until the peaks sprang to life under his touch, the once-soft flesh now taut and aching. Then his hands were at her shoulder, tugging at the gown until her breasts were bare.

His breath caught in his throat as his hazel eyes savored her. "Lovely . . ." And indeed she was, he thought, pausing to feast his eyes on the lush contours of her breasts. Wasted beauty, he thought. Wasted on a man who was so far away. Determinedly he pushed Enrique Navarro from his mind. The man didn't deserve her. He had let her grieve for his death while hiding in the lower levels of Jonathan's ship. Jonathan knew he would never have done such a thing. Never!

"I'd give you my heart and barter my soul for your love," he whispered.

Bending down, he worshipped her with his mouth, his lips traveling from one breast to the other in tender fascination. His tongue curled around the taut peaks, his teeth lightly grazing until she writhed beneath him. He savored the expressions that chased across her face, the wanting and the passion for him that were so clearly revealed.

Anne moved in sensuous fascination against him. Her hands crept around Jonathan's neck, her fingers tangling and tousling the thick waves of his blond hair as she breathed a husky sigh. How wonderful it was to be loved! Oh, why had she wasted so much precious time being angry?

The cool morning air caressed Anne's skin as Jonathan undressed her, slipping her gown over her head. She caught fire wherever he touched her, burning with an all-consuming need. She shivered in his arms as he gathered her closer, covering her body even more tightly with his to keep out the chill. With tender concern, he tugged at the blanket, giving her the largest portion, tucking it beneath the firm curve of her buttocks.

"Anne . . ." A shudder racked through him as he pushed her away. Just for a moment. Quickly he stripped away his own clothes, and Anne took her turn to appraise him. The image of broad, bronzed shoulders, wide chest, flat belly, and well-formed legs would forever be branded in her mind. Reaching out, she touched him, her hands sliding over the hard smoothness of his shoulders, moving to the crisp hair of his chest. Jonathan had three scars—one on his arm, one on his chest, and a long scar on his stomach. She lightly traced each one with her finger.

His teeth nipped gently at her lip. "I wasn't always quick enough," he said pulling her closer, rolling her over until they were lying side by side. Anne felt a great pleasure in the warmth and power of the firmly muscled body straining so hungrily against hers.

He kissed her again, his knowing, seeking lips moving with tender urgency across hers, his tongue finding again the inner warmth and sweetness of her mouth. His large body covered hers with a blanket of warmth. Anne felt the rasp of his chest hair against her breasts and answered his kiss with sweet, aching desire. But kisses weren't enough. . . .

"Jonathan . . . love me . . ." she cried.

"In due time." His hands caressed her, warming her with their heat. They took sheer delight in the texture and pressure of each other's body. Sensuously he undulated his hips between her legs, and every time their bodies caressed, each experienced a shock of raw desire that encompassed them in fiery, pulsating sensations. Then his hands were between their bodies, sliding down the velvety flesh of her belly, moving to that place between her thighs that ached for his entry. His gentle probing brought sweet fire, curling deep inside her with spirals of pulsating sensations. Then his hands left her, to be replaced by the hardness she had glimpsed before, entering her just a little, then pausing.

"You're still . . ."

"We . . . we were waiting to arrive in England before consummating our vows," she said. Every inch of her tingled with an intense arousing awareness of his body.

Bending his head to kiss her again, he moved his body, pushing deep within her, fusing their bodies. There was only a brief moment of pain, but the other sensations pushed it away. Anne was conscious only of the hard length of him creating unbearable sensations as he began to move within her. Capturing the firm flesh of her hips, he caressed her in the most intimate of embraces. His rhythmic plunges aroused a tingling fire, like nothing she had ever imagined. It was as if they were falling over the edge of a cliff together. Falling. Falling. Never quite hitting the ground.

Jonathan groaned softly, the blood pounding thickly in his head. His hold on her hips tightened as the throbbing shaft of his maleness possessed her again and again. Instinctively Anne tightened her legs around him, certain she could never withstand the ecstasy that was engulfing her body. It was as if the night shattered into a thousand stars, all bursting within her. Arching her hips, she rode the storm with him. As spasms overtook her, she dug her nails into the skin of his back, whispering his name.

A sweet shaft of ecstasy shot through Jonathan, and he closed his eyes, whispering her name. Even when the intensity of their passion was spent, they still clung to each other, unable to let this magical moment end. They touched each other gently, wonderingly.

"Now you are truly mine, Anne." And he would challenge any man who said otherwise!

Chapter Twenty

Dark clouds floated in the sky, threatening a storm as Jonathan and Anne slowly made their way back to her brother's manor. It was humid, the air chilled by the approaching rain, yet neither one seemed to notice. Riding next to each other, they both felt a sense of well-being and the inner glow that happiness brings.

"Are you certain that you are all right? You don't feel faint or dizzy . . . ?"

She did, but not from the bump on her head. Anne knew the feeling of light-headedness and the breathless excitement she felt every time she thought about their lovemaking had nothing do with her injury. The poets had a word for it, and that word was love.

"I'm fine. Except for the small lump on my head, I feel better than I have ever felt before," she answered. Jonathan had been very attentive, seeing to her every need. He had found a pair of his trousers and a doublet that would keep her warm on the journey home. He had in fact been very thoughtful and attentive in a dozen ways.

"Do you need to stop . . . to rest? Or are you cold? Do you need a drink of water . . . or . . ."

"I don't need anything except you."

"You have me now, tomorrow, and always." Anne felt her heart skip a beat as Jonathan looked over at her and smiled.

So this is love, Anne thought, a feeling that not even a poet's verse could fully express. Nothing could have prepared her for this breathtaking ride on air, or the warmth she felt deep within. She had never realized just how incomplete she had felt without him until the moment she had known the glorious satisfaction of being loved.

Anne felt her face flush as she remembered how tenderly he had learned every inch of her body with his hands and mouth. What had passed between them had been beautiful, incredibly so. Romantics said that love made the world spin and the angels sing. Perhaps it was true.

She paused to look regretfully from the direction they had come. Being with him brought her a deep sense of contentment. Going home meant being without him again. It meant a certain sense of loneliness. "I wish we could go back . . ."

"So do I. It took all my resolve to act like a gentleman." Just looking at her brought forth a renewed desire. Jonathan wanted to make love to her again, but unselfishly he thought about Anne's reputation. He didn't want her to be the victim of gossipy chatter.

They rode the rest of the way in silence, but the looks that passed between them said far more than words could ever tell. Jonathan knew that from this moment on, Anne would be branded into his heart, his soul.

When they reached the stables, Jonathan's hands lingered on the soft curves of her body as he helped her dismount. It seemed perfectly natural to drape his arm possessively across her shoulders as they walked. She was his. From this moment on, she always would be in his heart.

Anne paused to look up at the sky, letting her breath out in a long, deep sigh. "I'm so happy, Jonathan! I never knew that it was possible to feel like this."

"Nor I!" He felt as if the years had been swept away

and he was but a boy again. He gazed intently at Anne, wanting to engrave every detail of her beauty upon his memory. The arch of her brows, the upward tilt of her mouth, the way the early morning sunlight danced upon her dark, brown hair.

Anne took a deep breath. Strange, but in her current frame of mind even the smell of the horses was sweet. There was something magical about her surroundings. The grass seemed to sparkle with diamonds; the branches of the trees were entwined as if embracing; the breeze seemed to be humming a love song. She felt light of heart. Carefree. Perhaps it was always that way when someone deeply cared for another.

Jonathan pulled her to him. "Anne! Anne! I've waited for you all my life." His lips went along her forehead, brushing gently along the heavy brush of her dark lashes, teasing the line of her jaw, then caressing her neck. "I don't want to let you go!" His emotions caused his throat to tighten, making his voice husky. "I want to make love to you again and again."

"And I would have you love me again, my dear captain, now that I know to what delights you can take me!" Anne arched against him in sensual pleasure, her hands sliding over the muscles of his arms down to the taut flesh of his stomach.

"Oh, how you tempt me." Jonathan's eyes moved up to the loft, where the hard wood was covered with a soft bed of straw. His strong fingers stroked and fondled her breast as he struggled with his longing. "But you will be a bit sore after our loving, Anne." Especially since they had made love a second time, a mating even more passionate than the first. "I want to be the most considerate of lovers." He playfully touched the end of her nose. "But tomorrow night . . . !"

"Tomorrow night!" The words made her tingle as if a gentle wind caressed her.

"And the next and the next. . . ." For an endless moment he held her against him; then, as if fearing to test his resolve, he let her go. "Come, my love. It grows late in the morning, and as much as I regret it I must return you to your family."

"You must . . ." Anne had put Edward out of her thoughts, but now his fate plagued her mind. Had his journey to Chartley gone unhindered? Had he been cautious in any dealings he might have had with Mary Stuart?

He and I must have a talk when he returns. I'll tell him what I overheard and warn him to distance himself from any further intrigue. It was perilous to become involved in politics, as their father and mother knew well.

Worry over her brother spoiled her previous good mood, but as she and Jonathan left the stables, his show of affection and the way he took her hand soon lightened her mood again.

"I hope your servants are too busy to notice us," Jonathan said now as he opened the thick wooden back door and they tiptoed in. Jonathan was determined to protect Anne's reputation at all costs; therefore he looked cautiously about the room before he was satisfied that they could enter.

"Deserted! Everyone must be abed."

"At this hour?" Anne whispered. "Hardly. My brother has trained them all to get up at the crack of dawn."

"Mmmmm . . ." Jonathan suspected that they were taking advantage of her brother's absence as servants were often prone to do. They needed a captain to discipline them. Still, at the moment he wasn't going to complain.

Anne paused to look around and listen before following Jonathan in. As she moved she tried to tread lightly so as not to set the floorboards creaking, but each step seemed to explode in the silence.

Jonathan led her to the stairs. "Be careful. No more midnight rides. . . ."

"Only if I am coming to see you."

Their fingers moved over each other's faces. "Jonathan . . ." She lifted her arms to encircle his neck. She clung to him, her breasts pressed against his chest, wishing they didn't have to say good night.

Jonathan buried his face in the dark cloud of her hair,

inhaling the rose scent she always used. "No matter what I'm doing, I will be thinking of you and how you should be beside me. Oh, how I wish—"

"So do I." Her body arched against his as he caressed her. His fingers seemed to be everywhere, touching her, setting her body ablaze with desire. But Jonathan was a man true to his word. He repeated the word, "Tomorrow."

"If I can wait that long. Now that I know what I have been missing, I feel the need to make up for lost hours."

"And indeed you shall if I have my way. But upstairs with you now."

Mutely Anne nodded, a smile trembling on her lips. She leaned against him, outlining the shape of his mouth with her fingertips. "And are you doubly certain you do not want to join me there?"

"And have your brother cry out for my head when he returns?"

"Tomorrow then." She disappeared up the stairs.

Jonathan stood there for several minutes after she had gone. A smile lit up his eyes, and for a moment he was tempted to follow her, to change his mind about making love to her in her room. Then, with a shrug of his shoulders, he turned away.

"Strange how desolate I feel being alone now," he whispered to himself. But he was not alone, nor was their entrance unobserved.

"It looks as if you have worked yourself into her confidence. Walsingham will be pleased," a voice said softly. Sitting in the shadows was a man Jonathan thought he recognized. One of Walsingham's former servants. So, Anne's household had been infiltrated. He would have to tell her to be careful.

Jonathan tried to control the anger raging through him, but he was certain that the man could read everything that had happened in the glow that effused his face. "Walsingham is wasting time spying on her. She is loyal to the queen."

"That's what they all say."

"Anne speaks the truth."

"And yet there was a time when *you* doubted her. Surely you must have had a reason."

"I was a fool!"

"No, you were wise. Like a bloodhound you sensed a plot and averted a tragedy. Unfortunately, such schemes are as plentiful as weeds and crop up just as quickly."

"There are no weeds here." Jonathan clenched his jaw. "You can tell Walsingham that there is no reason to assume that Anne's husband will come out of hiding. There was nothing between them." For which he thanked God. "Stafford is unfertile ground for conspiracies."

"Quite the contrary. Stafford is filled to the brim with Stuart sympathizers, and it is but a stone's throw from Chartley and temptation." Slowly the man stood up. He stiffened his back as he looked up at Jonathan. "Do you know, sir, of any letters being passed between Mary Stuart and her followers?"

"Letters?" Jonathan spoke earnestly. "No."

"Nevertheless, they do exist, for they have been intercepted."

Jonathan knew a moment of stark fear, not for himself but for the woman he loved. Not all of the people whom Walsingham had ensnared were guilty. "And just what do these letters contain?"

"Wishful thinking, jibberish, childish plans of escape. Walsingham, however, is certain that soon there will be more."

Jonathan stood quietly for a long, long time, assimilating what Walsingham's spy had said. Mary Stuart was smuggling letters out of Chartley, little knowing that they were being read by her enemies. But what had that to do with Anne? Was she suspect? Or was this man merely chattering?

"What has all this to do with me?"

The man's eyebrows furled, his eyes glowed, and in that moment Jonathan had the feeling that Walsingham's web was far more encompassing than he had ever supposed.

"You are to keep your eye on everyone in this household!"

Jonathan was adamant, wanting to put an end to the matter. "I am not a hired spy. I told Walsingham that I would keep watch for Enrique Navarro and let him know if the man set foot on English soil. I did not say that I would act like a mole."

Jonathan turned to leave, but as he made his way to the door he heard the man say, "Then if a tragedy befalls, you must join in the consequences."

Anne tiptoed up the stairs, keeping her eyes focused on the haven of her bedroom door, mindful of the fact that she needed to change her clothes and comb her hair. Just a few more steps and she would be safe from any inquiries about her whereabouts last night. If any questions were asked as to why she hadn't come downstairs for breakfast, she would simply say that she had been plagued by a headache. Knowing Margaret, there would not be any prying, for her sister-in-law had always been the kind of person to honor another person's privacy.

"And yet . . ."

Never in all her life had Anne been in such need of someone to talk to. The necessity of discussing Jonathan and the way she felt about him coiled within her, winding itself so tightly that she was certain she was going to burst. She just had to tell someone how wonderful it felt to walk on air.

"No, I can't say anything, at least not yet . . ." There were still a few uncertainties concerning her relationship with Jonathan. Things that had to be ironed out before Anne shared her joy with anyone.

"Merry-go-up!" Exiting her daughter's room, a doll clutched in her hand, Margaret startled her. "Are you coming or going, Anne?" She regarded her with upraised brows.

Realizing she was wearing Jonathan's garments, Anne sheepishly brushed at her trousers. She told a half truth. "I was out riding."

"Riding?" There was a hint of laughter in Margaret's voice. Her eyes were all-knowing.

Anne flushed as she remembered the passion she and Jonathan had shared. The glow in her eyes and her tousled appearance had surely revealed her secret.

Looking down to adjust the farthingale of the doll, Margaret said softly, "It's all right, Anne. We'll speak no more until you wish it."

Anne sensed that Margaret would be glad that she had found someone, but she wasn't ready to talk woman-talk just yet. Besides, there were other things on her mind besides lovemaking.

"Margaret . . . ?" Anne paused. How could she question her sister-in-law about her brother's activities without revealing something he might not want Margaret to know? "Where is Edward?"

"He's out and about. Business as usual." She paused. "You're frowning. What is it?"

Anne was remembering that Jonathan had told her he had found out her brother had ridden to Chartley. After overhearing the clandestine conversation of Edward's visitors, she was apprehensive. Chartley was where Mary Stuart was incarcerated. Coincidence? No, of course it wasn't. "It's . . . it's nothing!"

"Nothing?" Margaret's eyebrows shot up in disbelief.

Anne was quick to respond. "I was just concerned that he is working much too hard. He just got back from London, and within a wink he's at travel again." She looked at Margaret out of the corner of her eye. Was Margaret involved in the scheme? She decided to test her. "And after staying up so late last night and all."

"Late?" Margaret seemed to be puzzled. "Edward went to bed early last night. We both did."

"Really. . . ." Anne shrugged. Her sister-in-law's expression was too forthright for her to have any suspicion. "Then I must have been mistaken. I thought I heard voices downstairs."

"Taddie and Mary!" Licking her index finger, Margaret

tried to wipe a smudge of dirt from the doll's face. "Mischievous little mice. I told them that the next time they crept downstairs after bedtime, I'd have their heads."

Not wishing to get her niece and nephew in trouble, Anne said quickly, "I don't think it was the children. The servants perhaps. Or mayhap I was dreaming. Don't trouble yourself any more about it." Anne gave her sister-in-law a quick kiss on the cheek, then hurried to her room.

Slipping off Jonathan's trousers and doublet, Anne puzzled over her brother's clandestine meeting. *Whatever Edward is doing, he is keeping it from Margaret,* she thought. To protect her from involvement in case something went amiss? That would be her brother's way of doing things. Edward was always a gentleman and always considerate of the people he loved. Unfortunately, he was also very sympathetic to those he felt were the tragic victims of destiny, particularly the imprisoned former queen of Scotland.

"Mary has been most unfortunate, and there are many who grieve for her in private," she had told him over and over again, "but there is nothing you can do." Anne had thought that Edward had put Mary Stuart's tragic circumstances out of his thoughts, but she had been wrong.

"A pox on Babington!"

Thinking about it, Anne remembered that Edward had always been impressed by Anthony Babington, who like himself was a young, married country gentleman. They had met in a London tavern in Edward's wilder days and coincidentally been at court at the same time. Babington was a well-to-do scion of a well-established Northumberland family of the Catholic faith, who had settled in Derbyshire.

Babington had always flaunted his lineage, and being of an impressionable nature, Edward had been in awe of his new friend. Anne remembered how the young man had been overdressed in an elaborately decorated red-velvet doublet, red trunk hose, and gold hosen the one time she had met him several years ago. Babington was rich, his family having benefited from two marriages to heiresses. His income was well over one thousand pounds a year, or so Edward had said. But was he wealthy enough to finance a rescue in such a manner that he would not get caught? Anne doubted it.

There were several idealistic young men who were likewise moved by Mary Stuart's circumstances. A few had allowed their chivalrous sentiment to lead them to the block. Better men than Babington had tried and failed and ended up with their heads atop London Bridge.

Anne was determined that her brother would not be one of them.

Jonathan's thoughts were troubled as he rode back to his manor. He had to get Anne away from Walsingham's scrutiny and intrigue. He had to find a way to make her safe. But how? His ships had been confiscated for the time being. He couldn't sweep her up in his arms and spirit her away no matter how much he wanted to. How then?

I must find out what Walsingham is planning, why he has someone spying on Anne's family, and second-guess him. He had to find a way to spy upon the spymaster. I'm surrounded by spies in my own household but I'll find a way to turn the tables and find out information from them.

In the meantime, Jonathan threw himself into work with a purposeful fury. After stabling his horse, he forced himself to do the work of three men so as to vent his anger and frustrations. He repaired the bridge that crossed the stream, dug a well, put up a fence, and chopped enough firewood to last all winter long.

"Oh, how I wish things were different," he whispered, assessing his hard work. "This place would be perfect to raise a family." *A family! A loving wife, a son, a daughter!*

Though he had been a wanderer, Jonathan wanted to settle down. All his life he had wanted someone to love, someone who would love him in return. He had found that with Anne.

I've found what I was so desperately searching for in all the ports of the world. He'd found a dream, his dream. He didn't need to sail the world any longer. He'd found his world with Anne. What was more, he wanted to marry her.

It was the only way they could be truly happy. And the one way he could protect her.

There was only one problem. Her husband. Deep in his heart, Jonathan knew they could not live a lie. He had to tell her the truth. No matter what Walsingham wanted, Anne had to know that Enrique Navarro was still alive.

Anne looked down at the sewing she held in her hands and tried to concentrate once again upon the stitches. Her brother had been gone a long time. Much longer than it took to go to Chartley and back. Where was he? In agitation she stuck the needle into the coarse cloth, then cried out as she pricked her finger. She stared at the blood, hoping against hope that it was the only blood shed today.

"Oh, Edward . . . pray to God that you are safe!"

As if in answer to her prayer, she heard the faint sound of wheels hitting against the stones outside and the clop of hooves. Unless Margaret and the children had returned from the village, it had to be Edward. Anne cocked her head to listen attentively to the sounds outside the window. Hearing Edward's whistle, she threw down her sewing and hurried to meet him at the door.

Anne could feel the blood rising in her cheeks as her brother bounded through the door, nearly colliding with her. "Annie Blythe!" He eyed her quizzically, sensing a purpose for her greeting. "Where are my other two girls? And my boy?"

"Margaret, Mary, and Taddie went to the village to visit the cobbler."

"And you didn't go?" He grinned. "Can I assume then that you have enough pairs of slippers?"

"A woman never has enough shoes," she answered, nearly giving in to his banter. "But I'll go another time. I stayed behind so that I can talk with you."

Edward wrinkled up his face. "By the tone of your voice, I'm about to get a scolding."

Anne sighed. "Not a scolding, a warning." Putting her

arms around his neck she hugged him tightly for several minutes, then stepped away. "I love you, Ned. I don't want anything to happen. . . ."

He took her hand, squeezing it gently. "And I love you . . . but . . . ?"

Anne blurted it out. "I heard voices last night, and I followed."

"Blast it all!" Furtively looking over his shoulder, he tugged her towards the stairs. "We don't want to talk downstairs. Servants have big ears and all too often mouths to match, I fear."

Their footsteps blended together on the stairs, Edward's heavy tread and Anne's lighter step. He led her into the sitting room next to the master bedroom and closed the door behind them.

"What did you hear and what did you see?" His eyes bored into hers.

"I recognized Babington, and I heard him introduce you to the bearded ruffian. I heard enough to know that overdressed peacock is trying to involve you in a plot to help Mary Stuart escape. Oh, Edward, don't! Margaret deserves better than to be made a widow by the headsman's axe."

"I owe Babington a favor."

"A favor?"

He shrugged. "He used his inflence in London to put me on the road to wealth and security."

"You have no need of him!"

"But I do." When she started to speak, he held up his hand. "You don't know a wit about commerce. There are those who have established monopolies. Prices are rising. It is exceedingly competitive. Except at fairs, no one is allowed to sell goods unless he is a resident." His tone became boastful. "Babington has pulled a few strings so that I am now accredited as a resident of several towns. Besides that, under his tutelage I am going to move my goods by water rather than by road, thus improving the time it takes to deliver what I have promised. And Babington has given me an inroad to buying and selling overseas. He has helped me to form my own merchant company to sell goods abroad.''

"Fie! You didn't need Babington. Your own resourcefulness would have aided you. Why, just look at what you have on your own—your ideas of selling goods from the New World and . . . putting your own people to work right here." Her eyes implored him, "As for aid, why didn't you turn to Father?"

Edward turned his back on her. "Father lives in the past. He is old-fashioned. He doesn't realize that in these times it is foreign commerce that puts coins in a man's purse."

"Father does not live in the past, Ned! He is wise."

"He is over-cautious."

"Because he knows danger . . . as do I!" Taking his arm, she tugged him around to face her. "Elizabeth has eyes in the back of her head, and even if she didn't, she has Walsingham to tattle." She wagged her finger in his face. "Babington or no Babington, you must cease any involvement in Mary Stuart's cause."

"I can't!"

Anne was taken aback. Usually Edward listened to her, but he was being unusually stubborn. "Can't or won't?"

"I'm not a schoolboy, Anne Blythe. I'm not your little brother. I'm a man. I have to make my own decisions."

"Whether they are wrong or right, even if what you do might bring heartache to those who love you?" Her eyes filled with tears. "Ned, we all love you. We don't want—"

"I know that." His tone softened. "I promise you, I will be careful."

Chapter Twenty-One

Muted rays of sunlight filtered through an opening in the bedroom shutters. From beneath the window the sound of the first cock's crow reminded Anne all too jarringly that morning had come, much too early for her liking.

"I'm going to pull the covers over my head and stay in bed all morning," she mumbled rebelliously. Oh, but she knew that she couldn't. Today Margaret had planned on gathering together all of the foodstuffs, both pickled and dried, and securing them in the cellar. Winter's icy breath had at last warned them that not only was it coming but it intended to stay. *I can't be lazy. I have to help. . . .*

Stretching her arms, she opened her eyes just a slit as her hand made contact with solid flesh. Only at that moment did she remember that she wasn't home, she wasn't in her bed, and she wasn't alone. Jonathan was beside her. Last night he had come to spirit her away, making good on his promise of "tomorrow." Now his arm lay heavy across her stomach, the heat of his body warming hers as they lay entwined.

The sound of his steady breathing made her heart begin to pound wildly. A flush of color stained her cheeks as she remembered the words she had said, the things she had done. Things she had never even imagined before. Intimate things. Things that would have seemed so wrong and embarrassing even with Enrique and yet seemed so natural with Jonathan.

Beneath Jonathan's hands and mouth, her body had come alive and she had been lost in a heat of desire she had never believed possible. His hands against her aching breasts had warmed her through the fabric of her gown. Never had she removed her garments so quickly or so frantically. A pain had formed so taut in her belly that she had feared she would explode with want of him.

Undeniably she had been bold last night, but caring about him had thoroughly thawed the ice that supposedly encased her heart. Many suitors had accused her of being cold and uncaring, and Anne had feared that it might be true, but last night Jonathan had ignited a sensual fire that had proved the others to be wrong.

It seemed a wanton lived inside her body, an ardent woman who responded unashamedly to Jonathan. Despite the heat of their passion, however, he had been gentle with her, hurrying nothing, taking his time. He had savored the silk of her flesh, his fingers sliding over her skin so tenderly that she had tingled with a prickly fire. But when he had touched the softness between her legs, she could wait no longer. Arching upward, straining against him, she had moved her legs apart and he had entered so smoothly, so easily, that she had wondered if she were dreaming.

'Twas no dream. . . . The lovemaking that had followed had been too memorable, too heated, too stimulating, to be unreal.

"Amour . . . love. . . ." she whispered. It sounded just as remarkable in either language. *I love him . . . we love each other . . . we are lovers.*

Once Anne might have thought the word had a tawdry ring to it, but feeling as she did about him, she couldn't believe that the passion and joy they found together was wrong. He knew just how to touch her, knew all her sensitive spots. In a tender assault of kissing, stroking, and teasing her with his tongue, he knew how to bring her again and again to a heart-stopping crest of pleasure.

If I had known it would be like this, I never would have jumped from the portal. I would have welcomed Jonathan's lovemaking the very first time I laid eyes on him. No, she couldn't have opened her heart, mind, and body to him then. Love was something that had to grow even in the grip of adversity. Besides, there had been Enrique.

Enrique! Closing her eyes, she tried to imagine what it might have been like to have his hands upon her, his lips caressing hers, his . . .

No. She could never have been so intimate with Enrique. Something had been lacking. Something that had caused her to put off the consummation of their marriage again and again. She had thought it was because she was frigid, but Jonathan had dispelled any such thoughts from her mind.

Jonathan's lovemaking made her forget anything else, made her feel as if everything would work out for the best in the long run. Her only worry was Edward, but he had promised that he would be careful. To ensure this, she would watch over him just as she had when they were children. Determinedly she shoved aside the misgivings that entered her mind and clung to her optimistic feelings.

The world could be a much happier place when two people were in love. Love was not tangible, yet Anne thought at times that she could nearly reach out and touch it. It seemed to enfold her, warming her. Right now that was the only important thing.

Rising on one elbow, Anne looked at Jonathan with aching tenderness. He looked so much younger and more vulnerable when asleep, not at all like the formidable captain she had once attacked with a sword. He snuggled up against her, his powerful body sprawled across the bed as if he didn't have a worry in the world. Reaching out to touch a stray lock of his tawny hair, she felt just as protective of him somehow as she felt of Edward. She would never let any harm come to either of them.

She'd given her whole heart to Jonathan. Just being with

him made her smile. There was a romantic side to Jonathan that deeply touched her. When she was with him, she felt special. He said over and over again that there was only one woman in the world for him and that it was she. He said he would never let her go.

Though Anne longed for a firmer commitment from him, wanted with all her heart to be his wife, his love was enough for now. Ties of the heart were forever binding. Margaret had said many times that men were secretly terrified of marriage. Perhaps that was why she had proposed to Edward over and over again before he had said yes.

"What would you do, Captain Jonathan Leighton, if I proposed . . . ?"

Leaning forward, she touched his mouth lightly in a kiss, laughing softly as his lips began to twitch. She'd teased him about crying out orders in his sleep. She had told him that he would always be a ship's captain, but he had firmly denied the desire to feel the deck of a ship beneath him again. He had told her that he wanted to take up a "landlubber's life" and build up the manor house with the same dedication that he had given the *White Griffin.*

"Anne?" Jonathan cherished the blessing of finding her cradled in his arms, her mane of dark hair spread like a cloak over her shoulders. He felt an aching tenderness and drew her closer. "What a welcome surprise."

"For me as well as for you." She snuggled into his arms, laying her head on his shoulder, curling into his hard, strong body. "You were calling out orders again," she said with a laugh.

"Was I?"

"You were telling imaginary sailors to get to their battle stations. You were fighting a battle with someone. And . . . you were calling out Walsingham's name." She nuzzled his neck. "I don't think you meant Falkhearst's tabby."

"I'd like to blast Walsingham right out of the waters. I'd like to—" He tensed. Though he had put it off for a moment, he knew that now was the time to confide in Anne. "I need to tell you—"

She hushed him with a kiss, just content being with him for the moment. "We'll talk later. Right now I want to take advantage of being together before we have to return to my brother's."

"But . . ."

Touching his face with her hands, she kissed him, a potent kiss that stopped the world from turning, at least for a moment.

Time froze as they explored each other's lips with infinite appreciation. Anne locked her arms around his neck, her hands kneading the muscles of his back as if commiting them to memory. She couldn't help thinking how right it felt to be in his arms.

"Mmmm." A moan slid from his throat as he silently worshipped her body with his hands. He stroked her breasts, kissing each in turn. His tongue tasted the sweet honey of her flesh. His hand moved lightly over her hip and down her leg as he spoke. Weeks of frustration and worry seemed to have melted away. She was his! At last he had come to know the glorious sweetness of her body. Oh, but her body had been pure heaven, her genuine outpouring of love a precious gift. Whenever they were together, she made him the happiest man alive.

"I'd like to wake up every morning and find you next to me," he confided, nibbling at her earlobe playfully. But he was not sure just what destiny had in store for them. He wanted to hide out from the world forever, but could he? He wanted to spit in Walsingham's eye, but did he dare? Despite his smile there was just a hint of a furl to his brow. "Anne . . ."

"Hush!" She didn't want to spoil the morning by letting reality intrude upon her dreams.

Without another word he reached for her, a primal growl in his throat. Cupping her chin in his hands, he kissed her hard. Pleasure jolted through him, a rush of emotion. As she arched her body and sighed, he knew it to be the same for her. Her response to him gave him a heady feeling. He had been able to bring her deep satisfaction not once but several times during the night.

Jonathan moved his hands over her body, stroking lightly—her throat, her breasts, her belly, her thighs. With reverence, he moved his hands over her breasts, gently and slowly, until they swelled beneath his fingers. He outlined the rosy-peaked mound, watching as the velvet flesh hardened.

Anne closed her eyes to the sensations she was becoming familiar with now. Wanting to bring him the same sensations, she touched him, one hand sliding down over the muscles of his chest, sensuously stroking his flesh.

"Just think of the time we wasted," he whispered in her ear. "Aren't you sorry you hit me over the head?"

"You needed your comeuppance at the time."

"Aye, perhaps I did . . . but now . . ."

Their eyes met and held as an unspoken communication passed between them. He was ready for lovemaking and so was she. In a surge of physical power, he rolled her under him. Then they were rolling over and over in the bed, sinking into the warmth and softness. Anne sighed in delight at the feel of his hard, lithe body atop hers.

A flicker of arousal spread to the core of her body. Being with Jonathan encompassed every emotion she had ever known. She was passionately in love, recklessly so.

"Anne, my love . . ." he said again, his voice thick with desire. But kissing didn't satisfy the blazing hunger that raged between them. Slowly, sensuously, Jonathan let his hand slid up her thigh, his fingers questing, seeking that most intimate part of her. His legs moved between hers and pressed to spread her thighs.

Anne moved her body against him, feeling the burning flesh touching hers. He inflamed more than just her body. Indeed he sparked a flame in her heart and soul. The touch of his hands caused a fluttery feeling in her stomach. A shiver danced up and down her spine. She leaned against his hand, giving in to the stirring sensations.

Caressing her, kissing her, he left no part of her free from his touch, and she responded with a natural passion that was kindled by his love. Her entire body quivered with the intoxicating sensations he always aroused in her. She would never get tired of feeling Jonathan's hands on her skin, of tasting his kisses.

Reaching out, she boldly explored Jonathan's body—his hard-muscled chest and arms, his stomach. His flesh was warm to her touch, pulsating with the strength of his maleness. As her fingers closed around him, Jonathan groaned.

"Anne!" Desire raged like an inferno, pounding hotly in his veins. Her skin felt hot against his as he entwined his legs with hers.

Her body arched up to his, searing him with the heat of her passion. Warm, damp, and inviting, she welcomed him as he entered her.

Feeling him inside her, joining with him in love, Anne felt her heart move. With Jonathan she always felt first astonishment, then delight in the joy of being together. It was as if the whole world was whirling and spinning around her as she moved in rhythm with him. Bringing her hips up to meet his, her body quickened its movements. Her body was aflame; then it was as if it burst into a hundred tiny flames. She felt as if she were floating, hovering above the earth.

Love was an exquisite journey. Writhing in pleasure, she was silken fire beneath him, rising and falling with him as he moved with the relentless rhythm of their love. They were spiraling together into the ultimate passion. Climbing together. Soaring. Sweet, hot desire fused their bodies together, yet there was an aching sweetness mingling with the fury and the fire. They spoke with their hearts and hands and bodies words they had never uttered before in the final outpouring of their love.

In the aftermath, when all their passion had ebbed and they lay entwined, they sealed their vows of love with whispered words. Sighing with happiness, Anne snuggled within the cradle of Jonathan's arms once again, happy and content.

"I love being with you." Jonathan placed soft kisses on her forehead. She mumbled sleepily and stretched lazily, her soft thighs brushing against his hair-roughened ones in a motion that stirred him again. Even so, he knew they had to talk. "Anne . . ."

He couldn't keep putting it off. He had tried to be honorable, but his good intentions had fallen by the wayside when he had seen her lying like a broken doll on the grass. He had meant only to soothe her, but he had given in to his feelings then and now.

When I'm with you, I forget about everything but you. . . . I want to feel you lying beside me now, tomorrow, always. I want to spend my life with you . . . grow old with you . . . share my heartaches and my dreams. First however, he had to make her understand how he could have made love to her knowing about her husband.

Anne stared into his eyes. He had that look again. That look that told her he was hiding something. "Jonathan? What is it?"

Fearing that he might lose a newfound paradise Jonathan gently cupped her face with his hands. "Remember the aftermath of the sea battle? You came after me with a sword calling me a pirate. We argued, so engrossed in our own verbal battle that we both failed to notice that your husband was—"

A loud pounding at the door interrupted his confession.

"Bloody damn!" He wondered who in the hell it could be. Surely even Walsingham's servants wouldn't be so brash as to intrude in his bedroom. "Go away!"

"There is a messenger downstairs." Jonathan recognized the servant's voice.

"He can wait!" Jonathan looked towards the door, then at Anne, then back at the door again. "I want to go back to sleep."

"He cannot. He is in a hurry to get back with your reply."

"Reply? I'll give him my reply." Jonathan angrily wrapped a sheet around his lower body. He pushed open the bedroom door and took the stairs two at a time, muttering under his breath all the while. He wanted nothing more than to forget about traitors, spies, and plots. He wanted to get on with his life, with this woman, and to hell with anything else.

"I've come from London," a boy not more than thirteen proclaimed, handing Jonathan a folded paper that was embossed with Walsingham's seal.

Tearing the missive open, Jonathan swore beneath his breath as he read the message. It was sent in code with no references at all to Anne's husband; even so, he knew what Walsingham was saying. He was warning Jonathan, forbidding him again to tell anyone that "the rooster" was alive until the proper moment. A moment that Walsingham would determine. In return Walsingham promised that the secret about the "rooster's" fate would be kept and that the "hen" would be given amnesty for any misdeeds.

"Jonathan, what is it?" Having hurriedly slipped on a robe, Anne stood in the hallway.

Jonathan was too busy reading to reply. The message stated that someone had given one of the Spanish prisoners aid in escape from England to Spain. Someone living in Stafford. Someone with an uncle who was a priest. Jonathan had no doubt that Walsingham meant Anne. Thus the promise of amnesty. In other words, Walsingham was gagging Jonathan and blackmailing him into silence.

"Jonathan. Tell me!" For just a moment Anne panicked, fearing that someone in London had found out about her brother's involvement with Babington.

"It's just about my ships. They ran into a storm and there was some minor damage." He hated to have to lie, yet what else could he do?

"Your ships . . ." She was relieved, yet worried about his troubles at the same time. "I'm sorry."

"It's nothing that can't be fixed. Money is only money, after all."

He tried hard to smile, but the smile didn't reach his eyes. For all intents and purposes Walsingham's ultimatum tied Jonathan's hands. He couldn't ask Anne to marry him because by law she was already married, nor could he ask her to petition the pope for an annulment because she thought herself a widow. Their future was in limbo, much as if some evil sorcerer had cast a spell on them. And indeed perhaps an evil sorcerer had.

"I have to go to London." To have it out with Walsingham once and for all.

Chapter Twenty-Two

The cobbled streets of London were dark and eerie. It was that time of night when thieves and other miscreants prowled. The rooftops and towers of the city looked ominous at night, like sentinels on guard for any who would seek to betray England's queen. Above them the awesome Tower of London hovered with its ever-threatening promise of imprisonment.

Jonathan looked over his shoulder from time to time and clutched at his sword as he rode into London. Trying to blend with the shadows, he made his way towards Walsingham's apartments to pay him a long-overdue visit.

"I'll tell him what he can do with his cryptic message! I won't live my life with an axe poised over my head, or Anne's," he mumbled. He had to know once and for all what Walsingham intended and perhaps make a bargain or two, even if it was with the devil himself.

He can do anything he wants with me, but he must stay away from Anne. In return Jonathan would help him fight against Enrique Navarro, Philip of Spain, and indeed the whole of Europe if need be, to keep England safe.

A sudden wind chilled his body—or was it a sense of

foreboding? Jonathan tugged his cloak more firmly around him as he left the stables, remembering how warm and contented he had felt cradled in Anne's arms. Oh, how he wished for her softness now. Instead he was walking all alone, going to meet a man he detested. What made it even more annoying was his intuition that he was being followed. A small dark figure tagged along behind him, walking when he walked, stopping when he stopped.

Jonathan was cautious. Footpads roamed the streets, keeping a close watch for simple countrymen and unsuspecting foreigners. Was he being followed with theft in mind? Well, he would soon send the fellow on a merry chase. With that intent, he wove an intricate pathway of escape, up one narrow twisting roadway, down another. Pausing, he listened for any sound of footsteps and satisfied himself that whoever had been following was now left behind. With a satisfied smile, he continued on his way.

The Thames was dotted with boats and barges that looked like leaves floating towards the shore. Jonathan hired one of the boatmen to take him upriver, feeling relieved the moment he stepped into the boat. The water seemed by far a safer way to travel.

The Thames, with its dock systems, snaked eastwards to elegant Greenwich, the palace where Elizabeth and her councilors were now in residence. It was a slow journey, the heavy boat awkward against the current. Jonathan was therefore doubly glad when at last the barge drew up at the dock that led to Greenwich. Handing the boatman several coins, he stepped out of the boat and hurried down the pathway.

Though the hour was late, every window in Greenwich was lit. Elizabeth and her court were said to keep late hours. Lifting his arm, Jonathan Leighton knocked upon the intricately carved wooden door. He was anxious to get this matter over with as quickly as possible so that he could return to Stafford and Anne's waiting arms.

A young page in the Tudor livery of green and white answered the door. "Yes?" The voice was far from friendly.

"I'm Captain Jonathan Leighton. I've come all the way from Stafford to see Sir Francis Walsingham on a matter of urgency."

"Was he expecting you?"

Jonathan answered truthfully, "No, but I am certain he will want to see me."

"Very well, sir. You may enter." Jonathan followed the page through a maze of corridors that smelled of cloves and perfume. The page stopped before one of the doors.

Jonathan passed through that portal. The door closed behind him with a sense of finality that urged him to caution. He wondered how many men had entered through that doorway only to find themselves the spymaster's prisoner because they were suspected of some plot or other.

Jonathan was ushered to a small, dark room. As he entered, Walsingham looked up with a grimace Jonathan supposed was his idea of a smile. "How good to see you again, Captain Leighton. I assume you got my message."

"I did and rode post haste to discuss it with you."

"Discuss? Why? I would think there is very little reason for any words between us. You know what I mean in the missive."

"I do. You want to blackmail me into becoming one of your spies," Jonathan said beneath his breath. "Well, you can go to the devil—"

Walsingham heard his whispered mumbling and was angered. "Go to the devil. I think not. The devil comes to me and does *my* bidding."

His words chilled Jonathan to the very bone. Still, he had to speak his mind. "In your missive you aluded to the fact that Anne Morgan Navarro was somehow suspected of freeing one of the Spanish sailors. You are wrong!"

Walsingham shook his head. "I have it on good authority that she most definitely gave an enemy aid."

If what Walsingham was saying was true, that information put Anne in severe jeopardy. "I know Anne. She would never go against her country. If she transgressed in any way, it was a tragic mistake."

"A mistake?" Walsingham's smile was evil incarnate. "What would you do if I told you that she helped your enemy escape, a man who took vengeance upon you by burning your ship, the *White Griffin,* to ashes."

"My ship?" Jonathan paled. "No. . . Anne wouldn't . . ."

"So, I see that when you are personally involved, it becomes a different matter." Seeing that he had struck a nerve, he continued. "After your ship was destroyed, I conducted an investigation. I was told that a sailor named Juan de Vega took revenge upon you by torching your ship."

"Anne would not have had any part in that."

"Not in the actual act of setting the fire, but in helping the arsonist escape the country and thus his just punishment."

Jonathan felt as if a heavy weight had suddenly been placed on his shoulders? "How did she help him?"

"They traveled together to Canterbury. There her uncle took the man in, dressed him like a priest, and smuggled him out of the country."

Jonathan could sense that Walsingham was purposefully trying to make him angry at Anne. What was more, it worked. When he thought about his ship going up in flames, he was incensed. Did she know what the sailor had done? Had she been a part of the act of vengeance that had nearly destroyed all that he had built? Clenching and unclenching his fists, he tried to calm his anger by remembering that he loved her. He wanted to protect her. Because of this he somehow had to come to terms with her actions. What was done was done. He had told Anne that he wanted to forget about the past. Now he had to live by that vow.

"I know what you are trying to do, but it won't work. What happened has already happened. I will not dredge up any old suspicions." He had made his share of mistakes. He would leave it to Anne to come to terms with her conscience. "If you want my help, and it is obvious that you do, then I want your word of honor that Anne Morgan Navarro will not be harmed in any way and that this matter will be forgotten."

"Forgetfulness has a price."

Jonathan was trapped by his love for Anne. He knew that, and so did Walsingham. "I want your promise that you will not drag Anne into any of this spying business. In return . . . in return I will do everything within my power to uncover any plot or scheme that either Philip or Enrique Navarro has put in place."

Walsingham's eyes narrowed. "That is no bargain. As a loyal Englishman, you would be expected to do everything in your power to protect England and the queen."

"But a willing and loyal servant is far more valuable than one acting under duress." He could see that his words had hit home, for Walsingham's expression softened. Jonathan continued, "I want your assurance that Anne will be protected."

"As you wish. I won't let the Queen harm one hair on her dark-haired head," Walsingham answered, forcing a smile. "In return you will be on the watch for Navarro and will inform me immediately if he tries to see his wife."

"She is not his wife," Jonathan shot back. "At least not in the full sense of the word." Jonathan revealed to Walsingham that the marriage was never consummated. "Because of this I am asking that you allow me to tell her that he is alive so that she can go about the business of getting herself free from her marriage vows."

"So that she can marry you?" Walsingham's look was smug, as if he knew that there was more to the tale.

"Yes."

"The answer is no! You may not tell her. The widow Navarro is a Catholic. All Catholics are suspected of being in sympathy with the captive Scottish queen." There were several papers on Walsingham's desk. Picking one up, he crumpled it viciously, mumbling beneath his breath, "Mary of Scots. Mary of Scots. How I loath that woman and all who seek to give her solace."

"As do I. But upon my oath as a captain, Anne is not one of them!" Jonathan came staunchly to her defense. "If she—if she gave the man who burned my ship a helping hand to escape, then she did it without knowledge of what he had done.''

Walsingham grunted.

"All the time she was under my watchful eye aboard ship, she never once gave me cause to suspect anything amiss," he lied, thinking about the time she had hit him over the head to get the keys to the hold. "That I want to marry her should be proof enough of her loyalty, for I would never marry a traitor or anyone who would willfully harm Elizabeth.''

"Again you say that you want to marry her. . . ." Walsingham's eyes were piercing as he stroked his dark beard.

"Yes, by God!" Jonathan was impatient, so much so that he could not hide it any longer. "But I cannot ask her to marry me until I tell her about her hus—"

"No! Absolutely not. I forbid it!" The stern, unrelenting expression on Walsingham's face made argument futile. Even so, Jonathan had to plead for his happiness.

"Anne has a right to know!"

"And I have a duty to decide what may and may not be revealed!''

The sudden stark silence as the two men glared at each other was long and drawn out. At last Walsingham spoke.

"Marry Navarro's widow and tell her after the fact. You and I are the only ones in England who know he is alive." He turned his back upon Jonathan, and it appeared that the interview was at an end.

"No!" Jonathan took Walsingham by the arm. "To do so would make our marriage a lie. I want to marry her legally.''

"Then you will have to wait—for an eternity or until Navarro reveals himself to his widow." Disengaging Jonathan's hand from his sleeve, Walsingham brushed at his doublet.

Jonathan's conscience was sorely tested. He wanted Anne with all his heart and soul, but at what price? Still, as he deliberated the matter he was able to soothe his sense of right and wrong. Navarro had disappeared of his own volition, faked his own death, and made his wife a widow for all intents and purposes. He had stayed away from her for three years. Perhaps he would be too fearful to ever show his face. Could Jonathan take the risk? "Would our marriage be legal in England?"

Walsingham's expression hardened dangerously for just a moment, but then he shrugged. "I suppose it could be arranged." His eyes glittered with a sudden idea. "As a matter of fact, that is perfect, for it might well bring Navarro here when he learns of his wife's intentions."

Jonathan hoped that it did not bring Navarro to England, for he wanted no more trouble from the man. He wanted Anne to forget about every minute she had been married to Navarro. He wanted her to continue to think Enrique had died, for it would make everything much simpler. "If I keep my promise not to tell her, will you assure me that if Navarro risks coming to England, he will be intercepted before he reaches Anne?"

"She will be none the wiser. Indeed, she will continue to believe that her husband drowned. In return you will cooperate."

"Yes. . . ." Jonathan soothed his conscience by telling himself that he could and would make Anne happy. Anne's knowledge of Navarro's escape from death would ruin their newfound happiness. "In return I will do everything within my power to aid you in your fight against Enrique Navarro."

"And against the enemies of the queen?"

"Of course. The queen's enemies are my enemies," Jonathan said, and he meant it.

"Then there is something else that you can do to ensure my silence on the matter of Navarro's return from the dead." Walsingham reached up to adjust his collar. "There is a great fool, Anthony Babington by name, who has been instrumental in furthering Mary Stuart's secret correspondence with foreign parties, King Philip in particular. This loquacious, chivalric would-be rescuer of the exiled Scottish queen has been recruiting adherents from among his friends and acquaintances to form a strange little circle of conspirators, including a fanatical priest named Ballard, or 'Savage,' as some call him.''

Jonathan braced himself. Walsingham was going to ask him to spy, and he would be honor bound to say no. Spying was ugly business. When he started to refuse, however, Walsingham held up his hand.

"These men with more money than brains envision cloudy dreams of heroism and have plotted to bring Mary the gift of liberty.''

This time Jonathan did speak. "There have been many such attempts, most of them impotent.'' And some of them justified, he thought, remembering his brief visit with the aging Scottish queen who had not seemed at all threatening to England or to Elizabeth.

Walsingham shrugged. "Ah, and indeed one might have assumed it would be the same this time except for the latest adherents to the plot, among whom is a certain Gifford, a hothead who cries out for Elizabeth's death.''

"He what?'' Jonathan's anger was ignited by this bit of information.

"Your 'friend' Navarro and the Spanish ambassador have been in touch with the conspirators. My agents have reported to me that King Philip is agreeable that four Catholic gentlemen will gain entry to Elizabeth's court to make an end of her with poison or dagger.''

Walsingham's words had the desired effect. Jonathan reached for his sword. "Tell me who they are. They will never get within a hundred yards of her, I will see to that.''

Reaching out, Walsingham touched his arm. "Hold your temper in check. We do not yet know who they are, but we will find out. Meanwhile the snare is already being fastened at one end. When the time comes, I will have my hounds upon them with but the snap of my fingers. All I ask of you is to watch and to listen, not only for Navarro's return but for suspicious doings on this Babington's part.''

Jonathan shook his head. "I'm sorry, I would be of little help to you there. I would not know that man if he stumbled over my foot.''

"Then by all means I shall see that he is pointed out to you." Walking over to his desk, Walsingham wrote down a name, then handed a scrap of paper to Jonathan. "This Babington is well traveled. He and his followers have several designated meeting places. Sometimes in Giles Field, other times in Stafford. They meet often in Babington's house in Barbican. And then again, the Devil's Thumb seems to be their haven now and again."

"The Devil's Thumb?"

Walsingham laughed softly, an ominous sound. "I see you know of it. Well, then, a man would be exceedingly thirsty after a long ride from the country. A visit to the Devil's Thumb might indeed be in order tonight."

"Tonight?" Jonathan could tell by Walsingham's tone of voice that it was more of a command than a suggestion. He looked down at the piece of paper, stunned to see a woman's name. "Gwen?"

"She is a tavern maid as well as a paid informer. It has been duly reported that Babington and some of his fools have recently returned from Stafford and are there celebrating. If you tell her that I sent you, she will point Babington out to you so that you will know him the next time that you see him."

The night had quickly turned cold, wet, and miserable. The taproom of the Devil's Thumb was thick with smoke and packed with a multitude of patrons fighting to get closer to the fire that burned brightly in the great hearth. Jonathan moved through the crowded room greeting those he recognized, taking note of those he did not, wondering which one was Babington.

Damn Walsingham! Jonathan was angry at himself for having been so easily pulled into the act of spying. If it was the price for his happiness with Anne, however, it seemed a paltry price. Besides, he would not have been a loyal Englishman had he not been determined to guard the queen from any harm.

The tavern was a hive of activity, with friends and foes alike rubbing elbows as they sought to keep warm and at the same time quench their thirst. Firelight danced and sparked, illuminating the faces of the tavern's patrons as if through a fog. It was an uproariously boistrous throng. The laughter and chatter was deafening, so much so that Jonathan could barely concentrate on his thoughts as he wound himself through the crowd.

Several ships had put into the London port, which added to the tumult. The sound of foreign tongues blended with those of their English-speaking counterparts. Hoping against hope to find Enrique Navarro amongst the crowd, Jonathan sharpened his eyes and his ears, but he was soon to be disappointed.

Well, what did I expect? That Enrique Navarro would put into London and brazenly announce himself? No, if Navarro was in England, he would be well disguised.

"Cap'n?"

The sound of a friendly voice promised to lift Jonathan's mood. Turning around, he came elbow to elbow and nose to nose with Edmund Falkhearst.

"What are ye doing in London? Why, ye were in the country but a wink ago." The corners of Falkhearst's mouth tugged up in a grin. "Not that I'm not happy to see ye, Cap'n." The grin just as quickly soured. "Ye didn't—didn't have another spat with Annie, did ye?"

It seemed to be the only good news Jonathan could report. "No, as a matter of fact I came to London to make certain that there is no more quarreling between us and to ... to settle a few things that will make it possible for me to ask her to become my wife!"

"Wife?" Falkhearst was elated. He patted Jonathan on the back, took a long swig from his mug of ale, choked, then burst into a fit of inebriated giggling. "I knew it. I knew it. Ye are as made for each other as two peas in a pod."

"So to speak," Jonathan replied, trying to quiet Falkhurst's outburst. He didn't want to draw attention to himself. He hadn't taken into account Edmund's exuberance.

"Gweneth . . . Gwenith . . ." With a hiccup and then a belch, Edmund beckoned a buxom, red-haired tavern maid.

"Gwenith . . . Gwen . . ." Jonathan repeated. Strange, he had seen the full-figured young woman a dozen times or more and paid her little attention. Now he needed her.

"What will you have, good sirs?" Gwen sauntered up with a swish of her skirts, eyeing Jonathan up and down..

"Ale all around, if you please. . . ." Falkhearst announced.

"Ale it will be." Gwen looked at the handsome blond man.

"Oh, no, no. Keep yer eyes off of him. He's getting married!" Falkhearst giggled again. "And I couldn't be happier."

"Married . . ." If Falkhearst was openly elated by the news, the tavern maid named Gwen was equally disappointed. Before Jonathan could say a word to her, she hurried off.

"So that's Gwen," Jonathan exclaimed.

"Aye, and ye had best stay clear of her if ye don't want Annie to chop off yer head. Gwen isn't the type to keep a secret, just in case ye wondered. So toe the line, me boy."

Gwen returned with a tray of cups and tankards that she balanced with skillful aplomb. Moving about, she filled and refilled the drinking utensils in a flirtatious manner.

Suddenly Falkhearst nudged Jonathan in the ribs. He pointed towards a table where three velvet-cloaked gentlemen sat talking and drinking. "The tall skinny man with the thatch of black hair and the nose like a bird's beak. He is one of Walsingham's spies. A vicious man. John Rothingham by name."

"Rothingham." Not Babington. Even so, Jonathan took due note, studying the man intently.

"He thinks himself a clever man indeed, yet everyone knows him for what he is—a devil!" Gwen whispered in Jonathan's ear as she noticed the direction of his stare. She pointed to another man. Shorter. Fatter. Pockmarked. An unpleasant-looking character if there ever was one. "That one is called Selby. He is Rothingham's creature. Deadly."

"Is that so?" Jonathan realized in that moment that Gweneth was afraid of Walsingham and was obviously spying for him not so much for profit as out of fear. But where did her loyalties really lie? Perhaps he should be cautious lest he find himself caught up in some sort of trap.

Gwen refilled Falkhearst's mug. She revealed that Rothingham and his cronies often met at the Devil's Thumb to plot and to plan. "The men who sit at the table with Rothingham and the two men disguised as sailors." She patted his hand. "Avoid their company as you would the rats that plague this city, for that is what they are."

"Rats?" Jonathan asked. It was strange how Enrique Navarro came to mind.

"Rats!"

Jonathan took a long sip of ale, then whispered in her ear. "I will heed your advice." He paused, deciding not to tell her that Walsingham had sent him, for he could tell that she was trying to protect him from the spymaster for some reason or other. "It seems you might know a great many patrons here."

She beamed from ear to ear. "Oh, indeed I do!"

"Including a man named Babington?"

For just a moment she stiffened; then, deciding that she could trust him because of his friendship with Falkhearst, she pointed to a table in the far corner of the tavern. "The man in purple and silver. That's him!"

Jonathan's eyes turned to look upon a young gallant dressed in a doublet the color of the richest wine, the sleeves slashed and embroidered with silver showing the fine Holland linen of his shirt underneath. His trunk hose and hosen were ornately embroidered in silk threads of various colors. His light brown hair was worn long, brushing the collar. As was the fashion, he wore a single gold earring in his left ear, a gesture to style that Jonathan had made himself once or twice.

"So that is Anthony Babington," he said softly. Staring intently, he emblazoned the young man's image in his mind and had no doubt that the next time he saw him, he would remember him.

Cups, mugs, and glasses were filled and refilled over and over again with wine, whiskey, and ale. Falkhearst had made certain that it was a riotous evening in celebration of Jonathan's decision to renounce his freedom and become a married man.

"If she will have me!" Jonathan declared, knowing how unpredictable Anne could be.

"Does she know yet that ye snore?" Falkhearst grinned as Jonathan started to deny it, having forgotten that they had shared Edmund's cabin when Anne had been Jonathan's "guest." "Or that ye have a stubborn streak as wide as London Bridge? Or that ye have the devil's own temper? Or that ye have a wandering eye?"

"Had a wandering eye," Jonathan insisted, focusing his eyes on his mug of whiskey instead of on the tavern maid, who kept brushing up against him.

"Had a wandering eye . . . ha!" Pulling up a chair, Ryan Paxton, the sea captain who owned the Devil's Thumb, insisted that one woman could never be enough for a man. "When you are away from home, in some foreign port, we'll see if you can resist temptation."

Falkhearst used his hands to outline the silhouette of a very curvy woman. "You wouldn't be doubtful if ye had ever seen Annie." He whistled. "What's more, she's a lady through and through, she is." He hiccuped. "Makes me wish I was younger so that I could marry her myself!"

"Marriage . . . bah!" A sailor who had sailed several times with Jonathan grimaced. "Why settle for beef when the whole forest abounds with deer?"

"Aye, the only reason to put a leash around your neck is if the woman is over-sexed and comes with a huge dowry," chimed in another sailor.

"Or if she's a rich widow who can cook . . ."

"Is this Anne rich?"

Jonathan shrugged. "To tell you the truth, I don't know, nor do I care! I'd marry her if she didn't have a farthing. She's spirited, beautiful, and everything I have ever wanted."

"Being spirited is a good quality for a horse but trouble in a woman. As for a woman's comeliness, there is nothing as fleeting nor as fragile as a woman's looks. Even the loveliest of women can't stop the march of time. Today's beauty is tomorrow's crone!"

"With Anne, I'll delight in growing old beside her, and I will love her until the day I die!" Jonathan took a gulp of whiskey, then drained his glass. He could only hope that he would be allowed to grow old with Anne as his wife and that Enrique Navarro would never surface to ruin their happiness.

Oh, Anne, forgive me, he thought. *I have no other choice but to play the game with Walsingham's dice.* Trying to soothe his guilt, he took another glass of whiskey and then another, listening only halfheartedly as the men sitting around the table with him talked heatedly on the virtues and disadvantages of marriage.

When at last half the evening had passed, the dark-beamed taproom was in a shambles of spilled liquor and food. Jonathan's drinking partners warbled lewd songs, sprawled upon the benches, or snored as they cradled their heads on their hands.

The flames engulfing the huge logs in the hearth sputtered and burned low. One by one the smoking candles and torches that had brightened the taproom flickered, hissed, and died out. Darkness gathered quickly under the tavern's low-beamed ceiling.

Jonathan knew he had had too much to drink, and he swore it would be the last time. He was not too inebriated, however, to be deaf to the whispering that came from a table in the corner of the room.

"The Queen of Scots has been put exactly where she belongs."

"Aye, Paulet will put end to her scheming. There will be no more smuggled letters now that she is under his surveillance."

"No more schemes and treachery."

"Ha! Believe that and you are a fool," whispered another. "As long as Elizabeth holds the Scottish queen like a canary, there will be trouble. Young romantic fools will feel it their duty to free her."

"Fools like Edward Morgan . . ."

Recognizing Anne's brother's name, Jonathan attuned his ears to what the men were saying.

"She has been put in an inescapable cage. Paulet watches her like a veritable hawk. She will never be free."

"Don't say never. The Catholics are a devious lot."

"Care to make a wager?" A beady-eyed man took out a money pouch and hefted it on the table. "I say that Mary of Scotland will die being Elizabeth's captive and that she will not go to the scaffold alone. . . ."

Chapter Twenty-Three

Though spring was quickly approaching, the window pane in Anne's bedroom was lightly iced with frost. Stretching lazily and opening her eyes, she thought what a lovely morning it was in spite of the slight chill to the air. But then, perhaps every day was beautiful when one was in love. Love seemed to make a person glow inwardly even when the sun did not shine.

Slipping from the bed and putting on her robe, she was in a very positive mood as she walked to the window and wrote Jonathan's name in the frost. *He's become part of my life,* she thought.

Oh, how she had missed him. Just knowing that he was nearby had been exciting and brought unpredictability to her life. Now, although he had been gone less than a week, it seemed much longer. She was anxious for him to come back. In addition to her longing to see him, however, she was troubled and more than a bit puzzled about his hasty departure. Woman's intuition told her that Jonathan's reason for leaving so abruptly had something to do with a far more serious matter than he had confided. She could only hope that he would trust her enough to tell her the whole story when he returned.

I hope there wasn't anything seriously wrong in London. I hope that it didn't involve the queen. Anne knew Elizabeth was possessive when it came to handsome courtiers. ''Good Queen Bess'' was loath to have them marry or find happiness. She wanted every eligible male to vie for her attentions only, and she punished them severely when they strayed.

Was that why Jonathan had kept silent on the subject of marriage? Or was he secretly fearful of tying himself down? Was the sea an even fiercer rival than she had supposed?

Anne knew she was attractive, intelligent, and very eligible, yet it seemed that Jonathan had paled when she had teasingly brought up the subject of matrimony. Something was standing in the way of his asking her to marry him, but what?

I'm being ridiculously impatient and unreasonable, she thought. Her love affair with Jonathan had been sudden, passionate, and impetuous. Though it seemed now as if they belonged together, they had in reality just been reunited after a tumultuous relationship aboard his ship and three years apart from each other. Anne told herself she had to give him time.

''A woman knows in her heart very early in the courting period if she wants to spend the rest of her life with a man. A man on the other hand is a bit slower to come to that same conclusion,'' her mother had once told her. ''Women are by nature nesters; a man is hesitant about giving up his freedom. But if love is true and meant to be, it will triumph in the end.''

Love had triumphed for her mother and father in the face of insurmountable odds. Richard Morgan had been trapped in a loveless marriage to a woman with a child's mind. Anne's mother, Heather, had been betrothed to a violent, hateful man who wanted to marry her to enact vengeance. Anne's father had interrupted the wedding and literally swept his beloved up in his arms and kidnapped her from her own wedding ceremony. And that had been just the beginning of the obstacles in their way.

Jonathan did not have a wife and she was not betrothed. Any problems that might stand in the way of their marriage seemed unimportant by comparison. *Love will find a way if I am patient.*

Though Anne didn't consider herself to be overly sentimental, she wrote her own name in the frost under Jonathan's. She crossed out the letters they had in common, then ticked off the remainder to the chant, "Love, marry, hate, adore." It was a method that some superstitious young women used to determine the odds of marriage to a certain young man.

"I tried that the first time I laid eyes on Edward and it came up 'hate,' so I ignored it and took matters into my own hands. I asked him to marry me."

Anne turned and saw Margaret standing in the doorway. Blushing at being caught in a silly deed, Anne wiped the frost away with her hand.

"You could also try 'tinker, tailor, soldier, sailor, rich man, poor man, beggermen, thief' . . ."

Anne laughed softly. "I did once when I was a girl, and it came up thief."

"Ah, ha! Your handsome privateer!"

"Once I called him a pirate, but I have long since learned that Elizabeth not only condones acts of piracy, she fosters it and takes her share of the profits. I was naïve."

"I would say that you were very idealistic and perhaps a *bit* naïve." Margaret tugged at her skirt. "I . . . I don't want you to be hurt, Anne. All too often men can be rogues."

"I am not as naïve as you may think. I know what I am doing." Anne squared her shoulders as if settling in for a verbal fight. "Besides, I love him, Margaret."

Though it was obvious that Margaret wanted to discuss the matter at length, she kept silent, saying only, "In the long run, that's really all that counts." She walked to the window deep in contemplation and opened the curtains wide. At last having made her decision, she said, "If you are expecting a lecture from me on morality, you will not get it. Life is much too short and happiness too brief not to follow your heart.''

Anne was a little bit embarrassed that Margaret knew of her trysts with Jonathan, but she knew that she was open-minded and would not judge her harshly. ''Once I thought I'd never fall in love, so I married for the sake of prestige. Now I realize what a poor substitute that was for caring deeply about someone.''

Margaret agreed. ''Forsooth, how I pity all those women who are forced to follow their father's ambitious dictates instead of listening to their own feelings. It must make for a very dismal marriage bed.'' She patted her protruding stomach. ''As you can see, I followed where my passion and my heart guided me, and I will never regret it, even if Edward does have a few faults . . .''

Such as letting the wrong people lead him into trouble and being much too sympathetic and kind for his own good, Anne thought. She started to ask Margaret if Edward was going to London again, but they were interrupted.

''Mother, Auntie Anne . . .'' Mary stood in the doorway, her eyes wide as she announced, ''There's . . . there's a visitor downstairs. He wants to see Aunt Anne.''

''Visitor? So early in the morning?'' Anne's hair was tangled, and she was still in her nightgown. ''Whoever it is, send them away.''

''But he's come from London. . . .''

''London?'' At first Anne thought of Edmund Falkhearst, then her heart soared. ''This man . . . what does he look like?''

''He's tall and very handsome. Like Sir Lancelot!''

''Jonathan!'' Anne had never gotten dressed so quickly. Her hands seemed to be all thumbs and no fingers as she slipped on her corset, chemise, and a sapphire-blue dress. Hurriedly brushing her hair and piling it atop her head with pearl pins, she ran down the stairs barefooted, but paused before she turned the corner to compose herself. Taking a deep breath, she picked up her skirts and swept towards him in greeting.

"You look lovely as usual, Anne." He spoke her name softly, caressingly.

Jonathan looked haggard. Though nothing could mar his rugged good looks, he had dark circles beneath his eyes, his hair was mussed, his beard was in need of a trim, and his expression was pained. "Jonathan, what's wrong?"

"Nothing now that I'm with you," he said softly. The truth was, he had ridden all the way from London without stopping. Worse yet, he had a hangover. Was it any wonder, he swore to himself? He would never drink so much whiskey again!

Anne felt a sudden need to comfort him, so she put her arms around him and held him close. Though she had several questions, she held off asking a single one and just enjoyed the warmth of his body next to hers. "I missed you. . . ."

"Not half as much as I missed you."

"You're the one who went away." She nuzzled his neck, wondering how she could ever bear to have him go away to sea. It would seem like an eternity of loneliness.

"And I paid dearly for it. . . ." Despite his fatigue, Jonathan felt aroused by her nearness. Bending his head down to hers, he caressed her mouth with his tongue, pressing her lips apart, then molding their mouths together. Their kisses were tender at first, but the burning spark of their desire burst into flame.

Suddenly Jonathan pulled away. "We must finish what we have started when we are alone. . . ."

Anne was brought back to reality with a thud. For just a moment she had nearly forgotten where they were and that there were other people in the world. Gently she reached up and touched his face. "Then by all means, let's go somewhere devoid of watchful eyes."

"Not yet! I have something to ask you first." He didn't want to take the chance that something could or would come between them. What was more, he didn't trust Walsingham. He had to ask her now.

Bending down on one knee and taking her hand, Jonathan made a romantic request. He told her that he knew beyond a doubt that he loved her, that he wanted to wake up each morning and find her beside him, wanted to see her swell with his child, wanted to grow old with her. He said that there was no other woman who could ever make such a thorough claim on his heart.

"Anne, will you marry me?"

Anne hesitated only for a moment. Jonathan was a man who made her feel loved, contented, and happy. A man whose lovemaking took her to the stars and back again. What more could she ask for than that?

"I will!"

Anne was breathless as she climbed the stairs and swept into her sister-in-law's room. "He's asked me to marry him!"

"I suspected as much. You are positively glowing." Margaret hugged Anne tightly. "Are you going to tell Edward or shall I?"

"Jonathan is coming for supper tonight so that we can tell Edward together and then discuss the details of the wedding. And then, of course, we must tell Mother and Father."

"That you are going to marry the man who held you captive . . ." Margaret threw her hands up in the air. "Papa Richard will throw a fit! The last thing he heard about Jonathan Leighton was that he was the scourge of the ocean."

"That's what I thought at the time! I will have to change his mind. Besides, my father has nothing to say about whom I marry, considering that I am a widow. And he has always wanted me to be happy and now I will be!"

"Even so, you know that your father is very protective of you. The only reason that he has smiled upon your being here is that he knew Edward would watch over you."

"Watch over me, ha!" Anne knew it was the other way

around. "I have always watched over him and tried to keep him out of trouble." Thinking about Anthony Babington, she frowned. Despite her advice, Edward had met with the young scoundrel two more times. He was courting trouble.

"Alas, so have I. At times I feel I am as much a mother as a wife, but I love him anyway."

"So do I."

Anne wanted everything to be perfect. She wanted her father to respect Jonathan. She wanted them to like each other. In some ways Jonathan reminded her of her father. They were both strong, handsome, determined men.

"He will charm my mother. . . ."

"Perhaps, and then again your mother may be even more difficult than your father to sway."

"If they are open-minded about his being a privateer, they will both see that he is the man for me!" Anne was determined on that subject. She wanted her family to look kindly on her marriage to Jonathan, but if they did not then she would marry him anyway. And that was that!

Immersed in a warm, hazy glow, Anne drifted dreamily through the morning hours, remembering Jonathan's love-making. The water in the brass tub felt warm and wonderful. She lingered over her bath, sponging herself, imagining the cloth to be Jonathan's caress. Remembering that he had once spoken of his love for violets, she asked Margaret if she could borrow her bar of soap that held that fragrance. Leaning back, she closed her eyes and luxuriated in her bath, sighing with pleasure as a sheer rapture spread through her body.

Stepping from the tub, she wrapped herself in a large towel, then dried herself and set about finding just the right dress to wear. She chose a simple beige gown of linen with a neckline just high enough to be decent but low enough to be interesting. Always one to scorn corsets before, Anne had a change of heart, asking Mary to lace her up tightly. As to her hair, she remembered Jonathan admiring its length, so she decided to let it just hang free. To make certain the dark waves were shiny, she brushed it a hundred times.

Viewing herself in the mirror, she smiled, pleased with her choice of dress and coiffure.

"Your gentleman is here!" Mary couldn't hide her breathless tone. "Oh, I hope I find someone like him someday. He's so—so dashing. Is he really a privateer?"

"He is."

"And did he really kidnap you, Aunt Annie?"

"Someone has been talking. . . ."

Mary giggled. "I eavesdropped."

Anne hurried to explain. " He boarded the ship I was on rather . . . forcibly and . . . made me be his guest."

"Had I been you, I would have kidnapped *him!*" Mary was determined and obviously smitten. "When I grow up, I want to marry a privateer too!"

Anne touched her niece gently on the tip of the nose with her finger. "Oh, you will, will you?" After a last look in the mirror, she descended the stairs very slowly.

Anne was a vision of loveliness, so breathtaking that Jonathan could only stare.

"I've had my cook prepare sturgeon with sauce," Edward Morgan was saying. "I thought since you are a sailor, you might enjoy fish."

"Captain, Ned. Jonathan is a captain."

"Captain . . ." Edward held out his hand, greeting Jonathan with a firm handshake. "Anne tells me that you have a bit of news for me. Could it be about your ships? If so I can tell you right now that I would be interested in entering into a partnership with you that could be very profitable for both of us."

Jonathan winked at Anne. "I've come here to talk about a partnership with Anne."

"With Anne?" Edward wrinkled his nose. "She doesn't have the least idea about what goods to buy or sell. But I have some ideas on how to better market goods from the New World." He offered Jonathan some whiskey, but Jonathan declined. He intended to stay sober tonight.

Catching sight of Walsingham's informer, who had disguised himself as a servant, Jonathan grimaced. The thought that Walsingham was having the household watched bothered his conscience. He wanted to tell Anne but feared that revealing the information might in some way put her in jeopardy. He had to trust that she and her family would prove to Walsingham just how foolish his constant spying really was.

Like a practiced and most gracious host, Edward Morgan saw that Jonathan's plate was filled with succulent pieces of fish, small onions, carrots, and potatoes. Sherry, port, and claret were served continuously through the meal causing Jonathan to remark that if he weakened and did indulge himself, he would be too much "in his cups" to return home. All the while Anne's wide blue eyes held him captive. He wished with all his heart that they were alone.

He was conscious of a fierce urge to throw caution to the four winds, sweep her up in his arms, and elope with her. Convention be damned! His feelings for her were all that mattered. Even as the thought crossed his mind, he knew that it was important to Anne to have a proper wedding. But what about Walsingham? Could he be trusted to keep a bargain? Or would he make Anne pay the price for helping the sailor esape?

It was my ship that burned. If I can forgive and forget . . .

"Jonathan . . . ?" Anne noticed the way he was staring at her, with an intensity that unnerved her slightly. There was something forced in his smile. The sparkle in his eyes had turned to a pensive glow. Something was wrong, but she wasn't certain just what.

"Is everything all right?"

"Fine. Everything is delicious."

They talked of many things, at last settling on the subject of an upcoming wedding as they retired to the drawing room.

"Wedding? Wedding? Whose wedding?" Edward furrowed his brows suspiciously.

"Mine!"

Edward didn't need to ask to whom the marriage would be. "Annie Blythe. How? When? Are you sure?"

"As sure as a woman can be." Her expression told him there could be no argument.

"But what about the times he's out to sea?"

"I'll wait for him to come back to me." Anne smiled mischievously. "And then again, perhaps I'll go with him. I've always wanted to see the New World!"

"You would do that too, wouldn't you." Though Edward stiffened, he did take Jonathan's hand, pumping it up and down. "Congratulations. I guess I could tell you that Annie is strong-willed and will give you nothing but trouble, but then, you were on board ship with her in close quarters and so you probably already know that."

"Edward!"

Turning to his sister, Edward Morgan reached up and tugged at a strand of her hair, much as he had done when they were children. "I wish you every happiness."

For just a moment Anne waited warily for him to argue against Jonathan. When he didn't, she said sweetly, "Thank you. I hope with all my heart that we will be just as happy as you and Margaret. That's what I want, Ned ... more than anything."

"Then you shall have happiness. . . ." He stared at Jonathan as if daring him to make her unhappy even for a moment.

When at last they were alone, Jonathan pulled her into the warmth of his embrace and she put her head on his shoulder just as she had last night. "Whew! I hope that I passed that test."

"I think you did. Besides, Ned's bark is much worse than his bite. Now you have to meet my mother and father."

"God's blood, woman, I hope I survive." Mesmerized, his lips slowly found hers, kissing her with all the tenderness and gentleness in his soul. "The pounding in my blood tells me we had best set the date for our wedding very quickly," he whispered at last.

"I was afraid you might have changed your mind," she teased. "I was afraid Ned would scare you off."

"Changed my mind?" As he thought about her husband,

he frowned. "No. I want you to belong to me too much to do that."

"I'm glad. All I could think about when you were in London was you." There was no cunning in her voice, no coquetry in her smile.

He laughed softly. "I don't know how much longer I can act the proper gentleman." Pulling her into the shadows, away from her brother's watchful eyes, he pulled her up against him, his mouth hungrily finding hers again. His kiss was urgent, his lips hard and demanding against hers.

Anne pressed tightly against him, kissing him back eagerly as their bodies strained together. It was heaven to have her in his embrace. As her arms wound around his neck, any doubts or qualms Jonathan might have had about Enrique Navarro or Sir Francis Walsingham melted away.

The journey to the Morgan estates in Norfolk was long and tiring. Anxious to arrive as quickly as possible, Anne and Jonathan traveled at a bone-jiggling pace, stopping only at night. Often they made love, but just as often they would fall asleep cradled in each other's arms.

In an effort to make the best impression possible, Jonathan had brought his best clothes for when he arrived at the Morgan estate, a black-velvet doublet laced with silver, the garment cut to emphasize his broad shoulders and narrow waist. Black hosen, silver trunkhose, and high black-leather boots completed the outfit. Jonathan had packed just one traveling bag. Anne, on the other hand, had been undecided on what she should wear once they arrived and had therefore packed three.

"Women's garments remind me of a fortress," Jonathan said with a wry smile. "They make of a woman an impenetrable mystery. It seems to me that half the day must be spent putting them on and then taking them off. Why, a ship is sooner rigged than a woman."

"All too true," Anne had countered, brushing at her brown doublet, "which is why I chose to travel in men's attire. Once we get to Norfolk, however, I want to look my very best.''

"You always look lovely. Even dressed in a potato sack, you would turn any man's eye. Don't worry, my love.''

When at last they arrived at the manor house, it was Jonathan who was a bundle of nerves. Richard Morgan had a formidable reputation and was a man greatly honored throughout England. Jonathan couldn't help but be a bit nervous about what his prospective father-in-law would think about this match. It had been rumored at court that Richard Morgan hadn't thought any man good enough for his daughter, not even a future king.

"Smile, my dearest. My father will not bite.''

"I'm not so sure. I've heard talk. . . .'' He helped her from her horse, then unloaded her traveling bags.

"Father followed his heart. He can not wish any less for me,'' Anne retorted as she led the way to the double oaken doors. Her gentle knock was answered by a plump, gray-haired woman in a black dress and white apron.

"Anne!'' The two women dissolved into each other's arms, hugging tightly for several minutes. At last Anne broke away. "Kibby, this is Jonathan Leighton. Jonathan, this is Kibby Henslowe. She was once my nanny.'' Mischievously she whispered in his ear, " 'Tis Kibby you should be worrying about, for she will be ever more formidable than my father will be.''

Jonathan answered the challenge by taking Kibby's hand and giving it a warm squeeze. "It is a pleasure to meet you,'' he whispered, in the voice that made every woman swoon.

Kibby didn't succumb to Jonathan's charm immediately, however. Crossing her ample arms across her well-bosomed chest, she stood evaluating Jonathan. At last, as if she fully accepted him, she smiled. "And just why, may I ask, are you accompanying my little girl here?''

Jonathan liked the woman at once. There was warmth and a natural charm about Kibby. Jonathan's smile was genuine as he took off his cloak. Answering the questioning look on the woman's face, he told her that he had come to see Richard Morgan. "For some man-to-man talk concerning his daughter," Jonathan added.

Thick gray brows shot up in surprise. Kibby tilted her head to one side, studying Jonathan. She seemed to like what she saw. "Well then, I'll lead you to him while Annie changes her garments." Motioning with her head, she led Jonathan to the warmth of the hall's hearth.

Two figures stood there, framed by the carved posts of the inner doorway. Their pose was as perfect as if they had been painted upon a canvas. Richard Morgan and the Lady Heather. The man was tall, handsome, and muscular, with a strength and grace that belied his age. Only the wings of gray at the temples of his dark hair and the wisps of gray in his beard revealed that he was a man of later years. His wife equaled her daughter in loveliness. Her figure was still slim, her face flawless. There were only a few strands of silver in her thick auburn hair. Jonathan thought them to be by far the handsomest couple he had seen in quite a while.

The sound of his footsteps roused the Morgans from their reverie. As he and Kibby approached, they both looked up to greet Jonathan, but it was the woman who spoke. Heather. Jonathan remembered her name. She had been named for an evergreen that bloomed with small lavender flowers.

"Who have you here, Kibby?" Her voice was as soothing as an angel's, just as Anne's could be when she was calm.

"An Englishman! Captain, so he told me as we walked. Wants to see Master Richard about an important matter."

"Captain Leighton." Jonathan bowed politely, though he could not take his eyes from her face. It was like looking at Anne. Except for the color of her eyes and hair, Heather Bowen was a striking replica. The reminder quickened his heart.

Heather Morgan's smile was warm. "Welcome, Captain Leighton." She held out her hands in greeting,

Richard Morgan, unlike his wife, was not as welcoming. "Captain Leighton!" He glowered as he said Jonathan's name. "I remember hearing of you. It was upon your ship that my daughter was held against her will."

"For which I have made amends," Jonathan answered dryly. Obviously this meeting was not going to go at all smoothly.

"Amends?" Richard Morgan perused him up and down with a critical eye. "A gentleman would have brought her back before amends were needed."

Jonathan did not want to argue. How could he when he knew that he was in the wrong. "Circumstances were such that I regret that I could not. I have made many mistakes in my life, but know this, angering your daughter was one of the greatest."

"I'm sure that it was." Despite himself, Richard Morgan smiled slightly.

Heather Morgan, sensing the tension between the two men, tried to soothe the ill will. "Whatever happened three years ago is in the past. If Anne has forgiven and hopefully forgotten, then how can we do otherwise?"

Richard Morgan shrugged. "I am a reasonable man. I am willing to let bygones be bygones." He raised his eyebrows in question. "That being so, may I ask just why you have come to talk with me, sir? I doubt it is to rehash past errors."

"I've come to get your blessing on our upcoming marriage."

Richard Morgan could seemingly do nothing but stare.

Heather Morgan gasped. "Marriage?"

At last Richard Morgan found his voice. "So first you take her captive and now you want to make her your wife? God's teeth, man, what are your motives?"

"I love her. I want to spend the rest of my life with her."

Richard Morgan's voice rose to a shout "Fie! You are a wanderer. My daughter will spend long days and nights waiting for you to come home. That's not what I want for her."

"And yet you could see her married to a man who could jump over the railing of a ship and leave her behind to God-only-knew what fate?"

"Enrique Navarro was a gentleman."

"Enrique Navarro was a coward."

For a moment Richard looked as if the argument might escalate, but Heather Bowen stepped between them. "Richard . . . Jonathan . . ."

"Unlike Navarro, I would give my life to protect Anne. As for wandering, now that I have met her, I want a more settled life. More than anything else in my life, I want to be a good husband."

Heather Morgan smiled. "He sounds so much like you, Richard." She took Jonathan's hands in hers. "How does my daughter feel about you?"

"Your daughter loves him as much as you love my father." It was Anne who answered. Having quickly changed into a plain beige dress with no farthingale beneath, she swept into the room. "Jonathan is right. Enrique was a coward. The day of the sea battle, he thought only of himself, but I do truly believe that had Jonathan been my husband, he would have protected me with his life if need be." She looked down at her hands. "Enrique was never a husband to me in the true sense of the word. And even if he had been, he is dead. And I am very much alive! More so now that I am truly in love!"

"So, you love him, do you?" Richard Morgan sighed. When he looked at his daughter, there was so much love in his eyes that Jonathan was touched.

"I do!"

For a long moment no one spoke; then suddenly Richard Morgan turned to Jonathan. "How are you at chess?"

"I've played once or twice, but unfortunately I lost."

Morgan patted him on the shoulder. "Then allow me to give you a few pointers. It will give us something challenging to do when the family is together ere the evening."

Chapter Twenty-Four

The wedding day dawned bright and clear without even a hint that it might rain. Anne and Jonathan had chosen the last day of April. According to convention they could not marry during Lent, and the month of May, which was traditionally the month for remembering the dead, was ill-omened for lovers. Nor did they want to wait until June. Jonathan was eager to make Anne his wife and get on with their lives. Besides, he did not want Enrique Navarro to have time to find out about the coming nuptials in time to prevent the ceremony.

Though Anne had been calm and completely unruffled at her first marriage, she was inwardly trembling this time. She wanted everything to go smoothly without any quarrels between her father and Jonathan, whose temperaments were so similar that they always seemed to be at odds the last several days.

Anne had not time for a special bridal costume, but she had chosen a special gown of pale blue with gold trim and gold undergown of a style introduced by the queen. The skirt was long and trailed at the back, the sleeves bulged and the waist was cut long and triangular to a sharp apex below the waist. Anne wore a large ruff at her neck and small ruffs at her wrists. As usual, the skirt of her gown was spread out from the hips by a farthingale, which looked as though she had a large hoop beneath the hem and a smaller hoop around the hips. Though false hair was all the rage, Anne had no need for it, for her hair was thick, dark, and long. It was her "crowning glory," Jonathan said, so she wore it long and flowing.

Attended by her grandmother, Blythe Bowen, her mother, and Kibby, Anne was soon fully dressed, even to the silk stockings on her legs and fine leather shoes upon her feet, a gift from Jonathan's cousins, the MacKinnons. She wore a bridal garland woven of wheat, rosemary, myrtle, and early-blooming flowers that was borrowed from her mother, and gold-and-pearl earrings that she had borrowed from her grandmother. A bouquet of white roses and forget-me-nots sent by courier from Edward and Margaret, who were unable to attend due to Margaret's delicate condition, completed her ensemble.

Every bride included something old, something new, something borrowed, and something blue on her wedding gown. The old maintained her link with the past, the new symbolized the future, the borrowed gave her a link with the present, and the blue symbolized her purity.

"The wheat in the bridal garland is a symbol of fertility," Heather Morgan whispered in her daughter's ear as she tied the bridal knots. "I hope I'm not being selfish in hoping that this marriage will bring forth many children, for your sake as well as mine."

"There will be children, mother, but in due time. . . ." Anne chided gently. She confided her greatest dream. "I want to sail the world with Jonathan before we truly settle down to raise a family."

"Sail the world . . . ?" Heather shook her head. "Anne dear, will you never change?"

"As you have said a hundred times, I'm just like my father. I long for adventure, Mother, and with Jonathan I know I will have that and so much more. . . ."

Walking down the stairs, Anne found a large throng of guests awaiting her. They would accompany the bridal party to the church. Her eyes touched upon each one, but upon seeing Jonathan her gaze was unwavering. Jonathan was dressed in his best, a dark-brown doublet, tan hose, white shirt with ruffs at the wrist and neck, brown trunk hose, and leather shoes. For the occasion, he wore a gold earring in his left ear, his only conformity to current fashion. He smiled as he watched her walk down the stairs.

Coming up behind her, Richard Morgan kissed Anne gently on the cheek. "And so I lose you once again, but by the look in your eyes as you gaze upon him, I can see that you truly do love him."

"He'll bring me happiness."

"He'd better. . . ." It was obvious that Richard Morgan was concerned that his future son-in-law was not only a seaman but also a Protestant. He had openly confessed that he would have preferred that Anne marry a man of her own faith.

"Father!" Anne's voice was stern. She did not want anything to spoil her wedding day.

"All right, by God. I'll say no more, but I hope he's a better husband than a chess player," Richard said beneath his breath. Taking her arm, he escorted her into the large parlor where a small troop of minstrels preceded the wedding party, playing on flute, viol, harp, and bagpipe. Jonathan had paid the musicians, knowing how much Anne loved music. Even Anne's father admitted that it added just the right touch.

"Well, at least he does seem to have a romantic streak. . . ." Richard Morgan grumbled, turning his head to look at Jonathan, who was walking beside Heather Morgan in the procession. They were laughing and talking and it was obvious how much the captain charmed her. "But he had best forget such romanticism when he's out to sea and away from you."

Anne paused as they reached the steps, gently reassuring

him. "Don't be worried, Father. I am not. A woman knows in her heart if she is truly loved."

Outside the walls of the Morgan estates, the people of the village had gathered to watch the procession. Those who remembered Anne from her girlhood waved and called out to her; others had no doubt joined the crowd just because they loved the pomp and ceremony.

It was a long, tedious walk to the church. When at last they arrived at the square in front of the church, Anne's feet were aching and sore. The new shoes pinched her toes and rubbed at her ankles. She could hardly wait to slip them off during the ceremony and give her feet a much-needed rest.

"Thank God for long skirts," she mumbled, slipping the slippers off as the priest stepped out from the portico.

Richard Morgan's eyes glistened as he took his daughter's hand and put it in Jonathan's. "I give her to thee. . . ."

"For which I will always be grateful," Jonathan declared. He turned to Anne. "You look lovely. I thank God that you will soon belong to me." Their eyes moved towards the gold wedding ring that rested on a white satin pillow. Soon it would be placed on Anne's finger.

Together they faced the priest who asked the standard questions—if she was of age, if she swore that she and her betrothed were not within the forbidden degree of consanguinity, if the banns had been published, and finally if she herself and her groom both gave free consent to the match. He then began his intonation of Latin words in a deep, resonant voice that gave Anne chills. As the Mass progressed, she felt peace and love in her heart. She had found the man her heart had longed for.

Anne felt the gold ring touch first one finger and then another, to rest on the third finger of her left hand in an unending symbol of eternity. She would belong to Jonathan forever and would make him happy—this she vowed, even if it meant standing at the dock and watching as he sailed off on one of his adventures.

I will never interfere with Jonathan's freedom, she thought. Nor would he interfere with hers. That and love were the reasons the marriage would hold together through thick and through thin.

With a deep sigh, Anne sank to her knees to receive the wine from the priest's brimming chalice, watching as her father nodded to Jonathan, who was unfamiliar with Catholic rites, to alert him that he should kneel also.

The ceremony was long but hauntingly beautiful for Anne, more so because she knew that Jonathan had risked censure and prejudice by those unfavorable to Catholics.

When at last the priest ended the ceremony, motioning with his palms stretched out for Jonathan and Anne to rise, Jonathan slid his arms around her waist and before all assembled, kissed her.

"At last . . . you belong to me. . . ." he said when he drew away.

"Look at how gentle he is with her, Richard. They are perfect together . . . can't you see?" Anne heard Heather Morgan say before dissolving in a flood of happy tears.

Wiping at his eyes, it was obvious that Richard Morgan was deeply touched, yet stubbornly he wouldn't go towards the happy couple until his wife gave him a gentle push.

"Go on . . . he's part of the family now . . . your son-in-law."

"A pirate!" Even so, Richard held out his hand in a gesture of camaraderie. Jonathan shook his hand firmly, smiling all the while.

"You daughter has made of me a contented and very happy man."

As the couple left the church for the walk back towards the Morgan manor, they were showered with confetti and rice to bless the marriage with fertility. Similarly, another old custom was followed for the bride and groom to have to overcome an obstacle as they left the church. Some of the onlookers held a rope trimmed with flowers in their path so that Jonathan and Anne had to jump over it before continuing on their way. The jump symbolized their leap into a new life.

The wedding feast that followed the ceremony was a lively

affair. Edmund Falkhearst and Kibby had stayed behind to decorate the manor and oversee the preparation. There was music, dancing, wine, and an array of delicacies. Most important of all, however, was the wedding cake, whose richness again symbolized fertility. The cake was broken apart over Anne's head, then the guests scrambled for the fragments that would give them good luck.

Anne and Jonathan noticed that Falkhearst and Kibby seemed to have eyes only for each other, so they were not surprised when she picked up a piece of wedding cake to put under her pillow.

After partaking of the food, the guests engaged in the dancing, a whirling, high-stepping jubilant merriment. Then, amidst jovial laughter and shouted congratulations, the newly wedded couple were escorted up the stairs to the bedroom that contained their nuptial bed.

Though several pairs of eyes watched as they took their places in the large feather bed, they barely noticed, nor did they hear the drone of the priest as he gave the blessing. They had eyes only for each other. Then at last they were alone.

"My lovely, lovely wife. I love you so very much," Jonathan whispered.

"Show me!" Anne's eyes were boldly challenging, in the manner he had come to love.

Jonathan's intense gaze clung to her as he beheld her naked beauty. He ran his hand lovingly over the softness of her shoulder, down to the peaks of her full breasts. This was his bride, his mate forever and ever. She was worth the lie he had to tell because of Walsingham's stubbornness.

She is my wife now. Not Navarro's. Never his! he thought.

With a quick, indrawn breath, he drew Anne to his chest, molding his mouth to hers in a sweetly scorching kiss. His hands stroked her body, gently igniting the searing flame she always felt at his touch.

A blazing fire consumed them both as their bodies met and caressed. With hands and lips and words, they gave full vent to their love. Jonathan caught her in his arms and pulled her down, rolling with her until her slender form was beneath his. They were entwined in love, in flesh, in heart, and with their very souls.

Warm rays of sunshine awoke Anne and she stirred, stretching her arms and legs in slow, easy motions. There was something different about the morning—she sensed it yet didn't remember what had happened until she looked across the room and saw her blue gown draped haphazardly across a wooden chair.

"The wedding. My wedding!" Now and forever, she truly belonged to Jonathan and that thought made her feel warm, contented, and secure.

Before the priest, her family, and God, he had made her his wife and tied their lives together for eternity. What greater proof could there be of his love?

"Love . . ." she whispered. No wonder the minstrels and bards honored the very word. Love had a way of bringing gentleness to the heart, radiating out to others like rays of sunshine. Though her knowledge of courtship and lovemaking was limited to him, she still knew that he had always taken her with the greatest of tenderness. Aye, she loved him. There could never be doubt of that henceforth. Even now she could feel the whole world whirling and spinning around her when she imagined his hands upon her.

"Forever . . . !" As long as they lived, they would belong to each other. "Husband and wife." A sense of well-being radiated through her, and she knew that this was only the beginning. They had a whole lifetime to look forward to.

Cautiously, so as not to awaken him, she turned over on her side and watched Jonathan as he slept, her eyes touching gently on his fair-haired head, his lashes, and his well-molded lips. She found herself really looking at him as she never had before—noting the line of his brows, the angle of his jaw, the way his golden hair waved touching his neck and temples. With his eyes shut, he looked boyish, almost innocent, but in truth he was a passionate lover.

Last night they had made love not once but several times, and each time had been more stirring and satisfying than the time before. Closing her eyes, Anne recalled the husky cry of passion as he had whispered her name, "Anne," with as much reverence as he had said his vows.

Whispering his name, Anne stroked the expanse of his shoulders and chest, remembering the passion they had shared. His skin was warm and smooth, roughened by a thatch of hair on his chest. Against her breasts it had been more pleasurable than she might ever have imagined.

"Anne?" Jonathan's voice asked sleepily. Still half asleep, he smiled. Their gazes locked. She couldn't look away. Then he was rolling her over, pinning her beneath him as if he were not whole without her there. His hands moved over her back, sending a tingling sensation along her spine. "What a pleasant surprise to wake up and find you beside me." His voice was husky, his breath warm in her ear.

"I will be by your side as long as you want me there."

"That will be forever."

He caught her lips, gently nibbling with his teeth. His tongue touched hers, her mouth opening to allow him entrance.

They lay motionless until she could hardly bear it; then slowly he began the caressing motions that had so deeply stirred her last night. He touched her from the curve of her neck to the soft flesh behind her knees and up again, caressing the flat plane of her belly. Moving to her breast, he cupped the soft flesh, squeezing gently. Her breast filled his palm as his fingers stroked and fondled. Lowering his head, he buried his face between the soft mounds.

For just a moment Anne imagined what it would be like to have Jonathan's child. Before it had been a fear, but now that they were married it was something that she looked forward to. She wanted to have a son or a daughter with the strength and handsomeness this man possessed.

"My husband!" she said again. "Who would ever have imagined that our first harrowing meeting would end up in wedded bliss!'' She smiled sensuously as he moved his mouth and tongue over her breasts. ''Now no one can ever come between us.''

For just a moment, Jonathan stiffened. There was only one person, one man who could. He tried to push Enrique Navarro from his thoughts, but for a moment he was like a ghost, hovering there between them.

''Jonathan?'' Anne moved her palms over the muscles and tight flesh of his body. ''What is it? Are you tired?''

''No!'' A long, shuddering sigh wracked through him. Her hands pushed any lingering images of Navarro away. ''Oh, how I love your hands upon me.''

She could feel the reaction of his body to her touch, knew he was aroused. ''So it seems.'' She continued her exploration, wanting to learn every inch of him. In response she felt his hard body tremble against hers.

''Ahhhh . . .'' The sound came from deep in his throat.

Stretching her arms up, she entwined them around his neck, pulling his head down. Their lips met in a long kiss that sealed the promise of their love. His mouth played seductively on hers, his tongue thrusting into her mouth at the same moment his maleness entered the softness nestled between her thighs. She felt his hardness entering her, moving slowly inside her until she gasped with the pleasure.

This time their lovemaking was not quite as gentle but nonetheless satisfying. Anne couldn't help marveling at how their bodies fit together as perfectly as if they had been made one for the other. Her arms locked around him, and she arched herself up to him, joining Jonathan in expressing their love.

Afterwards she cuddled happily in his arms, her head against his chest, her legs entwined with his. Noticing that he was tense, she gazed into his face, disconcerted to see a frown there. How could he be even remotely unhappy after the bliss they had just shared?

''Jonathan?''

''I was just wishing that we could find a cocoon somewhere and stay there together like two caterpillars, away from the outside world.'' Jonathan gathered her close, as if he could shield her from the world's harsh realities. ''The queen sent her good wishes for our marriage—at least we have that—but there are rumblings.''

''That we are not a part of.''

''I've heard about a plot to harm Elizabeth.''

Reaching out, Anne touched his lips with her fingers, silencing him. ''Hush. Elizabeth has Walsingham. She has no need of you. And we most certainly have no need of him!'' At the very thought of Walsingham, she shuddered. *Oh, Edward, I hope when all is said and done you have listened to my advice. I hope you have had nothing more to do with Babington.*

''You're right. We won't speak anymore of such things.''

Touching her face, he kissed her. ''I love you, Anne. Very much. Please remember that no matter what happens. . . .'' As if to give proof, he held her tightly against him as if he would never let her go, then slowly made love to her again, molding her, shaping her. When he entered her, she felt her heart move. It was as if he were draining her soul, then pouring it back again, filling her to overflowing. Her joyous cries mingled with his as they joined together in a fiery union. For the moment at least, the world was held at bay.

The noise of pounding hammers, the scraping of shovels, and the low hum of men's voices floated on the breeze to Anne's ears as she stood at the well. They were home after an exhausting ride across England back to Stafford.

''Home!'' She smiled. The day she had first come to look at Jonathan's new lands, she had never realized that they would one day be her home, and yet they were now. A home she and Jonathan were building up together.

For the first few days after they returned, they had been so busy that they had seldom seen one another except at bedtime. Each one was hard at work on their own chores, Anne supervising the interior of the house and Jonathan supervising the exterior work and the manor's finances.

There seemed to be a hundred things to do. Anne could see that the manor definitely needed a woman's touch, and so she set herself to the task of spring cleaning.

In rooms without carpets, fresh rushes mixed with herbs were strewn, the old rushes thrown out and burned. New sacks of grain were bought from local farmers to replenish the grain that had been used. She planted a large garden right outside the kitchen door for vegetables and herbs. In addition, Anne set about redecorating the entire manor from room to room, smiling as she remembered how she had once redecorated Jonathan's cabin aboard the *White Griffin*.

I have changed since then. Now she chose the furniture, drapes, and other household decorations very carefully, having given in to her "nesting" instincts. Before she had been hell-bent on revenge.

Anne cringed as she remembered how stubborn, headstrong, and spoiled she had been then. She had grown just as her love had grown until now she was truly the kind of woman she wanted to be, still strong but with a strength that could bend when necessary.

Filling a large bucket with water for the new workers Jonathan had hired and Falkhearst was supervising to renovate the estate, she waved to Jonathan, who was deeply engaged in lively conversation with Edmund. He was grinning, looking happier than she had ever seen him. Happiness seemed to be contagious, for even Falkhearst talked on and on about settling down, perhaps with Kibby if she was so inclined.

Now that Anne was mistress, the household staff had grown by one. First there was Millie, the cook, and secondly Eleanor, who was in charge of the heavy household cleaning. They replaced Jonathan's former housekeeper, whom Anne had promptly dismissed upon taking charge of matters. There had been something devious about the woman which, when coupled with the disrespect she had shown Anne whenever they crossed paths, made her quick departure a necessity.

Following her lead, Jonathan had fired the stablehand and replaced him with a young man who used to be one of his sailors. Lastly, the gardener had suffered a like fate and been sent packing and replaced by one of Falkhearst's friends. Jonathan had insisted that from now on only those who were completely within their trust would become part of the household.

Anne sniffed at the air, relishing the perfume of the flowers that were blossoming nearby. Suddenly she realized that the fragrance was mixed with another smell. Something was burning.

"The milk!" Hurrying inside she saw that Millie had rescued her frumenty, a pudding she was making for tonight's dinner. Frumenty was made of wheat boiled with milk, currants, raisins, and spices, and had been a dish that her father was inordinately fond of. She hoped Jonathan would be pleasantly surprised.

"Aunt Mary!"

Anne whirled around, happy to see her niece standing in the doorway. "You've come just in time to lick the bowl," she exclaimed.

"I won't have time. I've come to get you."

"The baby! It's coming—my God, it's early!"

Mary shook her head. "Not the baby. Mummy told me to tell you that it has something to do with Papa."

"Edward?" Somehow Anne knew that her brother was in a world of trouble. That intuition sent her spirits hurling downward.

Anne's worst fears were realized. Hurrying to her brother's manor, she was met by a visibly shaken Margaret. "The fool! The blundering simpleton. He's ruined us all! He'll be lucky if he keeps his head!"

Taking Margaret's hand, Anne forced her to be calm. "Relax . . . get your emotions under control. Your baby . . . you'll bring it too soon." Giving orders for one of the servants to brew a cup of herbal tea, Anne listened to the fearful details.

"Edward is hiding down in the cellar. He's frightened

out of his wits, and I am in nearly as sorry a state. Walsingham ... Walsingham ..."

"Has done what?"

Taking deep breaths from time to time, Margaret somehow got the story out. Anthony Babington had been secretly corresponding with the exiled queen, Mary Stuart. Thinking that no one would find the letters hidden in a barrel, he had been rash, telling her about a plot to get rid of Elizabeth once and for all. Six Catholic nobles had agreed to do the grisly deed if she would but give her approval of the plan. In a letter that had been intercepted by Walsingham's agents only a few days ago, she had done so, jeopardizing not only her own life but the lives of all those involved.

"My dear Lord!" Only by the greatest effort was Anne able to keep her own emotions under control. It was even worse than she had feared. "I can't believe that Mary would be so reckless. Did she really give her blessing to the murder of our queen?"

"She promised rewards for the success of the undertaking. Worse yet, the messenger to whom her secretary entrusted this reply was a secret agent of Walsingham. Now a man named Ballard has been arrested."

"Perhaps that will be the end of it?" Anne knew she was being overly optimistic.

"Edward fears otherwise!"

Trembling all over, Anne ran to the stairs and hurried to the cellar. Her brother met her at the secret door. "Ballard's been taken!"

"Ballard?" Anne thought long and hard and at last remembered the man who had looked like a vagabond.

With intellectual zeal she and Edward tried to figure the situation out, concluding that there was nothing that could tie Edward to the zealot.

"But will he betray me? Babington has said that Ballard is one of the bravest, staunchest Catholics he knows. He said that no matter what they put him through, he will keep silent but I—I can't say for sure. Besides, for all his staunch babblings about bravery and continuing with the Enterprise,

Babington let it slip that he is going to apply to Walsingham for a passport to France.'' He nervously twisted his hands. "I'm going to ask him to get one for me as well.''

"No!'' Anne's voice was as loud as thunder. "You can't leave Margaret when she's about to have your child; nor can you take the risk of being entrapped. Trying to run from England could be construed as an admission of guilt on your part.''

"But what can I do, Annie Blythe. What?''

"You will do nothing, and you will wait and see what happens.''

Edward took Anne's advice. Meanwhile, he told her, the request for a passport had been sent to Walsingham but that he did not reply immediately. This was a source of worry to all the young men involved with Babington.

Then quickly the axe fell. News from London said that Anthony Babington had made his way to St. John's Wood, a few miles from London. There he had found a hut and stayed for a night. He had changed his complexion by staining it with walnut juice, had cut off his hair, changed garments with his servant and sent that unfortunate man back to Barbican. Moving on to Harrow, he had decided to lie low with a Catholic friend until the hunt was over.

Babington was a wanted man and all who sheltered him in dire peril. Again Anne and Edward waited anxiously to see if he would escape. They found out in a few weeks that he had not. His capture was not long delayed despite his cleverness. Babington was taken from Harrow as Walsingham's prisoner and lodged in the tower. The hunt was over.

Or had it, as Anne feared, just begun?

Chapter Twenty-Five

Bells all over England rang, pealing Walsingham's triumph. They chimed atop church spires, clamored from the decks of ships, rang from ordinary citizens' windows. Bonfires were lit. Throngs of people made merry in the street, sang psalms, marched about with tabor and pipe, and shouted out the news to any who might not have heard. Their cause for celebration was that a wicked plot to kill their beloved queen had been squelched and the conspirators apprehended. Messengers let it be known that a procession in London had been inaugurated to celebrate the rescue of Elizabeth and the imminent destruction of Mary Stuart.

If Mary's enemies celebrated, however, Anne viewed the events with trepidation. Walsingham had rounded up the conspirators one by one, aided by the tortured chattering of Babington, who had made his confessions on the rack. Confronted with the evidence, a decipher of his letter to Mary and her impassioned reply, he had admitted the authenticity of both. Moreover, he had babbled about ''the Enterprise.'' Every detail of the conspiracy was placed in the hands of the great spymaster. More than one man was fatally incriminated. Anne feared that her brother would be among them.

Walsingham had struck quickly and he had struck hard. Anne heard that Babington and his members of "the Enterprise" were led back in chains through the streets of London. There was no hope for them. Walsingham was not the kind of man who would listen to a denial of guilt. The verdict could not be anything but guilty.

"They're going to be coming after me! And I didn't do anything, Annie, I swear it!" her brother cried as they crouched together in the celler where Edward was spending more and more time in hiding. "I would never have had anything to do with the murder of Elizabeth, you have to believe me!" He was frightened out of his wits.

"I do believe you, Ned." Anne comforted him much as she had when they were children. "I'm your sister and I love you." *Others will not be so easily swayed to your innocence. Walsingham is ruthless and cruel. If you are named as one of the guilty ones, he will not stop at any means to ruin you,* she thought but did not say.

"I carried a few letters to Mary once or twice and met with Babington and the others a few times. That's all! Surely that is not enough to hang a man. Is it?"

Anne knew that it was. Walsingham had ruined men for less. She wanted to tell her brother, "I told you so," but realizing how frightened he already was, she didn't think it would help matters. Instead she said, "We will need help. You must let me tell Father."

"Never!"

"Father may be able to use his influence with the Queen."

Edward shook his head. "I don't want him to know. He and Mother are away from court intrigue and danger. Besides . . . I don't want him to hate me."

"You're his son. No matter what you might do, he would never hate you."

"Even so, I don't want you to tell him."

"Then let me tell Jonathan. . . ."

"No!" Edward was adamant on the subject. "I don't

know much about him. He could be in league with Walsingham for all I know. Besides, there are cases where bosom friends have been persuaded to turn against each other when faced with the rack.'' He shuddered.

"Jonathan is my husband, Ned. He loves me. And you as my brother are part of his family. He may be able to intercede on your behalf.''

"Family or not, Jonathan is Protestant, and just like all the others he will be against Mary and therefore against me. I can't take the chance. I'll wait and I'll hide out. If anyone asks where I am, tell them I'm in London. . . .''

Anne waited and kept Edward's secret. Meanwhile things got much worse. It was like a nightmare, pitting Protestant against Catholic again, as in the past. The trials of Babington and Ballard and their confederates resulted in the terrifying verdict of hanging and quartering, the sentence for treason. All those who had witnessed such an execution knew the procedure well. England had nothing to learn from Spain about cruelty. To deter further plotting, the worst possible death was planned for those found guilty. It was always the way of the lawgivers that the populace must see that just vengeance was brought down on traitors in order to curtail any further problems.

Even thinking about the punishment made Anne's insides roil. It would be gruesome and bloody. The condemned would be split open alive so that the heart and intestines could be wrenched out. The end was always death, but the severity of the sentence depended on whether the victim was cut down alive or allowed to remain hanging until he was dead so that the butchering was done on the corpse.

Through rumors, Anne and Edward had heard what was happening in London. The crowd had assembled in a field at the upper end of Holborn, St. Giles as it was known. There a scaffold had been erected with a pair of extraordinarily tall gallows. After being placed on hurdles and drawn through the city, Babington, Ballard, Savage, Chidiock Tichbourne, Henry Donn, Thomas Salisbury, and Robert Barnwell awaited their deaths.

Ballard had been first. True to Edward's prediction, he had been brave to the very end, even though he was subjected to unspeakable agonies. Babington had been next. It was rumored that he had suffered, and because of this had called out for mercy again and again. None had been shown. One by one the others Edward had mingled with suffered a like fate, though Elizabeth had shown mercy at the end and given the command that they be allowed to hang until dead before being cut down.

Because the northwest and northeast counties were mainly Catholic, it was quiet in Stafford, but in the areas of England where Protestants ruled, rhymes, ballads, and pamphlets circulated everywhere. It seemed in the city as well as the country, the words to several ballads were changed so that all of England was acquainted with the terrible conspiracy.

"London is a ghastly city of unspeakable men," Edward said when reading one of the gory verses. He was certain his own end was near. Of all the conspirators, only four had not yet been arrested.

"I should flee or I will be likewise doomed," Edward said to Anne over and over again.

Though Anne was fearful for her brother, she was determined to use her head. "No. Walsingham will be expecting the guilty to panic. Even if he does not have any evidence against you, he will assume the worst if you flee. You will lose any hope you might have had of being exonerated," she insisted. Soon it was a moot point. The roads were blocked; the ports were being watched. It was in that moment that Edward panicked and changed his mind concerning Jonathan. It appeared that his brother-in-law was his only hope. In spite of his wife and children, Edward had decided to get as far from England as possible.

"Mother has relatives in Spain. I'll go there, and then Margaret and the children can follow."

"Ned, don't be a fool. You will get caught and then your fate will be assured." It was a warning Anne seemed to have to say over and over again. Meanwhile, just in case escape proved to be the only way, she made provisions to help her brother.

Jonathan would have had to be blind not to notice the visible effects the Babington executions had on Anne. She was withdrawn and distant, except when she was in his arms. In those moments she clung to him as if fearing to let him go, yet when he questioned her about what was wrong she always changed the subject.

" 'Tis nothing. I'm nervous about Margaret's baby, that's all. It's due any day."

Jonathan knew Anne was hiding something. What it was or who it involved he could not say. Thus, hoping to get information from Anne's brother, he saddled up his horse and rode over to Edward Bowen's estates. He was told that Edward was not there despite the fact that Jonathan could see his reflection in the mirror and knew that he was hiding behind the door. To Jonathan's mind, it was a confession of Edward's guilt, but what was Anne's part in all of this?

It troubled Jonathan that Anne had once helped the Spanish sailor escape. Though he loved her with all his heart, he was plagued by suspicions. Was she involved in the conspiracy? He had to find out, and if she was he had to offer up his very soul to keep her out of trouble. Therefore he saddled his horse and rode at bone-rattling speed towards London.

After a harrowing ride that took a night and a day, Jonathan found Elizabeth's counselor sitting at his desk, scratching with a pen upon a piece of parchment. Suddenly aware of his heated regard, Walsingham raised his head. "Ah, Captain Leighton. I thought you would come."

"Is Anne in any danger? Because if she is, I will remind you of your bargain."

"Bargain?" Walsingham's smile was cold. "Oh, yes. It comes to me now." As if assuming that because Jonathan lived in the country, he was totally ignorant of what had been going on, Walsingham detailed the events that had gripped all of England. He squinted dangerously as he added, "It seems my victory held many surprises, however, including your wife's brother and three cousins of yours."

"Cousins?"

The look chilled Jonathan to the very bone. "Moira— Roarke MacKinnon's daughter—and her brothers. But then, I seem to remember that they were the black sheep of your family."

Jonathan felt the need to assert his loyalty. "My family and I have always been loyal to Elizabeth. And Anne has—"

"Has been much too besotted with you of late to do any conniving. She is innocent, at least this time." Opening a compartment in his desk, he brought forth a piece of paper. "But as to her brother, I cannot say the same." Walsingham spoke in measured tones. "I have here some very damaging evidence. It seems young Ned Morgan has been keeping some very bad company."

"Bad company?" Jonathan feared the worst.

"He was seen with Babington. Not once but several times."

Though he was trembling inwardly at the very thought of what might happen now, Jonathan somehow kept his outward visage calm. "You made a bargain that if I helped you capture Enrique Navarro, you would protect Anne."

"That protection does not extend to her brother."

"Yes, it does! She loves him. Were anything to happen to him, it would destroy a part of her."

Walsingham rose abruptly. Putting his hands behind his back, he paced up and down. At last he spoke, lowering his voice discreetly. "All right. I have no need to catch and kill a puppy. Enough blood has been spilled for the moment. But accordingly you will be indebted to me, Captain Leighton. You owe me a favor. Is that understood?"

"What kind of favor?" Jonathan was wary. Oh, how he hated being indebted to Walsingham for anything.

Walsingham didn't answer for a long, long time, letting

the silence stretch out. The only sound was the tap, tap of his fingers as he drummed them on his desk. At last he spoke, but very softly, as if afraid someone besides Jonathan might hear. "Navarro has been spotted. He's in England headed for Stafford. Bring me his head!"

It looked as if it were going to be a perfect day. The early morning sun slanted down in golden rays upon the land, touching the greenery with a fiery warmth. In the forests, sunlight streamed through the branches of the trees playing hide-and-seek with the shadows. Brooks and streams meandered through pasture land, glistening with reflected sunbeams. Birds twittered tunefully as they flew from tree to tree, competing with the melodic whisper of the breeze.

Sitting on the window seat of the library, gazing out over her husband's vast domain, Anne was melancholy. She missed Jonathan and feared that something she had said or done had driven him away. He had hurried off to London much too quickly.

I have to tell him about Edward. Secrets destroy trust and slowly destroy a marriage. Somehow she had to make Edward see that they had no other choice but to confide in Jonathan.

From across the room, Mary, at play with her spaniels, looked up. "Aunt Anne, something's the matter with Cider. He's been barking for the longest time now." Mary picked little Wart up in her arms and cradled him tightly.

Strange, Anne thought; she had been so immersed in thinking about Jonathan that she hadn't heard the dog, but she did hear the loud barking now as Wart joined in the chorus.

"What is it? Who's out there, little ones?" Remembering the part the dogs had in her reunion with Jonathan, Anne felt a surge of sentimentality. Jonathan had brought so much to her life. What if they had never found each other again? What if she were still alone?

"There's someone out there, Aunt Mary."

"No, dear. I think the dogs are just nervous about being away from home. They have to get used to—"

"Someone sneaking around."

Thinking it to be Edward in some sort of disguise and that he might have come to the manor to avoid apprehension, Anne opened the front door and followed the dogs, who headed immediately to the barn.

Pushing open the door, Anne called out softly. "Edward?" Seeing a man's silhouette crouching near the hayloft, she hurried forward to intercept him before he could run away. "Edward—what is it?"

As Anne crept closer, she gasped. It wasn't Edward!

"So we meet again, dearest *wife!*"

For a long, disbelieving moment Anne stared at the phantom. It couldn't be! She was imagining things. But no! It was he. Enrique Navarro. Like a ghost from the past, he stared back at her.

"No!" It couldn't be, she thought again. Enrique was dead. She had seen him fall over the railing, had seen him swallowed up by the sea.

"Sí, it is me, *querida.* You have not lost your mind."

"But how . . . I . . . I thought . . ." Anne stood deathly still as realization dawned over her. Enrique was alive. She didn't know how he had survived the jump or why there had been no sight of him in the ocean or where he had gone after he had jumped, but he had not died. "Enrique . . ." She moved towards him, her eyes sparkling with tears. "I thought . . ."

He didn't even touch her, just stood there looking at her coldly. "That I had made you a widow . . ."

Anne paled. Realization that her marriage to Jonathan was invalid tore at her heart. "Why didn't you get in touch with me, Enrique?" If she had known that he was alive, so many things would have been different.

His smile was cynical in the extreme. "Why? It didn't look to me as if you were lonely, my dear."

"Oh!" Guilt washed over her, threatening to drown the happiness she felt. "Let me explain." Somehow she wanted to make Enrique understand that although she had great affection for him, she truly loved Jonathan. But how?

"Explain?" For just a moment there was a flicker of emotion in his eyes, but then once more he regained his icy control. "There is no need. In all fairness, you had every reason to think that you were free."

"It's been over three years. Where have you been all this time? Why didn't you let me know—"

"I could not set foot in England lest I be thrown into the Tower. We Spaniards are not very popular at the moment, you see. But I did think of you often."

"How good of you!" Anne felt hot and cold at the same time. Her newfound happiness with Jonathan was now tarnished and illicit. Worse yet, because her husband still lived, she had committed adultery in the eyes of the Church.

"You are a romantic, my dear Ana, if you think that I would have risked my life and my freedom in the name of love."

"No, instead you thought only of yourself when you jumped. You didn't care what might have happened to me!"

"You were with your own kind." He said the word "English," like a swear word. "You just wouldn't understand that there are some things that take precedence over everything else." He shrugged. "Perhaps things might have worked out differently if . . ." For a moment he seemed regretful; then all traces of remorse vanished. "But what has happened has happened, and now you know."

It was as if a blindfold had been removed from Anne's eyes. "Yes, I do know. You used me. You planned to get closer to Elizabeth through me and then murder her!"

He didn't bother to deny it. "Ah, yes. But your captain ruined everything, and thus we had a change in plans."

"Babington! And the others. The poor fools!"

"Fools? They would have been rewarded handsomely if things had gone as they should have. If not for that *bastardo,* Walsingham!"

For once she thought kindly of the spymaster. "He saved the Queen's life!"

"At least for the moment."

Anne's blood ran cold. "What do you mean? What are you saying?"

Enrique's laugh was evil personified. "Elizabeth's rescue is merely a momentary respite. I shall take matters into my own hands, only this time I will have my dearest wife to aid me."

"Never!"

Enrique looked her right in the eye. "To the contrary, Ana, if you do not wish to see your brother executed like the others, then you must do as I say!"

Chapter Twenty-Six

The die had been cast. There was no turning back now. Anne was on her way on horseback to London with Enrique Navarro for a twofold purpose—to save her brother and to somehow warn the queen.

Turning to look back, Anne watched as the home she had shared with Jonathan got smaller and smaller behind her. She tried not to think, not to let the thought of Jonathan start a storm of tears. She had to think of Elizabeth, of her brother, and of herself. It would do no good to cry nor to think of what might have been. Enrique was alive. He was her husband. That changed everything. No matter what he was planning, no matter what he had done, she was his wife until the Church said otherwise. Even so, she could not keep Jonathan from intruding on her thoughts, not once but many times, as she continued on her journey.

"Why are you stopping? I told you we must get to London as soon as possible." Enrique Navarro was an unsympathetic taskmaster who had little care for Anne's well-being. He goaded her into riding at a furious pace, with the intent of reaching London by daybreak. Meanwhile Anne's body ached in a hundred different places.

She had been riding hard, the flanks of the horse heaving in rhythm to the hoofbeats. Anne felt each pulsation. The stallion was lathered; there was foam on the animal's neck and spittle dripping from its jaws. This and not her own misery at last forced Navarro to slow his pace.

"I did not realize that you would be such a hindrance," he chided.

Anne was incensed by his attitude. "Nor did I realize that you were so cruel and devious. And to think that I believed you to be a good man . . . and that I defended your honor when all the time you plotted to assassinate the queen."

"Henry the Eighth's bastard daughter, you mean. The true Queen of England languishes in Elizabeth's clutches." His eyes were glittering coals. "Did you know that she has been implicated in Señor Babington's plot and taken to Fotheringay?"

Anne shook her head.

"Well she has. And all the while that pig, Walsingham, plots her death. But little does he know that we will strike first and then rally the whole of England to put the crown on Mary's head."

"Mary's or Philip's?" Anne retorted sarcastically. She was troubled by Mary's incarceration but loyal to Elizabeth. Despite her faults, Elizabeth had been a good queen and she said as much to Enrique Navarro.

"She is a lying whore who smiled at our ambassador at the same time she was allowing pirates to steal and plunder our colonies. But all she accomplished was to convince all of Spain that in our self-defense we must crush England."

"Crush . . . ?"

"We are building over one hundred ships that will sail into the Englaish Channel and march all the way to London. The invincible Armada!"

"Dear God!" It was even worse than Anne had ever dreamed. "When are they sailing?" She had to find out and alert Jonathan. Perhaps he could think of a way to protect the coastlines from such an invasion.

"That is not your concern!" Enrique looked daggers at

her, as if reading her mind. "I should not have let you in on our little secret. Come, we have rested long enough."

Anne was defiant. "I will not go on! I'm going back."

Taking off his belt, he looped it over her wrists, then tugged her towards his horse. "If you give me any trouble, I will strangle you!"

Anne jumped back. It was dark, and they were all alone. Even so, she said with bravado, "Do and my father and husband will hunt you down like the dog that I now know you to be!"

"I'm your husband!"

The reminder tore at Anne's heart. What a fool she had been to tie her life to such a man. A myriad of emotions coursed through Anne's veins. "In name only, sir!"

"That can soon be rectified," he replied, looking her over from head to toe with eyes that stripped her bare.

She was repulsed and showed it in her expression. "I would die first!" Having known Jonathan's gentle yet passionate touch, she knew she could never allow Enrique to be intimate with her. Even if it meant putting up a fight.

"You are my wife!" Enrique said again.

"You deserted me for three years, and in that time I divorced you in my heart and in my mind."

His dark eyes were unrelenting. "I will never agree to a dissolution of our marriage. It suits me to have an English wife."

"What a vile bastard you are!"

Navarro shrugged her insult off. "You are angry now, but once we are victorious and England returns to the old ways, you will feel differently."

Anne reassessed the situation. Clearly he was determined to make her obey. If she did not, then she and her brother would obviously suffer for it. So be it then; she would pretend to give in to his wishes, at least for the moment.

"Perhaps I will feel differently later," she said softly, even going so far as to manage a smile. Oh, yes, she would be submissive now, but he would regret taking her with him in the end.

Enrique studied her for a moment, then said, "Come, we must hurry. Already I am behind the schedule I have set for myself."

"Of course. We must hurry . . ." she echoed, her mind whirling with schemes and plans.

"But remember that if you are going to travel with me, then you must learn to keep pace." Without another word, he slapped her horse on the rump, sending the weary beast galloping down the rutted road, guiding his own horse to follow close behind.

The journey was grueling. Anne's backside ached, and every muscle in her body throbbed when at last they reached the door of the townhouse of Roger Pembroke, a man Anne knew to be a current favorite of the Queen's.

"What are we doing here?" Enrique didn't have to answer her. Immediately she knew. Pembroke was an opportunist who obviously thought the Spanish were going to be victorious. So much for loyalty.

"Do you think I can just walk about freely on the streets?" Enrique was scornful. "I am a wanted man. Pembroke has aided me in remaining anonymous."

"Pembroke." She remembered Jonathan telling her that once Pembroke had been his arch rival.

Jonathan. . . . Lack of sleep and worry clouded her brain. What would he be thinking now to find that she was not at home? Enrique had not allowed her to write even a sentence of explanation as to why she had left or where she had gone. He would be fitful, frantic, overcome with worry and concern. How could she have ridden off without at least leaving him some sort of clue as to her circumstances? Had she but scribbled at least a brief line on a napkin, tablecloth, or even on the mirror, he might think of some way to help her. As it was, she had just disappeared. Now she realized that she was right in the middle of a conspiracy and that the situation was far more harrowing than she had anticipated.

*   *   *

A strong wind blew fiercely, whipping Jonathan's cloak wildly about him as he rode up the pathway to Stafford. Never had it seemed so good to be home. Home. Strange, he thought, how London or the deck of his ship had always felt like home before. Now his home was right here because he knew that *she* would be waiting for him.

Jonathan felt more at peace than he had in a long while, secure in knowing that Walsingham would not harm Anne or her brother. For the first time in weeks, he felt hopeful that he and Anne could find happiness without fear. Somehow that blessed emotion had always seemed to elude him until now. Now, for the first time, he held a hope that the turmoil of the past could truly be forgotten. With that thought in mind, he stabled his horse and strode down the pathway that would take him home.

There were a hundred things to do, odd jobs that he wanted to do himself that would make the place more comfortable. He enumerated them as he walked along. The cellar door needed fixing, there were two stones missing in the hearth of the bedroom's fireplace, he wanted to put up a fence around the garden Anne had planted, he needed to cut down the old tree whose roots threatened to undermine the foundation of the south parlor wall.

Jonathan pulled the heavy door of the manor open. The usual melee of laughter and chatter met his ears as Falkhearst and the servants celebrated the end of the day. Once he might have joined them but today he had other things on his mind. Walking from room to room, he scanned all those assembled for the familiar figure of his wife. She was nowhere in sight, so he supposed her to be upstairs in their bedroom.

I will surprise her, he thought, touching the emerald ring he wore on his little finger. He had bought it in London for her and intended on giving it to her this very night. I will take her into my arms and never let her go again.

Jonathan headed for the stairs, surprised when he heard Falkhearst say, "She isn't here!"

Jonathan looked at him, asking, "Not upstairs? Then where?"

"I don't know, Cap'n. I thought maybe she had gone to London to return with you."

"What are you saying, Edmund?"

"She is gone! She's not at the manor."

Jonathan felt a sudden jolt of fear. What if Walsingham had doublecrossed him? What if . . . ?

Hurrying up the stairs, taking them two at a time, he ran to their room and flung open the door. He searched for Anne's traveling bags. They were missing. So were several of her best gowns. Wherever she had gone, she had packed to go there.

Although he doubted she would pack just to spend some time at her brother's, Jonathan saddled his horse and rode over there, but Margaret said that she hadn't seen Anne since Friday and it was Wednesday now.

"Did she say where she might have gone? To her mother and father's?"

Margaret doubted it. If Anne had gone to Norfolk, she surely would have told them. Besides, she would most likely have taken Edward with her.

Puzzled, Jonathan returned home. "Where is she?" All sorts of thoughts ran through his head. His fear turned to anger. She couldn't wait until he returned before she wandered away.

Jonathan fought against his temper, but it reared its ugly head nonetheless. Damn! He felt betrayed, angry. Resentment turned to fear again as he listened to what Falkhearst had to tell him.

"Tom the stable boy said he saw Anne coming out of the barn with a dark-haired stranger. He told me when I questioned him that he saw the man saddle two horses, one for Anne and one for himself. They rode away together."

"A dark-haired man?" Jonathan and Falkhearst thought the same thing at the very same time. "Navarro!"

* * *

It was warm in the bedchamber of Roger Pembroke's townhouse. Anne slipped out of bed and padded across the wooden floor on bare feet, thankful that at least she wasn't being guarded while she was sleeping. Going to the window, she opened the shutters wide to get a breath of cool night air.

"Mary, Mary, quite contrary, how does your garden grow," sang a group of girls, their high-pitched voices in perfect unison. "With silver bells and cockle shells and pretty maids all in a row . . ."

Anne knew the rhyme to be about Mary, Queen of Scots. At dinner she had heard the news. Walsingham had put the Queen of Scots on trial. Worse yet, they had found her privy to conspiracy and of "imagining and compassing" her majesty's death, as they had worded it.

Guilty, Anne thought. But then, hadn't that been a foregone conclusion? Walsingham would not have gone to so much trouble to hang the others if he hadn't targeted Mary. Enrique had been so enraged by the outcome that he had nearly choked to death on a piece of beef when the messenger announced the news. Anne had heard him and Pembroke discussing the matter. They had debated the merits of putting their plan into action ahead of schedule

"How can you think of killing Elizabeth when you know she will never put her cousin to death?" she had asked.

"Never say never," Pembroke had replied. "I think this time she will comply with Walsingham's wishes, for although Elizabeth has been fearful of chopping off a queen's head, lest a few of her detractors get the idea and try to separate her head from her shoulders, she realizes that as long as Mary lives she will be a threat not only to her crown but to her life. That's why we must act and act quickly."

The plan that had been discussed was a simple one. Anne's part in the scheme was to make certain that she was invited to the masque that was being presented at Whitehall. Due to her husband's absence because of business matters, she would bring an escort with her. That escort would be Enrique in disguise. It would be Enrique's duty to signal the assassin, who would be a player in the masque, when to strike.

"I have to warn the queen. She must cancel the masque." Surely Elizabeth would be grateful for the information and would show mercy to Edward for his prior foolishness. The Morgan family had always been loyal to the reigning monarch, even when they didn't always agree with them.

But how was she going to warn her? The Pembroke household was on the alert to watch Anne's every move. *I will have to wait until the masque is underway and then call out the alarm. Somehow. Some way.*

Shutting the window, Anne returned to her bed. She had to learn all the details of the plot so that she would know just when to sound the alarm. Timing was of the essence. Snuggling amidst the pillows and blankets, she knew she had to be successful if she wanted to have any hope of ever being truly happy again. If Pembroke and Enrique were successful, then everything would be different in England. Enrique would be powerful and there would be no hope of ending their marriage. Jonathan would be lost to her.

"Jonathan . . ." He was always in her dreams, pleasant visions of the times they had been together or darker times when they had been at odds yet secretly attracted to each other. She didn't want to believe that the love they had shared was over. There had to be hope. It was the last thing on her mind as she closed her eyes to sleep.

Jonathan and Edmund Falkhearst rode all the way to London without stopping, only to know the fierce stab of disappointment upon their arrival. They had been so intent upon reaching their destination that they hadn't allowed the hard reality of the situation to penetrate their brains. That reality was that, except for the fact that they knew Navarro had abducted Anne, they knew nothing else.

They weaved in and out among the crowd; merchants' wives who had come to stroll the docks and take quick

inventory of their husbands' goods; warehouse workers with
their ropes, hammers, and grappling hooks flung over their
shoulders and around their waists; sailors hurrying back to
their ships after spending the day ashore. Two still-inebriated
sailors wound their way up the docks, and the air rang with
their drunken laughter. Though they questioned each and
every one, no one had seen anyone fitting Navarro's or
Anne's description.

"We might as well be looking for a thimble in a hay
loft, Cap'n," Falkhearst said with an exhausted sigh. "The
answer is always no. Once they left your manor they seem
to have just disappeared."

What he said was true. Anne had vanished into thin air,
and Jonathan didn't have one clue as to where Navarro
might have taken her. He wasn't even certain that they had
gone to London.

"I felt so certain Navarro would come here, but what if
that nagging feeling I had all along the road was wrong,
Edmund? What if Navarro headed farther north of Stafford,
or west, or east? What if he went all the way to Edinburgh
to seek refuge with King James in Scotland?"

"He's here! I feel it in my bones. We both can't be
wrong."

"But even if we are right, how are we going to find them?
Navarro was cunning enough to hide from me aboard my
own ship. How can I expect to find him in a city filled with
people?"

"You can't, Cap'n." Falkhearst sighed again. "But perhaps Walsingham can."

"Walsingham be damned. God's teeth, I don't want to
have anything to do with him! I'd just as soon cut off my
left ear." Yet even as he defiantly answered Falkhearst's
suggestion, he knew that the little man was right. If anyone
had caught wind of Navarro's whereabouts it would be the
spymaster.

Grumbling all the while, Jonathan led Falkhearst to a
vacant barge and instructed the bargeman to take them to
Walsingham's residence.

As the boat floated up the river, Jonathan had an excellent view of London, of its turreted towers, church spires, and steeply pitched roofs rising through the chimney smoke. The thick, grayish-white mist billowed about like thick clouds. London was a crammed commercial huddle that smelt of the river. A huge town swarming with people. Even the river itself was crowded, with the city's citizens crossing by boat-taxi, boats, barges, and wherries, all trafficking up and down the river.

People. People everywhere. And in all probability Anne was among them, somewhere.

The barge sailed past buildings of all shapes and sizes, at last stopping in front of a building Jonathan knew all too well. "Here ye go, sir."

Jonathan and Edmund stepped out of the boat and made their way to Walsingham's office, hoping against hope that he would be there.

Walsingham was said to be busy at work, but it was also said that he was in an ugly mood. Jonathan's need of him couldn't have come at a worse time.

"Well, what do you want this time?" Walsingham's expression gave warning that those who said he was acting surly hadn't lied.

"Navarro came to Stafford."

"By God! I knew he would eventually." Walsingham was anxious, fidgety. "Well, where is he? Did you nab him?"

Jonathan hated to admit the truth. "No! He eluded me."

"Damn it all, man. It was your duty to capture him. That was our bargain."

Jonathan knew he had to be humble, so as much as it irked him, he bowed his head. "I apologize. He was two jumps ahead of me. He came while I was in London talking with you and took off with my wife! I was hoping beyond hope that your network of spies might have caught wind of where he has taken her."

"Well, they have not!" Sir Francis Walsingham closed his mouth with a snap of teeth.

"Then I fear I am at a loss, for I have no idea where Navarro has gone or what he is plotting."

Walsingham had been sitting in a high backed chair but now he sprang to his feet. "What is he plotting? I do know that!" He looked at Falkhearst. "Can this man be trusted?"

Jonathan nodded. "I would trust him with my life."

"Which won't be worth a farthing if I take him into my confidence based upon your recommendation and he turns out to be a traitor."

Falkhearst spoke up. "I am as loyal an Englishman as ever lived, so help me God."

Walsingham grunted, then beckoned them closer. "A sailor back from a journey to Italy spoke of Spanish activities all across the Continent. They are buying in large quantities—foodstuffs, munitions, cannonball, sailcloth—in amounts that can only mean one thing."

"Invasion!"

"Exactly. Coupled with the rumors of a huge number of ships being built, that seems to be the answer. They are assembling a powerful fleet to sail against us, and Navarro has a part to play in it. But what?"

"His skill is as a diplomat. He must be trying to maneuver assistance from Englishmen who put profit above honor."

Walsingham's head bobbed back and forth in agreement. "Yes, yes. . . ."

"Give me back my ships. Call them back from wherever they are. We have to act and act quicky. This Armada must be ruined before it ever sets to sea."

"No. We have to wait for Philip to act."

Jonathan was incredulous. "Wait? To wait is to court defeat. The threat must be met early."

"The Queen wants to try a diplomatic approach." Sir Francis Walsingham smiled, though it was more a sinister grimace than a reassuring gesture.

"She is wrong!"

"On that we both agree." His eyes slowly widened. "How would you propose to change her mind?"

"I would talk with her and tell her what I have seen with my own eyes of how Spain treats her enemies."

Walsingham shrugged. "She is beset with problems. There are other men like you who are anxious for war but she ignores them. She yearns for peace and has taken every step in that direction. Every effort has been taken to prevent Spain from concluding favorable alliances that would further isolate England—alliances with Scotland, for example, or with France—and she has been involved in making cautious and indirect overtures to Philip and the Duke of Parma. She wants time to manipulate diplomatically and thus swing the pendulum of power in England's favor."

"Spain doesn't want peace—she wants England."

"To convert we so-called Protestant heretics in England to the Church of Rome? I don't think Philip really cares a fig for all of that, nor do I think he is as favorable to Mary Stuart as he pretends. Or favorable enough only to enter into a war." When Jonathan started to speak, he held up his hand. "Spain rules, has colonized and has exercised influence over much of the known world. Why would Philip want our little island?"

"To eliminate a major seagoing rival for economic reasons. Money talks, Sir Francis. It always has and always will."

"Exactly!" It was obvious that Walsingham wanted war and not peace. "Again we agree. But Elizabeth will not listen. She is a woman, and women abhor war, even if it is the only answer."

"She will listen to me! I'll find a way to make her understand the importance of striking out instead of waiting to be attacked. From what I have seen, we have a strong navy thanks to John Hawkins. I'll suggest a meeting of the queen and all her sea captains and fleet commanders."

"If you are to set up a meeting, it will have to be without my intervention. The Queen is testy over the—uh, matter of the Scottish Queen. However, there is to be a masque tomorrow night at Whitehall. Were you to come across her when she is in a good mood, she might be more easily persuaded." Walsingham lifted his brows suggestively.

"A masque?" Jonathan shook his head. "I have to find Anne first."

"First the queen and then your wife," Walsingham hissed. "Meanwhile, I promise to engage every spy I have at my command to find out where Navarro is hiding. Is that a bargain?"

Jonathan had no other choice. "It is a bargain."

Torches and tapers shone brightly, casting a glow on the brightly bedecked lords and ladies who gracefully made their entrance into Whitehall. As Anne mingled among them, she could only hope that the light was so bright that Enrique's light brown wig and newly shaved face would be so well illuminated that someone would recognize him despite his disguise.

As if reading her mind, Enrique grasped her arm so tightly that she winced. "Don't get any ideas, my dearest wife," he hissed in her ear. "If I am recognized, there is someone else who will take my place. As for you and your brother, I will make certain that if I go down in defeat, so will you. I have documents that will prove beyond a doubt that you and your precious brother are part of this little scheme. You will be safe only if I am successful."

Safe. . . . Anne didn't trust him for a minute. She would never be safe as long as Enrique was anywhere near her. Even so, she had done as he asked and solicited an invitation for the night's entertainment. Somehow she would find a way to save the queen's life and at the same time expose not only Enrique and Roger Pembroke, but all the others engaged in the plot to assassinate the queen.

"You are. . . . ?" It had been so long since she was at court that the page did not recognize her.

"Mistress Anne Morgan *Navarro* Leighton," she answered to his question. "And this is my—my escort." She waited, hoping there would be questions, but the young man didn't even blink before announcing them to the assemblage.

"Very good," Enrique whispered, giving her a light push as they entered the banquet room.

The air was pungent with the fragrance of spices and perfume. It was also noisy. The laughter, chatter, and whispering got on Anne's already edgy nerves as they swept by the queen, who as usual was dressed all in white. It was a startling contrast to Anne's gown of red. Anne had purposely chosen a color that would make her noticeable even from a distance.

"So, Anne, you have seen fit at last to leave your little country hideaway—but *without* your loving husband," was all Elizabeth said to Anne as she passed. All the while she eyed Enrique up and down with a look that clearly said she did not consider him attractive enough to suspect Anne's behavior to be scandalous.

Anne hoped beyond all hope that the queen would question Enrique so that his accent would give him away, but she directed her questions to Anne.

"Where is my handsome captain?"

"Jonathan had business to attend to and thus could not attend tonight's masque," Anne answered, "but he sends his regards."

"Business?" Elizabeth was curious, just as Anne intended. "What business could there be that I do not know about?"

Enrique jabbed Anne in the ribs, warning her. "There are many trees on our land and he seeks a market for the lumber."

"And who is this?"

Once again Enrique's pressure on Anne's rib cage conveyed a warning.

"In Jonathan's absence, I am fortunate enough to be escorted by his uncle, Edward Leighton." She paused, hoping that the queen would take a long look at Enrique and realize that it was not the elderly statesman.

"Edward Leighton. . . ." For just a moment the Queen

acted puzzled, but she shrugged as if accepting the lie. Then, before she could ask any further questions, she was distracted by a handsome young man with flaming red hair who had just entered the room.

"Your majesty!" Like all the others, the courtier was deferential to the queen, though Anne was sure she saw him wink. "Each time I see you, I am stunned by how much more beautiful you become."

Anne knew how much Elizabeth enjoyed perennial adulation. She was vain, yet at the same time distrustful of her waning physical charms; thus she dressed herself in costly dresses, varying them every day. It was rumored that she had at least two thousand dresses. For all her finery, however, her manners could be alarming, just as they were now as she tickled the young courtier on the back as he passed her by. She was also known to publicly swear.

The Queen's procession passed through the line of groveling courtiers, but not a one even looked askance at Enrique Navarro. They were too self-centered, Anne supposed. The court was filled with ambition, jealousy, and intrigue. They were too busy appraising the red-haired courtier to notice an enemy in their midst.

It seemed to be a never-ending march past doublets and gowns, but at last Elizabeth reached the far side of the room and seated herself gracefully upon her high-backed chair despite the hindrance of the wheeled farthingale beneath her gown. Motioning to the place beside her, she didn't surprise Anne when she chose the new courtier to sit beside her.

"So much for your friend, Roger Pembroke," Anne exclaimed to Enrique, taking satisfaction in the fact that he had been supplanted in the queen's favor. Even now Anne could see Pembroke's eyes flashing fire at his opponent.

Elizabeth noted the animosity too. Her mouth curved up in a smile, cherishing the rivalry. It obviously made her feel omnipotent and furthered her longing to be desired. To fuel the competition between two handsome gallants, Elizabeth gestured to Pembroke.

"Come closer. . . ."

"Yes, your majesty."

Anne watched as the haughty, lithe-framed, elegantly dressed nobleman hastened to the queen's side as soon as he was beckoned, sweeping low in a graceful bow. For just a moment it was obvious that he felt a prick to his self-esteem, felt threatened by the gloating smile upon his rival's lips. As the queen motioned for him to sit in the other chair vacant beside her, however, his ego was soothed.

"I believe your Majesty will be pleased by my little masque," Anne heard Roger Pembroke saying. He nodded his head to that spot across the room where the costumed and masked revelers awaited.

Anne looked in the same direction, wondering which one had been hired to murder the queen. She had to find out and quickly so that she could raise the alarm and see that the culprit was apprehended—along with Enrique and Pembroke.

"Which one is it? I can hear your brain ticking in wonderment," Enrique buzzed in her ear. "Well, you will have to wait. Meanwhile, relax and enjoy the entertainment. . . ."

"Let the masque begin!" The queen declared.

With the beating of the timpani, the masque was unraveled, beginning with the courtier-dancers, those carefully costumed and masked aristocrats. Perhaps nothing suited the courtiers' love of intrigue and admiration for personal cleverness as did the masque, Anne thought. It had a spirit of intrigue about it. More often than not these guileless-appearing performances hid a sinister intent, making light of court scandals or secrets. Tonight, however, there was something even more perilous planned. Murder!

The theme seemed innocent enough, depicting the scene of the interior of a sailing ship. Anne noted that the garments of satin that clothed the young actor's body were hardly appropriate and were not the kind of garments the sailors on Jonathan's ship had worn, but then, costumes were always lavish, audacious, and flamboyant at court entertainments. Roger Pembroke was a man of incomparable wealth who could well afford the extravagance.

The stage was resplendent with color—reds, blues, yellows, and greens—as the dancers began the main dance, accompanied by the torchbearers. Pembroke had chosen to give a double masque so that the dancers were equally balanced between men and women, which gave the men something lovely to look at. Twirling and whirling, the young women passed by him with a smile. Though professional actors had been hired, the masque used a minimum of dialogue, for no speaking was really needed. By gesture and mime, the story unfolded quite clearly.

A dancer dressed in white and gold, wearing a red wig, joined the sea captain on the stage. Only a fool would not have recognized that this young woman was portraying Elizabeth. Anne sat up in her chair with a start, clenching her jaw in indignation and alarm as another dancer, dressed like a ship's captain, came on stage.

Dressed all in black and wearing a gold crown, obviously portraying Philip, King of Spain, another male dancer leaped about the stage holding what appeared to be gold in his hands. Bowing low, he paid homage to the dancer portraying the queen; then, as his head was bowed, the dancer dressed as a sea captain attacked him from behind and stole his gold.

Elizabeth was incensed. "What foul infamy is this?" she growled, looking Lord Pembroke's way.

"Please, your gracious majesty, give the dancers time to complete the masque before you pass judgment."

Reluctantly she nodded her head just as a female dancer dressed in Scottish plaid and likewise wearing a crown jumped up on stage. Dancers dressed in gray formed a circle around the dancer representing Mary of Scotland, swaying back and forth to the music.

Anne felt as if a fist was gripping her stomach. She sensed that the moment of Elizabeth's demise was at hand. Enrique rose to his feet—a knife hidden up his sleeve, she knew for certain. Enrique was not going to give a signal. He was going to kill the queen himself!

Watching as if in slow motion, Anne realized that Enrique

was dancing, heading towards the Queen as if he were part of the masque. She knew she had to act and act quickly.

"Roger! Roger, what is the meaning of this—this—?" Elizabeth was saying, her full attention on Roger Pembroke. She didn't realize that Enrique Navarro was coming towards her, but Anne did.

Rising from her chair, Anne ran forward, hurling herself at Enrique just as he slashed out with the dagger. "Your majesty!" Anne winced in pain as the blade of the knife punctured her upper arm.

A gasp hissed through the crowd. An expression of horror contorted their faces as they realized what was happening. Sympathetic onlookers stared at Anne, then changed their focus to Roger Pembroke. The stares were accusing and condemning. In that one moment, all of his self-control snapped. Bolting from his chair and reaching out, he grabbed Enrique by the front of his doublet as if trying to rescue the queen.

"By God, whoever you are, you will rue the day that you were born!"

First one man and then another drew his own sword, their faces a mask of concern. The room exploded into a melee of angry shouts and threats. And all the while Anne held her wounded arm and fought to keep from fainting.

"God's teeth, he tried to kill the queen!"

"Who is he?"

"Anne!" Like a rampaging wild boar, Jonathan plunged through the crowd. Tearing the sleeve of his shirt, he wrapped it tightly around her arm to keep it from bleeding. "You'll be all right. I'm here now. I won't let anything happen to you."

Anne could feel the gentle pressure of his fingers as they stroked her hair. Despite her pain, she smiled. "Jonathan. You found me!" She tried to say more but he silenced her.

"Later. You can explain it to me later."

Jonathan whirled around, bracing himself for a fight just as Roger Pembroke took a step forward, a sword clenched in his hand.

"No!" Anne was horrified. It seemed as if the entire room was fighting. It was difficult to tell who was on which side, for the queen or against her. From the corner of her eye, she could see that Enrique Navarro was taking advantage of the turmoil and was moving towards the door. He was going to get away.

Jonathan saw the direction of her stare and sensed that the man, whoever he was, was one of the guilty ones. "Halt!" Leaving Roger Pembroke to another swordsman, he went after the retreating man.

Enrique Navarro brandished his own sword with deadly intent. "I've always wondered what it would be like to spill your blood. Now I will find out."

"Navarro!" Despite the disguise, Jonathan recognized his adversary's voice.

Fearing the outcome of such a battle, Anne stepped in front of Jonathan, only to be gently but firmly pushed aside. "I will not hide behind a woman's skirts, most especially yours. Keep out of the way." Jonathan had just enough time to block the Spaniard's blow. "So I see you will not talk reason."

"Reason? You Englishmen know nothing of reason, only of piracy." Navarro struck out again. The blow was parried just in time. A cry of anger was Navarro's reaction as he lunged again. Once again the thrust was parried.

The sound of sword on sword rent the air as the two fought a furious battle, a test of strength and of skill. Though at first Anne had worried about Jonathan's fate, she had to admit that he was making his usual show of prowess. Reacting to the warning of his senses, his sword arm swung forward again and again as she watched in horror-struck fascination.

"You are a pirate! But you will not steal my wife."

"I won't have to. I'll kill you and make Anne a widow. . . ."

"To the contrary, Señor Leighton, I will kill you!"

"Halt!" Elizabeth's shrill voice pierced the air. "I don't want any more fighting here." It seemed the battle would not progress long enough to see who would be the victor, for Elizabeth ordered Navarro to be taken away by the guards she had summoned to restore law and order.

"The headsman's axe will do just as well in ridding me of you," Jonathan exclaimed as he put down his sword.

"I won't lose my head!" In a scene reminiscent of that time aboard Jonathan's ship, Navarro headed for one of the windows and balanced on the ledge.

"Arrest him in the queen's name!" one of the guards yelled out. "Put all the traitorous bastards in chains." His glare at Pembroke said that he wanted him to be the first.

Fearing that somehow Navarro would escape, Jonathan took several steps in his direction. The Spaniard was bluffing. He wouldn't jump. More than anything in the world he wanted to see him poised beneath the headsman's axe, even if he had to apprehend Enrique Navarro himself.

"You won't jump. It would be instant death."

"Ah, but you are wrong, Señor!" In one daring leap, Navarro jumped from the open window, his arms spread out like a bird's wings as he sailed through the air.

Chapter Twenty-Seven

Enrique Navarro had more lives than a cat! Leaning out the window, Jonathan watched as he hit a bush, rolled off onto the ground with a thud, lay stunned for a moment, then got up, limping severely and holding his side as he ran.

"God's teeth, he survived! And he's getting away!"

Jonathan watched in helpless frustration as the man he hated above all men headed for King Street, the road that divided the palace in two. Pushing and shoving at anyone who got in his way, he was outdistancing the guards who ran in pursuit.

"I want that man!" Elizabeth shouted, breaking into the swear words she was known to use quite frequently when provoked.

"So do I," Jonathan growled, feeling the primitive emotion of hatred totally engulf him. God help him, he had wanted the man dead. It seemed, however, that once more Navarro had triumphed.

"Send for Walsingham! I want him to enlist every spy in his employ to find that horrible man." Though she was making a show at bravery, it was obvious that Elizabeth was shaken by the attempt on her life.

"If not for Anne . . ." Hurrying to Anne's side, Jonathan was the epitome of tender concern as he cradled her in his arms. "How is your arm? Did it stop bleeding?"

"Not yet!" Anne's eyes met Jonathan's and she steeled herself for the moment that was to come. A moment far more painful than her wound. "Jonathan . . ."

"Hush . . . don't talk. Just lie still, my love. Elizabeth's own physician has been called to help you."

"He'll want to bleed me, but I have lost enough blood. I just want to lie here until I regain some strength, and then I want to go home!"

Home! The word tore at her heart. She couldn't go home with Jonathan. She wasn't his wife. In truth, she never had been, and yet she loved him. Perhaps she had never really realized how much until this very minute.

"I'll take you home. I'll help Margaret nurse you. You'll soon be as good as new." Bending down, he kissed her forehead. "You saved Elizabeth's life! No man has ever been more brave!"

Clenching her fingers, trying to ignore the painful tightening in her stomach and in her heart, Anne looked him in the eye. There was only one thing to do, one thing she could say, though it broke her heart to even contemplate it. "I can't go with you, Jonathan."

He shook his head, denying the truth. "You can and you will!"

"No. Enrique is alive, and that means that I am *not* your wife."

"You are in my heart!"

"That doesn't matter. . . ." The words died in her throat as she fought a sob.

"Then I will be content being lovers until we can wed again."

"No." Tearfully Anne explained that there was a difference now that she knew Enrique was alive. "Until my vows to my husband are torn asunder, I will not commit adultery, not even in my heart."

Jonathan was thunderstruck. "You can't mean it!" His

fingers grasped her hand. He felt her quiver at his touch. "I love you. I would never do anything to cause you shame."

Tears spilled down her flushed face as she confided to him all that had happened since she had first come face to face with her husband. She blamed herself, whispering over and over that somehow she should have known Enrique was alive.

"Walsingham knew. All along he knew," Jonathan confessed, trying to soothe her feeling of self-condemnation.

"Walsingham?"

"Aye. Don't blame yourself, blame him for keeping such a secret for his own selfish purposes." Jonathan didn't realize that he was condemning himself as he talked, by unwittingly revealing Walsingham's plan to her. Until he saw the pained look in her eyes.

"And what of you? Did you know too?"

Jonathan couldn't lie. Not now. He told her the whole story, including Walsingham's insistence that he keep the truth from her. "I hoped that Navarro would just disappear so that we could be happy!"

"Happy!" Anne jerked her hand away. "How could we ever be happy when our marriage was a lie?" As she looked up at him, she knew she could never forgive him for keeping such information from her. He had made a bigamist of her, an adulteress and a whore. She whispered, "Love means trust. There can be no secrets."

"But Walsingham had information on your brother." Oh, why couldn't she see. "I wanted to save you and save him!"

"It doesn't matter. Whatever we shared has been destroyed."

"Anne . . ." He tried to take her in his arms, to comfort her, but she flung herself free of his embrace.

"Leave me alone! Your touch cheapens me. You knew. All along you knew we were not man and wife. You knew, and yet you let me go on thinking . . . dreaming . . . hoping for the future. . . ."

"There can still be a future for us, Anne. The Queen can

have your marriage declared invalid and we can say our vows again."

"No! She cannot. It is far more complicated than that. You don't understand. . . ." She turned over on her side, pulling her knees up beneath her chin. All her life Anne had been a devout Catholic, as fervent in her beliefs as she was in loyalty to her country and her queen. She did not want to be damned in God's eyes.

"I understand that I love you!" Jonathan was a brave man, yet this encounter had left him shaken. It was as if he was watching his life crumble into ashes. "Anne, let me explain. . . ."

"No . . . I don't want to hear." Putting her hands over her ears, Anne tried to sort things out in her mind, wondering why God would bring Jonathan Leighton into her life only to torment her with unfulfilled dreams.

I was a fool to enter into marriage with Enrique Navarro! And yet I am tied to him until the Church says otherwise. That could take a very long time.

"Anne!" He nearly screamed her name.

She could never have expected that pushing him away could cause her such pain, such longing, and yet it did. A soft groan of despair tore from her throat. Their gazes locked again in silence for the length of a heartbeat.

"I do not want to see you again, Jonathan. I have to think . . ."

"You don't want to see me?" He had feared she would be angry, but he had never thought she would banish him from her life.

"Not until matters are settled concerning my marriage." A spasm of pain passed briefly across her face.

"Then I will do as you ask, Anne." Somehow he managed the words. "But if you ever have need of me, remember that above all I will always care about you. First and foremost, I am your friend."

"I have no need of your friendship, sir," Anne retorted, regretting the words as soon as they left her lips. She did need him to care, so very much. More so now that her world had been turned upside down.

Jonathan's eyes burned into hers like blue flames. "Then from this moment on, I will cease to be in your presence. The queen has need of able seamen to aid her against the armada Spain is building. I'll spend my days on board my ship. That is where I truly belong."

Jonathan's features appeared to be carved in stone, except where a muscle in his jaw twitched with suppressed anger, not at her as much as at himself. He should have told her the truth and the devil with Walsingham. But he hadn't. And now all was lost.

PART THREE

THE GOLDEN HEART

ENGLAND, 1588

"What stronger breastplate than a heart untainted!"

—Shakespeare, *Henry VI, Part Two, III, 2*

Chapter Twenty-Eight

It was a tumultuous time in England. Once again the city rang with bells, this time warning of impending danger from Spain. Anne remembered, however, another chime of bells as the citizens of London heard about Mary Stuart's fate. Feeling that she could hesitate no longer, Elizabeth had signed the death warrant for the imprisoned queen; then, in a hurried ceremony held in the great hall of Fotheringay, Mary had been beheaded. Two masked executioners, asking her forgiveness, had been instrumental in taking her life. It was said that the wig fell from her severed head and disclosed her white hair. So much grief and heartache had aged her that, although she was only forty-two, she had looked much older.

"Mary. . . ." Though Anne had never even seen Mary Stuart, though she considered herself a loyal Englishwoman, she nevertheless felt a deep sadness. In some ways Mary Stuart had been a pawn in a fatal game of chess that had cost her life.

In the wake of the execution, a rider from Fotheringay had ridden in to London with the news. An intolerable cloud had been lifted; a great dread was gone forever. The continued threat to Elizabeth had been banished with the rival queen's death, he had proclaimed. As long as Mary lived, the chances were high that she might outlive her cousin, take the throne, and restore the old religion and the old times. So fretted the people in the southern and eastern counties and London, who had been nurtured on the English Bible and Cranmer's *Book of Common Prayer*. People who had learned to fear and hate papists, Spaniards, and the thought of foreign domination.

"God bless good Queen Bess!" Anne had heard the people cry out.

For years many English had been haunted by the fear that a failure in the Tudor line would toss the crown back into the arena to be fought for by contending factions, a recurrence of the anarchy called the Wars of the Roses. The Protestants had heard bloody tales from merchants and refugees of what had happened to the Huguenots in France and about the unfortunates who had been tortured by the Inquisition, and they feared a similar fate if Catholicism returned to the land. As long as Elizabeth reigned, they need not fear. They did not seem to understand that most Catholics of the realm would have been just as horrified by such acts of violence.

The last few years had been turbulent. There had been plots and rumors of plots as long as Anne could remember. A half-crazed youth who had boasted he would kill the queen had been taken, pistol in hand, within a hundred yards of her. Then the papers found on Francis Throckmorton revealed a widespread Catholic plot for a rising, the liberation of Mary, the assassination of the queen, and the invasion of the realm by Guisard troops. Then had come William Parry's cold-blooded revelation that he had been promised plenary absolution from Rome for the murder of the queen, besides substantial earthly benefits. The Babington conspiracy had been fresh in their minds when the murder of the Prince of Orange, another champion of Protestantism, had occurred.

England was still shuddering at the dangers when Elizabeth's life had again been endangered, and Anne had averted tragedy by stepping in the way of the dagger. Anne had been proclaimed a true heroine. All suspicion against her and her brother had dissolved. Anne had been rewarded with money, a London townhouse, and the Queen's gratitude and favor. Even so, Anne felt a deep sadness. No amount of adulation could ever equal the happiness she had felt with Jonathan.

Would she ever see him again? She had begun to fear that he would make good on his promise to leave her alone. It had already been over a year since she last saw him, though she had heard about his daring strikes against the Spaniards. He and Sir Francis Drake had cruised off the coast of Spain and, contrary to Elizabeth's wish, had attacked Spanish shipping, burnt the half-finished and unmanned ships at Cadiz, and enacted enormous damage to the Spanish navy. Unfortunately, however, the Spaniards had recouped their losses.

As Anne watched from the window of the townhouse she had made her home, she saw the bonfires, heard the bells, and both heard and saw the salvos that illuminated the sky. The citizens of London gave one collective groan as they realized the threat of Spanish invasion was real. The Spanish Armada, under the command of the Duke of Medina Sidonia, had sailed from Portugal and was heading for the British Isles.

The bells pealed louder and louder as more people heard the news. Most felt betrayed, for they had believed a new era had begun with Mary Stuart's death and that now all men would live in peace. Elizabeth had won the battle of the queens, they chattered. And yet they were wrong, for just as the Queen of Scots had envisioned, Mary's brave death seemed to have made her a martyr all over Europe and in the northern and western counties of England.

The beheading of Mary Stuart would not be the end of turmoil but the beginning. The execution had caused Catholics everywhere to sympathize with Spain and regard the Armada that was being built as a crusade against the most dangerous enemy of the Faith. Pope Sixtus V agreed to renew the excommunication of the queen and to grant a large subsidy to "la Armada Invencible," as it was being called. Worse yet, the beheading of Mary Stuart had seemingly made it more difficult for Anne to have her marriage to Enrique Navarro declared invalid, particularly because of her wish to marry a Protestant who had not only been favored by the English queen but had been one of her privateers.

Tired of hearing the tumult outside, Anne closed and latched the window in her bedchamber. She felt depressed and on edge. Her world was empty. Having experienced love only to be alone made the coming spring, that time of love and frolic, only a mockery. How could she even pretend to be happy?

All her life Anne had been stubborn and too quick to scold. Now she was paying for it dearly. She had verbally lashed out at Jonathan because he had not told her Enrique was alive, and in so doing, she had jeopardized her future happiness. Her despair went beyond tears. She felt hollow inside. Alone.

"I love him. I should have been content just being in his arms, even if it was as his mistress. . . ." Instead she had been so self-righteous.

Looking down at the scar on her arm, a vivid reminder of that day, Anne could barely control her grief for what might have been. Her dreams had been shattered and the future appeared to be filled with loneliness.

Every time she saw a ship coming into London, her heart lurched in her breast, hoping that it was Jonathan, that he had returned for her. Alas, each time she was disappointed. It seemed that even the breeze called out his name. Closing her eyes, she remembered their nights together, her body tingling with the very thought of it. He had made her a woman, had made her body come alive. That memory was more precious to her than gold. Would she ever see him again? Dear God, how she wanted to.

In sad dejection, Anne slid down in the chair by the window. Wrapping her arms about her knees, she drew them against her chest, resting her chin on top. *Oh, Jonathan,* she thought, sighing deeply. *I do love you so.* She hugged herself, pretending for a moment that her arms were his. Had she experienced love only to lose it? That and not the threat of the Armada was her greatest fear.

The waters of the ocean were a crystal clear blue, shimmering as far as the eye could see. From the deck of the *Red Dragon* all looked peaceful. London basked tranquilly in the late afternoon sun, or so it seemed. Deceptive. Fraudulent, Jonathan Leighton thought as he stood at the rail. In truth the city was in a state of turbulence. Throughout the city, nay the very country, there was a sense of imminent peril. The alarm had been raised that Philip II of Spain, ruler of the most powerful empire the world had ever seen and foremost defender of the Holy Roman Church, had marshaled all his forces hoping to alter the shape of the world and the manner in which men thought and worshipped. To this end he had sent the Spanish Armada, the greatest battle fleet the world had ever known.

Rumors had spread and dire forebodings were heard. The Armada, it was said, consisted of some five-hundred ships, galleons, and towering carracks, all heavily cannoned and carrying one-hundred thousand veteran fighting men who were more than sufficient to wreak havoc and end England's freedom.

"Are ye nervous, Cap'n?" Falkhearst's quaking knees proved that if Jonathan wasn't, he was.

"Either we will win or we will lose. I am prepared for either," Jonathan answered, "though to be truthful, I would much rather win."

"How can we, Cap'n? They're expert with dagger and pike. And you know yourself that their ships are twice again as large as ours. We're doomed."

"We're not! Not unless we lose faith in ourselves." Jonathan and Drake knew that their ships were smaller, lighter, and more maneuverable than the Spanish ships. What was more, John Hawkins had seen to the refurbishing and building of the queen's warships for the last ten years. Jonathan had an idea—to send in fireships among the great wooden galleons and burn them to hell. If the Armada sailed into the Channel itself, all England would be imperiled.

Jonathan knew what hung in the balance. The battle would determine whether Philip could achieve his dream of bringing all Europe under Catholic rule. It would decide if France would remain a sovereign power, and even more far-reaching, if Spain could gain complete control over the Americas. It also would decide if Anne was lost to him forever, for if Philip won, there would be no hope of wrenching her from the matrimonial bonds that tied her to Enrique Navarro.

The blue sky was veiled by swirling storms. The wind was a tormenting, powerful force, blowing first from the east, then the north, then south and just as quickly east again. High, foam-capped waves crashed against the shores, swelling the waters of the Channel. It was a punishing sea. The Spaniards had picked a hell of a time for a fight, Jonathan noted as he adjusted his spyglass. But then, they had undoubtedly been expecting a tranquil spring tide.

Jonathan had heard reports that the Armada had found it necessary to put back in the harbor of Corunna to refit, but now they had appeared, taunting him on the horizon. Tension crackled on deck. Tempers were short.

"We should have taken the offensive long ago and attacked at a time and place of our own choosing," he said aloud. But they hadn't, and now all he and his men could do was to watch as the stage was set and the players readied themselves for the inevitable conflict. A conflict of ideologies in which the future of the world hung in the balance.

"They're sailing in a strange formation," one of the sailors exclaimed.

"The ominous crescent. It's a formation designed to crush all opposition. They close in on the enemy, grapple, and then board. They think they will overwhelm us."

"What should we do, Cap'n?"

Jonathan could see the bows of the warships pitch and roll and yaw as great sprays of white burst across the decks. Just as it did on his own ships, the masts swept the horizon as the wind whistled through the rigging. Men scrabbled not to be washed overboard.

"What shall we do? Whatever it takes to keep from being obliged to grapple." Jonathan thought a moment. "We'll attack the wings of the crescent, where the strongest galleons are placed."

"Are you sure, Cap'n?" Falkhearst grabbed for a rope and hung on for dear life as the violent rolling of the ship nearly knocked him down. He gasped as some of the ship's equipment that was not lashed to the deck went skittering from one rail to the other.

Jonathan looked Falkhearst right in the eye. "I'm sure." He gave the order to sail out in a line. "For God, for the Queen, and for England."

The Armada was impressive, the number of ships far greater than anything Jonathan had ever seen before. The galleons were huge and heavily gunned, the variety of ships stunning and worrisome. *But never underrate the courage and seamanship of an Englishman,* he thought.

"Look, Cap'n . . . on the shore."

Jonathan was distracted by Falkhurt's gasp long enough to see that all along the shore, smoke had begun to rise.

Signal fires . . . summoning Englishmen to arms as well as sending the news of the Spanish fleet inland.

"At least the Spaniards will have a run for their money if they get by us," an old sailor exclaimed.

"They won't get by us!" On that, Jonathan was determined, yet puzzled too. It was strange that the Spaniards had made no effort to attack yet. Now why was that? Overconfidence? Undoubtedly. But Jonathan would soon show them. He would give the order to attack.

Crewmen scuttled back and forth across the deck as Jonathan and Falkhearst shouted orders. "Ready the cannons and send our Spaniard friends a welcome." Several rousing loud booms and a cloud of smoke began the battle. Under

Jonathan's orders, the ship bore down on King Philip's vessels.

Thunder growled. Jagged flashes of lightning cut through the sky. The wind whipped at the skirts of Anne's gown as she stood on the dock watching the English ships prepared for battle.

"Jonathan is out there." She could see the carved head of a dragon that decorated his ship and felt her pulse quicken. Next to Drake and Hawkins, Jonathan was the queen's most revered naval commander. But could he work miracles?

"The winds favor our ships," she heard an old wizzened sailor mumble to himself. "We can win if we are patient."

"We can win?" Anne wanted reassurance.

"Aye, that we can, young woman." He was flattered by her attention. "Elizabeth has spent a pretty penny on ships and the like. Hawkins has been building men-of-war for the queen's navy for just such an emergency. And I should know. I'm London's foremost shipbuilder."

"But their ships are so much larger. . . ." If Jonathan didn't feel intimidated, Anne did just looking at them.

"By God, that doesn't mean a wit. My ships are built to low lines and narrow beam. The Spanish decks are too high. Their guns will fire above our English ships and will only do minor damage. You'll see." He grinned. "If anything, those Spanish monstrosities will be so much slower than our sleek little vessels that we will make them look like buffoons."

The man was so sure of himself, so determined that the English would win, that Anne felt a great sense of relief. Besides, when she thought back to the encounter of Jonathan's *White Griffin* with the Spanish ship she and Enrique had been on so long ago, she remembered how the English had skillfully outmaneuvered the galleon.

"Jonathan will be victorious. . . ." She had to believe that because even a flicker of doubt or the thought of Jonathan's defeat and possible demise filled her with too much grief.

We'll be reunited again someday. . . . She had to have that dream.

All over London the streets buzzed with excitement and fear. As Anne stood at the dock, she was joined by more and more people who wanted to cheer their men on to victory. Elizabeth had made her aims very clear. Any invasion would be met with the full force of English strength from all the people, she had said.

"We shall defend our island, whatever the cost may be. We shall fight in the fields and in the streets. We shall fight in the hills. We shall never surrender," she had said in an address to her troops and to her people.

In truth, there were more volunteers signing up for the militia than a man, or woman, could ever count. Catholic and Protestant alike had put aside their differences for the moment and come to the defense of their motherland.

Squinting her eyes, Anne stared out to sea, watching the preparations for a giant chess game. It appeared that the Spaniards were waiting for the English to come close enough for grappling. Instead, the light English vessels scurried around the heavy Spanish galleons, firing broadsides as they went.

"Does this bring back memories, *querida?*" The sound of Enrique Navarro's voice chilled Anne's blood.

"What are you doing here?" she asked, turning around to face him.

"I wanted to be with my wife to watch Spain's victory," he answered, seemingly unafraid of being completely surrounded by Englishmen.

"You means Spain's defeat!"

"Of course, the battle could go either way. That's why I intend to be prepared." Something in his voice filled Anne with fear.

"What do you mean?"

"Only that I wish for my wife to join me on a ship waiting to sail out of England for Spain."

From out of the crowd four men came forward to join

Navarro, all brandishing daggers. That they meant to menace Anne was obvious by their expressions.

"You can't even think to abduct me. All I have to do is to call out, and I'll have the whole of London down on your head."

"Ah, *querida* . . . I think not. You see, my timing was perfect. No one will even notice what I do."

The ship's cannons roared like a continuous roll of drums. The air grew thick with smoke. The smell of rancid gunpowder made Anne cough and sneeze. Enrique was right. It was the perfect time for a kidnapping. Not only was the air rumbling with cannon fire, the people's excited shouts and cries drowned out any sound she might have made.

Anne's eyes darted left and right. She wouldn't let Enrique take her away. She'd fight with every bit of strength she had, even if she was outnumbered.

"Come with me peacefully, Ana. I do not want to hurt you."

"Go to the devil!" Anne started to scream, but Enrique's hand muffled the sound. Her hands were pinioned behind her back, a strong arm wrapped around her waist as she was pushed, pulled, and dragged towards a waiting ship.

Chapter Twenty-Nine

Jonathan's eyes were slits of weariness as he stood on the deck. It had been an exhausting battle that had taken the English ships from the Channel to Plymouth to Calais and back again. Still, the fighting continued.

The Spaniards had waited for the English to come close enough for grappling, but the ships under Jonathan's command had surprised them and scurried around the heavy Spanish galleons, firing broadsides as they went. The Spanish had fired back, but their decks were too high and their guns fired far above the *Red Dragon* and other English ships, doing only minor damage.

The English ships were easily maneuvered and this, coupled with their speed, made it easy for them to sail beneath the cannon fire, leaving the Spaniards helpless and confused. As night had fallen, they had fled before the wind, leaving one of their ships to be taken by Drake. Another was blown up, reportedly by a mutinous German gunner, and the wreck had fallen into English hands. As luck would have it, both ships contained ammunition, which was promptly transferred to Jonathan's and Drake's ships. Even so, Jonathan knew they had only enough ammunition left for a day's fighting.

"But we will make the most of it," he swore to Falkhearst. "We have to prevent a landing on English soil at all costs." Jonathan feared that the aim of the Spaniards was to take over one of the English coastal towns to use as a base for their ships.

Jonathan had heard that Howard, fighting near the Isle of Wight, had sailed his flagship into the center of the Armada, exchanging broadsides with every galleon that he passed. That daring, and the accuracy of the English cannon fire, had seemingly broken the Spanish morale.

"We'll show them how to fight, won't we, Cap'n. . . ."

"That we will! We'll make them feel like old men, slow and crippled with gout, while we sprint through the water like sea sprites." At the very thought of the upcoming skirmish, Jonathan felt rejuvenated. Splashing water from the rain barrel onto his face, he prepared for another battle.

"Captain Howard has sent me a message. He vows we have to deal a death blow to the Spaniards."

"How, Cap'n?"

"Fire ships!"

"Fire ships?"

"He wants to set fire to eight small and dispensable vessels and sail them into the Spanish fleet. We need ships and combustibles to accomplish the deed."

The original plan was to wait until ships could be found for the mission, but hoping to take advantage of the south-west wind and to strike quickly, the captains offered up their own ships to the cause. Drake offered one of his ships, Hawkins one of his, Jonathan gave his newly bestowed *Golden Lion* to add to five other ships contributed. The work of getting the ships ready had begun.

"I'll need volunteers to go with me while Falkhearst mans the *Red Dragon* in my absence."

"I'll go, Captain." A sailor named Farnsworth stepped forward.

"And I." Another sailor named Bates, raised his hand.

"Don't leave me behind!" A small but daring young sailor stepped in front of the other two.

Jonathan's smile displayed his gratitude for their loyalty and bravery. "Let's go!"

Crewmen scuttled back and forth across the deck as Falkhearst now shouted orders. The plan was to engage the Spaniards in a minor skirmish to distract them from the preparations under way for the real mission to come.

"Ready the cannons and send our Spanish friends a welcome." Several rousing loud booms and a cloud of smoke began another battle. Under Falkhearst's orders, the ship bore down on the Spanish Fleet.

Water barrels and stores were removed, and in their place were packed anything and everything that could be burned. The guns were left in place and loaded so that they would go off when the flames became hot enough, to intensify the destruction and thereby create terror among the enemy crews.

By midnight all preparations were made and the fireships stood in line, floating incendiaries. Skeleton crews were aboard each ship awaiting the musket shot that would signal the beginning of the attack.

Jonathan watched and waited. When the tide was running powerfully inshore, toward the anchored enemy fleet, when the wind was blowing in the direction to favor the fire ships, the signal was given.

"Let's go."

Eight ships were fired and set free, their crews scrambling into waiting longboats to sail to safety. Close abreast, the fireships moved toward the Spanish fleet, flames licking at the riggings as they sailed. Sparks danced along the decks; flames climbed the masts. In an eerie combination of smoke and fire, the vessels plowed through the night with ghostly brilliance.

"That will give them something to talk about!" Jonathan exclaimed, thankful that everything had worked out perfectly. As the burning vessels came closer to the Spanish ships, the fires grew hotter, igniting the first guns. Soon the sound of explosions rocked the air.

"We did it, Cap'n! Or rather, you did it!" Falkhearst danced a little jig. But the fight was just beginning. "Fire!"

The roar of cannons shattered the silence of the sea. The air was filled with the suffocating stench of smoke and powder. The sound of cannon fire was deafening, nearly drowning out Jonathan's commands as he strode back and forth across the deck waving his arms.

"Again, fire!" A volley of cannon balls cut to pieces everything in their path, damaging the hull and deck of one of the galleons before the Spaniards had time to counterattack. So far, so good, Jonathan thought. "Reload!"

Though he kept his silence, not even baring his soul to Falkhearst, who had been his first mate since he could remember, Jonathan knew that if the Spanish were given a chance to retaliate in full force, they could well blast the *Red Dragon* out of the water. He could not allow that to happen.

Aiding the men himself, Jonathan worked frantically, cramming the cannon with powder and ball, ramming it down the muzzle again and again. The huge guns were fired with deadly accuracy, shrouding the ship in cannon smoke.

"She's hit, Cap'n," Falkhearst called out.

It was total pandemonium. Some of the Spaniards jumped ship; others cried out in fear. In a scene of mounting confusion, ships crashed blindly into one another. Most were unable to maneuver and drifted with the tide. Puffs of smoke billowed from the enemy vessels as the crashing creak of wood splintered the railings

"We'll teach them to sail into English waters!" Jonathan shouted.

The strategy of the fireships had worked to perfection. With eight small ships the English had managed to break Spanish discipline, shatter the heretofore impregnable crescent, and scatter the world's mightiest sea force. At the same time they had struck fear into the hearts of King Philip's fighting men.

"And that's only the beginning. . . ."

Jonathan watched as Elizabeth's Lord Admiral ordered his captains to move in for the kill, their sails ballooning in the wind, their guns run out, and musketmen at the rails.

"For God, for the Queen, and for England!"

It was a cry that was repeated again and again until at last, after a battle off the French coast at Gravelines, the Armada was disabled. Ships had been sunk, men killed, and the threat to England subdued—but at a heavy price. As Jonathan looked out at the ocean, he could see blood flowing from the decks into the sea.

"Look, Cap'n, they're running away . . . retreating." Falkhearst pounded on his chest as if he and he alone had sent them fleeing.

"They *are* withdrawing." What was more, they were headed into the North Sea. Jonathan and several of the ships followed as far as the Firth of Forth, just to make certain the Spaniards were not planning anything coy. Lacking food and ammunition, however, they returned to port.

"They are going back to Spain where they belong!" Falkhearst announced to the crew amidst cheers.

The taste of victory was sweet. Jonathan felt proud of his men, proud of England, and proud of himself. His satisfaction was to be short-lived, however, when one of the faltering Spanish ships signaled with flags from the deck that they wanted to talk with the captain of the *Red Dragon*.

"Talk? What about? Do they want an escort back to Spain?" Jonathan said amidst loud guffaws from his men.

"Careful, Cap'n. It could be a trap. . . ." He reached out. "Give me that spyglass." Squinting through the eyepiece, he gasped, then swore. "It can't be!"

"What is it?" Jonathan took the spyglass and held it to his eye. "God's teeth . . . I must be imagining things. No!" He stared in awed trepidation. "No! No! It can't be," he said again. Oh, but it was. Dressed all in red, her dark hair blowing in the wind, Anne stood at the railing of one of the Spanish ships. Beside her stood a man Jonathan knew only too well. "Navarro!"

There could be no hesitation, no other choice. Jonathan had to ensure Anne's safety no matter what terms Navarro might propose.

"What shall we do, Captain ? About the woman on board that ship, I mean?" a young sailor asked.

"We honor the Spaniard's request to talk." The decision was made. Jonathan gave the order to sail towards the Spanish ship.

Anne felt sick to her stomach. She had watched the ongoing battle in apprehension and horror, fearing Jonathan would be killed at any moment. That he had not been slaughtered, maimed, or wounded had seemed a miracle. Now, as she stared at the English ship and saw his familiar blond-haired, broad-shouldered figure staring back at her, she felt a shiver of dread that went all the way down to her bones.

"What are you planning, Enrique? Something sinister, I would suppose."

"To the contrary, I am merely seeing to my well-being, *querida!*"

"Your well-being?"

With a snarl he explained, "I brought you aboard just in case the worst happened and the English managed to hold their own." He grabbed her arm. "You see, you are my key to getting back to Spain safely."

"I'm your hostage!"

"You are my guest. . . ." He smiled apologetically. "And my bait."

"You've set a trap for him."

"His ships are angling to cut off all escape. What other choice did I have?" His smile was evil. "Besides, it would seem to me that he and I have an old score to settle."

Anne's defiance softened in the face of reality. She swallowed her pride. "Please, Enrique. Don't harm him." She struck her own bargain. "If you let him be, I'll gladly be your hostage all the way to Spain without giving you any trouble."

He thought for a moment, then shook his head. "I do not want to insult you, *querida,* but the truth is, I do not care if you give me trouble or not, but I do desire above all things to see your captain dead! It would make me a hero in Philip's eyes, you see, and soothe my shattered pride." He revealed his plan to her with smug satisfaction. "I am going to lure your captain towards this ship using you as the prize. When the ship draws close enough, boom—we will blow her out of the water!"

Navarro's words were echoed by a thunderous explosion and belching smoke as the combat began.

"What the devil?" The *Red Dragon* shuddered. Falkhearst and Jonathan were knocked to the deck. The shattered mainmast came down in a deadly hail of splinters.

"The ship's been hit!" Pandemonium broke loose, but Jonathan quickly staggered to his feet and regained order, just as the ship lurched again. "We're hit again." The mainsail flopped about like a broken wing. "Shall we fire back, Captain?"

"No." Jonathan couldn't take a chance on Anne being harmed.

"But Captain—"

"The woman is English. I don't want to take the chance of her being killed." Jonathan had to think of a way to save Anne *and* his ship.

"But what if things get worse? Cap'n?"

"We'll deal with the worst when it happens," Jonathan answered, hoping that Edmund understood.

And then the worst did happen as the Spanish ship closed in. There was a boom of cannon fire, a splinter of wood, and a gasp of pain as Falkhearst stepped right in front of Jonathan, pushing him out of the way of danger.

Everything moved in slow motion. Jonathan saw Falkhearst fall, knew he had taken the brunt of the explosion in order to save him. Then he was kneeling down beside him. "No!" Blood gushed from a wound in Edmund's shoulder and side, and though he desperately tried to staunch the flow with torn fragments of his doublet, Jonathan feared that Edmund Falkhearst was dying.

"Cap'n. . . ." he breathed. "Don't worry about me. You've got to save Annie . . ."

"Hush. I'll worry about what to do as soon as you are patched up." Unshed tears stung Jonathan's eyes as he remembered how good to him Falkhearst had always been. Like a father, like a brother, like a trusted friend. He couldn't see him die.

"No. I . . . I've . . ." He winced with pain. ". . . sailed me last . . ."

"Don't say such a thing. You'll be right beside me when we sail to the New World, just as we always planned."

Falkhearst tried to smile. "I want to see the dragons. . ."

"The alligators . . ."

"The ones you told me about that gobbled up—" He gasped at the pain that shot through him. "Take care of Walsingham for me . . . promise?"

"I'll take care of Walsingham and *you.*"

A barrage of cannon fire shattered the railing. Jonathan was distracted for just a moment. When he turned back to Falkhearst he could see that he had closed his eyes.

"Edmund!" Fearing the worst, he gently nudged him. "Don't you die, do you hear? I'm going to need your help in freeing Anne from that devil."

Falkhearst's eyes popped open. "It's simple, Cap'n. We . . . we can't shoot at the ship as . . . as long as . . . she . . ." He paused, fighting against the pain.

Jonathan finished for him. "As long as she's aboard." He gave a whoop of triumph. "That's it!" Anne had jumped from his ship and been able to swim from the harbor all the way to dry dock. It would be a much shorter distance from ship to ship. But how could he make her understand what he wanted her to do?

* * *

With a shout of victory, the crew of the ship congratulated each other on having hit the *Red Dragon,* while Anne looked on in horror and fear. "God, please listen. Don't let him be dead! Please don't let him be dead." So praying, she propelled herself past the cheering sailors on the forecastle deck and stood at the railing.

Where was he? And why, oh why, had he so foolishly decided not to fight or flee? The answer was simple. Because of *her.*

"Just as Enrique perceived . . ." Well, she wouldn't allow such a sacrifice! Jonathan thought to protect her, but she would be the one to protect him! If she could only think of a way.

"He's dead. I saw him fall. . . ." Enrique put an arm around Anne's waist as if to protect her, but Anne was belligerent, shrugging off his arm. "He's not dead! I'd feel it if he were."

"Well, if he is not, he soon will be. The captain is giving orders to fire again."

"Is he?" Anne acted quickly. Before Enrique could sense her intentions, she reached for the handle of his sword and pulled it free of its sheath. Staring right into Enrique's eyes, she said, "Tell the captain not to fire."

"I will not!" Enrique Navarro squared his shoulders, assuming Anne's actions to be nothing but a bluff.

Anne pressed the tip of the sword against his throat so tightly that she drew blood. She knew from experience that when it came to danger, Enrique was a coward. "Tell him not to fire."

"You will not kill me!"

"That is your hope, but are you certain?" Anne increased the pressure of the sword against his flesh.

For just a moment Navarro's bravado wavered. "Even if you kill me, you can't kill all the others."

"No, I can't, but I will have the grim satisfaction of making myself a widow once and for all!"

Her voice was so determined, so cold, that Enrique Navarro shivered. "You hate me so much?"

"If you harm one hair on Jonathan's head, I will hate you forever." Her voice was stern. "Call off the fighting—now!"

He shrugged apologetically. "Alas, I fear that I cannot," he said, calling her bluff, "for I am not the only one who cries out for revenge. There were many killed."

Anne tensed. Out of the corner of her eye, she could see the Spaniards closing in around Enrique, around her. She felt a surge of desperation and confusion. What could she do now?

For just a fleeting moment she turned around and stared out at the *Red Dragon*. Jonathan was at the railing, and as their eyes met, he made a diving gesture with his hand. That gave her an idea.

"Give me the sword, *querida*. I will see that no harm comes to you," Enrique was saying.

Anne looked at Enrique, then back at Jonathan, and in that moment she made up her mind.

"Ana . . . please . . . give it to me!"

Relaxing her grip on the sword, Anne pretended to give in to Enrique's command. Then as he reached for the sword, she moved towards the railing, grabbed the wood firmly to hoist herself up and, balancing for just a heartbeat, she jumped.

For a brief instant, Anne's skirts slowed her descent to the ocean, and she felt as if she were floating on air. Then, as she hit the water with a thud, her heavy, water-soaked skirts dragged her under. She cried out, but her voice was muffled by the water.

"Anne!" Jonathan's voice was a scream as he leaned over the rail. She was going to be dragged under by the sea! She was going to drown. "No"! He gasped and tried to speak, but the agony in his soul at the very thought of losing her was too severe for words.

"Captain . . . Shall we lower a boat?" a young sailor asked.

Jonathan scarcely heard him. His only thought was Anne. Ignoring the danger, Jonathan tugged off his boots, climbed up on the railing, and dove into the ocean as cannon fire exploded around him.

Holding his breath, Jonathan plunged into the water's depths. Then, with strong, bold strokes, he swam towards the spot where Anne had dived into the water, searching everywhere. There was no sign of her. He had seen her go over the side, but she had quickly disappeared beneath the waves.

Anne! Anne! He called out her name mentally and vocally as he came up for air, hoping that somehow she might be able to sense his presence. Then, taking a deep breath, he dove deep into the sea again, stubborn in his resolve to find her. He stayed under until his lungs were screaming for air, then surfaced. Treading water, he continued his search, but he was growing winded and fatigued. His strength was giving out. And all the while there was the added danger of getting caught in the crossfire. Even so, he wouldn't give up.

Keeping his head above water, Jonathan looked around him, taking note of a dark shape looming in front of him. At first he tried to avoid it, then his senses alerted him to a frightening reality. It was a body.

"Anne!" She was unconscious, and he could only suppose that she had struck her head on something when she hit the water. Pushing away all thought that she might be dead, he called upon renewed strength. Propelling his body through the water, he moved towards her, gathering her into the safety of his arms.

Several crewman of the *Red Dragon* lowered a rope. With one arm firmly around Anne's waist, Jonathan managed to climb up and pull them aboard the ship. Gently he lowered Anne to the deck. Reaching out, he stroked her hair, tears flooding his eyes. "Please God, don't let her die."

"She doesn't seem to be breathing, Captain. . . ."

"Then I'll breathe for her," Jonathan whispered. Putting his mouth to hers, he forced air into her lungs. *Live,* he thought. *Please live.* More than anything in the world, he wanted her to open her eyes, wanted her to move. "Anne

... I love you. ..." He whispered in her ear ... and then she stirred. "Anne." He felt the slight pulsating of her blood at her wrist. She was alive. Thankfully he wrapped his arms around her and held her as if he would never let her go.

"All hands to battle stations!" Jonathan's knuckles whitened as he gripped the rail, shouting orders. His face was contorted in anger at Enrique Navarro. The devious coward's actions had almost killed Anne, and the attack on the ship that he had masterminded had come perilously close to taking Falkhearst's life as well. Well, if he wanted a fight, Jonathan would give him one!

Jonathan watched as his skilled sailors maneuvered the sails of the *Red Dragon* so that the ship moved in to almost point-blank range.

"Fire!" he ordered.

Obeying his orders, the crewmen sent forth a hail of cannon balls that bored into the thick hull of the enemy ship. The impact caused debris and men to be hurled in the air. Navarro's ship was wounded, but that didn't mean an end to the fighting. Indeed, it seemed to spur Navarro on. Striding back and forth across the deck, he shouted out orders as if he, and not the ship's captain, was in command.

"By God, look at him ... the pompous popinjay." Though Jonathan tried to control his emotions, a jolt of pure hatred flooded over him, prodding him to yell out, "Again, fire!"

A volley of cannon balls answered him, cutting to pieces everything in their path. And all the while Jonathan vowed vengeance. Even so, he was stunned when one of his crewmen took aim at Navarro and shot the Spaniard in the head.

Jonathan grimaced as blood poured from his enemy's wound, knowing at once from the extent of the damage done to his face that the blow was mortal. Running to the railing, he watched as Enrique Navarro slumped to the deck.

"This time he won't come back from the dead," Jonathan whispered.

Yelling and shouting, the Spanish sailors surrounded their fallen diplomat; then, as if his death somehow shattered their morale or destroyed their purpose, they stopped firing at the *Red Dragon*. Some even panicked and scurried over the deck like frightened ants. Only moments later, the ship was in the hands of the English. The war against the Spanish Armada was over.

It was quiet. All vestiges of warfare had been replaced by tranquility and a sense of peace. The moon was a globe of liquid silver, its pale light shimmering over the waves. A whispering breeze, as soft as silk, caressed Anne's face as she stood hand-in-hand with Jonathan on the deck of the *Red Dragon*, looking out at the ocean. Staring into the azure depths, her eyes focused on the water as if somehow she might read her fate there. What she saw beckoned alluringly. Her life, her heart, entwined with Jonathan Leighton.

"Anne. . . ." He spoke her name in a whisper that was swallowed by the breeze.

The air crackled with anticipation, pulsated with expectancy, surged with promise. A shiver danced up and down her spine as he put his arm around her waist and turned his head. For a timeless moment, they stared at each other; then he took a step closer.

"I thought I had lost you."

"But you didn't. I'm a much stronger woman than you realize."

"And much more stubborn," he said huskily, a smile touching the corners of his mouth. "Oh, Anne, a part of me died when you disappeared in the ocean. You risked your life. . . ."

"I had to get off that ship. I knew you wouldn't fire as long as Enrique held me captive. Enrique knew that too. He was using your love for me to manipulate your destruction. So . . . I took matters into my own hands."

"And saved us all. You're a very brave woman." Slowly

his hands closed around her shoulders, pulling her to him. "And very beautiful . . ."

At first he simply held her, his hands exerting a gentle pressure to draw her into the warmth of his embrace. Capturing her lips, he kissed her gently at first, then increased the pressure of his mouth against hers. Opening her lips under his, she gave herself up to the passionate sensations that flowed through her.

Jonathan's tongue moved against hers, savoring the warm softness. His hands moved lower to encompass her small waist, then slide over the curve of her hips in sensuous fascination. Anne put her arms around Jonathan's neck, her fingers tangling in his thick golden hair. Their bodies touched, intensifying the emotions churning within them. Breathless, her head whirling, she allowed herself to be drawn up into the mists of the spell.

Jonathan's lips parted the soft, yielding flesh beneath his, searching out the honey of her mouth. With a low moan, he thrust his fingers within the soft, silken waterfall of her hair, drawing her closer. Desire choked him, all the hungry prompting of his fantasies warring with his reason. His lips grew demanding, changing from gentleness to passion as his hands moved down her shoulders and began to roam at will with increasing familiarity. More than anything in the world he wanted to make love to her. Even so, he pulled away. It seemed that even though he was dead, Enrique Navarro still stood between them.

"Jonathan, what's wrong?"

"I was thinking of the violent way your husband died. Perhaps . . . perhaps you need time. . . ."

Anne shook her head. "I dutifully mourned Enrique three years ago when I thought he had died. I need mourn him no more." She reached up to touch his face. "Besides, in my heart *you* are my husband."

"I will be once we get back to London, in your heart and in all ways." Taking both her hands in his, he asked, "Will you marry me again?"

Anne answered before he had even finished the question. "Yes!"

"Then I am the happiest man alive!" Sweeping her up in his arms, Jonathan carried her to his cabin and laid her gently down on the bed.

Like a spark, his lovemaking ignited a fire in her blood. Her heart skipped a beat as he brought his head down and traced the bare curve of her neck with his lips. Then he was tugging at her garments nearly as frantically as she was pulling at his.

"I'm all thumbs!"

"So am I! Oh, Jonathan, it's been so long."

With a deftness born of desire, he removed her garments, leaving her body bared to his gaze. "You are even more seductive than I remembered." He let his eyes wander for a long moment, then reached out to caress her, sliding his hand over her stomach.

"Oh, Jonathan . . ." She ached for him, longed for him to be naked against her, to make love to her as he had so many times before in their bedroom at home.

Jonathan removed his breeches, tore off his shirt, and lay down beside her. Bending his head, he worshipped her with his mouth, his lips traveling from one breast to the other in tender fascination. His tongue curled around the taut peaks, his teeth lightly grazing until she writhed beneath him. He savored the expressions that chased across her face, the wanting and the passion for him that were so clearly revealed.

A sudden tidal wave swept over them, intensifying the passion that flowed between them. They were like two pagan lovers in the moonlight. Jonathan crushed her against his chest, shivering as he felt her nipples harden against his skin. Their bodies were crushed together as both simultaneously reveled in the delight of the texture and pressure of the other.

He kissed her again, his tongue searching and demanding as it explored. His fingers moved freely, leaving no part of her free of his touch, caressing her, loving her, learning her body as well as he knew his own.

"It seems so right, being here together like this," he whispered. Burying his face in the soft, silky strands of her hair, he breathed in the fragrant scent of her and was lost.

Anne's arms entwined around Jonathan's neck, her fingers tangling in his thick blond hair. Fascinated, she let her hands explore his body as his had done to hers. He uttered a moan as her hands moved over the smoothly corded muscles of his shoulders.

"Ah, how I always love you to touch me. . . ."

"Jonathan . . ." Closing her eyes, Anne awaited another kiss, her mouth opening to him like the soft petals of a flower as he caressed her lips with all the passionate hunger they both yearned for. Anne loved the taste of him, the tender urgency of his mouth. Her lips opened to him for a seemingly endless passionate onslaught of kisses. It was as if they were breathing one breath, living at that moment just for each other. Mutual hunger brought their lips back together time after time. She craved his kisses and returned them with trembling pleasure, exploring the inner softness of his mouth.

Desire that had been coiling within Anne for so long only to be unfulfilled, sparked to renewed fire, and she could feel his passion likewise building, searing her with its heat. They shared a joy of touching and caressing, arms against arms, legs touching legs, fingers entwining and wandering to explore.

Anne was lost in a sensual dream. A dream that intensified her daring. Giving in to her imagination, she slowly rolled over on top of him, sliding her body downward. As his muscled body strained hungrily against hers, she put the hardening length of his manhood between her breasts, sighing as she felt him shudder.

Jonathan felt the shock of raw desire as she undulated her body.

Back and forth, her breasts stroking him erotically. "Oh, yes . . ." He moaned aloud as he was gripped by the most powerful desire he had ever experienced in all his life. All coherent thought fled quickly from his mind, replaced by his need to possess her. Completely.

"Anne!"

Oh, how she loved the way he said her name. Looking up at his face, she saw that his eyes were closed. How strange that his expression made him look as if he were nearly suffering, yet he was smiling all the while as if in sweet torment. Then he was reaching down, grasping her hips firmly yet gently, moving her body upward. She could feel the insistent pressure of his swollen manhood moving closer to the warm, moist core of her body as she spread her legs.

His hands were between their bodies, sliding down the velvety flesh of her belly, moving to that place between her thighs that ached for his entry. His gentle probing brought sweet fire, curling deep inside her with spirals of pulsating sensations. Then his hands left her, to be replaced by the hardness she had glimpsed before, entering her just a little, then pausing as he whispered her name.

Remembering the way he had moved upon her when they had made love, Anne slowly, provocatively moved downward, taking him fully inside her. Capturing the firm flesh of him, she caressed him in the most intimate of embraces. Arching herself up to him, she fully expressed her fully inflamed emotions.

Jonathan groaned softly, the blood pounding thickly in his head. She was so warm, so tight, that he closed his eyes with agonized pleasure. His hold on her hips tightened as the throbbing shaft of his maleness possessed her again and again.

Instinctively Anne tightened her legs around him, certain she could never withstand the ecstasy that was engulfing her body. It was as if the night shattered into a thousand stars, all bursting within her. Arching her hips, she rode the storm with him. As spasms overtook her, she dug her nails into the skin of his back. Wave after wave lashed through them as they came close to mutual fulfillment.

A sweet shaft of ecstasy shot through Jonathan, and he

closed his eyes, whispering her name again and again. He
wanted to make love to her all night. Again and again.
Wanted to taste her, touch her, feel her tight softness sheath-
ing him.

For a moment Anne felt as if her heart had stopped, as
if she had stopped breathing. She was shattered by the pulsating explosion, the wonderous feelings that surged through
her. Even when the intensity of their passion was spent, she
still clung to him, unable to let this magical moment end.
She touched him gently, wonderingly. In that moment she
knew that she would never let Jonathan Leighton go.

Chapter Thirty

Richmond Palace was a noisy mass of confusion. In the wake of the Armada's defeat, the great hall was filled with men and women anxious to catch sight of the heroes who had accomplished what some had said was impossible. That one of the victors was accompanied by his lady caused an even greater stir as Anne and Jonathan entered.

"That's Anne Morgan Navarro and Jonathan Leighton," a tall woman said behind her hand. "They fought side by side, or so I heard, and brought down the Armada together."

"Forsooth, it was the storm that destroyed the Armada, not any man or woman." said the man by her side.

"It was divine intervention, that's what it was," echoed a nobleman who had overheard.

"Perhaps it was a little of both. That's why the queen's Armada medal reads, 'God Breathed and They Were Scattered.' "

"If you ask me, it was courage that saved us."

"Perhaps it was love," Gweneth Carleton said, looking in Jonathan's direction as if remembering her own feelings. "Merry-go-up, I'd march off to battle if it meant going there with him."

It seemed that everyone in the hall had their own opinion of what had occurred. In truth, all sorts of stories and myths had been concocted and spread during the fighting and in the aftermath of the battle. There were even rumors that some Spaniards had survived the fighting only to be massacred by wild men in Ireland when a storm wrecked their ships on that country's shores.

Jonathan shrugged such stories off. He knew the truth, and that was all that mattered. After Enrique Navarro's death, the Spanish commander had found himself in danger of total defeat and had made a fateful decision to return to Spain via the North of Scotland and Ireland. The Spaniards had run into a storm off the coast and several ships had been destroyed. In the end, King Philip had paid a terrible price for trying to subdue the English.

"Whatever happened, we were victorious," Henry Carleton said, as if he had been involved in the fighting.

"What's all this chattering about?" Dressed in a gown of oyster, embroidered with brown and gold, an interesting design that looked as if a thousand eyes were staring out from her bodice and the folds of the skirt, Elizabeth swept forward. "Ah, Jonathan. I should have known that it was you. Only Sir Walter Raleigh and you can cause such a stir."

Elizabeth's gaze swept over them. Anne and Jonathan made a striking sight. He was dressed all in white and gold, his garments a contrast to his blond hair. For the occassion he had hastily procured a new dress for Anne, of gold velvet to match his gold lacings.

"And why not?" The queen continued. "You are of a certainty one of the most dashing men for miles around." Looking at Anne as if she wished that she would disappear so that she could be alone with Jonathan, Elizabeth walked towards her chair. "But come, I have something for you."

That "something" was a great honor for Jonathan that made Anne very proud. He was given the title of knight.

Regal, humorless, and unsmiling, the queen conducted the audience with her usual competence and very little display of emotion, but Anne felt as if an inner warmth and gratitude radiated out to her as Elizabeth spoke Jonathan's name.

"I've rewarded Drake, Howard, and Hawkins already with lands, gold, and titles. What reward would you have, Sir Jonathan?"

"All I ask is your blessing on my upcoming marriage to Anne," Jonathan answered, brushing Anne's face with his hand.

"Marriage?" Elizabeth's eyes lit upon Anne, and there was jealousy in her eyes. "And are you certain that she is a widow this time?"

Jonathan nodded. "I saw her husband die."

Elizabeth stiffened. "Then there must be a period of mourning, during which time I have just the adventure for you. I'm taking you up on your offer to start a colony in the New World."

"A colony!" Jonathan couldn't hide his elation.

"And five ships. I want a large colony!"

"It will be very large, your majesty," Jonathan replied.

Elizabeth's mood was gradually improving, and her fond smiles clearly affirmed that Jonathan was in her good graces again. "A ship and a title before your name. Tell me, Jonathan, is there anything else that would make you happy?"

Jonathan squeezed Anne's hand. "Truthfully, your majesty?"

"Of course truthfully."

"I wish to marry Anne Morgan Navarro, and I wish to marry her today." There was no use beating around the bush. "I intend to take her with me to the New World."

Elizabeth eyed him coolly. "Marry her today?" She didn't try to hide the fact that she abhored the idea.

"We were very happy together as man and wife before. I want to feel that kind of happiness again."

"Indeed." Elizabeth reached out with her fan, touching Anne's chin, turning her face this way and that with the soft feathers. "I had rather been fond of the idea of marrying her off to Lord Vickery." Was she joking or was she serious? Anne didn't know. "What think you of that, Sir Jonathan?"

"Over my dead body!" Jonathan replied, then bowed to temper his show of anger. "Your majesty."

"So, I see. That is the way that it is." Elizabeth's eyes darted back and forth between them, taking note of the glow in their eyes whenever they looked at each other. She sighed regretfully. "True love, I suppose you would call it."

"True love it is," Jonathan answered. He might have asked for the world at that moment, but all he wanted was Anne.

"And I suppose, were I to deny you this request, you would do as Sir Walter Raleigh did and marry her anyway." The queen could be most unforgiving where matters of the heart were concerned. Raleigh and his bride had been condemned to the Tower when they had married secretly. Elizabeth had always coveted Jonathan's affection most heatedly. Was there hope she might then say no?

"I must confess that I would elope with her at the very first chance, your majesty." Jonathan's confession was met by stern silence. For a moment he was certain that he would be stripped of his newly bestowed title.

"I think you would do just that." The queen shook her head in exasperation. "Such an impetuous man! But then, I have always liked men of daring." Elizabeth put her hand to her temple and pondered the matter for a long, long time. "You know how much I favor you. Of all the lords, you are among those I hold most dear, except for Drake, that is."

"Your majesty does me too much honor," Jonathan whispered. Cautiously he waited, crossing his fingers behind his back.

"I had plans for you!" Again there was a long silence. "Even so I do not see how I can do otherwise than say yes." She turned to Anne. "You have, as you reminded me already, spent time in mourning. Besides, Enrique Navarro was a wicked man!"

"A very wicked man, your majesty."

"And it would tweak Philip's beard if I granted your

request." Elizabeth laughed softly. "And as you know, I will do almost anything for Philip."

"Yes, your majesty." Jonathan could barely contain his joy. The queen had consented to their marriage. "Sweet love, did you hear that?" he whispered in Anne's ear. Fearing that the queen might change her mind, as she was wont to do on occasion, he hurriedly and politely took his leave, dragging Anne behind him. Only when they were beyond Richmond's door did he dare let out a thunderous shout.

"What a wedding it will be, Cap'n." Coming up behind them, swathed in bandages, was Edmund Falkhearst. "Why, you could get married on the ship with England's coastline at your back. What do you say?"

Anne thought about it, at last deciding that she liked the idea.

"That's my Annie," Falkhearst exclaimed. "Ah, young love. What I wouldn't do to feel such vibrant feelings again." Falkhearst cocked his head and winked in Anne's direction, only to see that she was kissing Jonathan with all the tenderness of her heart.

The night air was filled with the fragrance of the flowers that covered the *Red Dragon* from bow to stern. The wedding music was the roar of the ocean and the sound of waves breaking over the ship's bow. The light of the moon and thousands of stars illuminated the makeshift altar. The guests were the crewmen of Jonathan's ships.

Standing at the helm, dressed in a gown of white velvet shimmering with glass beads, Anne smiled up at Jonathan, standing beside her at the rail. Her eyes appraised him lovingly. His white linen shirt and blue velvet doublet were molded to his arms and upper body; his tight hosen and breeches emphasized his physique. Oh, he was a handsome devil, all right. Strong. Stubborn. A man with a wanderlust. Being married to him certainly wouldn't be boring.

For one hushed moment, his eyes met Anne's and he

grinned. "I'm a lucky man," she heard him say, and knew that sentiment to be in her heart as well.

And lucky they certainly were. Anxious to establish colonies in the New World that would be equal to yet surpass those inhabited by the Spanish, Elizabeth had gifted Jonathan with *seven* ships manned by five-hundred men, of which one-hundred and eight were colonists. She had also given him box upon box and sack upon sack of supplies. Enough to last for at least four years—if Walsingham and the other ship's cats proved to be good ratters.

"Are we ready, Cap'n?" Falkhearst was all smiles. Not only had Jonathan asked him to be best man, he had also made Edmund the captain of one of the ships.

"We are!" Jonathan answered. Taking Anne's hand in his, they faced the priest.

The ceremony was brief. Anne felt the gold ring come to rest on the third finger of her left hand, an unending symbol of eternity. Relishing the ritual kiss, she thrilled with passion to know that this handsome, daring man belonged to her at last. The future awaited them with the promise of deep, eternal love.

Merlin's Legacy

A Series From
Quinn Taylor Evans